Sunnyside Blues

Books by Mary Carter

SHE'LL TAKE IT

ACCIDENTALLY ENGAGED

SUNNYSIDE BLUES

Published by Kensington Publishing Corporation

Sunnyside Blues

Mary Carter

KENSINGTON BOOKS
http://www.kensingtonbooks.com

KENSINGTON BOOKS are published by

Kensington Publishing Corp.
119 West 40th Street
New York, NY 10018

All Kensington titles, imprints, and distributed lines are available at special quantity discounts for bulk purchases for sales promotion, premiums, fund-raising, educational, or institutional use.

Special book excerpts or customized printings can also be created to fit specific needs. For details, write or phone the office of the Kensington Special Sales Manager: Kensington Publishing Corp., 119 West 40th Street, New York, NY 10018. Attn. Special Sales Department. Phone: 1-800-221-2647.

Kensington and the K logo Reg. U.S. Pat. & TM Off.

ISBN-13: 978-0-7582-2919-9
ISBN-10: 0-7582-2919-4

First Kensington Trade Paperback Printing: July 2009
10 9 8 7 6 5 4 3 2 1

Printed in the United States of America

Chapter 1

Present day
Police Precinct
Sunnyside, Queens

There was nothing remarkable about the police interrogation room. If it were a bar, the sign on the wall would have read: TWO PERSONS MAXIMUM. Eggshell walls and a brown tile floor. Andes suddenly wished she were wearing yellow; she'd complete the metaphor: the yolk in the middle. Perhaps they were going for that effect, as if they wanted her to crack, or hatch her confession. Was there really anyone behind the one-way mirror? It too had cracks, and scratches, and particles of dust at the edges that begged for a healthy dose of Windex. Who was watching them from behind the mirror? Were they clutching little notepads and slurping strong black coffee? Andes thought she caught a whiff of it, but she hadn't been offered any. The tape recorder was running.

"I'm telling you right now, this is one big misunderstanding. I didn't kidnap anyone." The officer, who looked like a kindly old grandfather, if your kindly old grandfather was the type to pick you up by your neck and give you a good shake while slowly but surely cutting off your oxygen with his gnarled knuckles, didn't say a word. Having grown up among them, Andes was no stranger to the strong, silent type. Men with deep voices hiding behind their common-man exterior, vocal cords covered up by flannel shirts, wool scarves, and social norms. The quiet workingman, who, instead of a word, would just as soon give you a nod or a grunt, despite an eternal spring of sound, and thoughts, and jokes, hidden deep within.

Voices that could shout, sing, and speak in tongues. Voices ragged from years of working in coal mines and smoking cigarettes would somehow transform, melt into deep, dark, silk when the Lord moved on them to preach. The quiet whisper of their day voices would open up into a world of sound that both enchanted and commanded. Sitting here, on the verge of arrest, Andes could taste their voices on the tip of her tongue, catch them like snowflakes. Yet like these strong, silent men, she was suddenly at a loss for words. And it was looking like Andes, the self-proclaimed atheist, was in desperate need of an act of God.

But even if he was a religious man, it didn't look like the Lord or anything else was going to move on the police officer sitting across from her anytime soon, so she pushed her memories aside and continued with her confession. "In the beginning, I didn't even want to baby-sit the kid. Not that I'm not a kid person, because I am. Kids adore me, and I've always tolerated them extremely well." Andes paused again just in case he wanted to jump in, lead the interrogation. She didn't need a lawyer; she'd already told him that, this was just one big misunderstanding.

And people who asked for lawyers always looked guilty, everybody knew that. Still, Andes was keeping an ear out for what her lawyer might be objecting to if she had one. Since the officer had done little more than turn on a tape recorder and stare at her as if she were guilty until proved innocent, she'd done all the talking. Her little voice was whispering for her to stop, but her big voice plowed on.

"That sounded awful—tolerating them—didn't it? I just mean they've always liked me a little bit more than I've liked them. But if you saw how kids take to me, you'd realize it's not a fair comparison. Basically, they fall madly in love with me, and

I fall 'normally' in love with them. That's what I should have said. And I did fall madly in love with the kid. But I won't lie; in the beginning I wanted to kill him."

The officer raised an eyebrow. "Not literally, of course," Andes jumped in. "That would be wrong." The eyebrow went back down. Andes held her breath. Officer Friendly was starting to look bored. Andes wished again for a cup of coffee and this time added a chocolate cream–filled doughnut to her silent wish list as well.

"But that's okay, because at first the kid hated me too. I know, I just told you children fall madly in love with me. Well, the kid was the exception. The first time we met, he mortified me in front of an entire dock of people. I'm sorry." Andes apologized for the tears, now spilling out of her eyes and rolling down her cheeks.

She patted down her pockets for a tissue. Ever since she'd met the kid, she'd taken to carrying tissues in her pockets—who would have ever believed that? But she didn't find one, he'd taken her last one, so instead she sniffed, inhaled, and topped her fantasy cup of coffee off with a shot of Baileys. But her doughnut, once sweet and decadent, now had an arsenic-centered filling. She imagined sliding it across the table to the overweight mute in blue. A glazed Trojan horse. Would she smile as he ate it? Make polite conversation? Would he recognize her betrayal seconds before the poison infiltrated his body? Poison doughnuts, poison pens, poison lipstick. Poppies, apples, parades. A harsh look from a lover. Painted toys from China. The single bite of a deadly snake. Kill him with kindness. *Hello, Juliet. Wake me up when Romeo's dead.*

Andes bit her lip and tried to remember if she'd given to the policemen's ball last year. "I'm sorry. I don't normally cry in front of people. But the kid and I—we've come a long way, baby." Andes laughed. "Oh. Don't misunderstand that either. I don't smoke and neither does the kid. Believe me, if I was going to start, it would have been in here (not that you would have offered me one), and if the kid ever started, I'd kill him. Not literally, of course—"

"That would be wrong," the officer finished for her. He heaved forward and snapped off the tape recorder. Andes, who had become accustomed to him being seen and not heard, was startled when he started speaking.

"You don't smoke?" he asked.

"No."

"Then why all these?" The officer reached into his lap, brought up a plastic Foodtown bag, and shook the contents onto the table. Once again, he clicked Record on the tape recorder. Andes stared at her matchbook collection, obscenely splayed across the table for the world to see. She curled her fingers around the side of her chair and squeezed, fighting the urge to sweep the matchbooks onto her lap and caress them.

"Do these belong to you?" the officer asked. The tiniest flicker of apprehension manifested itself on Andes's upper lip in the form of a little bead of sweat.

"Where did you get them?" she asked. Her voice sounded hollow and foreign in her ears. It wasn't really what she wanted to know anyway. What she really wanted to know was what had happened to the carved wooden box in which her collection belonged. It was an old snake box Brother Elliot carved by hand forty years ago. It once housed cottonmouths, diamondbacks, and timber snakes, but Andes didn't bother to mention that either. "Where's the box? Didn't they come in a wooden box?" She was aware of her voice rising and cracking, but compared to the out-and-out fit she wanted to throw, she was holding it together remarkably well. Who would take those beautiful little works of fire art out of a hand-carved box and toss them into a plastic Foodtown bag?

How many people had touched her gems, how much oil from how many fingers had seeped into the miniature works of art, marring their individuality with anonymous fingerprints? As if wanting to ratchet up her distress, the officer grabbed her matchbook from Barcelona and flicked it open with his fat thumb. He was going to ruin the cover! Had he no respect for the vibrant orange cover and tiny flamenco dancers?

"Can you please—" Andes said, bringing her hands up and clutching at air. The officer stared at her, matchbook in hand.

He didn't drop it, but at least he stopped rubbing it between his dirty fingers. "I know they might not look like much to you—"

"What? These?"

"But they are part of a collection."

"I can see that."

"And I would really appreciate it if you wouldn't bend the cover like that." There, she'd said it. Andes watched incredulity invade the officer's face only to be swallowed up by a shake of his head. It was just as she thought; he had no clue how precious they were to her, how gorgeous, how priceless. Each little packet a painting, a purse of potential fire, the start of something, a flick, a flame. Matchbooks with names of places she'd been; the snapshot of the traveler's life.

"You don't mind if I . . . ?" The officer feigned taking a match out of the book.

"I do, I do. As you can see, none of the matches have ever been used. Not a single one." Andes, who minutes ago had been crouched over in a self-pitying pose, was now sitting ramrod straight. The officer threw the matchbook down and crossed his arms across his stonewall chest. He'd been waiting for this.

"I know that. I've had them thoroughly checked out." Andes couldn't have been more mortified if he'd passed her panties around the precinct for New York's finest to sniff. She had to remind herself to focus on the kid. He was her first priority here, no matter what was being done to her. The officer was just trying to bait her. *Calm down and focus on the kid.*

"Is Chase okay? I need to know he's okay."

"This ain't Guantanamo." The officer laughed at his little joke, a chuckle that rose sharply and died down just as quickly when he realized he, alone, found it humorous.

"It's just, the kid can really bottle it up," Andes tried to explain. "I thought I was bad, but you've never seen someone stuff down feelings like that kid."

"Ah. That explains the hunger strike." The stress of the day, coupled with the thought of Chase going on a hunger strike for her, struck Andes as absurdly funny. This time it was her turn to laugh, and the officer's turn to shame her into silence.

"I'm sorry. It's just that—he never would have done anything like that before he met me. I think I've really helped him express his feelings in productive ways. Not that starving is necessarily productive—but it's creative, don't you think? And—how long have I been here?"

The officer looked at his watch. "Thirty minutes."

"Oh. It seems like longer. He likes cheese pizza."

"That's what we offered him."

"Oh. Well, did you cut it into circles?"

The officer raised an eyebrow.

"That's the only way he'll eat it," Andes explained. "He's diametrically opposed to triangles. Get it? He likes circles. Never mind. And squares are—well—square. I've never tried a rhombus or an octagon, so feel free, but I'm doubtful. After all, even a kid like Chase likes routine. I'm sorry, but can I have some tissues?" *And maybe a fucking cup of coffee and a motherfucking glazed doughnut, you fat fuck?*

The officer spread his hands out in an I-have-nothing type of way. Andes nodded and wiped the back of her hand against her nose. "I'm sorry. This has been a very emotional day. And that woman out there. I don't care what you call her. She is not his mother. Do you hear me? She's a horrible person who doesn't even know that kid, let alone love him. And if you let her walk out of here with him, I'm going to the newspapers and I'm going to let everyone know that you turned an innocent ten-year-old boy over to a gold-digging crack whore." Andes leaned down and shouted the last bit into the tape recorder before putting her head down on the table and sobbing. After a few moments she lifted her head and tried to calm herself in her sea of matchbooks, spread out on the table like stepping-stones to unseen worlds.

"Have you called his dad yet?"

"Are you speaking of Dave Jensen or Jay Freeman?"

Andes bit her lip. Apparently, the officer had been talking to people. What had they told him? Pick a father. Any father.

"Jay," she said at last. Then, "How long am I going to be here?"

"That's up to you."

"How so?" The officer had another surprise waiting for her underneath the table, and he wasted no time producing it. It was extremely disorienting seeing his thick hand wrapped around her slim neck. It was her doll, Rose. Or what used to be her.

The left half of her body was completely charred; only one eye was still twinkly and blue, the other was seared out of its socket except for a single eyelash pointing straight up like the last stick standing in a desperate attempt to spell out "HELP" on a deserted beach. Gone was all but a few wisps of her silky blond hair, plastered against a blackened plastic head, and the remains of her purple dress were singed beyond repair. She was barely recognizable; Jane Doe, Jane Doll. Andes stared. The officer leaned in.

"Who did this, Emily?" he said. "Who's been setting the fires?" Andes looked at her matches. She looked at the one-way mirror. She looked at the wall. She wanted to yell at him that he wasn't supposed to call her Emily. Nobody had called her Emily for a long, long time. And okay, maybe she never legally changed her name, but a person should be called what they want to be called. Of course he couldn't have known that. And even now she wasn't opening her mouth to explain it to him. Because deep down, she was still Emily; she hadn't run far enough or fast enough, she had always been Emily. The thought, while bringing tears to her eyes, brought with it a surprising sense of relief, of letting go. She thought about all the chances some people got in life, and then she thought about the kid out there and all that he'd already been through in his ten young years. Maybe it was too late for her, but she could still save him. "I used to be a peaceful world traveler," Andes said. "Did you know that?"

"I asked the kid who's been starting the fires. Do you want to know what *he* said?"

"Would you please go and cut that pizza in circles before it gets cold?"

"Why don't you answer my question and then you can go and cut it yourself?"

"And remind him Gandhi was a lot older than ten, okay? But don't say it like that—like he doesn't already know exactly how old he was, because as you've probably figured out by now, the kid is a genius. And I'm not using that term lightly. But he does need emotional support."

"What does Satya—oh what was he saying?"

"Satyagraha."

"Yeah. Who's that?"

"He's trying to tell you he's taking a nonviolent stand to my arrest. Ahimsa. You gotta love that kid. But you tell him he's gotta eat. Just get a glass or a bowl or something and turn it upside down on the pizza and cut. But don't make it an oval. He won't eat an oval. Believe me, I learned that the hard way." With that, Emily Tomlin leaned forward and snapped off the tape recorder.

"So what are you saying here?" the officer asked.

"I'd like to call that lawyer now," Andes answered.

Chapter 2

"**P**edophile!" he screamed at her from the middle of the dock. "Pedophile!"

Andes Lane, a petite twenty-five-year-old world traveler, was standing on the dock with a worn green yoga mat clutched in one hand and a shiny penny outstretched in the other. In her split-second fantasy, the kid had taken the penny out of her hand and treated her to a dazzling smile, so in the moment, she was immobilized not only by the accusation hurled at her by the red-faced boy, but by the simple realization that no matter how Andes imagined people reacting, they always disappointed her.

And not only did the kid have a healthy set of lungs, but his declaration was buoyed by the water that surrounded them; Lake Union acted as a giant aqua echo chamber that amplified the boy's voice, carrying his cry of "pedophile" out to every sailboat, house barge, and Fourth of July reveler on deck, as well as the boat full of Canadian tourists who were at that very moment passing by in Stanley's Steamship, sipping on Stanley's signature chocolate root beer floats and angling their digital cameras to get a better shot of the *Sleepless in Seattle* houseboat. When his cries of "pedophile" reached their finely tuned Canadian ears, they craned their necks to get a better look at *her*, the aforementioned pedophile, as they simultaneously praised and blamed the fall of the American dollar for the spectacle she had become. All that was missing was a bugle call and a posse of foxhounds unleashed for the hunt.

Instantly Andes's mind conjured up horrible images: young, scraggly, long-haired convicts dangling puppies as they lured children into beat-up vans decorated with dancing bear bumper stickers, and middle-aged, potbellied perverts, palms stained with Skittles, sweet-talking innocent children into doing more than just sitting on Santa's lap. She glanced down her body just to make sure she still had breasts, as the dock full of pale half-dressed Seattleites looked at her as if they were watching a live episode of *To Catch A Predator*.

Not that women couldn't be pedophiles. In fact, she suddenly remembered it was in the Seattle area—Mary Kay someone—not the makeup lady, but the teacher who slept with her student and went on to have two children with him—shit—Letourneau—that was it, Mary Kay Letourneau, she remembered how sorry she felt for Mary Kay's husband and her four children—although he'd since taken the kids to Alaska and remarried—all useless information at the moment—although fleeing to Alaska was starting to look like an attractive possibility. After all, she was fond of layering up and wouldn't mind living in a place where at any given moment you could spot a moose or a bear ambling down the road.

Andes racked her brain for what she should say in her defense—*I'm not a pedophile* of course came to mind, but then she wondered if that would be like declaring you weren't an alcoholic to your AA group. So instead she raised her yoga mat high above her head like an offering, as if a faithful practicer of Downward Facing Dog couldn't possibly be expected to defend such drivel. My God. All she tried to do was give the boy the shiny penny she'd plucked off the dock—*find a penny, pick it up, and all day long you'll have good luck; a penny for your thoughts,* and all that jazz. Would she be standing here humiliated if she had offered the kid a quarter instead? There was even a Sacagawea dollar in her fanny pack, but it was too late now.

If she *were* a pedophile, what would she say? She often played this mental game with directions, since she had no sense of them; if she reached a fork in the road, she would ask herself which way her instincts told her to go, and then she would go in the opposite direction, since her instincts usually led her astray. But if she *were* a pedophile, she would deny it, of course, so that was of little use in this situation. What Andes didn't know as she stood there utterly humiliated was that she was about the tenth person the boy had called a pedophile that week, in part due to a recent school assembly on the subject, but mostly because the kid didn't know how to scream at the person he was really angry with, the man who was currently bobbing in a rowboat underneath the dock. So instead, he unleashed his rage on strangers, giving him a shot of pleasure that often lasted the whole day.

Andes flipped the offending penny out onto Lake Union and held up the Houseboat for Rent advertisement she had torn off the bulletin board in the laundromat. "I'm looking for Jay," she said. Suddenly, several people on the dock immediately looked at their feet. It struck her as odd, yet Andes couldn't help but follow suit and look at her own feet. They were housed in bright pink flip-flops, and turning slightly pink, most likely because like her fingernails, her toenails were painted black, drawing the sun directly to them, roasting her little piggies one by one. She wiggled her toes and wondered if anyone would let her buy a hot dog or hamburger; it seemed as if every single sailboat was sporting a hibachi, and the smell of barbecue tugged at her hunger. She hadn't eaten a single thing all day. It had been the last leg of her Greyhound trek from San Diego, and by the time the journey was done, she'd lost her appetite. But now that she was on land, even if by the sea, her hunger was returning with a vengeance. Just then one of the gatherers stomped on the dock.

"Jay," the voice belonging to the stomping foot said. "You

have company." Seconds later, a pair of hands emerged from underneath the dock, gripped the wooden planks, and pulled. The tip of a rowboat slid out, and Andes found herself looking at a good-looking head in his early thirties. He had a strong, tanned face, sandy hair, and blue eyes that reminded her of a summer sky.

"Yes?" he asked, looking directly at Andes.

"Are you Jay?" she asked, jostling the advertisement.

"I am," he answered. Then, before she could inquire about the houseboat, he said, "You don't look like a pedophile to me." Those who hadn't ambled back to sunning themselves, or flipping burgers, or whatever else it was the residence of West-lake Marina did on the Fourth of July, laughed easily at the man's joke. Andes did not. "Although I guess you never can tell these days," Jay continued.

"I'm not a pedophile," Andes said, but it was barely a whisper. Before she could explain or defend herself any further, a woman drowning in a flowered sundress, floppy orange hat, and oversized sunglasses descended on them. She was sloshing champagne from a crystal flute precariously balanced in her manicured hand. She tapped a long fingernail at the head in the rowboat.

"Jay," she said. "I assume you got my message?" Jay pushed out a little farther, so that now he was a head, arms, and a chest. He crushed a can of Miller beer in his left fist and closed his eyes. "Jay?" the woman demanded. There was no reply. The woman turned and stared at Andes as if she were to blame. Even though his eyes were closed and he couldn't possibly see her, Andes held the advertisement in Jay's direction and jostled it up and down again.

"I was wondering if the houseboat was still for rent?"

"Be careful what you wish for, dear," the woman said, push-ing down on Andes's forearm. She smelled like a field where a hundred gardenias had come to die. "Now, you listen to me, Jay. Did you or did you not get the message?"

"I did."

"So we have an understanding?"

"We do." Jay let the woman get a few steps away before continuing. "You left me a message, and I got it. That's our understanding." The woman stopped, turned on her red heels, and click-clacked back the few steps she had gained.

"I mean it, mister. If you urinate in my flowers again this year, I swear to God, I'll—I'll—"

"You'll what?"

"I'll call Child Protective Services!" the woman screamed. Andes first thought was: *I didn't know Child Protective Services handled plants.* Her mind was already conjuring up overwrought social workers swarming in to protect verbally abused petunias. Then she followed the woman's gaze down the dock in the direction of the kid. Andes let out a little gasp, but Jay just laughed.

"You promise, Mrs. Mueller?" he toyed. Mrs. Muller's hand fluttered up to her sunglasses and she fiddled with them, even though they were perfectly snug around her face. A white line wrapped around her wedding finger, as if a well-worn ring had recently been removed. Jay must have been following her gaze, for he turned to Andes and said, "Do you know how many women chuck their engagement and wedding rings into this lake?"

An old man sitting on the deck of a yacht behind them shot up and shouted, "Betty!"

"If you take Stanley's tour along the lake, he'll tell you all about the heartbroken brides-to-be and brides who have tossed their tiny little diamonds into the lake. Now, men would never be that stupid, even if the thing is tiny. We'd pawn it." Andes was trying politely to listen to the story, but it was rather difficult given the fact that she'd never actually seen another human being vibrate without the help of any electronics. But Betty Mueller's body was literally shaking.

"I mean it, Jay. Any drunk and disorderly behavior out of you today and I'm calling the police."

"Betty," the old man shouted again. "You said you lost that ring!" Mrs. Mueller click-clacked away again, even ignoring the old man in the yacht, leaving Andes to wonder who was talking to whom. Jay looked up at Andes and smiled.

"Now, if I pee in the kid's Kool-Aid, I can see calling CPS. Or his science project. He made a volcano last year. Come to think of it, pissing on it would have been brilliant! It would have given it the extra spurt it needed. Thing didn't explode whatsoever. Just kind of gurgled and then popped." Andes held up the flier again, for she had nothing to say on the subject of pissing or premature-ejaculating volcanoes, and her fair skin was at the mercy of the sun.

"I want to rent this houseboat," she said.

"Finally," he said. "I've put up dozens of those fliers, and had just about given up."

Dozens? Andes tried to feign surprise, but the reality was she'd spent the entire morning taking down every one of them within a three-mile radius so nobody else could beat her to it. Now, standing on the dock, looking out toward the lake, she spotted several houseboats, shoebox-shaped barges gently bobbing in the water. She prayed the blue one in the middle was the one for rent.

"So it's still available?" Andes asked.

"It will be," Jay said. "After tonight, of course."

"Oh." As Andes wondered where she would spend the night, Jay pushed off with his hands, sending the entire rowboat into view. Instead of pulling himself up onto the dock, he simply floated in front of her and studied her. Full six-packs of Miller Lite rested on either side of him, and empty cans formed little mountains at his feet. Andes took a moment to gaze out onto the lake. It was a perfect July day. Lake Union looked custom-made for the celebration, glittering like a giant sparkler, bouncing pins of light off the water and shooting them into to the sky.

Andes's eyes feasted on the houseboats once again. She'd already fallen in love; it had to be the little blue one in the middle. She stood on the dock, not knowing whether she was coming or going, her body stiff and still, as if she were waiting for a gust of wind to come along and make up her mind. Up ahead the kid was kneeling on the dock, his shoulders hunched over to such a degree that the tip of his runny nose was practically kissing the lake, his lips almost brushing against the discarded debris the lake had gathered into its core. It was standing here taking in his collapsed frame that Andes felt a surge of pity for the boy, and something akin to a motherly instinct grabbed her so hard she swayed on the dock and had to do a little two-step to keep from keeling over.

"Easy there," Jay said. "And here I was going to offer you a beer." At this the kid's head shot up, although how he could have possibly heard that all the way down the dock, she didn't know, but suddenly he was glaring at her, and she half expected him to scream obscenities at her again, only this time instead of hating him, she felt tender toward the boy. But he didn't scream at her, he simply lasered her with a lifetime of hatred and then stomped out of sight. Without turning his head in that direction, Jay shrugged an apology.

"He's been a little bastard lately," he said. Andes didn't return the smile Jay offered; whereas moments ago she'd hated the kid, now she didn't want to be complicit in putting him down.

"Is he your son?" she asked.

"Guess that would make me the big bastard, huh?" Jay joked. "I'm Big Bastard Senior, he's Little Bastard Junior." Andes didn't laugh. She found whenever she laughed at men's jokes, they fell instantly in love with her. She did have a magical laugh, and those in the presence of it often yearned for more. But she was turning over a new leaf, looking for a home, a place to settle down. She needed the attention of a sarcastic boozer like she needed another hole in her thong.

"Are you sprouting roots?" Jay asked, hauling himself onto the dock.

"What?"

"Let's move. I'll show you Luna."

"*Luna?*"

"The house barge. That's what we call her." Andes fell in step behind Jay, wondering as she watched him walk if he always swaggered like that, or if it was because of the slight movement of the dock, or was it the beer? After all, he was putting the beers away pretty fast, but it was a holiday, America's birthday, as good a time to get sauced before noon as any, she guessed. She wasn't a big drinker herself. She did like an occasional glass of spirits, but something of her upbringing must have stuck with her, for she never wanted to imbibe to the point where she lost control and thus increased her chances of committing a mortal sin. God was her parents' drug of choice, and as it turned out quite an unforgiving one at that.

But everyone on the dock was drinking or halfway to drunk, so why was she being so judgmental? Jay probably didn't drink much at all, which was why he was going a little overboard today, everything in moderation, and that probably included overdoing it.

As they drew closer to the houseboats, Andes's excitement grew. This was a dream come true. She thought of all the crappy apartments she'd been living in the last nine years, ever since she left home at the age of sixteen. This was it, this was finally her "making it," this was going to be home. It was a choice, she realized. Not something you stumbled upon, or found, or forced. It was simply a choice to land somewhere and say. *This is where I'm going to stay. No matter what, this is where I'm going to make the best of things.* Kind of like a marriage. She'd been waiting too long to find a place where she felt like she belonged; it was time to just settle. Make it so.

Jay stopped short of the house barges, and climbed into a twenty-four-foot sailboat docked at the end of the dock. The houseboat was off to the left, they should be turning left. Then it hit her. It wasn't one of those cute little houseboats he was trying to rent out, it was this sailboat. She'd fallen for the old bait-and-switch. Sure, as sailboats went, it was something to see. Its wood was stained a deep red, the sides curved like a giant whale. White sails soared into the sky, wrapped tight like cocoons, bursting to spread their wings and sail. The deck was all wood, with built-in benches. A table in the middle was cluttered with a half-full ashtray, the board game Clue, the *Seattle Times,* an open box of chocolate chip cookies, and numerous cans of Miller beer. Its charm wasn't lost on Andes; it was probably enticing to those who sailed. Andes didn't sail.

What a racket, trying to rent a sailboat to someone who didn't sail. What a waste of rent to let that beauty just sit there like a floating Motel 6. Besides, the house barges, sitting just feet away, were real little homes, real regular-people spaces with bedrooms and kitchens and roof decks. Roof decks. She was not going to get swept away in the romanticism of a sailboat. Besides, she knew what BOAT stood for—a hundred drunks on the dock had already told her, "break out another thousand," that's what a boat was.

Although she had always entertained the idea of learning to sail. What if it was her destiny, to sail around the world? She might even be able to make a career out it, combine her wanderlust with an actual paying job. She could become a sailing instructor. Or a journalist. She could sail to distant ports and write about them! A travel blogger. The possibilities were endless. Here she was, ready to settle, but lo and behold, fate had other plans. Still, she'd have to put up an argument, she couldn't let the man think she was some naïve, hopelessly romantic little thing who didn't know the difference between a sailboat and a houseboat.

She would let him think she hated it, even though she knew it was her destiny to sail around the world. Maybe she could get him to teach her. How could she have missed it? After all, one of her favorite books, *Dove,* was about a sixteen-year-old boy who sailed around the world all by himself. By himself. With two cats.

"Excuse me," she said to the back of Jay's head disappearing down a ladder and into the belly of the sailboat. Andes held on to the edge of the sailboat and threw her leg over the side and onto the deck like mounting a horse. She was a small person, she didn't need much room, and she was meant to be on the move. Sailing into open waters. She could send her mother a postcard. *Ghost Daughter Sails Around the World.*

Suddenly the need to live in a houseboat was replaced tenfold by the need to sail around the world, fulfill her destiny. But she'd better not let him get one whiff of her need; human beings could sniff out desperation the way dogs could smell fear.

"Are you serious?" she yelled down to Jay. "You expect me to fall for this shit?" She glanced around as she cussed, forgetting there was a kid lurking about. She'd made a conscious decision to start incorporating cuss words into her vocabulary the minute the number twenty-nine bus left the Blue Ridge Mountains of West Virginia far behind her. Still, she didn't mean to swear in front of his child. On the other hand, it was completely appropriate for a sailor to cuss, although she hadn't quite earned her sea legs yet, had she?

"Do you think I'm stupid?" Andes yelled. Jay's head suddenly appeared from underneath the ladder. From where she stood, peering down the rabbit hole of her new home, she could make out a tiny little stove and fridge. Jay had another six-pack in his hand.

"Do you want one?" At that moment, as Andes stood on a rich man's rental, she wanted much more than she could articulate. She wanted to be one of those wealthy families with sailboats and yachts they visited on weekends. She could imagine the house Jay lived in, probably one of the old Victorians on Queen Anne Hill. No wonder his kid was such a brat. Yet strangely enough, she suddenly imagined herself in the mix. She could see herself in their Victorian house, she could see them as a family. She was crazy. And tired. She'd been traveling so much lately, had barely had time to stop and take a breath.

"Your ad said a houseboat. Houseboat. Not sailboat."

"Uh-huh. Is that a yes or no on the brewski?"

"You can't expect me to live on this wreck of a sailboat." Jay's eyes narrowed and his jaw tightened. He was short, probably just 5'8", but exuded such strong energy he seemed six foot something. *Napoleon complex,* Andes thought, *but boy are those angry men sexy.* She realized too, from the look she was getting, that this wasn't just a rental for him, and she'd stepped on something holy, had gone too far, oh, she knew that look only too well. "It's not a complete wreck—it's just—not a houseboat is what I mean—and I'm willing to live here, but you'll have to do something about the rent."

"Uh."

"And what is that smell?" Andes said, taking the plunge and making her way down the ladder. "It smells like sweat and beer. No place for a lady."

"No, I guess it's not." Andes was thrilled to see a little built-in table, a bed, and a whole other sleeping space in the back, partially hidden by a makeshift sheet hanging on a clothesline. She loved it. Although it could probably use a washing.

"I'm willing to work with this—but you have to realize, I'd be one of the few open minded enough to see this as a place to call home." Jay slammed the six-pack into the sink and descended on her without warning. Andes was still perched on the ladder, and he came so close, inches from her face, and trapped her by placing a hand on either side of her head, grasping the rails of the ladder like a prisoner clutching at his bars. She could smell the beer on his breath, but surprisingly, it wasn't unpleasant; neither was the stubble on his face. His eyes, she noted for the second time, were a beautiful shade of blue. They looked like the ocean on an ideal day, they were eyes you could sail away on.

"This 'wreck' is not for rent. This 'wreck' is our home." It took Andes a moment to understand that "our" meant him and the kid, not him and her.

"Idiot," a small voice in the corner said. There was the kid, sitting at the table, listening to every word.

"I'm sorry," she said. "I love it. I've always wanted to sail around the world." Neither of them commented. "You can't blame me. You said you were going to show me the houseboat and then you lured me down here." Jay removed one of his hands and reached around to the wall nearest it. He removed a key from a nail and dangled it in front of her face.

"I was just stopping in to get the key to the house barge." *And get another six-pack*, Andes thought. "And nobody even asked you in," he added.

"I'd love a brewski," Andes said, even though what she really wanted was a bacon cheeseburger.

"Offer's off the table," Jay answered. "Now turn your little self around, march up the ladder, and get the hell out of our home." The boy snorted and turned his attention back to the thick book that lay in front of him on the table.

"Harry Potter?" Andes asked. She was red with humiliation, and burning from the way Jay had just spoken to her, but he was like an angry dog. It was better to coddle them into calmness.

"*Moby-Dick,*" the boy replied, emphasizing the latter.

"That's impressive," Andes said.

"Not on a gorgeous day like this, it isn't," Jay said. "Go outside. It's a holiday. Act like a kid your own age and play."

Andes didn't like the tone Jay was taking with the boy, but she certainly wasn't going to open her mouth again. The tiny space shrunk even more, and she had a sudden yearning to get out into the fresh air herself. She turned around on the ladder, and since Jay didn't move, she had no choice but to let her ass pass across his face as she climbed up, yet even then he didn't bother to move. Once on deck, she felt a thousand pounds lighter. It was a beautiful day, a day that if she believed in God, she'd be giving thanks to him for it. Jay was right, the kid should be outside, but she still felt sorry for him. Jay's tone walked a razor's edge, and there was no way the kid hadn't picked up on it.

But he wasn't her problem. She needed to get back to her dream of living in a houseboat, even if she couldn't sail it around the world. Andes's best trait, in her opinion, was her chameleonlike nature, her ability to easily blend into the circumstances life threw at her.

"It is impressive that a kid his age is reading *Moby-Dick,*" she said as Jay followed her out. It couldn't hurt to subtly boost the kid up; maybe Jay would realize he'd been too harsh. Then again, she wasn't crazy about the kid either. The only words he'd ever spoken to her were "pedophile," "idiot," and "dick."

Jay unlocked the door to the houseboat, and the minute Andes stepped inside, she forgot all about her destiny to live on a sailboat. It was adorable. The walls and floors were made out of wood, the ceilings boasted big beams that curved into the shape of a dome, and each and every wall had two windows overlooking Lake Union. She was on a home floating on the lake! Of course she was parked at a dock, not literally in the middle of the lake, but still she was in a different world. The type of world where you could open the door to the deck from your living room, sit out on the little front porch, and watch ducks float up to you. The kind of world where a gentle bobbing motion was your constant companion. There were two porches, one at the back where you stepped from the dock right into the bedroom, and one off the living room facing Lake Union. In between lay a narrow hallway, a small office (which would be perfect for her jewelry making), a tiny bathroom (which, yes, was emitting a faint, faint sewage smell, but she could get some special chemicals or potpourri to take care of that), and a galley kitchen. She was amazed to see the kitchen had a built-in microwave, a closet with a small stacked washer and dryer, and a ladder that pulled down and led to the best part about the house barge: the large roof deck.

Andes was so lost in dreamland, she barely noticed Jay hadn't said two words to her. But he did ascend the ladder to the roof deck, opened the hatch, and waited expectantly for her to follow. As she stepped into the Seattle skyline, she felt like a queen stepping into her throne. The view was breathtaking, the water below sparkled, and the sunshine soaked into her skin. For a moment she forgot how often it rained in Seattle, and in her imagination, she saw herself sunning on the roof deck 365 days a year, not stuck inside with rain pelting and beating the little house barge from side to side like a child's plastic toy in a tub.

Andes looked to her left, away from the Seattle skyline, and from here she could see the little blue bridge known as the Fremont Bridge, and the expansive curve of the Ballard Bridge behind it. It popped into her head that Seattle had one of the highest suicide rates in the country, and she silently prayed any potential jumpers would have the good manners to wait until after sundown to take their fatal leaps off the bridges.

In the center of the roof deck was a plastic table and chairs, perfect for sitting and sipping a glass of wine, or having an early dinner. On this day Lake Union was littered with sailboats, yachts, and kayaks. This was the one day a year where boats were allowed to drop anchor and wait for the fireworks, which would be set off from a barge in the middle of the lake. Andes was deliriously happy until she remembered her future floating dream home had already been rented for the Fourth. She wondered if she could either suck up to the interlopers or find a way to scare them off.

"I'll take it," she said, spreading her arms and tilting her face to the sun.

"Who says we'll take you?" Jay said.

"I'm sorry I insulted your sailboat," Andes said. "I was trying to." She stopped short of confessing. Would admitting to putting it down just so she could finagle a deal on the rent really help her case?

"I'll need references," Jay was saying. "And pay stubs." References and pay stubs. Seeing as how she'd just arrived in the Emerald City and didn't have a job, that was going to be tricky.

"I'm new in town," she said as if that should excuse everything. "But I have a savings. I can pay you first and security."

"References and pay stubs," Jay repeated.

"But I just got here—"

"From your old job, then. Wherever you came from."

"I was in Tokyo. And Kyoto. And Hong Kong. I was traveling, I wasn't working."

"Look, I'll give you the application and you'll just have to fill in your last employer—you have worked at some point in your life, haven't you?" A litany of jobs paraded through Andes's memory, including but not limited to: waitress, mistress, plant caretaker, dishwasher, and fairground liaison—if passing out fliers and having a quickie with a carnie behind the Ferris wheel could be considered a real job . . .

"Well yes, but—"

"Great. Put it down. And I'm sure there's someone I can call here in the good old US of A who can be a reference. Actually I'll need at least three."

Andes nodded as if this were a request she was capable of accommodating. *How about the Father, the Son, and the Holy Ghost?*

"And then I'll be approved?"

"We'll see, won't we? Drop off the application and I'll get back to you by the end of next week."

"End of the week? I can't wait that long."

"Look. You're lucky I even showed it to you today. Look around you. It's a holiday."

"I think we got off on the wrong foot," Andes said, bringing out her flirtatious tone. "Why don't I just hop down the dock and buy us some brewskis, then we can chat and enjoy the day?" Andes had passed a deli on her way to the marina. Plying Jay with beer beat the alternative of trying to find a hotel near Lake Union on the Fourth of July. Jay didn't answer right away; instead he turned to her, his eyes on high beam. She couldn't remember the last time anyone had ever stared at her so intently, if ever.

"Where are you from?" he asked. "Originally?" Unaware that she was even doing it, Andes took a couple of steps back.

"Almost heaven," she whispered.

Chapter 3

Starling, West Virginia
Fifteen years earlier

Emily Tomlin wasn't afraid when he first lowered her into the well. Her behind fit snugly into the horse harness as if it were a swing, and because her mother had threatened bodily violence if she got her new pink dress dirty, he lowered her until she dangled just a foot from the muddy bottom. Not that she had any sense of measurement or had given any thought to the distance between her and the end of the well, but she did know if she stretched her foot out she could just touch the tip of her shoe to the sludge below. But even this she did not find out until a good hour had passed, until the cross-slice of orange above her had squeezed out an angry red, seeping blood across the sky before surrendering to an inky blue. Emily conjured up a trio of witches gathered above her. They swiped at the night air with tall, gnarled sticks, swinging them high above their heads. Puffs of green smoke ignited from the tips of the sticks, unleashing a spell of pitch black across the sky. It was then, as the darkness fell down and down, and down the well, that Emily felt the first vestiges of fear. He wasn't really going to leave her down here, was he? He wasn't going to drop serpents on her, was he? She'd seen enough piles of bones in the woods to know that sometimes living things lay on the ground undiscovered for years. Would she sit here, undiscovered for years? Would she become a pile of rags and bones at the muddy bottom? Who would find her?

She had a sharp longing for her new doll. When her mother had reached for it, she pushed it away; she didn't want it to get dirty or scared. Now she wanted it. She knew it was evil to let your doll become a pile of bones, but still, she wanted her. Now that the sky had slammed down its dull, dark, cover, she could no longer even see the tips of her black shoes. Her hands were getting sore from gripping the rope, but if she let go she would either get the back of her dress dirty from the side of the well, or flip upside down, maybe even crack her head on the bottom.

This Emily was well aware of. She'd been flipped over by men time and again; seeing as how she was small, she attracted many unwelcome attacks in the form of flips: men's arms picking her up and flinging her into the sky as if she were a doll, only to be caught by the ankles and barely saved from smashing her head against the ground. Maybe that's why Emily had such a unique take on everything that happened to her—she was accustomed to seeing the world tipped upside down. So despite the stinging in her palms, Emily Tomlin clung on to the rope. Her teeth were starting to chatter.

She really had to use the outhouse, too; her bladder was bursting. She squeezed her legs together as hard as she could and felt a tingly sensation from the place where she had to pee, even though she knew that feeling was a sin. Surely he was coming for her. If he was waiting for her to cry out and beg, he was going to wait all night. Despite a healthy fear of her father, Emily was resilient. Something inside her always resisted, always fought, always challenged. Enough time had passed that she could now see again, and she tried to pick out patterns in the curved stone wall while she gently placed her feet on the side of the well and pushed off, causing a swirling motion that was actually kind of fun. What kid didn't want to swing after dark? Still, it was very, very, cold. Her mother had tried to wrap a coat around her, but her father said no. *She won't learn her lesson if she's all bundled up,* he said.

But Emily couldn't remember what lesson she was supposed to be learning. If she did, maybe this time she might relent; call out to him, hurtle her voice up the well, throw up a cry of regret and absolution. What had she done? She remembered standing in the kitchen to show her mother her new dress while the pork chops fried on the stove and the corn on the cob filled her with its sweet scent. Somewhere on one of the countertops sat a chocolate cake waiting to be iced and then topped with red gumdrops. Emily had insisted they all be red, but now she didn't remember why this was so either. She liked the other colors too, she really did. Except for yellow, she didn't like the taste of yellow. She thought of her mother's thin hands picking out all the red drops without complaint. And she remembered what was in her own hand, the best birthday present ever. It was a doll with the most beautiful blond hair she had ever seen, and she should know, she had already brushed her hair a hundred times, until her mother gently took the brush out of her hands and told her it was time to set the table for dinner. It was Emily's tenth birthday.

Emily changed her mind yet again and came back around to being glad she didn't bring the doll down the well. The doll, who she had yet to name, wouldn't like it down in the well at all. She wouldn't like the cold, or the darkness, and she certainly wouldn't like the smell of mud and something rotting, or the occasional scraping and scurrying just below her foot that made Emily squeeze her eyes shut and pray whatever it was wouldn't crawl up her leg. And she didn't want the doll to get her dress dirty; it was the prettiest purple she'd ever seen in her life, something a princess would wear. Of course, this made sense—her doll was a princess. She was a princess who lived in a castle and wore pretty dresses and ate chocolate cake with red gumdrops every day.

And she didn't have to go to church—or "meetin's"—waiting for the moment when the wooden boxes lining the wall were opened and rattlesnakes would pour onto the floor in one giant slithering pile so you couldn't tell where the tail of one began and the other ended. Her doll was too sensitive, too delicate for this. But Emily was not. She loved when the snakes were draped across pulpits, offered up in the muscular arms of the men she knew, the same arms they used to flip her or tousle her hair, the same hands sometimes offering candy, or playing the guitar, or shaking a tambourine, as they read from the Bible—God-fearing, believing men, good and simple men who put their faith in the Lord. *"And these signs shall follow them that believe; in my name shall they cast out devils; they shall speak with new tongues; They shall take up serpents"*—Mark 16—

Exodus 20:5–6. That's why she was down there.

"Thou shalt not bow down thyself to them, nor serve them: for I the LORD thy God am a jealous God, visiting the iniquity of the fathers upon the children unto the third and fourth generation of them that hate me; And shewing mercy unto thousands of them that love me, and keep my commandments."

That was what her father expected her to recite when she was laying the third plate onto the table, but all she remembered was, *"Thou shalt not bow down nor serve, for I the father hate you who don't love me."* And so that's what she said. He picked her up so fast she was still clutching a butter knife and fork when he flung her over his shoulder. Where were those? Her mother must have taken them out of her hand as her father carried her out of the house, but she didn't remember this. She only remembered how the screen door slammed behind them, how the wind stung her surprised cheeks, how anxious and helpless were her mother's eyes as she staggered behind them, begging her husband Zachariah to at least allow Emily to wear her coat.

This was the first time he'd actually put her down the well, although he'd threatened it so many times Emily felt as if she'd been down here before. But what she didn't know was how she was ever going to memorize Exodus 20:5-6 down here. She now knew even less than she did an hour earlier, now the only line that remained and played and replayed in her head was: *I, the father, who hates you.*

The well had been empty for over five years now, the spring that fed it long dried up, and a newer well had been built thirty feet out. But Emily didn't know this, and even if she did, she wouldn't have cared. She just wanted out.

And then, just as she was contemplating letting her bladder go and soiling her new dress, her father loomed above her.

"I have to go to the outhouse," she said.

"Dinner is ready," he answered. "So you decide. Dinner or the outhouse." Emily crumpled, finally giving in to her sorrow, letting the tears roll down her face and listening to the angry voice in her head. It wasn't fair. It was her birthday. Why couldn't he be nice to her on her birthday of all days? Her mother had spent all day making her favorite foods, and the two of them had talked about the meal all week, visiting it before bed like a fairy tale. Pork chops, applesauce with real chunks of apple and cinnamon sprinkled on top, whipped potatoes that looked like whipped cream and tasted like heaven, and chocolate cake with red gumdrops for dessert.

"I'll touch a snake," Emily said.

"You will not. Only those anointed by the Lord shall handle."

"I really have to go to the outhouse."

"Well then," her father said as hand over hand he pulled on the rope. "Outhouse. Exodus 20 verse 5–6, and then bed."

That night, as Emily lay under the covers clutching her doll, whom she had decided to name Rose (for roses were pretty and sweet and red), and lightly chewing on the ends of her hair, the door creaked open and her mother tiptoed in. "Are you awake?" she asked, lowering herself onto the edge of the bed. As Emily sat up and nodded, her mother placed a tray on her lap. Tears welled in Emily's eyes. It was all there: pork chops, applesauce, whipped potatoes, and chocolate cake with red gumdrops. Emily's head jerked to the doorway, but her mother's hand wrapped behind her shoulders. "He's asleep," she said. "He won't be up again tonight." And then, "I'm sorry it's a little cold." Emily stared at her birthday dinner. Part of her wanted it more than anything else in the world, but there was another part of her that knew it was too late, it was spoiled. She should have been eating it at the table with her doll, in her new dress. They should have lit the candles and sung "Happy Birthday." Hating herself for doing it, Emily pushed the plate away.

"I don't want it," she said. An unbearable silence descended on Emily when her mother removed the tray and slipped out of the room. In her wake she left a cold spot where her warm body had once been, and the faint, lingering smell of pork chops.

Lake Union, Fourth of July
Fifteen years later

The Lake Union deli swarmed with so many people, Andes couldn't tell who was coming and going. Bacon sizzled on the grill, and for the few not participating in libations, the coffee was bottomless. Andes bent down, pretended to scratch her ankle, and removed twenty dollars from the sweaty bottom of her foot. She was starving too, but surely someone on the dock would be willing to sell her a hot dog, or with a little luck, give it to her as a neighborly gesture. Not that she could claim to be a neighbor yet, but it was going to happen, she was going to make it happen. It wasn't easy; she was famished now, and hunger always made her irritable. She needed meat.

She'd tried on numerous occasions to become a vegetarian, but she failed each and every time. She liked the idea of being one, but when it came right down to it, she couldn't deny her inner carnivore. But now it had been weeks since she'd had a real meal. Beef jerky and drinkable yogurt really didn't count. But beer and champagne came first. She needed them to get on Jay's good side. It wouldn't leave her enough for a proper meal, but she'd have a floating home.

She only had enough money to pay for one month of the houseboat, and despite what she assured Jay, she couldn't afford a security deposit on top of that. She'd work it. Somehow, she'd work it. Two little towheaded boys plowed by with something popping and burning in their wake. Sizzlers. She'd never seen a community so gung-ho for the Fourth of July. In West

Virginia you'd have a few kids setting off a few cheap fireworks
and numerous shotguns, but nothing like this. She hadn't been
in Seattle long enough to realize that any sunny day on the lake
was a gift to be devoured; when the sun shone in Seattle, even
the agnostics believed in God.

"Hey, girly girl," someone boomed. "You're next." A smiling
man at the counter looked at her expectantly. Andes set the
champagne and beer down and handed him the twenty. "Love
the hair," he said, not even reaching for the money.

"Thanks." Andes waited for him to ring her up, but he didn't.
He simply stood there, staring at her. Andes glanced at the line
behind her and back at him.

"Is that your natural color?" Andes ran through her usual re-
sponses in her head. *Yes. No. Maybe. Of course. What do you think?
And, that's between God and my gynecologist.* "Don't tell me," the
man said before she had a chance to pick an answer. "It's real, I
can tell. Won't even make you drop your drawers. But stay away
from the fireboats this afternoon!"

"Fireboats?"

"They come a-sprayin' about noon. But if they catch that
hair, they're liable to turn their big hoses on you." He was tall
and skinny, with spiky black hair and bright green eyes. He
stuck his hand out. "I'm Lenny."

"Andes." When their hands met, he squeezed hers and yanked
her forward across the counter before putting his mouth flush
against her ear.

"I certainly wouldn't mind them aiming their big hoses at
me, if you know what I mean." Andes laughed politely and
thrust the twenty at him again. "So, Red. Mind if I call you Red?
Andy doesn't suit you."

"It's not Andy, it's Andes. Like the Andes Mountains. They're
not as high as the Himalayas but they cover twice the distance—"

"Still callin' you Red. So. Red. What brings you to the Emerald City?"

"I'm traveling," Andes mumbled. "I like to travel."

"I wish I could travel," Lenny said with a sigh as he finally
rang her up. Then he dropped the banter along with her

change on the counter, looked past her, and yelled, "Next." Andes would have been a bit more startled by the change in his demeanor had he not treated her to a parting wink. She scrambled out of the deli and headed back to the sailboat.

"What are you doing here?" Chase yelled when she climbed down the ladder.

"Your dad said I could stay," Andes said, feeling childish. Chase eyed the six-pack in her hand.

"Is that for him?"

"Yes," she admitted.

"He doesn't need it. He's going to pace himself today."

"Okay. I'll just put it in the fridge." Andes made her way to the tiny refrigerator, but Chase beat her to it and barricaded himself against the little door.

"There's no room," he said. Andes sighed, set the beer in the sink, and began the process of twisting the top off the bottle of champagne. She was starting to see why this kid's father drank so much in the first place.

"Are you going to drink that?" Chase demanded.

"What do you think, kid?"

"I think you'd better leave."

"Why?" As Andes pried her fingers against it, the champagne cork suddenly popped, shooting out a little mist. Andes whooped, even though under the cloud of the kid's glare, it didn't give her the usual celebratory thrill.

"Do you like snakes?" The question was delivered with the menace of a mob boss asking her if she liked cement shoes and bottomless rivers.

"I love snakes," Andes lied. "Do you want to show me yours?"

"Sicko," the boy squealed, jumping up and down. Then, as she tipped the bottle of champagne to her lips and drank, he waved something compact and dark in her face and pushed a button.

"Do you want to show me yours?" Andes heard her own voice say.

"Pedophile," the kid said, snapping off the tape recorder and lighting up the ladder.

"Shit," Andes said. That kid was a piece of work. She drank some more champagne and then headed up the ladder herself. She needed sunshine and the company of sane adults.

The minute her eyes became level with the deck, she was startled by a slick triangular head and beady black eyes. It looked to be a good size, thick and at least four feet long. Its tail agitated back and forth and it was emitting a loud buzz. For a split second Andes thought the boy had actually turned himself into the snake. The hatred undulating off the reptile was eerily familiar. Its massive jaw opened and a pink tongue darted out from between two pointy teeth. Andes screamed, and in response the snake shook its tail even harder and opened its mouth so wide she could see pink at the back of its throat. Andes's breath caught in her chest, and before she could think to drop the bottle of champagne and hang on to the railing, she fell backward. The back of her head slammed into the floor as she landed in the belly of the boat. Remarkably, the champagne bottle was still upright in her hand; not a single drop had spilled.

The kid's head appeared above her, the snake dangling in his hand. "It's fake," he laughed, banging it against the ladder. "It's plastic!" He squeezed the neck of the thing and the snake slowly opened its jaw and hissed again. "Plastic!" he shouted.

Andes only thought, as she tried to lift her head to the champagne bottle and drink, was that if for no other reason than it would annoy the kid, she was definitely going to seduce the little bastard's father.

Chapter 4

"Shit," Jay said. He was peering over her, looking concerned. Andes, on the other hand, was feeling quite good, considering she didn't think she could move. Her head was pleasantly buzzing, and she was vaguely aware of giggling, but somehow it felt as if it were coming from outside of her, as if she was observing rather than participating, and she was powerless to stop it. "What did you do to her?" Jay yelled at Chase.

"Nothing! She's not a boat person," the kid yelled back.

I am too a boat person, Andes wanted to say. *Someday I'm going to sail around the world. With two cats.* Instead she just giggled.

"Shit," Jay said again. She was aware of them moving around her, and it wasn't altogether unpleasant until Chase plopped onto the built-in bed adjacent to where her body lay and dangled his stinky feet just above her face. Andes wanted to tell him to move, but her mouth wouldn't cooperate. Jay lit a cigarette and peered down at her from the other side. *Seriously. Stinky feet and cigarette smoke? That's how they treat a possible head trauma victim?* "Shit." How many times was he going to say that? Now Andes was starting to get slightly worried; maybe there *was* something wrong with her. "Hey," Jay was saying, waving the cigarette. "Hey." Andes's eyes moved in his direction. He wasn't as good looking upside down. She could see up his nostrils. "The houseboat is yours," Jay said like an announcer on a game show.

"Oh," Andes said as the feeling started to return to her body and the buzzing in her head eased.

"Don't sit up," Jay yelled as she lifted her head. "Just rest a bit." He took the champagne bottle out of her hand and slipped a pillow underneath her head.

"I'm fine."

"You're not a boat person," Chase said, leaning down and yelling at her as if she were ninety. *Birth control,* Andes thought. *He should be the poster child for birth control.* She closed her eyes and pretended she was in a raft in the Mediterranean surrounded by blue-green waters and kissed by the sun, as her sailboat with two cats bobbed just a few feet away. Chase's toe edged closer to her face. Just as his big toe was about to nudge the tip of her nose, Andes's hand shot out and she tickled the bottom of his foot. He yanked it away. "Freak!" he yelled.

"Go outside and play," Jay commanded. Andes was just sitting up when the first pair of long legs descended the ladder. Two more followed, attached to smiling, tanned women sporting skimpy bikinis. Two were tall with dark hair piled on top of their heads, one was sporting a blond bob, and it was obvious from the way they were circling him who their target was. Andes glanced at Chase to see how he was taking it, and because she couldn't see Jay's face through the wall of tanned backs and hair blocking him, and she was happy to see Chase looked as disgusted as she felt.

"Hey," Andes said as she managed to stand up. "I noticed you have the game Clue up there." Chase looked as if he wanted to say something sarcastic, but then nodded instead. Andes grabbed the champagne bottle and the two headed up to the deck. A few minutes later Andes was pleasantly surprised to find she was actually enjoying herself. The kid was way into the game, his eyes intent on each move she made, and a little smile played across his face as she put Miss Scarlet in the Study with the Rope. It was as if he knew she had both Miss Scarlet and the Study, which she did, and when he showed her the card for the rope and she marked it on her sheet, she noticed he marked something on his sheet as well before making his move. They were so into the game, in fact, Andes didn't even realize Jay and his posse of pussy had also joined them on deck, climbing one level above them, sunning themselves near the mast. Chase's glance at them wasn't lost on Andes.

"Hey," she said after Chase had figured out it was Colonel Mustard in the Library with the Candlestick, "do you know what this reminds me of?" Chase looked dubious as Andes held up the miniature candlestick.

"No," Chase said.

"Japan."

"Candlestick trading?" Chase asked with keen interest.

"What's that?"

"Japanese candle charts. They're used to predict the stock market."

"Oh," Andes said, feeling slightly inferior, not to mention irked he was taking the tablecloth out from underneath her story. "No. I meant the temples in Tokyo."

"Oh," Chase said, as if that was nowhere near as interesting as candlestick trading.

Andes continued anyway. "Everywhere you walked there were these magnificent temples. Some were massive. Like castles. Others were little bitty things like bird nests. I loved those the best. I would take long walks and venture down unknown streets. Some of them were dead ends leading right into a temple. Like hidden treasures. And inside the temples people put objects they held sacred. Symbols that made them feel closer to God, I guess."

"What kind of symbols?"

"All sorts of things. Candles, figurines, coins. Pictures of loved ones. Quiet expressions of spirituality."

"Ropes and knives too?" Chase asked, holding up the game pieces.

"Nope. Only humble and peaceful things. And the temples themselves were built out of all sorts of materials. Stone, stick, brick—"

"So you could huff and puff and blow them all down?" Chase inhaled deeply, unleashed his breath over the board game, and knocked Miss Scarlet on her ass.

Andes ignored him and continued her story. "You know what's really funny?"

"Roadkill?"

"I always felt at home there, even though I was an outsider, a gaijin." Andes held the tiny candlestick up to the sun and smiled when it gleamed. "Someday I'm going to build a temple. Something small. Maybe I'll hide it so nobody else will even know it's there. But I'll know. I'll know."

It wasn't Chase chewing on the miniature rope that snapped Andes out of her reverie, but Jay, standing a few feet away from her, watching her. How long had he been there?

"Hey, guys," he said. Chase spit the rope out and jumped up.

"You want to play, Dad? Please?" Jay looked at Andes as he took a seat beside Chase.

"Sure, little buddy," he said. "How about the three of us?" Chase didn't look like that was the number he had in mind, but being a smart kid, he kept his mouth shut. At least this one played games, even if she didn't know what candlestick trading was.

By the time Chase won another game, Andes had finished the bottle of champagne, which, given her empty stomach and small stature, was more than enough to carry her off. "He is so smart," she said over and over again about Chase. She turned to Jay, who was leaning back with his arms spread over the boat, watching her. "Do you have anything to eat? Like—meat?"

"We could fry up my snake," Chase said. "Mexicans eat snakes. Did you know that?"

"Let's get you to Gerry's boat," Jay said with a look to Chase. "He makes a feast every year."

"Tastes like chicken," Chase added.

"Gerry's boat?" Andes asked politely.

"Gerry's boat!" Chase yelled. "Did you say Gerry's boat?" Jay stopped him with another look before smiling at Andes. "It's technically a yacht," Chase added.

"Well, you're going to be out in the dinghy eating beans from a can if you don't watch your smart mouth," Jay said. Chase laughed despite the dead serious look on his father's face.

"Last one there's a rotten egg!" Chase yelled. He was off the boat and down the dock before Andes even stood up. Jay took her arm and helped her off the boat and they followed behind, walking much slower, watching the bottoms of Chase's bare feet fly up ahead of them. Andes wondered how on earth he didn't get splinters, wondered why Jay didn't tell him to wear his shoes. Maybe fathers made better mothers. Less nagging. Easygoing about things like shoes. Then again, if he did get a splinter or worse, step on a rusty nail, what kind of parent would he be then?

Not that telling the kid to put his shoes on would make Andes a parent. What was this squeezing feeling she had toward him, even though most of the time he was mean to her? Was it because he didn't seem to have a mother in his life? There'd been no mention of one, no pictures of a woman on the sailboat, and it was obvious Jay was much more than a weekend dad. Deep down did Andes have a maternal instinct after all? She'd been around kids growing up, of course. Neighbor kids and church members were family, everyone's door was open to everyone else, sometimes there would be as many as twelve kids in their three-room cabin. And during tent revivals, there were hundreds of kids running around, and often Emily, as she was known then, became the primary caretaker. But she never had this kind of protective feeling toward them; in fact, most of the time it was a burden watching them, but she had been fifteen then—not usually the age where you're thinking about babies.

And she'd dated a man with three kids, if you could call what she and Keith had "dating." But of course they had a mother, Keith's wife to be exact, so she never felt any emotional tugs watching them from a distance, or pretending to be just another waitress when he brought them in for lunch. No, whatever this was she felt for the kid was new and different, and she didn't exactly like it. It felt unfamiliar, and it made her feel off balance. Although hadn't she just called him the poster child for birth control? How was it she instantly loved and hated this kid? But whatever it was she was feeling, it didn't stop her from wanting to jump his father's bones, especially after a bottle of champagne. And it was the Fourth of July! What better day for seduction? Fireworks!

Oh, who was she kidding, she wasn't going to get involved with her landlord, that would be a huge mistake. She just needed some meat; that should return her to sanity. "He's a smart kid," Andes said.

"It's not genetic," Jay said. "His mom and I—well, we ain't that smart." Andes laughed, but not too loud. It was how they spoke where she grew up, so if he was making fun of it, she didn't want to laugh too loud. As a child it was how she spoke too, until her maternal grandmother insisted on speech lessons and a lot more. If not for her grandmother she'd probably still be in Starling, West Virginia. She'd be married. She'd have children. She'd be a Signs Follower. There wouldn't be a grave dug in her backyard. And her parents would still be speaking to her.

"He's my life," Jay was saying. "And I'd die for him." Andes was grateful they'd reached the yacht; she didn't want the serious tone the conversation had taken to ruin her Fourth of July buzz and seduction plans.

Chase slid open the back doors of the yacht and snuck into the living room. He glanced out the porthole. His father and the girl with the boy's name were far enough behind him to buy him a few minutes. The party was taking place on the top deck of the yacht; the living room was empty and open for inspection. But a full plate of cheese and crackers, and bottle of wine perched on the counter suggested someone might wander down at any minute. He had to be quick and on the ready! Guests would also be up and down to use the bathroom, so

Chase had better be prepared. He couldn't believe it when his dad said they were coming here. Just two days ago his dad had called Gerry a faggot in front of the whole dock. Chase had never thought of Gerry's sexual status until then. But lately he'd been thinking about it nonstop, going over every single thing he knew about Gerry. Was Gerry gay? Chase didn't really even care so much, other than the fact that he hadn't figured it out for himself. But now he was so intrigued, he had to find out once and for all.

Asking Gerry, of course, would have been an option. But that was for dummies, not supersleuths like Chase. Gerry had always been nice to Chase, even with all the trouble with his father. Gerry was a good cook too, was that the clue Chase overlooked? He started with the pictures on the bookshelf. Gerry liked to read. Books completely covered one wall of the yacht, stretching from floor to ceiling. Gerry liked true crime. Was that gay? Chase didn't think so, but he knew he had a lot to learn. He also had two books on fishing, and a couple on sailing. There was at least one Stephen King, which Chase highly approved of, and a couple of travel books on Costa Rica. Costa Rica. That did sound kind of gay. Chase picked book after book out of the shelves, as if the mere touch of the pages would reveal Gerry's orientation. Magazines, that's what he should be looking for. His father kept a stack of *Penthouse* in the closet. Maybe Gerry did too?

He was about to look for a closet when he passed several photos sitting on a table. He peered down and studied them. One was of Gerry and an old lady. One was of Gerry, the old lady, and a younger woman—his girlfriend? His sister? Three others were of Gerry and a man—about his age—thinner, always smiling. In every single one they were standing close together, and they were all on some kind of beach. Costa Gay-Rica? It could be his brother. Chase wanted to slip one of the photographs in his pocket, but Gerry would probably notice. He had to find something that was sort of proof, something he could take, something Gerry wouldn't miss.

Just as someone was coming down the ladder, he spotted a

black lighter with a Playboy Bunny on it. Chase's arm shot out and the lighter was in his pocket just as Gerry himself emerged into the living room. It was obvious he was startled to see Chase, but he quickly covered his surprise with a broad smile.

"Chase. The party's upstairs. Whatcha doin' down here?"

Chase smiled, feeling slightly sick. He pointed to the pictures, specifically to the ones of Gerry and the thinner man.

"Is that your brother?" he asked. Gerry's eyes slid to the picture for only a second before turning to the plate of cheese and bottle of wine.

"That," he said, "was a very good friend of mine. Paul."

"Was?"

Gerry dug into the cork with the wine opener, looking over Chase as he did so, as if Paul were standing right behind him. "He passed away a few years ago."

"Oh," Chase said.

Gerry pointed up to the deck. "There's some orange soda upstairs in the cooler. Coke too, I think. And plenty of food."

"That's why we came," Chase admitted.

"We?"

Chase glanced out the window, although by now his father and Andes were no longer visible through the little round window. "Dad and Little Red Riding Hood." Gerry threw his head back and laughed, which made Chase laugh too. He didn't even know why he said that. Was it because he thought of his dad as the Big Bad Wolf? Or maybe he was just naturally funny.

"How did he die?" Chase asked.

"Ow." Gerry yanked his hand back from the bottle of wine and sucked on his finger. "These darn wraps," Gerry said, indicating the partially removed foil on the neck of the bottle, sporting a few drops of blood. Chase thought he saw tears in Gerry's eyes. He stared at Gerry, sucking on his finger. *Gay*, Chase thought. "Why don't you run on upstairs. I'll be up in a jiffy," Gerry said, moving toward Chase and herding him to the ladder.

Gerry stood in his living room and waited until Chase was out of sight. What had the boy been doing in here? He headed to his desk. All the preparation he'd done for this party and now this. Jay crashing his party. Chase asking about Paul. And now he'd gone and cut himself just so Nancy Meyers could have her sixth glass of wine. He didn't care what he promised Richard. He'd start tomorrow. He needed a cigarette. Now where was his lighter?

Andes liked Gerry from the moment he introduced himself. He was one of those people you like straight away, whereas she was the type that had to grow on people. She was standing on deck a little lost since Jay had just disappeared, drinking yet another glass of something—she wasn't exactly sure what it was, just that it was pink and alcoholic—when Gerry found her. She didn't even mind that he called her Little Red Riding Hood, whereas normally she loathed all nicknames other than the one she gave herself. People, it seemed, were always trying to name or tag others, like their own personal graffiti wall. But Gerry had such a big smile you couldn't help but like him. He talked of the fireboats that were to come and spray any minute, the weather—a day like this was a gem—and he made sure she tasted every single appetizer that sailed by them on a tray carried by shirtless men in faux tuxedo shorts. It wasn't long before Andes was full, drunk, and uncommonly happy.

"I can't quite place your accent," Gerry said. "Where are you from?"

"West Virginia," Andes blurted out before she could think to lie.

"So how do our mountains compare?" Gerry asked, nodding in the direction of Mount Rainier.

"It's beautiful," she said, taking it in. It looked like the torso of a large, lumpy monster, with jagged shoulders and a snow-peaked head.

"It's amazing," Gerry said. "On a foggy or cloudy day it disappears. Like it's not there at all. And then—wham—she's back."

"I thought just boats were 'she,' " Andes said. Gerry laughed.

"You got me. Rainier could be a he. A big, bad, boy, eh? And then you have the Cascades, and the Olympic Mountains. God certainly smiled on us, didn't he?"

"If you believe in that sort of thing."

"Good point, good point. Still, they have a spiritual quality about them, nondenominational of course."

"Of course."

"You're an atheist, then?"

"I'm still working that out."

"Me too." Gerry laughed and they clinked glasses. "But when the sun is out, and the mountain is watching, and the water is shimmering—"

"And the mai tais are flowing," a male voice interjected.

"And the mai tais are flowing," Gerry repeated with a smile at the male intruder. "Then I'm inclined to believe." The newcomer smiled at Gerry, then turned to Andes and stuck his hand out.

"Richard Barns," he said as they shook. He was a tall man in his late fifties with a full head of silver hair and a tan that suggested he spent a great deal of time somewhere other than Seattle. He was wearing a Hawaiian shirt and khaki shorts. A diamond watch adorned his wrist, along with a huge gold ring.

"This is Andes. She's from West Virginia," Gerry informed him.

"Oh," Richard replied as if Gerry had said something fascinating. Then Gerry and Richard looked at Andes as if it were her turn to say something fascinating. She couldn't think of a single thing.

"Andes," Richard said after a while. "Short for Andrea?"

No, for the Andes Mountains, I'm from West Virginia, and I don't know if I believe in God.

"You got it."

"I've never seen you around. Are you just visiting?"

"I'm going to be renting that houseboat," Andes said, pointing at the blue barge. On top of the roof deck of her new houseboat, Jay's Fourth of July guests had descended. Andes could make out a set of parents and three teenage boys. She couldn't help but wish a big wave would topple them off the side, but given the calm waters, the only thing that was going to do that was the tequila in the father's hand.

"That's why you're hanging around Jay," Gerry observed. "That's a relief."

"Yeah," Richard added. "I thought you looked too smart to be another of his chippies."

"They've been very nice," Andes said, suddenly feeling protective of them.

"Who's been very nice?" Richard asked. "His chippies?"

"No," Andes said. "I meant Jay and Chase."

"Don't mind him," Gerry said, nudging Richard with his hip. "He's teasing you."

"Didn't mean to get you all fired up," Richard added with a wink.

"Speaking of fire," Gerry said, pointing down the lake. Had they been speaking of fire? Andes was drunk, that's why nothing was making any sense. In the distance a large red boat was chugging toward them, shooting columns of water into the air as if it were run by a pod of whales spouting on deck.

"The fireboat," Andes said, feeling like an insider.

"They should follow Chase around," Richard quipped. Gerry nudged him again, so hard this time he splashed his drink onto his Hawaiian shirt.

"Sorry, darling," Richard said. "Too many mai tais. But the kid's an aspiring pyro and you know it."

Gerry thought about his lighter and shrugged.

"He's a smart kid," Andes said, again wanting to come to his defense.

"He's been through a lot," Gerry said.

"Does he have a mother?" Andes couldn't help but ask. As she did so, she looked around for Jay, already a little bit afraid of him and not wanting him to know she was gossiping about them.

"We've never seen her," Gerry said. "But according to Jay, she's a cokehead."

"That's awful."

"Yeah. Imagine him being the good parent," Richard said.

"Richard," Gerry said.

"Come on, Gerry. He's a lunatic." Richard turned to Andes. "About once a week he causes some kind of scene on the dock. Now, we're a close-knit community. And none of us are perfect—"

"We're like the Melrose Place of Seattle," Gerry interjected.

"But Jay's trouble when he drinks. Last week he shoved Gerry and called him a faggot—"

"It was a gentle push—a bump—"

"It was a shove. And he called you a—"

"Yes, yes. Do we have to keep repeating it?"

"And this was after Gerry had just fished him out of Lake Union at three a.m."

"Now, Richard."

"Don't now Richard me. It's true, isn't it?"

"Like I said, none of us are perfect."

"Well," Andes said. "He seems to be a pretty good father, right?"

"That depends on your definition, I guess," Gerry said. "But despite their struggles, those two are definitely attached at the hip."

"Well, they need a hip replacement, if you ask me," Richard said. A collective whoop rose from the deck as the fireboat passed. Andes spotted Jay and Chase at the bow of the boat. Even from a distance Andes could see Chase was excited out of his mind and Jay was keeping a watchful eye on him. The kid was so wound up by the fireboat he was in danger of tumbling overboard. Andes felt guilty, as if just listening to Richard and Gerry made her complicit in putting him down.

"Excuse me," she said. Before she knew it, she was standing beside Jay and Chase and had slipped her hand into Jay's. He looked at her for a moment and smiled as if not at all surprised, and then he glanced over at Gerry and Richard before once again returning his attention to Chase. If Chase noticed them holding hands, he didn't comment.

You're holding hands with a homophobic drunk, Andes chided herself. *What are you doing?* Andes wasn't even sure how she felt about Jay, but she knew one thing. She wouldn't be over here holding hands if Richard and Gerry had spoken kindly about Jay and Chase. Because there was one thing she knew for sure: no matter how much she tried to deny it, and no matter how hard she tried to outrun them, she would always belong with the outsiders.

Chapter 5

The first time was an accident. A match was flicked and it landed on top of a discarded newspaper. Flames licked slowly along the edges, giving off pleasing bursts of orange and blue. It might have stayed harmless had it not been for the greasy rag underneath, dropped out of a lazy mechanic's pocket. It happened so fast, the mini-explosion. Terror struck first. Then something odd happened. The holder of the match felt an overwhelming feeling of satisfaction. A real accomplishment! The flames weren't just eating up the newspaper, they were eating up everything that was unfair in life. Loneliness, frustration, rage. It felt really good. As if the fire was a friend. A burning, destroying, friend. Still, the fire shouldn't spread too far. Not this time. Luckily, there was a hose lying nearby, hiding like a snake in the grass. Soon a very valuable lesson was learned. Putting out a fire felt nowhere near as good as starting it.

The fireworks didn't disappoint. Color exploded over the water, and the surface of the lake reflected the rainbow bombs like a magic mirror. Andes could feel the vibrations through her bare feet as she stood on Jay and Chase's sailboat. Chase was squatting on top near the mast, and Andes and Jay were standing down on deck; Jay was standing right behind Andes, as close to touching without actually touching as possible. Andes had already decided, as long as he had condoms, she was going to let whatever was going to happen, happen tonight. To her making love was no different than the evening meetings in the one-room churches back home: the "laying of hands," expressing ecstasy as the spirit moved through her, exulting in unabashed, raw feelings. But this time instead of Brother Bosley or Brother Hennessey laying their hard-worked hands on the crippled, or sick, or lame, they were the hands of boys trying to pleasure her, and it wasn't much of a leap, there didn't exist a colossal chasm between one or the other, they were just different; tiny steps she could trace from believing in God to handling a serpent, to allowing boys inside her, underneath her, on top of her. Even if like in church, she wasn't completely a believer, even if, those back home would damn her to hell for it, even if in God's eyes she was a sinner. Nevertheless, Andes was eternally hopeful, even if damned. And so, sex to Andes seemed incredibly familiar, almost like coming home—at least as long as it lasted. And like church, sometimes it moved her, and sometimes it left her lying in a disappointing void and wondering if that's all there was.

She'd already had five lovers, but that really wasn't that many when you considered she'd lost her virginity at sixteen. Her first was Keith in the Florida Keys; then the quickie with the carnival worker, which really shouldn't count; third, a sweet guy in New Orleans after too many Hurricanes; four, a computer programmer in Texas who wanted to marry her—she still felt kind of guilty for saying yes, then pawning the ring and taking off; and fifth, a man she thought she deeply loved, and had stayed with for three years until he decided to move to Spain with a girl from Brazil. And Andes went west, first to Oregon where the small towns were too reminiscent of home, and then to Seattle, where it was small enough to maneuver but big enough to get lost in.

Jay was a safe bet as far as lovers went. If she did it once and decided it was never going to happen again, he wouldn't cry or smother her with forkfuls of potential wedding cakes, or get down on his knees in the middle of a crowded Target and pledge his undying love in front of discount detergent.

Jay put his hand on her side, and Andes moved back until their bodies were touching. The fireworks were building up to their finale, the bursts of color now frenetic and loud. Jay pulled back her hair and kissed her neck, and Andes threw the remainder of her doubts overboard. Now all they had to do was find someplace alone, away from the kid. Wasn't it his beddie-bye time? All maternal feelings she'd had for the kid earlier in the day had vanished and now she was convinced she was missing the mother gene entirely. Still, she didn't want to upset the kid either; he was obviously already unstable, not to mention watching them like a hawk, so she stepped to the side and put physical distance between her and Jay. He didn't move close to her again, but he did look at her, the question hanging in the air.

"Your little boy has big eyes," she whispered. Jay locked eyes with her, igniting the heaviest jolt of sexual tension yet. He took a swig of his beer, plunked it on the rail, and looked away.

"That he does," he said. The fireworks were over. The air was still and quiet. Boats were pulling up their anchors, starting up their engines. The folks partying on the dock turned radios back on, pulled more liquor out of cabinets and coolers. Music, and voices, and laughter converged, blending into a continuous rising chorus that signified an all-nighter. Andes couldn't help but stare at the people renting her houseboat. There were now seven of them up on the roof deck, all large football-looking people, even the woman and two children. Jay saw her watching them and laughed. "You're stuck with us tonight," he said with another quick touch to his side. "Don't worry," he added, "Chase goes to bed at one."

As the night grew, it mattered less and less to Andes whether or not they were going to get intimate. She was feeling sleepy and subdued, her buzz was wearing off, and the constant bobbing of the boat was lulling her to sleep. She was aware of Jay watching her, and it made her feel attractive and interesting. There was something indefinably intimate about a man watching you sleep. She'd lost track of Chase, but Jay didn't seem to be worried, and if anything, it was whomever Chase was torturing that they should be concerned about. It was nice to know there was still a place besides home where communities existed where everyone was welcome and nobody was locking their doors. They would be celebrating in West Virginia too: meetings, music, and shotguns. It was a long way away, but their fireworks would be just as vibrant against the coal black sky and inky blue mountains.

The thought that she would never be with her family again delivered Andes such an unexpected blow of pain that she reached for another beer. She was having a good day, a good time. She tried not to think about her mother's face or her father's deep voice, which depending on his mood could lull her to sleep or fill her with fear. But there were times when being with them had filled her with such comfort, she couldn't have ever imagined leaving.

She'd written since she'd been gone. A letter a week, for the past nine years. They'd all come back to her, every single letter, to every PO box she'd ever set up.

"Are you okay?" Jay asked, his lips almost pressed against her ear.

"Sorry. Memory lane."

Jay stood up and grabbed Andes's hand. "Let's go for a walk," he said. "Perk you up a bit."

"Where's Chase?" Andes couldn't help but ask as Jay helped her off the boat and back onto the dock.

"Wherever they'll have him," Jay said with a wink. "Don't worry, he knows where he is and isn't allowed."

Andes nodded, although if it were *her* kid—

But he wasn't her kid. And the night was young, and so was Andes, and she did want to perk up, she wanted to have fun. In fact, she was on an upswing again, she felt light and giddy. She felt like skipping down the dock. Jay must have been feeling the same, for he started jogging in place. "Race ya," Jay called as he sprinted away from her.

"Hey," Andes laughed, spilling her beer as she ran. "No fair." He was fast, that sailboat boy, but she was no slouch. Mountain girls knew how to run and climb like the best of them. She set her beer on the deck of an unsuspecting speedboat and sped up herself. Just ahead, Jay was waiting for her by a rectangular gray building with dark windows.

"What's this?" Andes asked when she caught up.

"My office," Jay said. "I'll show you." He opened the door and Andes followed him into the pitch-black interior. She felt a twinge of panic—she'd never liked the dark, and she stood completely still, waiting for him to turn on the lights.

"Are you coming?" Jay's voice said from somewhere ahead of her.

"I need light," Andes said. Seconds later Andes heard the puff of a lighter and saw Jay's strong face lit by the little flame.

"Afraid of the dark?"

"Yes."

"Oh. Sorry." He reached out his hand, still faintly illuminated by the little flame. His fingers cast long shadows on the wall, stretching toward her like a giant spider. As soon as Andes took his hand, the lighter went out.

"I don't want to draw any attention to us," Jay explained. "It's better if we keep the lights out. Just stay with me." As Andes's eyes adjusted to the dark, she could make out a conglomeration of sawhorses and hanging tools, and random boat parts were scattered everywhere she looked. In the middle of the warehouse stood an old wooden yacht, propped up on cement blocks. Its paint was half stripped, and drop cloths surrounded it.

"You build boats?"

"Mostly fix them up," Jay said. Andes wanted to ask him more about his work, but he had other things in mind. His hands were on her waist, guiding her to a far corner where a cot was flush against the wall.

"It's not much," he said, pulling her toward him. "But we'll be alone." She didn't have time to respond; his mouth was on hers, and suddenly they were kissing. And even though she had wanted this minutes ago and knew it was coming, something was lost in the speed. She suddenly found herself instead of kissing, wanting to talk. She tried to shut off her thoughts and just concentrate on his mouth on hers, soft and insistent. He was maneuvering her toward the cot, gently pushing her down and climbing on top of her. His hands started to roam, and Andes tried to let it happen, but she was certain someone else was in the warehouse with them. She pulled away from Jay and sat up.

"What's wrong?" He sounded slightly irritated, and his attempt to sound conciliatory fell flat.

"I heard something," Andes said. It was a clanking sound. Something at the far end of the room had fallen over. In the distance she could hear the voices of those on the dock still celebrating, and from somewhere above them, the ticking of a clock.

"Probably a dock rat," Jay said, kissing her neck. His voice was deep and his laughter vibrated on her throat. His mouth found hers again, and his hand traveled to her breast and squeezed her nipple. Again, Andes closed her eyes and tried to freefall into mindless bliss. But now, in addition to thinking about dock rats and wondering where the kid was, she smelled gasoline. It was as strong as if someone had poured it all around the cot. She pulled back again.

"I'm getting mixed signals," Jay said, giving up all attempts to hide his annoyance.

"Do you smell that?" Andes asked. It was unmistakable now, the sharp, sweet scent of gasoline.

"It's boat fuel," Jay said. He was dismissing her, Andes knew the tone when she heard it. But before she could insist something was really wrong, a loud whoosh erupted from the opposite side of the warehouse and a ball of fire exploded along the base of the wall. Flames quickly shot up, greedily licking their way to the ceiling. It was happening so fast, it didn't seem real.

Andes screamed, but for a split second she was paralyzed. As hard as she tried, she couldn't move. *This is how people die*, she thought. *Their bodies refuse to move.* She was mesmerized by the giant cloud of smoke gathering above the flames like a tornado as the flames devoured the wall. *The warehouse is all wood and fuel*, Andes thought. *We're as good as dead.* Jay grabbed Andes's hand and yanked her to her feet.

"Get low," he said pushing her to the ground. "Crawl. Door's straight ahead, crawl as fast as you can," he shouted as he dropped to his knees behind her. Adrenaline pumped through Andes as she crawled, expecting the entire building to explode each time her palm or knee advanced another step. The floor was hard, and sharp things—nails, pebbles, coins?—were digging into her flesh. *Go, go, go*, she thought. *Just move.* Her lungs tightened as smoke curled around her nose and mouth. She had to cough, but she was afraid it would cause her to inhale more smoke, so she tried to hold her breath. She couldn't see the door, but they were moving, they had to be close.

At least we weren't in the middle of sex, Andes thought, choosing the most inopportune moments to be grateful for the small things. After all, if she did make it out alive, she didn't want to crawl onto the dock bare-ass naked. Finally, she could make out the edges of the door. She hesitated again, trying to remember fire-safety advice. Was it safe to open the door? Was she supposed to feel it for heat? Would the air from outside feed the fire even more? Before she could pick a course of action, Jay was on it. He moved past her, kicked the door open, and pushed her out on the dock.

She wasn't prepared for the audience that waited. The residents had already started to gather, huddling in numerous groups and shouting at each other as they watched the flames devour the side of the building. Andes could feel heat on her face, her palms and knees stung, and her chest felt a little tight, but otherwise she was okay. She turned to ask Jay if he was okay, but he was gone.

Someone ran by with a fire extinguisher, and then another someone, and soon small blasts of water were at war with the fire. The more they sprayed, the greater the smoke poured out. The extinguishers were way too small against the raging inferno, making no more of a dent than tossing a glass of water upon it, but the men continued their efforts nonetheless. Unseen hands grabbed Andes, ushering her farther and farther from the burning building, which is when she realized she was still too stunned to move herself. She hated this about herself, and knew it was probably a throwback to an earlier time, her propensity to turn into stone whenever faced with a real crisis. Whereas most people could depend on their fight-or-flight reflexes to kick in when they were terrified or in imminent danger, Andes's body, instead, turned to lead. Someone wrapped a blanket around her, but for some reason it made her shiver even more.

"It's okay," a woman said. "You're okay."

Andes nodded. *I'm okay,* she repeated to herself, but she didn't really believe it. She looked around, suddenly desperate to know where the kid was. She didn't have to wonder for long; she knew when she heard a man on the dock yell, "Get back, kid," he was shouting at Chase. This was the trigger that finally released her, and her body kicked into gear. She threw the blanket off and angled herself through the throng of people to get a better look. The man she heard yelling at Chase was holding a fire extinguisher in one hand and trying to restrain the kid with the other. Chase was thrashing about, wiggling as close to the fire as he could get. Finally Andes spotted Jay, who picked Chase up and flung him over his shoulder. As Jay walked toward Andes with the kid, he continued to kick and struggle.

"Almighty Jesus," someone behind her said. Andes turned and saw Gerry staring at the flames, shaking his head.

"He's going to get us all killed," Richard said, popping up behind him. "I told you he's going to get us all killed."

"Shh," Gerry said. "Don't start."

"Who?" Andes said. "Who's going to get us all killed?" Sirens wailed in the distance. The fire trucks were on their way. Jay set Chase down beside Andes. Backlit by the bright hue of the flames, Andes could see the boy's eyes were wide with excitement. *So that's where the expression "eyes wide as saucers" comes from,* Andes thought. His hair was matted and sticking up, his face was covered in small patches of dirt, and sweat was running down his flushed face. It was as if he had been in the building himself. Andes noticed Gerry and Richard exchange another look as they too studied Chase.

"Don't move," Jay said. Then he looked at Andes and touched her cheek. "Watch him for me?" Andes nodded and Jay disappeared again, toward the fire. Chase started to move, but Andes grabbed his arm.

"Let me go."

"You heard your father," Andes said. "Stay here." The words sounded ill and maternal in her mouth. The entire dock seemed to be gathered around the burning building; apparently it beat eating, dancing, and drinking, hands down. Were they going to find out she and Jay had been in the warehouse fooling around? She didn't need to earn that kind of reputation in her new home.

"What were you doing in there?" It took Andes a moment to realize the thoughts in her head were echoing. She looked down at Chase, stalling for time. He was standing with his hands on his hips and wearing an expression that demanded an answer. Andes didn't offer him one. She could leave tonight, she thought, catch a bus to anywhere. She could take the midnight train to Georgia. Maybe it was a gift, finding out Seattle wasn't the place for her after all, maybe all mountain communities were her Kryptonite. The kid was right about one thing, she wasn't a boat person, and she didn't owe him any explanations. Firemen were spilling onto the scene, forming a line of thick black jackets with yellow stripes, a medley of hats and boots pulling hoses. Some of the firemen were in charge of crowd control, pushing the onlookers back, as the others blasted away at the flames that were now angrily consuming the entire building. Chase, seeing that she was distracted, seized the opportunity and took off.

"Damn't," Andes said. One minute he was there and the next he was gone. She was being shoved too, by onlookers eager to get closer to the action. Where was Jay? Suddenly a scream rose a few boats behind her, and like a mother with eyes in the back of her head, Andes knew one of the Freeman men was responsible. She turned toward the screeching sound, and there bathed in the half-light of the dock, and spotlit by the red flashing lights of the fire engines, was Jay, pants down, penis in hand, unleashing an impressive stream of piss all over Mrs. Mueller's flowers.

Chapter 6

Gerry, Richard, and Lenny from the deli formed a protec-tive semicircle around Andes as excited gossip about the fire bandied back and forth above their heads. She distinctly heard Richard say, "It's the kid. Somebody's got to tell them it's the kid," and Gerry rushed to hush him. Andes turned to Richard.

"You think Chase set the fire?" she asked.

"Yes," he said over Gerry's attempt to hush him again. "I do."

"Why?" Andes demanded. "Why do you think it's Chase?" Richard didn't let Gerry answer; he pulled him out of earshot and began speaking to him privately. Andes tried to pretend she was no longer interested and forced herself to turn away from them.

"Drama!" Lenny yelled. "What I tell ya, Red? Never a dull moment. Bet you've never seen so much excitement in all your life, have you?"

Andes thought about Brother Howard, a sweet retired coal miner who once placed the head of a four-foot copperhead in his mouth and left it there for the entire rendition of "Walk

With Us, Oh Lord," while his wife, Mary Jo, stuck a blowtorch underneath her chin and didn't suffer a single burn.

"Never," she agreed. Lenny grinned and grabbed her as if they were best friends. Andes looked past them, wondering where Chase was now, and then looked behind her to see if Jay was still fertilizing the flowers, but he too had disappeared again. Andes felt a stab of jealousy, followed by self-pity. People all over the world were taking action, breaking out of the doldrums of their lives, yet what had she ever done? She'd stayed on the fringes, watching other people lead interesting and exciting lives, that's what she'd done.

Once in a while she felt it deep inside her, a taunting ache, daring her to *do something*. Become a doer instead of a watcher. She was doing something, she told herself, she was traveling, she was searching for a home, she was renting a houseboat. But it wasn't enough, it wasn't out of the ordinary, and it certainly didn't require any great leaps of faith. She could disappear off the planet tomorrow, and what had she really done, who would really mourn? Could you force yourself to become someone else simply by taking action?

What if right now she walked over to Mrs. Mueller's flowers, squatted, pulled down her panties, and peed? Andes did have to pee, all the champagne was catching up with her, but then she thought about the flowers. What had they done to deserve it? They were living things, after all; if she was going to piss on something, shouldn't she piss on something that at least deserved it? She looked around for Chase. Richard and Gerry, apparently done with their discussion, rejoined them.

"What are you looking at?" Richard asked Andes. She was doing it again, staring off into space.

"Were you in there when the fire started?" Gerry said out of nowhere. The three of them looked at Andes, waiting for an answer. Andes almost gave it. Instead she broke away, moving toward the firemen. It was a small act of rebellion, which Andes was famous for, but nevertheless walking away made her feel a little bit closer to being a doer.

She saw Jay first; he was hard to miss. He was arguing with

one of the firemen. The fire was now all but out, and several trucks were starting their engines and preparing to leave.

"That's my workshop," Jay yelled. "You have to let me in there."

"Nobody gets in until we say they get in," a fireman said. "You'll have to wait until after our investigation." Andes thought she saw Chase on the other side of Jay, and even though she couldn't see all of him, his body was rigid with excitement, and he was glued to the argument.

"Follow me in there, then," Jay said. "I have to check on my tools."

"First off, back up," the firemen said, poking Jay in the chest. "You're drunk and you're shouting."

Another fireman stepped forward.

"Trouble?" he asked his partner.

"This idiot wants to run in the burning building."

Jay, who had allowed them to poke and shove him with little resistance, now stepped forward.

"Who the fuck are you calling an idiot?" Jay said.

"Dad," Chase whispered. Andes heard Chase as loud as day, despite the impossibility of hearing a kid's whisper through firemen's suits and hoses and the railings of men in a pissing contest. She tried to throw a look of warning to him, but his intuition wasn't tuned on her at all, and he didn't even glance her way.

"Back up," the fireman barked. "Or you'll be talking to the cops."

"I'm not afraid of you," Jay said. "And I'm not afraid of them." Andes glanced over at the cops. There were four of them, standing wide-legged, hands on hips, crossed against chest, and playing with a toothpick, respectively.

"Dad," Chase whispered again. Andes had a feeling she was supposed to do something.

"Jay," she said. He ignored her and took a step toward the two firemen blocking his way. One of them shoved him back. He stumbled and bent over at the waist, as if he were going to be sick.

"Oh no," Chase whispered. Andes thought it was just the thing he needed, getting sick in public, a little social humiliation to sober him up.

"It's all right," Andes said. Chase gave her a look like she was the dumbest duck on the dock and then stomped on her foot. She yelped and was about to lash into him when she saw Jay sprint forward like a linebacker. It took everyone but the kid by surprise. Jay knocked through the firemen, sending them off balance; one teetered so close to the edge of the lake that he had to grab on to the nearest post to keep from plunging in, and before you knew it Jay had disappeared into the charred building. The fire was nearly out, but smoke still lingered inside, posing a considerable danger.

The firemen and the four police officers rushed in after Jay. Minutes later, they reemerged; it took three of them to drag him out of the building. Jay stopped resisting and they took their hands off him for a minute. Jay turned to the cop nearest him and threw a punch. "Oh my God," Andes said as all hell broke loose. Jay was thrown to the ground. Chase ran forward screaming and Andes followed.

"Dad, Dad," Chase yelled.

"It's okay, son," one of the cops told Chase as they jerked Jay to a standing position and cuffed him. Jay put his head back defiantly and looked at Chase.

"Hey, little buddy," he said. Andes's thoughts were whirling around so fast she remained mute. *Hey, little buddy?*

"Is this your sister?" Andes heard the cop ask Chase. It took a minute for Andes to realize he was talking about her.

"No," Chase said.

"Do you have any family here?" Chase pointed at Jay, who was being led down the dock toward the parking lot. The cop spoke into the radio.

"No worries," the cop said. "We'll get you a place to stay the night."

"She's my aunt," Chase said, putting his hand in Andes's. "She's my dad's sister." The cop looked at Andes. Oh God. Had he heard she and Jay were in the building before the fire started? Did he think she was in there with her brother? If he knew she was from West Virginia, the jokes would get even worse.

"Weren't you in the building?" he asked her.

"I haven't visited in a while," Andes said. "Jay was just showing me his—" She stopped short of saying "tools." "Workshop." There, she hadn't lied, she simply didn't confirm or deny they were related.

"I'm sure the fire chief is going to have some questions for you. In the meantime, are you assuming responsibility for the kid?"

"Of course," Andes heard herself say. The police officer handed her a business card.

"He'll be detained overnight," he said. "You can call us in the morning." He smiled at Chase and then disappeared. Andes wondered if anyone was going to question her tonight, but from the way they were wrapping things up, she didn't think so. Besides, there was nothing she could tell them, was there? She remembered she heard something, a clink, something knocking over. Was someone else in the building? Because she didn't hear a door opening or closing, nor had any of the shadows or the lights moved, which they certainly would have if a door had opened. What was the clink anyway? Maybe a sparkler had come through the roof or some such thing. Add that to the traces of boat fuel, and poof!

But Andes had heard something clinking, something toppling over, not sizzling and popping. Still, she couldn't have seen and heard everything that was happening with Jay's hands on her breasts and his mouth clamping over hers, could she? But why did he want back in the building so bad? The minute the police were out of sight, Chase dropped her hand and walked away from her.

"Hey," she yelled after him, but he didn't stop. As she followed him, she half expected him to disappear into someone else's boat, or even stop and pick another fight with her, but instead he headed straight for his sailboat. His shoulders sagged and he walked as if he were ready to fall asleep at any second.

Pity swallowed her once again; the kid was constantly surprising her. In the morning his father would be back, and Andes knew she would be out of there. The day had been too much for her, the events too strange, already tainting her dream of living in a houseboat. She had learned to listen to that nagging feeling, the one that whispered, *This isn't going to be home.* And did she really need to get involved with pyromaniacs and alcoholics? Was that really any better than serpents and the eternal fear of hell?

This too shall pass, Andes thought as she hauled herself over the side of the boat. She was feeling the effects of a day's worth of drinking and was already dreading the hangover. She descended the ladder and tried to think of what she could say to the kid to make him feel better. But he was already tucked away in his bed with the curtain firmly drawn. Andes could feel the boat swaying; not the ideal place to have a hangover, she thought as she tried to steady herself. She had no idea what to do now.

She made her way to the little sink and looked around for a glass. She found one, filled it with water, and looked around the crowded counter for aspirin. As her hands moved the objects in front of her—an ashtray, a marble, a set of keys—Richard's words came back to her. *Someone has to tell them it was the kid.*

Where *was* the kid during the fire? His face had been dirty and flushed. What if he had followed her and Jay in the building? That didn't necessarily mean he had anything to do with the fire. And wouldn't she have seen him in there? Just then, Chase let out a tight cough, as if he had been trying to hold it in. Andes stared at the curtain as she weighed her options. Should she insist on talking to him when the incident was still fresh? She should at least see if he was awake, and ask him if there was any aspirin. She had a sudden urge to make the kid prove he didn't have anything to do with the fire. After all, it was a tiny sailboat. Did she really feel safe falling asleep a few feet away from a pedo-pyromaniac?

And what about the rest of the people on the dock? If they

thought this kid had started the fire, why didn't they say something? Maybe it was Gerry she should go see—would it be safe to leave the kid alone?

Andes once again reminded herself he wasn't her kid, even as she approached the curtain and placed her hand on it. It was the kid's father she should speak with, in the morning when he was sober and sorry. He should know what people were saying about his son, shouldn't he? Andes had barely moved the curtain when the kid yelled out, "Go away." So, he was awake, and expecting her. This gave her the confidence she needed and she yanked open the curtain. Chase was sitting straight up in bed, fully clothed, as if awaiting a confrontation.

The careful way she planned on broaching the subject, and the inquiry of the aspirin, disappeared as she met his defiant glare. "Where were you during the fire?" she asked. To her surprise, Chase giggled. He thrust his index finger up.

"Where were you when Miss Scarlet was strangled with the rope?" he shouted.

"Chase."

"Inspector Clouseau!" He started humming the ditty from *The Pink Panther.* "Da dun da duh—"

"Chase—"

"Da duh, da duh da duh da duh—"

"Stop it."

"Da dun dah duhhhhhhhhhhhhhhh." Chase's rendition became a screaming fit. He had risen to his feet in the middle of the bed, his face as red as a beet. Andes was clutched with fear; the kid was going to have a heart attack.

"Okay, okay, okay," she said softly. She started singing because she couldn't think of anything else. A soft hymn—

"Oh Lord walk with me—"

"Da dun dah duhhhhhhhhhhhhhhh—"

"For I've lost my way—"

"Duh duh duh duh duh duh duh—"

"Oh Lord talk with me, I've had my say—"

"Where were you?"

"I've reached the end, and I'm alone—"

"Were you kissing my dad?'

"I need your love—"

"You, you, you, you, you."

"To guide me home." As the last soft verse reverberated through the tiny space, both of them came to a slamming stop. Chase slumped back on the bed, the redness slowly fading from his cheeks. He looked exhausted, and alone. He stared at the ceiling. Andes started the song again as she peeled off his tennis shoes. He didn't stop her. She could ask him about the fire in the morning, when he wasn't so exhausted.

"Do you have pajamas?" Chase didn't answer, he just burrowed himself underneath the covers. Had he brushed his teeth? She supposed shorts and a T-shirt wouldn't kill him, but should she get him to brush his teeth? But he was already closing his eyes.

"Sing," he demanded quietly. Andes hesitated only slightly. On the one hand, she hadn't sung these songs for nine years. On the other, she was comforting the kid. She closed her eyes and started the song again. It was nice, singing it without having to shout over him.

"Oh Lord walk with me, for I've lost my way. Oh Lord talk with me, I've had my say. I've reached the end, and I'm alone. I need your love, to guide me home." Chase sniffed and took a deep breath. Andes thought he might be on the verge of crying, but she certainly wasn't going to point that out.

"Would you like to hear about the time I watched the running of the bulls in Spain?" she asked softly. Chase studied her for a moment and then nodded. Andes sat on the edge of the bed and folded her hands in lap. "I'm sure you've heard about the narrow streets, thousands of people running as the bulls thunder past. But what most people don't think about is the amount of dust the stampede stirs up. It's like a sandstorm assaulting your eyes as the people fly past, fleeing from the bulls. But it's the collective energy you feel from the crowd that transforms you. It's one of those rare moments in life where every part of you feels alive. And the sound, oh the roar of their feet on the pavement, the screams from the crowd. So close
when the bulls charged past, I swear I felt their hot b

my neck." Andes stopped to touch her neck. She smiled at
Chase, and although it looked as if it required effort, he gave a
little smile back. "And afterward there was a huge celebration.
Music played from every corner of the street. Violins, and guitars, and drums, beating out a victory. In my bed that night I
could still feel the stampede, still hear their hooves thundering
in my ears."

"Like I feel the sailboat move even when I'm not on her,"
Chase interjected.

"Exactly," Andes said. She and Chase smiled in their mutual
understanding. "It was a magnificent day, the kind of day where
you could die happy because you had really lived." She closed
her eyes for what she thought was just a second. A few minutes
later she awoke with a start. She looked down at Chase, afraid
he would make fun of her for falling asleep just like that while
sitting up. But he was all lids and eyelashes. His chest moved
rhythmically up and down. The boy who had spent all day torturing her was also fast asleep.

Chapter 7

The second time, the fire was bigger and lasted twice as long. This time newspapers and rags were brought to the scene. It was an abandoned shed, standing alone, no one around. A fire extinguisher was on hand too, since a hose probably wouldn't be lying around this time. The speed at which the fire burned was unbelievable! Too fast, really. Rather disappointing. But it was fun standing as close to the heat as possible, testing it step by step, dancing with danger. It was a talent of sorts. Unfortunately, cars were starting to slow down and watch, so the fire had to be put out. It wasn't fair. It wasn't supposed to be open to the public. Next time (for there would be a next time, there had to be a next time), next time, the fire would be set in the middle of the night. There would be less traffic, and the midnight sky would be the perfect frame for the vibrant orange and red flames.

Chapter 8

Andes didn't remember when the last of the partiers died down, or when the nauseating rocking of the boat turned into a gentle sway, but she must have fallen asleep, for the next thing she knew, she was sitting up, trying to remember where she was. The problem with being a world traveler was that you often felt like an amnesia victim, and your first waking moments were filled with the task of sketching in who, what, where, when, and why. It was the why that often bothered her the most. Why Seattle? Why this sailboat? Why did she drink so much the night before? She patted the tiny bunk looking for the bottle of Aleve she'd finally found stashed in the bathroom. She was definitely going to need more. To her dismay, the bottle didn't rattle with pills; instead she shook and shook and managed only to dislodge one lone pill stuck to the side of the bottle. It wasn't going to be enough. She felt hungover and mean. Mean as a snake.

"You're awake," a voice shouted from somewhere. "You're awake!" It wasn't a question, or even a statement, it was a demand. Andes groaned. What time was it? What was the kid doing up so early? She could ignore him, of course, he couldn't possibly prove she was awake. She could be shaking out pills in her sleep. "Here." Something landed on her stomach. Andes opened one eye and saw another bottle of Aleve. The kid was holding a glass of milk. "Take three," he said. "You'll feel a little better in twenty minutes. Then you can have some burnt toast."

"Thanks." Andes inched up her head and set about trying to open the bottle without moving any other part of her body.

"If, after the toast, you still feel sick, you should drink a beer." Andes groaned. "Hair of the dog," Chase added. It was unconscionable allowing this boy to administer to her hangover, but she didn't have much of a choice. Giving everything she had, she managed to sit up and swallow the pills. No matter what, she wouldn't be drinking a beer. She looked at the kid, who was staring at her with an abundance of focused energy. Morning person, she never would have guessed.

"What?" she asked when the kid didn't look away. He flicked up his arm and fanned a wad of cash in front of her face.

"Let's go," he said like a gambler enticing her to Vegas.

"Go where?" she said, trying not to move her head too much in either direction.

"To bail out my dad," Chase said, the "duh" clearly back in his voice.

"Where did you get that?" Andes reached for the cash, but Chase jerked his hand away.

"It's mine," he said. "And my dad's."

"I see," Andes said, sliding out of the bunk and wincing when her feet hit the floor. He followed her to the bathroom door and continued to talk even after she firmly closed it in his face.

"The precinct is open. But they won't see us until after eight. It's six-thirty," he said through the door. Six-thirty. He was insane. His father would probably be passed out all day anyway. What was the rush? "He's got an old truck. We could go in that."

When Andes stepped out of the bathroom, he was holding a set of keys in addition to the cash.

"I don't drive," Andes said.

"What do you mean you don't drive?"

"I don't have a license," Andes admitted.

"Why not?"

"Because I've been traveling."

"So?"

"So, some people stay where they are in their stupid little towns and get their driver's licenses, other people backpack through Europe!"

"Oh," Chase said, throwing the keys across the room. They landed in the sink. "I've never been out of Washington state." Chase stuffed the cash in his pants pockets, a little in the right, a little in the left, and the remaining bills divided between his back pockets. Andes watched, fascinated. "Bus," he asked, marching toward the ladder, "or cab?"

"Chase. I'm not going to the police station."

Chase whirled around. From the look on his face, this thought had never occurred to him.

"You have to," he said, irritating her further.

"No, I don't."

"Fine. I'll go by myself." He scrambled up the ladder. Shit, she should have anticipated that one. Andes, head pounding, hurried after him.

"Wait." Smug, he turned. "You can't go by yourself."

"Then get a move on," he said.

"What about Gerry? Wouldn't he take you?"

"To bail out Dad?" Chase yelled. "Are you crazy?"

"Fine. Friends? Grandparents? Don't you have anybody?" Andes realized how harsh her words sounded the minute they came out of her mouth. She probably would have felt worse if the kid had crumpled into tears or some such thing. Instead his face remained passive.

"No," he said, matter-of-fact. "It's just me and Dad."

"Okay," she said. "I'll take you. But—can't you give me a minute?"

Chase looked at his watch.

"Do you need a beer?" he asked.

They took the bus downtown. Andes looked out the window and Chase fiddled with his watch, which seemed to have some kind of shooting game on it. Andes had read about Seattle on her bus trip here. The city was composed of a lot of little neighborhoods; Lake Union was central to Fremont, Capitol Hill, and downtown. The Aleve and milk had perked her up a little. Maybe after she sprang the kid's dad she could do a little exploring, hit Pike Place Market and Pioneer Square.

Chase led the way from the bus stop to the police station as if he'd taken the route on numerous occasions, as if he were going to school. When they reached the precinct, he ran up the stairs, pushed open the door, and marched up to the front desk. Coffee, Andes thought as she followed. That's what she needed. Wasn't there a rule about coffee before the pokey?

"We're here for Jay Freeman," Chase announced to the officer standing behind the counter. "We've got bail." The officer glanced at Andes. She simply nodded.

"Wait here," he said, disappearing into the back. Chase immediately turned to the row of chairs lining the wall behind them, plopped down, and picked up *Time* magazine. Andes reluctantly followed, wondering if she should pick up a magazine too, even though she didn't want to risk her headache returning by reading. The officer returned and called out to Andes.

"Miss?" he said. "Would you step up here for a moment?" Chase looked as if he wanted to sprint out of the chair, but he managed to remain sitting.

"Go," he hissed at Andes. Andes walked up to the desk.

"Are you the kid's mother?" he asked.

"No, just a family friend," Andes said.

"I'm going to let the kid see him, but I'm afraid Mr. Freeman's not going anywhere."

"What do you mean?"

"I'll let him tell you his business. But he's not going home today, or anytime soon." Andes could feel Chase's eyes boring into her, and it was as if she could almost feel his feet swinging into her back as he kicked them underneath his seat.

"I'll let you see him first," the officer said. "Then the kid." Andes turned to Chase with a little smile.

"I'm going in first," she said.

This time Chase did eject himself from the chair.

"Why?"

"She has to fill out some forms with your dad," the officer told Chase.

"What forms?"

"Standard paperwork."

"So? Why can't I go too?"

Andes knew, even if the officer didn't, that lying to the kid was just going to rile him up.

"Chase," she said. "I don't know what's going on, but your dad wants to talk to me first, okay? I think we'd better just be patient and do it their way." Chase's eyes narrowed and he crossed his arms against his chest, but after a moment he sat back down.

"Make it quick," he growled.

Andes turned to the officer. "You'll watch him?" she asked. The cop shrugged and then nodded. He picked up the phone and soon another officer came out and gestured for Andes to follow him. She was quickly frisked, led through a metal detector, and then taken down a long hallway until they reached a little room to the left. Jay was sitting at a table, looking as hungover as she felt.

"Hey," Andes said, feeling extremely awkward. Jay nodded. Andes sat down across from him.

"Chase woke me up at six," she said. "He has your bail money." Jay ran his hands along the table and sighed.

"I have a situation," Jay said. "It's not good." Andes felt herself go numb as he talked. At first she was listening politely, like you would do when a stranger regaled you with their problems. And then the pieces of what he was saying started to fall into place. He'd been in a bit of trouble in the past, and it had never quite been resolved, and if she was hearing him correctly, there had been a warrant out for his arrest. Some trouble in Oregon, of all places, he said, as if Oregon was to blame. After paying the fine for last night's misdemeanor in Seattle, he would be transferred to the Oregon authorities to sort things out. He talked fast and low; Andes had to lean forward to catch every word.

"What did you do?" Andes asked, even though technically it wasn't her business. Which was exactly the look Jay gave her. Then he shrugged, as if it were nothing.

"I failed to show up for a court date," he said, leaving it at that.

"Oh," Andes said. And then it dawned on her. "What about the kid?"

Jay ran his hands over his face, coughed, set them back down on the table, one clenched over the other. "Maybe he could to stay with my folks," he said. "In Oregon. But I need some time to look into that possibility."

"Oh."

"Do you think you could just look after him until I speak with them?"

"You haven't called them yet?"

"I've been a little busy," Jay said. "Don't worry, I'll do it soon."

"Okay."

"And I need a couple of other favors as well."

"Okay."

"You got something to write on?"

Andes shook her head and turned to the cop standing by the door. He looked put out but eventually summoned someone to bring a pad of paper and a pen. Jay took the notebook and started scribbling. It seemed to go on forever.

"You have to go see Chase's mother," he said as he wrote. "Bring her five hundred dollars in cash—"

"Wait. What?"

"Can I get through this list and then you can ask questions?" Jay asked with more than a touch of irritation. Andes thought it was rather ballsy of him, given all the favors he was racking up, but she let it go.

"She lives in Olympia," Jay said. "That's the capital—"

"Wait," Andes couldn't help but interrupt again. "You have custody—and you pay her?"

Jay nodded.

"She doesn't care about the kid. She cares about the cash. As long as I keep it coming, she doesn't fight for visitation."

"You don't want her to have visitation?"

"Wait 'til you meet her," Jay said and left it at that.

"Where do I get this cash?"

"Chase knows where I keep it," Jay said.

Andes couldn't believe she was just sitting here letting him make this list—pay off Chase's mother, wait to hear from the grandparents, look after the kid—was she really going to do any of this? Sure, she felt bad for the kid and all, who wouldn't, but that didn't mean she had to get sucked into the drama of their lives, did it? *Suckers, there's one born every minute, isn't that what they say? Wake up and smell the coffee, Andes.* Except she hadn't had any, which could very well be the reason she was sitting there saying okay, okay, instead of waking up and telling him that wasn't the way this was going to be.

Just say no. That's all she had to do. It's not like the kid would be out on the street. He'd probably go to a foster home for a few days, but that wouldn't be so bad, would it? Then someone could call the grandparents—all right, she could at least do that—they would come pick Chase up, and as far as the mother was concerned, couldn't he just mail a check? She thought it was totally crazy, him paying her, but again, this wasn't her mess to clean up. So why weren't her lips moving? Why was she taking the list, standing up, and shaking hands? She was at the door when he spoke again.

"Listen," he said. "I don't really know you." *Here it comes,* she thought. At least he was finally going to show some gratitude. "You seem okay," he continued. "But if you do anything—I mean *anything*—to fuck with my kid, you'll live to regret it." She stared at him. "No offense," he added. "But it had to be said."

"Okay," Andes said as her rubber legs carried her out of the room and back down the hall. She tried not to look at Chase as he took his turn to see his father. Call the kid's grandparents, pay off the kid's mother. It wasn't going to be fun by any stretch of the imagination, but it wasn't exactly the end of the world either. She would do these two little favors and that would be it. Then she would leave Seattle. Where would she go? Wherever it was, maybe, just maybe, it would be home. And even if it wasn't, it had to be better than this.

"Here," Chase said shoving a piece of paper at Andes the minute he came out. "He made you a list."

Andes stared at it. "I have a list," she protested, holding up her own.

"Well, now you have another one," Chase said, thrusting the paper in her hands. She opened it. There, listed in surprisingly neat print for a drunk and a convict, were ten additional "favors." Andes had the sudden urge to set fire to the paper, something, she reminded herself, she shouldn't do in front of the kid. She folded it and stuck it in the back pocket of her jean skirt. Chase was already heading out of the station.

Chapter 9

On the trip back, Andes spent the entire time thinking about Chase's mother. They were going to visit her that afternoon; it was the one thing on the list Andes had decided to do. Then somehow she would find somebody else to take care of the boy while he waited for his grandparents. That's when she started wondering if she shouldn't just leave him with his mother. Obviously something was going on with her, given the fact that her son wasn't living with her, but if Andes knew anything for sure, it was that there were always two sides to a story, always. What if she'd just given up fighting for custody because Jay had intimidated her? Now Andes was actually looking forward to meeting Vicky. This was something else that wasn't exactly a good sign—the kid was calling her Vicky, not "mom." Andes was formulating a plan, and it was going to start with the way they were dressed.

"Let's pick out what we're going to wear to your mom's," Andes said the minute they were back to the boat.

"I'm hungry," Chase said, throwing his backpack on the table.

Oh God. Some kind of interim caretaker she was. Of course the kid was hungry. They hadn't even eaten breakfast. She should have taken him out to eat after the police station. Taken him out for sorry-your-dad's-in-jail pancakes or some such thing. Well, they could go out now, and while the kid's mouth was full it would give Andes an opportunity to lay out her plan for reuniting him with his mother. Maybe that's why she was here—to repair a family leak. Sure, Jay might get a little pissed off, but after he'd "sorted out" his past, maybe he'd see the boy needed both a mother and a father, and the two of them would work out a mutual parenting plan like he should have done in the beginning.

"Let's go out to eat," Andes said, forcing a tone brighter than she felt. "Do you have a favorite restaurant?"

"Who's paying?" Andes eyed the cash stuffed in Chase's pockets. "Oh no," he said. "This is bail money."

"But there isn't going to be bail this time—" Andes cut herself off. What exactly had Jay told the kid? She'd have to find this out over pancakes too. "There isn't going to be a bail hearing today," she said.

"I think we have macaroni," Chase said, marching to the cabinets and flinging them open. "You can boil water, can't you?"

"It's ten-thirty."

"So?"

"So we should eat breakfast food."

"Conforming to the masses. I should have guessed."

"Excuse me?"

"You're a conformist. If everyone else was jumping off a bridge, would you?"

"That depends," Andes said. "Are you on it?"

"On what?"

Andes found her duffel bag and dug into the bottom.

"Look," she said. "I'll pay." She should have talked to Jay about spending money. At some point the kid was going to have to let go of his loot, or she would have to swipe it while he slept.

"What does it depend on? What would make you jump off a bridge?"

"You just never know, Chase. Every situation is unique."

"I'm just asking for one."

"I'm don't want to have this—"

"One!"

"Okay. Maybe the bridge is collapsing and my only chance of surviving is to jump. Okay, kid? What about that?"

Chase shrugged like he didn't care whether or not she jumped off a bridge, or they had macaroni or breakfast food. He just shook his head and said "conformist" again under his breath, but loud enough for her to hear. Then he flew up the ladder screaming "Pig Heaven!" which Andes could only hope was a restaurant.

Andes's plan was simple. They would eat breakfast. They would dress up. They would stop and buy flowers. They would go to Olympia and the kid would make actual conversation with his mother. Andes would brag about the kid to her, lie if she had to, and by the end of the visit surely she would invite Chase to stay with her instead of going all the way out to Oregon. Not that Andes wanted to deny the kid time with his grandparents, but so far the kid hadn't mentioned them at all, and really, if Andes was going to commit herself to this, she couldn't start feeling guilty about the grandparents. And then Andes would be off. She'd already decided Alaska was the place for her. She could find a little cabin to rent in Juneau, sell her jewelry, and maybe even teach yoga. She'd always wanted to see Alaska, and since she'd always had a little of the wild in her, why not go to the source? Just having an exit plan was getting her through the morning.

Pig Heaven was hell. Or rather it was a living demonstration of what hell would be like if it were run by kids under ten. After entering through a large pig mouth, you put your name on the Little Piggy list, waiting for a booth with a curly tail to be freed of the screaming children eating from heaping plates with their hands or mouths, for no utensils were allowed in Pig Heaven, not even for adults. Andes couldn't believe this was sanitary, or legal, but she couldn't imagine a judge in the land who'd want to take on these delirious, squealing children, happy as, well, pigs in shit. Speaking of which, there was actually a mud pit at the back door, where children who'd worn down their parents during the fat-, sugar-, and sodium-laced meal were allowed to roll in before rolling out the door.

"We're not staying here," Andes said as she observed the horror-stricken look each mother wore like a trauma victim. "Let's find a McDonald's with a playland."

"I'm too old for McDonald's. I want to eat here."

Andes's reply was preempted by a football slamming into her solar plexus.

"Pigskin!" Chase cried, scrambling for the football as Andes doubled over in pain.

"First time, huh?" a smiling waitress asked Andes as she attempted to straighten up.

"This is hell," Andes said. The waitress laughed.

"The kids love it," she said. "They get to be themselves."

Andes looked around again at the screaming children. Rules like no running, no screaming, no throwing food didn't apply at Pig Heaven. It was hard to tell whose children belonged to whom as they were all milling about, eating off paper plates from the buffet set up in the middle of the restaurant. The smell of bacon and ham was hot and heavy in the air.

"Is it his birthday?" the waitress asked brightly.

"I don't think so," Andes said.

"Then what's the occasion?"

"What do you mean?"

"Come on. No parent's gonna bring their kid here unless it's their birthday or the parent really fucked up." She said the last bit in a whisper in Andes's ear, followed by a laugh that came out like a snort.

"I must have really fucked up, then," Andes said in a normal voice. The waitress shrank back.

"Watch the language, lady. No bad wolves allowed in Piggyland."

Andes resisted the urge to huff and puff and blow the waitress down. She would rise above. Chase was testing her resolve. No matter what, she would survive Pig Heaven. She'd smile;

that would really freak the kid out. She'd act like she loved Pig Heaven even though at the moment she'd like nothing better than to unleash a pile of copperheads into the mix and show these little piggies what chaos really is. There it was again, her inner meanness rearing its ugly head.

"I don't suppose you have low-fat granola," Andes asked as she handed over the flat rate of ten bucks each. The waitress snorted again, and Andes didn't know if it was her real laugh or a job requirement. She found an empty seat and a large cup of coffee. With any luck, she'd never see the kid again. As the minutes ticked by, Andes gave up her plan to woo the kid's mother. She was simply going to drop him off with her, and that would be that. She was his mother, for God's sakes, she should be stuck in Pig Heaven with the kid, not her. In fact, she was taking him to her the minute he stuffed the last little piece of bacon in his face. She didn't owe this kid anything, and the mother would have no choice but to take her little piggy back. He could wee, wee, wee, all the way home. She legally had to take him. If his grandparents still wanted him, they could pick him up at her house. And now that she'd blown twenty bucks on breakfast, forget the flowers. She'd even let him roll in the mud, deliver him to her doorstep looking like a refugee—what did she care?

Andes looked up and saw the one father in the restaurant, most likely a weekend dad, giving children piggyback rides up and down the aisles. He looked like a prisoner on a chain gang, shuffling back and forth, the will to live drained from his body. Andes smiled when Chase caught her eye from a trough across the room, and felt a thrill when Chase's face contorted into puzzlement and then outright anger that he'd failed to break her spirit. It felt so good she even reached onto a kid's plate at the next table and swiped a piece of bacon. The kid cried out, and Andes snorted. Seconds later, Chase wanted to leave.

"Oh no, you don't," Andes said as Chase headed for the front door. "We're going out the back."

"You're embarrassing me," Chase yelled as Andes grabbed a piggy-tail straw off a table and held it to her ass.

"Tough," she said. "Deal."

"You're a freak," Chase yelled.

Andes whirled around so fast Chase would've rammed into her if not for the excess sugar and nitrates in his body temporarily quickening his reactions. Andes immediately sat on the edge of a booth where a family sat stuffing their faces, grabbed Chase's hands, and pulled him to her so that they were eye to eye.

"There are a lot of names you're free to call me," she said in a voice that hushed every pig within ten paces. "You can be as nasty as you like, and I won't say a word. You can push every single button I have and I'll just sew them back on. But you don't ever—I mean ever—call me a freak. If you do—if you even so much as mouth the word—I will bring the wrath of the universe down on you, and I promise you, you don't want to know what that feels like."

They stared at each other for a few seconds. Chase seemed to be weighing the words, digesting the tone. Then he looked away.

"Okay," he said.

"Okay," Andes said. "Now let's go roll through some mud."

Chase was smart enough, or afraid enough, to acquiesce.

Chapter 10

In the end, they didn't roll through mud. Chase didn't want to because Andes giving him permission took all the fun out of it, and Andes didn't want to because she was after all, a girl. And they did freshen up a bit and pick up pink carnations before boarding the bus for Olympia. Just like the short trip into downtown Seattle, they didn't speak much on the nearly four-hour ride. His mother lived a short distance from the bus stop, and once again Chase led the way. Soon they were standing in front of a dilapidated Victorian house with a large front yard.

If the yard had a voice, or a social worker, it would have yelled, *Clean me up*. It was so littered with toys and junk, Andes found herself looking for price tags, as if someone was preparing for a flea market. Amongst the broken and dirty toys were fast-food wrappers, soda cans, and what appeared to be car parts, digging into the ground and leaking rust. In between the detritus weeds grew. Andes stood still, as if a single step might cause an explosion of junk. Chase plunged straight ahead, maneuvering through the obstacles with little interest. Andes almost overlooked the obese orange tabby who, defying physics, had perched his large furry mass on the railing of the porch.

"Hey, kitty," Andes whispered as she moved toward him. Chase watched her. When Andes was a few feet from the cat and reaching out to pet it, Chase lunged forward.

"Don't touch him." Andes ignored Chase and moved closer. "He'll bite you." Just as Andes touched the tip of the fat cat's head, he let out a hiss that rivaled that of any snake Andes had ever heard. She tried to yank her hand away, but the cat's teeth had already sunk into the softest flesh of her palm. Andes screamed and the cat yowled as if the bite had hurt him worse than it hurt her. Then he leaped off the rail and landed somewhere in the jungle of the yard. Andes's palm was bleeding. It wasn't fair. Andes loved animals. When they didn't like her back she felt judged, and condemned, way more rejected than she would have by a human.

"I told you," Chase exclaimed as Andes studied her bloody palm. "Jesus."

Andes didn't know if he was drawing a religious comparison or simply swearing. Not that she really cared. She was too busy worrying about rabies and trying not to dwell on the memories the hiss and bite brought up of another time, another place— memories best kept locked away. She had to concentrate on the chipped paint of the porch to keep her mind from going there.

"Are you crying?" Chase asked. His voice sounded more curious than accusatory, but Andes had learned his moods swung like a weather vane, and she wasn't going to get lured into thinking he actually cared whether or not she was okay. And even though it wasn't the kid's fault she'd been bitten, in fact he'd even tried to warn her—*he told her so*—she was still pissed. There was something about him that pushed all her buttons. It was the same something that made her fiercely protective of him, and she neither understood nor welcomed either emotion. One thing was for sure—the kid was staying here, and she was going to Alaska. Or the emergency room.

Chase was pushing open the door. Andes wanted to scream at him to knock, but he was already inside. For a minute she thought maybe she wouldn't even go in. She was highly aware that all she had to do was turn around, go back through the maze of junk, and disappear forever. Really, could anybody

blame her? How terrible would the headlines be? GIRL ABAN-
DONS BOY SHE BARELY KNOWS WITH HIS BIOLOGICAL MOTHER. Shock-
ing. But she didn't leave; instead she walked up to the partially
opened door.

She could hear the blare of a television, a violent video game
with grunts and explosions. She stepped into a dim foyer where
she was met by a symphony of smells. Cigarette smoke, mold,
and something heavy and sweet, like burnt syrup. From the
other room a kid's voice cried out, "Motherfucker!" It was a
young boy's voice, but she was pretty sure it wasn't Chase.
Andes reminded herself it wasn't too late to turn around. And
why was she the one holding the pink carnations?

"Hello?" she called out. "Hello?" She didn't want to venture
any farther without a gas mask, but unless she was going to turn
around and leave, she had no choice. It was of little consolation
that she'd probably get used to the smell. Her hand was bleeding less, but it was throbbing, and she prayed Chase's mother
would know whether or not the devil cat had been vaccinated.

Chase and another boy, a pale skinny thing with white-blond
hair, were seated inches from a giant television screen. In its
day it had been the television to own, a huge screen that came
with the price of bulk; it was so chunky, it could have been a
china cabinet. Today's sleek plasmas made it obsolete, a tech-
nological dinosaur, but the four-year-old boy and Chase didn't
seem to care. The video game was on full blast; they were racing cars down a highway while animals darted across the road.

Andes averted her eyes and it took everything she had not to
yell at the children to turn it down and back off from the screen.
She paused for a moment wondering why mankind was so violent. Even children had this propensity deep inside to see things
crash, explode, and burn. Even if it was an innocent bunny rabbit crossing the street. Andes could probably make a fortune in-
venting a snake-handling video game, but you wouldn't see her
running out and acting on that impulse. Oh, wouldn't George
Turner have an orgasm over that.

She shut off her thoughts. She couldn't believe how often
she thought about George Turner as if it had happened yester-

day and not almost a decade ago. But he wasn't her problem anymore, and neither were the kids. *This is not my problem, this is not my problem, this is not my problem,* she chanted silently as she continued through the house, looking for the woman whose problem it was.

The kitchen was in shambles. Dishes were piled everywhere. In the sink. On the stove. On the table shoved into the corner. From behind the pile of dishes on the table Andes could see cigarette smoke curling up an invisible chimney, as if behind the pile of dishes there was a dollhouse fireplace. Either that or Barbie was hitting the fags.

Andes looked closer and could make out white, stringy blond hair. She crept forward until she could see over the dishes. Hunched over, with a cigarette in her mouth, was a teenage girl.

"Hello?" The girl's head shot up, and trembling hands hit the table as she jerked back, causing the wall of plates to wiggle precariously. Andes lunged forward just in case they were about to take a tumble, but miraculously they stayed in place. Now that she was close to the girl, she could see she wasn't a girl at all. Her face was skeletal, and the lines betrayed she was a grown woman. But she was so gaunt Andes couldn't tell her real age. She could have been twenty or fifty. Her eyes were red, her lips slightly swollen. Andes resisted the urge to recoil and attempted a smile.

"I'm Andes," she said in a soft voice. "I brought Chase."

"Chase?"

"Your son?"

Vicky brought her fist down on the table, but this time Andes didn't make a move to save the plates, which once again jostled but didn't crash to the floor.

"I told that motherfucker to stop calling him that."

"I'm sorry?" Andes said.

"His name is Hector."

"Hector?" Andes looked around as if there were a Hector hovering about, hidden somewhere in the messy kitchen as if they were playing a live game of "Where's Waldo."

"That motherfucker started calling him Chase because when

he was about two he had to chase him all over the place." Vicky snorted.

"Oh." Chase's name was Hector? *You must never use this against the kid, never, ever, ever,* Andes told herself, fearing she would break this promise the next time the kid did something obnoxious.

"Like you can really chase anyone on a motherfucking sail-boat!" Vicky shrieked. She had a point there, but Jay could have been chasing him around the dock instead. Andes didn't bother to throw this in.

"Hector is his grandfather."

Andes made sounds like she cared, but she was really looking around thinking, *This is America. People all over America sit in dirty kitchens while children become deaf, dumb, and blind from video games.* She wanted to ask how they could afford a giant *mother-fucking* television but not dish soap. This wasn't the America they showed on soap operas or movies of the week, unless it was about redemption, unless by the end the program the poverty-stricken folks were suddenly wealthy and clean. No, these were the homes you saw on Jerry Springer. Americans would only watch them if they were reduced to daytime sideshows.

"Did you bring the money?"

"Here it is, Vicky." Andes didn't know how long Chase had been standing there, but suddenly he was moving in front of her, trying to figure out where on the table to place the pile of cash. He didn't have to search long, Vicky reached out and grabbed it from him.

"Thank you, Hector," she said. Chase flinched, but simply nodded. He looked up at Andes as his mother counted the money. Andes found herself staring at the woman's trembling hands.

"Ready?" Chase said.

"For what?"

"To go. Let's go." Vicky didn't protest. She was still counting, silently mouthing the amount as she did. When she was fin-ished, she frowned and started again. Andes looked helplessly around the kitchen. Somebody should do the dishes. In fact, the whole place needed to be cleaned top to bottom. She was afraid to open the refrigerator, but she couldn't imagine it held anything good for the kid in the next room to eat.

"What's your brother's name?" she asked Chase.

"Half brother," Chase said. "Timmy."

Way better than Hector, Andes thought.

"How old is he?"

Chase shrugged. "Dunno. Let's go."

Should she do the dishes? Call Child Protective Services? At the thought, Andes looked at the carnations still planted in her hand. *Help! I've got starving carnations here with nowhere to go but a dirty vase. Bring reinforcements now!* Andes looked around for a place to set the carnations. She opened the cupboards. There weren't even any clean glasses big enough to hold the flowers. Realizing the futility, she dumped them on an old plate of spaghetti. Her plan to leave Chase here had gone out the window, and she'd almost forgotten that she might have rabies, could start frothing at the mouth at any second. Vicky, obviously dissatisfied with the cash count, pushed herself away from the table, stuck a cigarette in her mouth, and bent over the stove. Then she turned on the gas and leaned over until the tip of the cigarette touched the dancing orange and blue flame. Chase watched, fascinated. Wispy blond strands were so close to the fire, Andes lunged to turn off the gas.

Vicky jerked back, startled.

"Sorry," Andes said. "But your hair." She pointed at Vicky's hair and the burner. Vicky took a long draw on the cigarette and shrugged.

"I think we should help with the dishes," Andes said, turning to Chase. But where to begin? Did she even have sponges or dishwashing liquid?

"Don't bother," Vicky said.

"The next bus is in twenty minutes," Chase said. "We can catch it if we run really, really, really fast."

Andes pulled Chase aside, which wasn't really necessary since Vicky wasn't paying attention anyway; she was smoking and staring out the window like an episode of *When Good Mannequins Go Bad.*

"Is she always like this?" Andes whispered.

"Like what?" Chase was truly puzzled. Andes gestured at catatonic Vicky and then at the mess around them.

"Like this!" Chase shrugged again, a gesture that was starting to really irritate her, but she knew she was just cranky—how could she leave Timmy here with in this mess, with this woman?

"Does Timmy's father live here?"

"Sometimes," Chase said.

"Does she have other kids too?"

Another shrug.

"That you know of?"

"No."

"We'll go in a few hours," Andes said, digging in her purse for her cell phone.

"A few hours?"

"We're going to the store to buy some cleaning supplies, then we're making lunch for your brother—"

"Half brother—"

"Then I'm—making a phone call." There was no way she could leave without calling CPS. This was neglect, plain and simple; the filth in the house alone was reason to call.

But what if the little boy ended up in an abusive home? Or one without PlayStation? Andes knew either would terrorize the boy for life. Her thoughts were interrupted by Vicky pounding on the table.

"Motherfucker!" This time one of the plates escaped from its stack and crashed to the floor, splashing dried bits of tomato sauce—at least Andes hoped it was tomato sauce—all over the dirty linoleum. Vicky didn't even blink.

"Hector," Vicky said, in the first motherly tone Andes had heard out of her. "It's fifty dollars short." Chase started to move forward and speak, but Andes stopped him with her hand.

"Are you kidding me?" Andes said.

"Don't," Chase said quietly.

"And where's your father?" Vicky said glaring at Andes as if seeing her for the first time.

"He's—" Andes started to say.

"Working," Chase interjected quickly.

Vicky snorted. "Does he think I'm mother—"

"Watch your language," Andes warned. Vicky glared at her again. "You have children," Andes stated.

"Who I have to feed," Vicky said, shaking the wad of bills in Andes face. "He's fifty dollars short!"

Andes knelt down to Chase.

"Go in the other room," she whispered.

"What are you doing?" Chase whispered back.

"Just go." Chase gave her a look that equaled Vicky's in its capacity to shrink the receiver into a tinier version of themselves, but Andes held his gaze until he slumped out of the room.

"Do you have anybody you can call?" Andes asked Vicky.

"For money?"

"No. For help."

"I don't need help."

"Either you call someone or I will," Andes said.

"What do you mean?"

"I mean, either you call someone to come over and take care of your son—your other son—and help you clean up this mess and whatever else it is making you shake like that, or I'll have no choice but to call Child Protective Services." From the other room came the sound of a great explosion followed by both boys shouting, "Yes!" Vicky curled in on herself, crossing her legs tightly and hunching over as she puffed furiously on what was left of the cigarette.

"I'm just a little behind," she said, looking around. But the attitude was gone, and defeat had taken over her eyes. Andes almost felt relieved. Her instincts had been correct; Vicky wanted to be forced to get help. Andes marched over to the telephone on the wall, snatched it up, and brought it over to her.

"Well?"

Vicky took the phone. She dialed a number by heart. Andes went over to the sink, mostly to give her privacy, but also hoping to find soap. Vicky was soon mumbling into the phone, and the next thing Andes knew, Vicky was holding the phone out to her.

"She wants to talk to you." It only took Vicky's sister-in-law Beth a half an hour to arrive. And as Andes requested, she brought cleaning supplies. Vicky was onto another cigarette and barely looked up as Beth introduced herself to Andes. She was an attractive woman in her mid-thirties. She had short blond hair cut in a bob, and she was wearing what appeared to be surgical garb.

"Don't worry," she said when she caught Andes looking at her attire. "It's my day off, but I can't help it, I like to be comfy." She glanced at Vicky, then at the mess, and shook her head.

"I'm glad you made her call," she said. "She hasn't taken my calls in weeks. I should have just driven over, but"—she glanced toward the living room—"it's a lot to take on another kid."

"We could call CPS, but—"

"No. My nephew isn't going into foster care. I've taken him before. I'll do it again. And you," Beth said to Vicky. "Are you using again?"

"Does it look like I'm using?" Vicky shouted. "Look at me! Look at my hands!" She held her shaking hands up while keeping the cigarette clenched in her mouth.

"Withdrawals," Beth said. "They're a bitch."

"Go pack a suitcase for Timmy," Beth told her. Andes thought Vicky would protest, but instead she quietly left the room.

"I'll probably have to do it over, but she needs something to do." Beth and Andes started on the dishes. Beth began clearing a spot to pile the old ones and Andes started the water in the sink.

"So," Beth said, "I take it Jay has a new girlfriend." It took Andes a minute to realize Beth meant her.

"No," she said. "No. I'm just—a new neighbor."

"Right," Beth said with a derisive laugh as the first grouping of dishes disappeared into the suds. "So where is he?" she asked.

"Work," Andes said. Beth shook her head but didn't say anything.

"He had to go out of state, actually," Andes heard herself say. "He's going to help build a houseboat in Hawaii." Oh shit. Now why did she go and say that? Beth's laugh told her it didn't matter; she didn't believe her anyhow.

"I see," Beth said. "So who's going to take care of Hector?"

"I think he prefers 'Chase,' " Andes said as she scrubbed at a pot. "I am," she added. "I'm looking after Chase for a while." Andes didn't know why she just didn't tell her the truth, that Chase was going to stay with his grandparents in Oregon, but it was too late, the lie had already slipped out of her mouth.

"You're kidding," Beth said again. Andes stopped scrubbing and looked the woman in the eye. Where she came from, this was the only thing to do when others needed a "talkin' to." The woman held her gaze for a few seconds and then looked away. "That's a lot of responsibility for just a neighbor to take on, isn't it?"

"It's just until his grandparents come," Andes said.

"Jay's parents? You're kidding."

"You seem to think I do a lot of kidding," Andes said with an attempted laugh.

"Sorry. I just—I didn't even know Hector had grandparents."

"Well, he does. They live in Oregon."

"Have you met them?"

"Not yet." Beth made space next to Andes to dry the dishes.

"Hope they're not anything like him," Beth mumbled. Vicky entered the room with a handful of clothes.

"Like who?" she demanded.

"Jay's parents are going to watch Hector while his father's in Hawaii," Beth informed her.

"Hawaii!" The word came out as a screech. Vicky dropped the clothes on the floor. "That motherfucker's in Hawaii?" Chase ran into the room and stood in the doorway, but Andes and Beth were too busy trying to calm Vicky's shrieking to notice.

"It's for work," Andes said, quickly figuring it was easier to stick to the lie. "He's helping build a houseboat."

"He shorted me fifty bucks and he's in Hawaii!"

"Calm down," Beth said. "I'm sure 'Hawaii,' " she said, drawing quotes, "is a euphemism for rehab."

"That motherfucker," Vicky said, but quieter this time.

"You're the one who slept with him," Beth muttered.

"So?" Vicky said, the screech back in her voice. "Miss High and Mighty. I've slept with a ton of men."

"Good for you."

"Including your good-for-nothing brother!"

"Don't I know it."

"Who has a small dick!"

"Vicky, I swear to God—"

"Unlike Jay, who has a whopper."

"Vicky!"

"But he's not the biggest or best I've ever had. I had me a nice fireman once." At this Andes stiffened and glanced toward the living room. There was Chase, in the doorway. "It was a summer fling. Just a fly in and fuck for the weekend thing. I was sleeping with him at the same time I was sleeping with Jay."

"Vicky—" Andes tried to cut in.

"For all I know, he's Hector's real father! Dave Mother Fucking Jensen from Sunnyside, Queens!" Somebody gasped and the slippery glass Andes held in her hand crashed to the floor. She looked at Chase again, hoping beyond hope he'd gone away, but he was still standing there, riveted to the scene. And there was no doubt about it; Chase had heard every motherfucking word.

Chapter 11

By the time Andes and Chase left his mother, her house was clean and his half brother was safe, but Chase was a mess. His lips kept were constantly moving, silently rolling the name "Dave Jensen" over and over, once in a while shaking it up by adding the word "fireman" or "Queens." Andes was mouthing too, but hers was a simpler: "motherfucker." If anyone on the bus had cared to study the pair, they would have screamed for the bus driver to stop so they could drop the two off at the nearest mental institution. Andes found herself looking forward to getting back to the marina. She was exhausted, and the Fourth of July already felt like weeks ago. She and Chase could have a relaxing evening, play Clue, order a pizza, go to bed. In the morning she'd call his grandparents and they could figure out if they were coming to Seattle to pick him up, or if she and Chase had to go to Oregon.

She had yet to say anything to the kid about his mother's outburst, although it was sitting between them, making the stifling air in the bus all the more unbearable. He was a smart kid; he knew he couldn't trust a word that woman said, didn't he? On the other hand, what did Andes know about any of it anyhow? Nothing. Nor did she really want to know any more. She was starting to realize that the best thing for the kid would be if Jay were able to solve his little problems as quickly as possible and get back home to the kid. Andes glanced at him. He was leaning back against the seat; his eyes were half closed and his lips were moving. He appeared to be singing without an iPod. She turned back to the window and lost herself in the Olympic mountain range, so clear that when she put her hand on the window and traced the peaks, she could almost feel their sharp, cold points.

"How does pizza for dinner sound?" she finally asked.

"Perfect," Chase answered. Andes was slightly surprised at his casual acceptance; she had grown used to preparing herself for arguments. "Pizza and packing," Chase said.

Packing? Andes thought. "Packing heat" rose to mind.

"Your grandparents might come here, though," Andes said. "So we should wait on the packing."

"What grandparents?" Chase demanded. And there it was, attitude back, pleasantries obliterated.

"Your grandparents," Andes said. "Jay's parents." Chase looked at her like an evolutionist would look at a creationist after presenting insurmountable evidence on how the creatures of this planet, including humans, have come to exist, only to have the creationist reject it with a simple "Praise God."

"I don't know what he told you," Chase said. "But my paternal grandparents are dead."

"What?"

"So they're definitely not coming to get me," he continued. "But on the off chance they do, I'm going to run." Chase started laughing then, which is when Andes realized she'd never really heard him laugh. Had he not been somewhat laughing at her, she would have been taken with what an innocent, warm sound it was. It was also an honest laugh, which meant he was either telling the truth, or he *thought* he was telling the truth. Andes wasn't going to have it out now, it was Jay who needed a "talkin' to." She'd almost forgot what she and the kid had been talking about in the first place, and when she remembered she almost kept her mouth shut, but curiosity won out.

"Packing for what?" she asked.

"Queens," Chase said. "I'm going to Sunnyside, Queens."

It was Andes's turn to laugh, although she hadn't meant to.

"Since when did the pilot die and leave you in charge of the plane?" she said. This was something she'd once heard a little boy in her class say, when she was about Chase's age, and she'd gone around saying it for a full year—in school, at least, never at home or meetings. What was it about Chase that reduced her to a child? Still, it was an appropriate question—unless of course they had actually been on a plane, in which case it would have been totally inappropriate, and given today's sensitive flying climate, she would never say it on an actual plane. If a flight attendant heard her, she might be stripped of her free nuts or thrown off the plane altogether.

"That doesn't even make sense," Chase said. "We're on a bus."

"Fine. We're not going to Queens. Does that make more sense?"

"I don't care what you do," Chase said. "I'm going to Queens."

"We'll just see what your father has to say about that," Andes said.

"Which one?" Chase replied.

Andes had to admit, she liked sitting up on the deck of the sailboat, watching the world go by as it gently bobbed in the water. The pizza was on its way, but instead of playing Clue, true to his word, Chase was packing. Andes wished she didn't have to wait until morning to have it out with Jay. There were two very important things she intended to confront him with. One: the Alive or Dead game, starting with—your parents!

Two: Where is the key to my houseboat? The floating barge was locked up tight as a drum, and a cursory search of the sailboat hadn't turned up the key. He'd probably stuck it in his pocket after giving her the tour, and after that they were in a burning building, and then he was in jail. She thought maybe she could go to the warehouse and look, although it probably wasn't a good idea since the police had yet to take down the yellow crime scene tape. She wondered if they were close to figuring out how the fire started. When the pizza came, Andes paid the delivery boy with her last twenty dollars and called down to Chase. She set the pizza box on the built-in table, sat in a deck chair, and dug in. Moments later Chase joined her. She hadn't thought about getting a beer out of the fridge until she saw him. He was dressed in a purple cape and wearing a gold crown. Had it not been for the long, curly blond wig and bright red lipstick, she would have wondered why he was dressed as a king. A man carrying a case of beer in one arm and a poodle in the other stopped to stare. Chase smiled and waved at the man as if greeting his royal subjects. The man slightly frowned and then lifted his poodle in a wave before moving on. *That makes three things I'm going to have to talk to Jay about,* Andes thought. And why couldn't she have been stuck with a stray poodle instead?

Andes would have thought Jay wouldn't have been in any real position to be intimidating, but she was wrong. On their next visit he asked to speak to Chase alone first, and then Andes. She was hoping she'd get the chance to see the look on Jay's face when Chase walked into the holding room wearing his queen costume, but instead she sat in the lobby rifling through the newspaper that just held more of the world's woes. She expected Chase to come out dejectedly carrying his costume, but he didn't. He swept out, his cape trailing the ground, his head held high. But Andes saw the change and knew immediately from his red cheeks and slightly elevated breathing that the two had fought. He sat down next to her and started swinging his legs. An officer came out and motioned for her to follow him. The thought of leaving Chase like that without offering any words of comfort tore at her, yet she didn't know what to say. She would have given him money to get a snack out of the machine, but in her hurry that morning she'd left the last of her little stash at home. She followed the officer down the hall to where Jay was waiting, all the while preparing herself for a fight of her own.

"What's with the outfit?" Jay asked the minute she stepped into the room.

Andes looked down at her sundress. It was yellow with colored flowers. It came to just above her tanned knees, and on her feet she wore her usual pink flip-flops. Her hair was pulled back in a banana clip, and her large sunglasses were perched on her head. Her jewelry was made by her own two hands, faux emeralds interspersed with pearls, matching dangling earrings, and a chunky bracelet in which she had superglued all of her favorite stones: tiger eye, rose quartz, hematite, and amber. She took on a defensive posture and made a point of taking in Jay's government-issued jumper and two-day shadow.

"It's more than I can say for yours," Andes said, pulling out her chair and trying not to wince at the screeching sound it made across the linoleum floor. She was surprised to hear Jay laugh.

"Not yours," he said, still chuckling. He jerked his thumb out the door. "Chase."

"Oh." Andes laughed too until Jay managed to ruin it.

"Why is my son dressed like a fag?" Jay practically yelled, all humor off the table.

"Why are you teaching your son sexual orientation intolerance?" Andes yelled back. She was no longer afraid of this man, in part due to the guard posted outside the door. Jay sighed, drummed his fingers on the table.

"They don't let me smoke in here," he said.

"Chase said your parents are dead," Andes said.

"They're taking me to Oregon tomorrow," Jay said, changing the subject.

"You mean they're extraditing you. What did you do?" she asked.

Jay sighed and looked away. Then he looked back at her, and they engaged in a staredown.

"I think you owe me that much," Andes said.

"I had a friend in Oregon. Back in the day. I had my pilot's license. This was before Chase was born. For a little extra cash, my friend asked me to run some packages from him. From Oregon to Florida."

"Drugs?"

"It would seem so."

Andes took this in. She didn't know what the proper response was, she hadn't seen any Hallmark cards saying, "Sorry You Got Busted for Flying Drugs in Your Little Plane Across State Lines," so she kept her mouth shut.

"When my friend got caught, they put on the squeeze. Wanted to clean up Portland." Jay stopped to laugh. "They already had the big guy, see? They had him. He was the fucking drug lord. But no, that's not enough for this prick DA. He wants all the little fish too. He wants the fucking delivery boy. So I ran."

Not very far, Andes wanted to say. *You went one state over. Why not Mexico? Why not Alaska?*

She'd forgotten about Alaska. That's where she was going. As soon as they figured out what to do with the kid.

"So you get arrested for punching out a fireman and now Oregon comes knocking," Andes said, trying to fill in the gaps.

"Fireman? I hit a police officer," Jay said. Oh. Andes realized she had firemen on the brain. Now wasn't the time to bring that up either.

"So what about the charges here? Hitting the police officer?"

"Seems they're going to bat me back and forth. Oregon wants me first and Seattle has agreed because they're waiting to see if they're going to . . . add any charges. And then I may even have to stand trial in Florida."

"Let's take this a step at a time," Andes said. "The charges in Seattle are minor, right? What? Assaulting a policeman?"

"And possibly arson," Jay mumbled.

"What?"

"My dumb luck, that's what. It's the tenth marina fire in Seattle this season. Seems there's a serial arsonist on the loose." Andes stared at Jay as her mind tried to entertain her with inappropriate images, as it always did. Serial arsonist made her think cereal arsonist, and in her head Froot Loops were exploding and Cheerios were running down the street with flaming Mohawks. Jay suddenly leaned forward and grabbed Andes's arm.

"I know what the neighbors are saying," he said.

"You do?"

"They can check me out all they want. I'm not worried about that. But you gotta get Chase out of here for a while. They didn't dare bother him while I was there, but with me gone? No matter how friendly my neighbors seem, they've got an agenda, believe me."

Andes thought about Gerry and Richard, and their suggestion that Chase was a budding pyromaniac. Did this have anything to do with Vicky's revelation that Chase's other possible-father was a fireman?

Andes had assumed it was the first time Chase had heard such a declaration, but what if that wasn't the case? Didn't most drug addicts and alcoholics repeat themselves when they were high? Maybe Chase didn't even remember it. But he'd heard it before; it was in his subconscious. And thus began his obsession with all things fire. Andes couldn't be sure if her theory was correct, but it made sense to her. How much of this did Jay know?

"Chase is obsessed with fires," Andes said. She hadn't meant to say it out loud, or maybe she had, but this time she was slightly afraid of his reaction.

"What ten-year-old boy isn't?" Jay challenged.

Andes shrugged. What did she know about ten-year-old boys? She thought about the boys she grew up with. All jangling limbs: legs, and arms constantly moving, jerking, jumping, kicking. And despite gossip to the contrary, children weren't allowed to handle the serpents. Mothers kept them in the back room, although some were more lenient than others. Some held their children close to the open door, ready to bolt if the snakes went wild. Others barely noticed or became so lost when the spirit moved them that they didn't notice their boys creeping toward the front where a brother would be handling, drawn like a sweaty, jittering magnet to the snakes, the excitement, the danger. Andes had seen fire handling too, and yes, the boys lit up anytime the flames went poof!

Sometimes the boys would gather around the snake boxes

before and after meetings, if such a box was left unattended. Huddled masses of scabby knees and quivering excitement. Yes, boys were drawn to danger, she supposed. But Emily had loved the snakes more than any boy. That she had proven beyond a doubt.

"Hello? Are you there?"

"Sorry." Why was she apologizing to him? Why was he the one acting like he was being put out? "Are your parents dead?" she finally asked, although she already knew the answer.

"Yes."

"So how—why?"

"Because I needed time to think, okay? I need to figure out who is going to take care of my son while I'm dealing with this bullshit." The anger seemed to ignite a thought. "What did you tell Vicky?"

"That you were in Hawaii on a job."

Jay laughed, an out-and-out belly laugh.

"I'll bet she flipped."

"Her motherfucking lid," Andes agreed.

"I told her to stop saying that around him," Jay said. "I don't talk like that around Chase."

"You should have also told her to do the dishes, keep food around, stop smoking in the house, and vaccinate her cat."

"Cat?"

Andes held her palm up to him. "I could be rabid," she said. *But I can pray. If it's God's will, the bite won't harm me. We are the Sign Followers. And they shall take up felines—*

"Her sister-in-law came to take the other kid," Andes added, interrupting her own intrusive and ridiculous thoughts.

"You made her call?" Jay asked.

"Of course," Andes answered. "It was that or social services."

Jay slammed his hand on the table with gusto.

"I knew it," he exclaimed. "You have good instincts. I like you." He leaned forward again, almost daring her to break his gaze. "Chase likes you too," he said. "Don't be fooled by his behavior. I know my son. He likes you."

Normally Andes wanted to be liked. Normally when someone told you they, or someone close to them liked her, she felt happy. This was anything but. This was a guilt trip. She wasn't going to fall for it. She had the Alaskan frontier waiting for her.

"And your point is?" she asked.

"I'm just asking for a little more time."

"Look. Even if I wanted to take care of the kid—which I don't—I don't have the money."

"What are you talking about? I told you where the cash was. Didn't Chase get it?"

"Oh yeah. He got it all right. And he's not letting any of it go."

"Jesus."

"First it was supposed to be bail money for you. He wouldn't even cough any up at Pig Heaven."

"You took him to Pig Heaven? It's not his birthday!"

"I even paid for our bus tickets to Olympia."

"I'm sorry."

"And now you should be doing a drum roll—" Jay's fingers stopped drumming on the table at this. "He says he's not spending a penny of it unless we use it to go to Sunnyside, Queens." Andes finally spat it out, sure by now the kid hadn't told him anything about his "other father" or going to Queens. Jay had no idea why Chase was wearing a purple robe, a blond wig, a gold crown, and red lipstick. Jay was putting the pieces together now, and it was fascinating watching him do it. Facial expressions were so underrated in today's culture. Expressions were like paintings, or sunsets, even the horrified ones.

"Queens?" Jay finally said. "As in New York?"

"As in." Andes didn't offer any more. She was quite enjoying the role of Girl in the Know for once. If he wanted more, he'd have to painstakingly coax it out of her. Besides, this way she'd find out if Jay knew anything about this "other father suspect." When Jay didn't say anything, however, Andes felt some of her power slipping and caved a little.

"Vicky put the idea in his head," she said. Jay nodded and looked over Andes's shoulder at the wall behind her. This time his face was hard to read. She grew even more impatient. "Do you know where I'm going with this?"

"I never know where women are going with anything," Jay said. "Why don't you enlighten me?"

Andes took a deep breath. "She was angry."

"Don't sugarcoat it."

"I think she's going through some kind of withdrawal."

"Yes."

"And she said you were fifty dollars short—"

"What?"

"So she was really mad—"

"Andes!"

"She said you might not even be his real father. She was sleeping with another man at the time. Dave Jensen. A fireman. He lives in Sunnyside, Queens. Chase heard the whole thing."

She hadn't meant to keep talking, she was going to say a little at a time and give Jay a chance to respond. But once she started and he didn't cut in, it was like trying to drive your car over gravel—it was rough going, but she just had to get through it. Now his face was alive again, although he was battling to get it under control. It was like watching a slideshow: this is Anger, this is Grief, this is Jealousy. And just when she thought he was going to end it with Rage and Accusations, he ended it with, Be Careful What You Wish For. And she was pretty darn sure this wasn't the first time he'd heard of Dave Jensen either. Just like she suspected, Vicky had opened her mouth before.

"I see," he said.

Andes didn't ask him outright if he'd heard this before. This wasn't her soap opera.

"Look," she said. "I'm sorry."

"Go to Queens," Jay said.

"Excuse me?"

He pushed his chair back, and it too screeched. "Tell him you're in charge of the money. And I've got a little more. Enough for you guys to have a little fun, stay a couple of months."

Andes pushed her own chair back and stood.

"A couple of months?"

"He's not going to stop now. You don't know my son."

"This has nothing to do with me!"

"But don't let him anywhere near that man. Not for real."

"What?"

"Just pretend like you're trying to find him. He'll get bored and want to come home."

"He knows his name. He knows he's a fireman in Sunnyside. If he wanted to find him—if he's still there—he could find him."

"So stop him," Jay said. "It's up to you to stop him."

"Why don't you just get a blood test, show it to Chase and prove you're the father?"

"Because I'm going to prison. Who knows for how long. And the kid needs to get out of town. It's the perfect distraction."

"Distraction? You want the kid thinking some other man is his father just to distract him?"

"It's the only way he'll stop obsessing on getting me out of jail. You don't know him. You don't know how his mind works. Once he gets it set on something—"

"Aha!"

"Aha. What?" For a moment Jay looked and sounded exactly like Chase. She felt like freeze-framing Jay and marching Chase in to see it for himself.

"How do you expect me to keep a mind like that—once it gets set on something—away from Dave Jensen?" Had she been an attorney in a courtroom, Andes was sure the jury would be nodding their heads in admiration and agreement. Jay, however, looked less than impressed.

"You're still the adult, Andes. Besides, it's New York. There are plenty of other things you can distract him with once you're out there."

"Do you have any idea what you're asking me?'

"Obviously."

"This is a lot of responsibility."

"I know."

"I don't want this responsibility."

"Why? You have places to go?" Andes thought about Alaska. "Kids? A husband? A boyfriend even?" Andes knew her face was red, and no one was more surprised than her when she imagined the room filled with snakes, draped over her as she danced in front of him unafraid and moved by the spirit, moving closer and closer to the soft part of his neck with the fangs of a diamondback.

"Because that kid out there doesn't," Jay said, taking the venom out of her diamondback. "He has nobody but me. And if you think this is easy for me—"

"What's in it for me?" she asked before Jay burst into tears. His voice was cracking and he was exhausted. She couldn't handle tears from this one. God knew what he'd get her to agree to then.

"What do you want?"

Her plan worked; Jay's machismo was back full force.

"A salary."

"That can be arranged."

"Three months. Then I'm done. Period."

"Fine."

"Okay then. We'll go to Queens. But first you're going to have to sign something—some kind of contract giving me guardianship, whatever. Ask your lawyer to come up with something."

"Okay."

"Okay." Andes waved to the guard outside the door. When she had reached it, Jay called out to her again.

"And Andes?"

"Yes?"

"Don't mess with my kid."

"I—"

"I mean it. He's my son. Not yours. Not Dave Jensen's, not even Vicky's. He's mine. And if you fuck with that in any way, I promise you—"

"I'll live to regret it," Andes finished for him. And she had no doubt it was one promise he intended on keeping.

Chapter 12

Just because they were going to Queens didn't mean Andes was going to let the kid know right away. How could she ever establish any kind of authority if he thought all he had to do was put on a silly costume and everyone around him caved? And she also needed time to formulate a game plan. If she admitted now that Jay had given his permission for them to go to Queens, Chase would be at the airport in a flash. It had been a whirlwind couple of days and she just needed time to relax. So she was more than thrilled when Gerry saw them coming up the dock and shouted an invitation to dinner across the way. Andes immediately accepted for both of them, and Chase stomped off in obvious displeasure. So what. He could stay on the sailboat for all she cared; she was going to dinner on a yacht.

The way home from the prison hadn't gone well either. Andes got Chase to admit that yes, he understood "the man who says he's his father" was going to be sent to Oregon because he had failed to show up to court a long time ago for a "work project" and judges didn't look too kindly on those who didn't show up for their court dates. And of course, he wanted to know when they were going to go to Queens to search for his "biological" father. And then he gave the middle finger to a couple of teenage boys who sat behind them and were obviously making fun of his costume. Andes felt guilty for cheering him on on the inside while outwardly scolding him. But she couldn't just let him give the middle finger to people on city buses, could she?

Although she'd often felt like flipping off people on city buses, and the boys behind them were completely obnoxious, but this was about the kid and his manners, not about what felt right. Besides, what if she hadn't been there and those kids had decided to start a fight? They could have hurt him. And they did reach to grab his middle finger when he stuck it over the seat, but Andes was quick. She pulled Chase's hand back, and then looked at the boys. "Don't even think about it," she'd said. They didn't. She might be little, but she was tough. She was pretty sure she could have taken on the two of them if they'd wanted to push it further.

A nice dinner, some wine, and a clean, spacious yacht was all she needed. She'd noticed too that Gerry had a computer in the yacht, and she was hoping he'd let her use the Internet and check her e-mail. If they were in fact going to Queens, she'd have to do a little research. The more she actually thought about going to New York, the more excited she became. She'd avoided such a big city so far, but maybe it was meant to be. Alaska was cold anyway, and where better to make a living selling your jewelry than New York? She could probably make her entire living just selling at street fairs. Maybe the universe knew she was too afraid to go by herself and was sending her through Chase. Now, why they had to pick a stubborn ten-year-old to accompany her, she couldn't figure out. Maybe in addition to rewarding her with life in the most exciting city in the world (or so she'd heard), maybe they were also punishing her by sticking her with the kid—kind of a paying off your karmic debt while being rewarded type of thing. Either way, Internet access and a glass of wine was on the evening's agenda.

It started out as a beautiful evening. They sat on the deck, enjoying the last strands of daylight along with a perfect glass of Chardonnay. From here Andes could see Chase on the deck of the sailboat, swiping the air with a large stick.

"Did you come from a costume party?" Richard asked as they watched him.

"No," Andes replied. Then she turned her head slightly away from him. She wanted to pretend he wasn't there.

"I've got it!" Gerry said. "He's in theater camp?"

"No. Oh God, this cheese is amazing," Andes said, reaching for another piece.

"It's from Lyons," Richard said. "France. Have you ever been?"

"I've been to Paris," Andes said. "But not Lyons."

"We love Paris," Gerry said.

"Love it," Richard echoed emphatically.

"Me too," Andes said. "It's a magical city. Especially at night. All those lights twinkling. I loved strolling along the Left Bank with a croissant on a lazy Saturday."

Richard and Gerry nodded in unison.

"Have you done a lot of traveling, then?" Richard asked.

"Are you kidding? It's practically my vocation," Andes said. This was the perfect lead-in. "Which is why I often need to count on the kindness of strangers," she added.

"*Streetcar Named Desire!*" Gerry said, clapping.

"Ubiquitous, but still a good one," Richard said.

"Is there something you need?" Gerry asked.

"I was wondering if I could use your computer," Andes said. "I need to go online."

"But of course," Gerry said. "We have high-speed here too, can you believe it? Go on down. We'll keep an eye on Chase."

"Actually," Richard said. "I think we should stroll over there and coax him to dinner."

"Do you mind?" Gerry asked her.

Why would I mind? Andes thought. *He's not my kid!*

"Be my guest," she said. At least she'd have some time alone on the computer. Although there were more pertinent things she needed to look up, Andes went first to eBay to feed a little addiction. Of course she wasn't going to bid on anything—her credit card was to the max, and she didn't exactly have a shipping address yet—but still she just had to see the latest offerings. Not that she needed anymore, but there were a few items she would have liked to add to her collection. Next she checked e-mail, mostly spam, and an e-mail from a friend she'd made in Florida, and a distant cousin on her maternal grandmother's side, the few people she kept touch with in this world, and she quickly sent off replies hinting she might be headed to Alaska. She knew they thought her life was exciting—all that travel . . .

Andes took a deep breath and typed her next search item into the Google bar, feeling the familiar tug of excitement and anxiety as her fingers pecked the keys. She'd been doing this for nine years and there was never much to find. She found out a little—which neighbor kids had graduated from high school, who was getting married, who was having babies, simple things like that. But this time when Andes typed in *Starling, West Virginia,* a headline jumped out at her:

SNAKE CULT DEATH REVIVES DECADE-LONG MYSTERY.
MOVE OVER, AMELIA EARHART. WHERE IS EMILY TOMLIN?

Panic, even worse than the kind she felt in the warehouse fire, engulfed Andes. But she didn't get to read further. Gerry, Richard, and Chase were coming in from the deck. Andes quickly minimized the screen. The computer was in a little office space adjacent to the living room, so anyone walking behind her would be able to see what she was looking at. But the computer was hooked up to a printer. If she could somehow print this out without anyone seeing, she could read it later, privately. Or she could find an Internet café, somewhere private. Snake cult. Andes might not be a Sign Follower in her heart of hearts, but if there was one thing she knew, it was that they were not a cult. Or freaks, or lunatics, or weird in any way. They were practicing what they believed. They were living in a country founded on religious freedom, or so she'd liked to think.

Andes's heart was pounding out of her chest. Why? What had stirred this all up again? Or who? *Where is Emily Tomlin?* The only people who knew weren't talking. Apparently, they didn't care.

"Andes?" Gerry called to her as everyone took their seat at the small dining table. "Are you ready?"

"Sure—is it okay if I print something out first?" There was no way she'd be able to wait until tomorrow to read the article.

"Sure," Gerry said. "Do you need help?"

"No, I've got it," Andes said, hurrying to print.

Chase made a beeline to her.

"What are you printing?" he asked.

"Privacy, please," Andes said, shutting off the screen and keeping her eyes glued to the printer slowly spitting out the paper.

"Is it our plane tickets?"

"Plane tickets?" Richard asked.

"Nobody said we're going yet," Andes said, unable to resist. She couldn't think about the kid now. She had to deal with her crisis.

"Going where?" Richard persisted.

"Sunnyside, Queens," Chase said, marching back to the table.

"Queens?" Gerry said. "Is that why you're dressed like that?" Chase nodded and Gerry belted out a laugh. "Now I've heard of people wanting to go to Manhattan—but Queens?"

"Or Brooklyn," Richard added. "I hear Brooklyn is the new Manhattan."

"I have family in Queens," Chase said.

"Chase," Andes said sharply. When he met her eyes she shook her head no.

"Who wants salmon?" Gerry asked. For a few minutes they pretended to enjoy their meal. Andes could barely swallow, and it was taking all her concentration to keep her hands steady; they were shaking like a leaf. Andes was surprised to see Chase wholeheartedly digging into the salmon; she would have bet her life on him demanding a substitute. It just went to prove she didn't know anything about the kid at all. And Gerry and

Richard kept smiling at each other and Chase, which is when it hit her. He should stay with them! They lived just "down the street." They obviously liked the kid. They were even willing to overlook his homophobic father. Furthermore, Chase obviously liked the two of them. It was perfect. Chase would stay here and Andes would deal with her crisis. It seemed like the perfect plan until Chase asked if he could light the candle.

Andes had been so absorbed in her thoughts she hadn't noticed the fat hurricane candle standing prominently in the middle of the table surrounded by a delicate glass cover. It was deep red with orange stripes. Gerry and Richard reacted like actors eager to say their lines.

"Of course!" and "How could we have forgotten?" they cried together. Then they exchanged a satisfied look. But Andes didn't realize this until later either. At the time she simply smiled back and fussed over the candle, whereas she was really wondering whether or not to sneak away to the bathroom to read the rest of the article.

"My lighter is in that drawer over there," Gerry said, pointing to a little desk by the couch. Chase raced over to the desk while Gerry and Richard exchanged more nervous smiles.

"I can't find it," Chase said after pawing through the drawer.

"It's a black lighter with rabbit ears on it," Gerry encouraged. Something about his tone did get through to Andes then, and a faint bell jangled in her head.

"Nope," Chase said. "Not here."

"That's funny," Gerry said. "It was here the night of my party. On the Fourth."

"Well, it's not here now," Chase said. "Do you have another one?" Gerry pushed his large frame away from the table and joined Chase at the drawer.

"But it would be such a shame to lose that one," he said. "I've had it forever. And I always keep it in this drawer. Don't I, Richard?"

"Gerry is impeccable with his placements," Richard agreed. "It's always been in that drawer. That is, until after our party."

"Hey," Gerry exclaimed. "You were here that night, Chase.

Remember when I came downstairs and found you down here? Would you know anything about that lighter?" The faint bell in Andes head turned into a three-alarm fire. She too stood.

"What is going on here?" she asked.

"What about matches?" Chase asked. "I could use matches." Jay's warnings from the jail rang in her head. *The neighbors are starting to gossip about Chase. Believe me, they have an agenda. Without me there to protect him—*

There have been a series of marina fires lately. The police think there's a serial arsonist loose—

"Chase," Gerry said. "Think carefully. Is there any way you might have taken that lighter the night of our party?"

"Not necessarily on purpose," Richard chimed in. "Maybe one of the guests asked you to retrieve it for them?" Andes watched as Chase caught on to the little skit they were enveloped in. Then she watched him twist it to his advantage.

"Hmm," Chase said. "Let me think." Gerry and Richard both leaned forward anxiously.

"So many things going on that night," Gerry encouraged. "And then of course the fire that night. I would hate to think whoever ended up with our lighter started that fire. But I'll bet the firemen could trace things like that," he said as if it were an afterthought. "I'd feel just terrible if I thought our lighter was involved in any kind of arson."

"They'd never be able to trace that," Chase said. "Even if they found the lighter."

"Well, who knows what they can do nowadays," Richard said. "They're still investigating. And with Gerry's lighter missing just hours before the fire—"

"Chase," Andes said. "We're going."

"They won't—"

"Chase," Andes said. "Not another word."

"They won't what?" Richard asked.

"Thank you for the lovely dinner," Andes said. "But we have to be going now."

You could have been parents this summer, Andes telepathically tried to tell Gerry and Richard. *Instead you had to turn into the*

Aging Gay Hardy Boys. Leaving Chase with these two hell-bent on uncovering him as a pyromaniac was just as destructive as leaving him with his incompetent mother, jail-ridden father, or dead grandparents. She knew part of them meant well, may have even been trying to help the boy, but she still couldn't stop that fierce well of protection from rising up and flooding her. But what if they were right? What if the kid was a pyro?

Regardless, it was the other scenario rattling around her brain, the one that made her want to protect the kid. What if they were wrong? What kind of damage could they do to a young life that had already had its share of troubles? If there was one thing Andes knew, it was the damage that could be inflicted by accusations. She knew how deeply children processed the words and fears of adults, how quickly they could personalize things, and how heavy the weight of the world felt on ten-year-old shoulders. Jay was right. What ten-year-old boy wasn't interested in fires? For the first time since coming here, Andes saw Chase as someone in need. Someone who needed her.

"Don't go," Gerry said, sounding slightly guilty. "We have dessert."

"Bananas flambé," Richard said sheepishly.

"Sorry," Andes said. "We've lost our appetite."

"We shouldn't," Gerry said after they'd left.

"Why not?" Richard said. "Don't you want to know what she was looking at?"

"No," Gerry lied.

"We don't know anything about this girl. Who is she? Where did she come from? Why is she taking care of a boy she doesn't even know?"

"She seems like a perfectly nice girl."

"Look, I'm just going to have a glance. You can't stop me."

Gerry sighed as he cleared the table.

"Bingo," Richard said. "Listen to this. eBay—"

"Ooh, eBay. Let's call *America's Most Wanted.*"

"Don't you want to know what she was looking up?"

"Not necessarily," Gerry said, trying to sound as uninterested as possible. Richard told him anyway. Gerry stopped what he was doing and stood still.

"You're kidding," he said. "What else?" Richard read off the items. It only got stranger.

"It's odd," Gerry admitted. "But what do you suggest we do?"

"We don't take our eyes off that girl for a second," Richard said. "And we do a little bit more digging," he added as he sat at the computer and started to type.

Chapter 13

When night fell, Andes regaled Chase with a tale of her trip to Egypt. One morning, while shopping in a busy market, she was swindled by a salesman. He sold her a tiny, yet very expensive bottle of perfume. He said it would make the next man she kissed fall in love with her. Andes didn't believe in the tale, nor did she necessarily like the spicy odor of the perfume, but she loved the little heart-shaped bottle it came in. She put a few dabs on her wrists and her neck and then forgot all about it. Later, she rode a camel across the dessert. The guide couldn't believe how taken the camel was with Andes. They were the last in line because the camel kept stopping every few feet to look lovingly back at her. The guide finally asked her to step off the camel and leave the group. Grudgingly she did so, but as she was making her getaway, she felt the camel's snout on her neck. She turned around and the lovesick camel kissed her square on the lips. Andes threw the perfume into the nearest trash container and never did find true love in Egypt.

Next she sang Chase a hymn, and didn't scold him when he announced he was going to wear his queen costume to bed. She did, however, sneak back in and remove the crown from his head after he was fast asleep. Then she sat at the table and removed the printout of the newspaper article from her pocket. She took her time, as if slowing down would somehow mitigate her growing panic. She unfolded the article ever so carefully, and smoothed it over three times before actually reading it.

SNAKE CULT DEATH REVIVES DECADE-LONG MYSTERY.
Move Over, Amelia Earhart. Where is Emily Tomlin?

Nestled in the Appalachian Mountains of West Virginia, Starling has had a long tradition of serpent handling. Signs Followers, as they call themselves, of the Jesus Name Holiness Church, practice everything from snake handling and strychnine drinking to playing with fire in order to prove their allegiance to God. Normally a private town, bordering on secretive, all eyes were on them last week when a 19-year-old boy, Thomas Hunley, was bitten by a venomous four-foot timber rattlesnake. After refusing medical help, Thomas' hand swelled to four times its size, and he died four hours later on his living-room couch.

Andes looked up from the paper. Tommy. He used to sit in the back row with Johnny Helms. He was a mean kid, always sneaking into the snake boxes, and poking at them with sticks before meetings to get them all riled up. By the time he was done, the slumbering snakes would be thrashing and hissing. She tried to conjure up some empathy for him but couldn't. Except the publicity was going to hurt Starling once again, lead to snap judgments about a culture that outsiders couldn't possibly understand, and for that she was sorry. They were people, not freaks. They were musicians. They worked hard. In mines, in construction, in mills. They made quilts and home-made jam. They lived simple, devout lives. They knew the magic of a river, the beauty of the mountains, and every nook and cranny of the woods behind their homes. Their children were happy and free, their doors open and unlocked. Every religion had practices that seemed odd to outsiders. Even if others didn't agree with it, how could they judge a people whose beliefs were so strong they were willing to put their lives on the line for it? Andes continued to read.

> Although at 19 he was of legal age, it once again raises the question of the safety of the children of Starling, West Virginia. Although it's widely touted that no child has ever died of a snakebite in these cultlike religious practices, some are left to wonder if this is the whole truth and nothing but the truth. After all, children have been known to handle snakes—take the most famous example, that of Starling, West Virginia's Emily Tomlin, who was first photographed by me handling a copperhead at just 15 years of age—

As if this weren't horrifying enough, he had reprinted her picture. She stared at her fifteen-year-old self, smiling for the camera, proud of Millie, her secret name for the six-foot diamondback draped in the palms of her outstretched hands. She could still feel the cool, slick skin against her hot and sweaty palms. Millie didn't like the flash of the camera either; she reared her head back at the blinding light and opened her jaw in a hiss. Her fangs were a baby's breath away from Emily's neck. Everyone, especially George Turner, held their breath. He would have been to blame had the snake sunk its teeth into her tender, young flesh; he was the idiot using a flash. Quick as lightning, Brother Hensley came up behind Emily. His left hand wrapped around the snake just behind the neck, and his right gripped it farther down the body, allowing him to safely remove the agitated reptile and return it to the snake box. Andes couldn't bear to look at the picture, or think about the avalanche of consequences it unleashed. She covered the picture with her hand so she could read the rest of the article.

> Where is Emily Tomlin now? I tried visiting the Tomlins and although all family members refused to speak to me, I heard from Emily herself—

What??

Her voice spoke loud and clear from a simple wooden cross mounted in the Tomlins' backyard.

Andes's stomach lurched and she had to slap her hand across her mouth to keep from crying out.

From the dates carved into the cross, it appears that Emily Tomlin died at the age of 15. Although it hasn't been confirmed hers was a snakebite-related death, questions are being raised. Authorities have yet to make a decision on whether or not the body should be exhumed, but the normally quiet community is rallying against the suggestion, and has even hired a group attorney to fight my request.

There was a little bit more, but Andes dropped the article and ran to the bathroom, sure she would be sick. Nothing came up other than a deep sorrow that couldn't be purged. She couldn't think about that coffin, and she certainly couldn't think about that awful night. She sat on the floor of the sailboat's tiny bathroom for a long time before her body stopped shaking. She tried to blame the sickening feeling in her stomach on the rocking of the boat, but deep down she knew it was really the article causing her distress. Her past was coming back like bad weeds, burrowing underneath her skin and taking root. She squeezed her eyes shut, but it didn't matter, her lips were already repeating the words, *great harm, great harm, great harm,* and her mind was already drifting home, back to the past, back to Starling, West Virginia.

"Death is in that box," Brother McCullough said, pointing. Emily followed the trajectory of his finger to the wooden crate shoved up against the back wall. Death was not only in that box, death was alive and buzzing. Emily had sensitive ears, and a thrill rose in her stomach as she listened to death's rattle, staring at the box, silently daring it to move. It did not budge, of course, nor could she actually see the serpent from all the way across the room. She would have to be up close and peering into the tiny grate in the top to actually get a glimpse of the reptile. But she could feel it all right.

A pulse beat in her throat, and she rubbed her sweaty palms against her long wool skirt before curling her hands into half-fists and resting them at her knees. When was he going to take it out? Soon? She could hardly wait. Could everyone feel their hearts pounding inside their chests? Power running through the tips of their fingers? She had to grip her seat with both hands to keep from racing over to the box, throwing open the lid, and cradling the snake against her chest like a newborn baby. Was God talking to her? Was this how being anointed felt?

She wanted to touch them, oh, she wanted to touch them so bad! The right front tip of her new Mary Janes tapped silently against the concrete floor. Her grandmother's words swam in her head. *They're not handling snakes in those meetings, are they? Are they?*

"What we do at our meetings is none of her business," her mother told her. "If you tell her we handle serpents, she could bring great harm upon us, Emily." Great harm, great harm, great harm. *No,* Emily told her maternal grandmother. *They don't handle snakes.*

Death was in the room, just a few feet away, coiled and hissing in a pine box. What if she touched him? They normally didn't let children handle, but she knew of a fourteen-year-old girl in Tennessee who did. Emily was nine. There was no way she could wait a whole five years to handle. She would rather die. Emily wiggled in her seat. The sermon was quiet so far, but it wouldn't stay that way for long. Soon the music would start, and then the dancing, and before you knew it someone would be speaking in tongues. The entire room would shake with the spirit of the Lord and when that happened, Death watch out! When brothers and sisters were anointed by the spirit, anything could happen. They were truly God's army, armed with nothing but faith and the power of the Lord. She wasn't supposed to touch, only watch. But sometimes she felt the spirit move on her to handle, she felt it! She dreamt at night of snakes. Their cool, slippery skin, their darting pink-forked tongues, their deadly hiss and rattles. She imagined draping death around her neck like Cleopatra.

They don't handle snakes in those meetings, do they? No, Grandmother, they don't. Great harm, great harm, great harm. Emily wondered why her grandmother didn't ask if they swallowed strychnine or handled fire during the meetings, because they did that too. They drank strychnine and battery acid out of old tin coffee cans and fat glass jars. They held blowtorches up to their chins like children did with dandelions. Last week Brother Elliot opened the wood-burning stove while preaching, stuck his hand into the roaring beast, and scooped up a handful of red-hot coals. Then he walked up and down the aisle, cradling the burning coals in his palms as he preached. When he was finished, he returned the coals to the stove and held out his palms to his fellow brother and sisters. They were white and shining, even in the dim light of the meeting room. That stuck with Emily more than anything, the whiteness of those palms. It was a true miracle.

Emily snuck in and touched the coals later, after the fire had long died down, and they were nothing but hard black balls disintegrating in the belly of the stove. Still, she pretended they were hot and practiced carrying them up and down the aisles. When she was finished, her hands were covered in soot. She had to scrub them with a wire brush to get them clean, and even then, her hands were raw and red. From that moment on, it didn't matter to Emily what her grandmother said, or what her mother said, and even the harshest words from her father couldn't pierce Emily's new resolve. Because she was a believer. God had sown into her a miracle seed, and it was growing. She had been anointed, chosen by God to handle serpents. She coddled this secret like a best friend, whispered to it during her darkest hours in the well.

She imagined holding *two* blowtorches under her chin with a dozen snakes wrapped around her neck. There were twelve disciples in the Last Supper, and Emily would wear a snake for each of them. What would her father think of her then? He would see that the Lord moved on her, chose her. He would see that she was special. After all, God was the one person Zachariah Tomlin seemed to fear, if not love. Death was in that box. But it wasn't death that concerned Emily, it was the kind of life she could have if he could only see how the spirit moved on her. Some kids strived to make their parents proud by getting good grades or hitting a home run in baseball. But Emily knew nothing short of a miracle would make her father proud of her. But suddenly, that was possible. She would be the youngest child to ever handle a serpent. She would hold death in her arms, and only then would she know what it was like to really live. Even after all the hours she spent at her grandmother's house, subjected to special tutoring so she wouldn't talk like them, act like them, think like them, she still knew it was the only place she would ever belong. Almost Heaven, West Virginia. Not that she minded the schooling. The lessons were fine with Emily, and she was a good student, as her grandmother often remarked, a "quick learner." But deep down, she was like them. And one day, she would perform miracles that would far surpass the likes of anything Starling had ever seen.

They don't handle snakes in those meetings, do they? Do they?

"Andes?" She had fallen asleep on the bathroom floor. Chase's hand was on her shoulder. "What are you doing?" he asked.

"Nothing," she said. "Just." She dropped the thought, there was no "just," no excusing why she was lying on the bathroom floor. Where was her article? Terror rose in her at the thought of the kid getting his hands on it. She picked herself up off the floor and darted back to the little table. At first she didn't see it, and panic gripped her until she spied it underneath the table. She swiped it up and skimmed it again, this time bypassing everything but the name of the person who had done this to her again, the person ripping open her history. George Turner. *New York News,* New York, New York.

It was nine years later, but it was him all right. She remembered him. She remembered the large camera, the zoom lens, the friendly smile as he stood behind the crowd snapping the picture. Most of all she remembered her grandmother's reaction. A rage she had never seen on anyone but her father. And the mess it all started. The mess it was threatening to start again. All because of him, George Turner. She'd been too young then to know she was being manipulated, him with his story, Grandmother with her counselors, and her father—she'd never forget that day, that last day. All the harm she'd brought upon her family because of this man. George Turner. There was a grave in her backyard with a simple wooden cross bearing her name. And it was all because of him. Because of his picture. The chain of events he'd set in motion. A photograph. Publicity. Public outcry. A grandmother's reaction. A mother's cowardice. A father's rage.

And George Turner was at it again. Only Andes wasn't a naïve fifteen-year-old. She wasn't going to let him dig up her past. Her parents could have ended this once and for all, but they didn't. They didn't want any more attention, but they weren't letting him touch her again either. Did this mean they still loved her? Was there any chance? She couldn't let them bring her family any more pain. *Great harm, Emily, great harm. They don't handle snakes in those meetings, do they?*

When Chase came out of the bathroom he was wearing his queen costume again. "You can take that off now," Andes said. "We're going to Queens."

Chapter 14

Andes knew she should try to hide her fear of flying from a ten-year-old with more radar than the U.S. Air Force, and she tried her best, but in the end, it was a losing battle. She was found out.

"Are you sick?" Chase demanded without an ounce of empathy. She was stuffed in the middle seat, clutching the armrest on Chase's side because she didn't want to disturb the large man in the aisle seat next to her. Along with his snoring, his cologne was overpowering her. Still, she was grateful; it was keeping her from thinking about dying in a fiery crash. How could people think handling snakes was crazy, yet flying in an RV with wings was completely acceptable? Andes grew up among mechanics; she knew how many things could go wrong. People weren't birds, they weren't meant to fly. She hated thinking this, she hated the rapid trill of her heart, the sweat gathering in her palms, and the tears threatening to spill. Most of all she hated the fact that she had an overeager witness to her phobia; a high-beamed laser pointed right at her.

"Window," Andes whispered. What she meant to say was,

"Look out the window and leave me alone!" But only "window" came out.

"Do you need my puke bag?" Chase shouted. Passengers turned to stare and the large man next to her snorted and tried to maximize the distance between them, a futile but noble attempt.

"No," Andes said, pushing the little white bag away. Just when she thought he couldn't embarrass her anymore, Chase snapped open the bag and pretended he was throwing up. A flight attendant hurried over and the large man sprang from his seat just as the plane hit a nasty patch of turbulence. The massive man pinned the size-two flight attendant against the side of the seat. Chase dry-retched into the bag again. Valium, Andes thought. Did anybody on the plane have Valium? *Surely there's a doctor, or a housewife from the sixties aboard?*

The flight attendant wrenched herself free, lunged across Andes and handed Chase smashed saltines and a ginger ale. He smiled, and Andes noted with a touch of jealousy that he'd never smiled like that at her. She couldn't help but roll her eyes. The attendant noticed and frowned.

"I can get rid of the bag for you, darling," she told Chase, handing him a new one. Chase just looked at her. She waited, smiling like only one anticipating being handed a bag full of puke could smile. "Are you nervous about your play, sweetie?" she asked when Chase still didn't turn over the bag. Andes laughed, which, judging by the look from the attendant, was completely inappropriate. Chase was still wearing the cape and the crown. It cost them an extra hour checking in. Chase smiled and nodded.

"Can I have the bag, sweetie?" the attendant asked again with slightly less patience.

"I threw it out the window!" Chase said.

"I'm sorry, miss," Andes interrupted. "But he didn't actually throw up." The flight attendant looked like she didn't believe her. Andes grabbed the bag from Chase and showed her the evidence.

"Oh," the flight attendant said, less friendly now. "I see."

"I will if you want me to," Chase exclaimed, holding up the bag. The attendant gave Andes a look conveying what she thought of her mothering skills. No doubt she was lamenting the demise of first class, longing for the days when she could yank closed a curtain and cater only to those who paid enough to misbehave.

"I know this is your first time flying," Andes said when the flight attendant left. "But that was not good behavior."

"At least I finally got something to eat," Chase said. "I'm freakin' starving."

Andes eyed the crackers. She was starving too. She'd been too nervous going through security to think about packing them a lunch. How was she to know they were barely going to feed them?

"You know," Chase continued as he opened the saltines and poured the crumbs down his throat, "for a world traveler, you're a complete mess."

Andes didn't reply. Unfortunately, she agreed.

"You're kind of strange too," Chase added.

"This coming from the boy still dressed like a queen even after getting his way."

"Touché."

For a while they settled into the flight. Chase watched the small television in front of him, and Andes braced herself for hours of nonstop channel flipping. Instead, to her surprise, he remained immersed in the History Channel. A feeling close to motherly love enveloped her as she watched him study archeologists sifting through sand. Well, good for him. And they were going to New York, one of the most exciting cities in the world. She could take Chase to museums, and he would actually enjoy them. He would probably love the Egyptian exhibit at the Metropolitan Museum of Art and the dinosaurs at the Museum of Natural History. She bought a guide on New York City, and those pages were marked with paper clips. She'd also tucked Jay's parting note into her guide.

I'm his father. Don't mess with my kid. What did he think she was supposed to do? Sunnyside, Queens, was a very small community. They had a name, Dave Jensen, and his profession, fireman. Even if he wasn't Chase's father, once Chase heard the word "fireman," it was game over. Jay knew his son; did he think she was Superwoman? She was probably making a huge mistake. She should have never agreed to look after the kid. Sure, it would have left Chase in foster care, but why did she feel that was her problem?

Maybe it wouldn't be a problem. Who knew if Dave Jensen was even still around? People changed jobs all the time. And no matter what, Andes was not going on another "road trip." They weren't going to chase Dave Jensen all over the planet. Still, if Dave Jensen was still living in Sunnyside, Queens, what a shock the poor guy was in for. Maybe she should have contacted one of those reality shows. *Knock, knock, fireman, is this your pyromaniac kid?* Andes tried to settle into an uncomfortable nap against the back of her seat, but she was distracted by Chase, who was expressing his nervous energy by kicking the back of the seat in front of him. Nevertheless, she was too tired to scold him. She never would have dreamed that by the end of the flight *she'd* be the one throwing a first-class fit and facing the authorities.

Chapter 15

If anyone asked Andes when her collection had become as important to her as life and death, the oxygen she breathed, she would have been at a loss for words. Not that she would have wanted to mime her explanation either. It wasn't anyone's business. That was the problem with the world today; all the unlimited access to information had cultivated a society that demanded to know one's most innermost secrets. Couldn't Andes have a few, private little quirks? Couldn't everyone just mind their own business?

It started with a statement: "Send me a postcard." And the underlying message—*I don't care about you anymore.* That much she knew. She had just had the last outrageous fight with Keith. Their affair was over, he was insisting she get out of Dodge—or in this case the Florida Keys. Andes didn't want to leave. She had grown fond of rolling out of bed and strolling along the beach, permanently smelling like coconut, and living on a steady diet of Jolt and peel-'n-eat shrimp. But when Keith found a shell on the beach that looked so much like his wife's face, complete with the mole between her eyes, he took it as a sign. Andes thought the shell looked like a teenage boy battling his first pimple on prom night, but it would have been pointless to point this out. If there was one thing Andes knew, it was that you couldn't mess with other people's signs. In fact, the more people tried to convince you it wasn't a sign, the more devout you became. A crusty, mole-ridden seashell had spoken, and Keith was a new man, a faithful man. He vowed then and there he was going to be a better father and a doting husband. Apparently, that didn't jibe with a little waitress on the side. *I'm going to Rome*, Andes told him when he didn't even ask where she would go. *Send me a postcard*, he replied.

Of course the dots would be much easier to connect if she had started collecting postcards, but Andes's life had never been a linear, logical place. Matchbooks were way more exciting. Postcards smacked of cheap lies: *Having the time of my life, wish you were here.* Matchbooks spoke of faraway places, dimly lit lounges, crystal bowls protected by impeccably dressed hostesses, and urgent phone numbers scribbled by groping hands in secret alleyways. They boasted of sultry jazz clubs, and secret rendezvous. Little purses of potential fire, a flick, a flash, a flame.

She also didn't remember when her nightly ritual started, but as her collection grew, the little books became her bedtime stories, her salvation. She would touch them at night, passing them through her small hands like rosary beads, praying for a sign. Where should she go? Where was home? The matchbooks struck at Andes's imagination; they illuminated the women Andes could become, like filling in the empty spaces in an endless string of cut-out paper dolls.

And then there was the slight matter of where her collection was housed. To a nondiscerning eye, it was simply a wooden box. Perhaps something picked up at a roadside gift shop, with a tag that bragged of its local craftsmanship. A box to be purchased with homemade jam, maple syrup candies, and a couple of beeswax candles.

Upon closer inspection, most would notice it was made out of high-quality oak and carved by a patient and talented hand. Only a select few would know from the size and the markings, and the netted slots at the top, that it was indeed a snake box. It was the last thing she took on her way out of Starling. It used to be the box where she kept her doll Rose. Then came the first batches of matches, a collection from Spain and Portugal. Next came Italy, and Greece. Gorgeous Paris, London, and Dublin. Soon, she had most of Europe and was off to Africa and Asia. They were each unique, like characters in a story, personalities all their own. Since then, her collection had grown so you could barely see Rose beneath all the matches. Andes was grateful it fit the carry-on size restrictions; she had tucked the box perfectly into a black duffel bag she purchased for its transport.

But what she really couldn't figure out was what she needed out of her bag right then and there; what possessed her to open the box during flight? Of course that was a lie; she knew full well why. She was so stressed she needed to see them, touch them. She couldn't stand Chase making fun of her, clenching his hands against the side arms of the seat in imitation of her, and dry-retching into the puke bag. And the heavy man next to her was reeking with sweat and what smelled like two-dollar cologne. *Here I am, stuck in the middle with you.* Not to mention starvation and turbulence—

She just needed a little break, a little breather, a little prayer from her rosary books. Yet the reasons she went over the edge were irrelevant, knocked out of her head as her precious box was knocked over by a certain someone plowing into her. His body made impact with hers at the exact moment she was reaching to touch the first matchbook. Later, the airline would grill her mercilessly. How did she manage to get a wooden box full of matches through security, when the limit (as they would inform her later) was four matchbooks per passenger? Why they thought she had the answer to this security breach, she didn't know, and she would tell them this each and every time they asked her the same question in slightly different ways as if she were personally responsible for the sorry state of American airports.

How was she to know how a snake box full of matches passed

unseen through the X-ray machine? Maybe the workers were distracted by a pair of tits coming through X-ray—how was she to know? No, she wasn't one of those people trying to test the security of the airlines, although she'd heard of those people, and they'd managed to sneak some pretty scary items past security themselves, hadn't they? And even though it wasn't her aim, shouldn't they be thanking her for bringing more attention to the issue of national security?

She didn't know the limit was only four matchbooks per person or she would have checked the bag. She told them this with ease, although the very thought of being separated from her bag clutched and clawed at her stomach.

Still, she should have waited. She should have mentally fingered her matchbooks. Did she actually think her collection had disappeared midflight? But she was dying to see how her little books had arranged themselves from the motion of the plane. Was Das Beer Garten on top of Bahama Mama? Was the Flamenco Dancer from Argentina in flagrante delicto with the Black Sheep from Dublin? If she had waited until they reached New York, they might have shifted again and she would have missed out on their in-flight secret sex life. That would have driven her crazy.

Just a little peek, a quick look, that's all she meant to do. Her matches were living a life of their own, and she just wanted a quick glance, like catching up on a soap opera she'd fallen behind on. And she couldn't really blame the kid for what happened next, but it's true that if he hadn't jumped out of his seat and launched himself on her just as they caught a patch of turbulence, she wouldn't have tipped the box at all.

Chase was dying to know what was in that box. He'd asked her before, but she refused to tell him. She always kept it under lock and key, and she only opened it at night when she thought he was fast asleep. But sometimes, she was wrong. Sometimes, he was dead awake. His imagination had been running wild. At first he prayed she was carrying automatic machine guns, but that fantasy was dashed when she got through security without being thrown against the wall and body searched. Then he wondered if there was some kind of wild animal in there, but again, she probably couldn't have slipped it onto the plane, could she? Chase thought they put all the animals underneath the plane. In all likelihood it was something boring, like more of those skirts and hot pink flip-flops she liked to wear, but if that was the case, why all the secrecy? If there was anything that captured Chase's imagination, it was a good secret. He had a few of his own, but those were kept under the lock and key of his mind. It was a cool box too, made of wood with carvings on it. There was also a cool net on the top, like a tiny screen door, and he should have been able to see inside, but she had placed a piece of black felt behind it, obscuring his view. He couldn't believe it when she actually got up during the flight and took out the box. This was his chance.

The first time he tried to jump out of his seat he almost killed himself on the seat belt. If he didn't hurry, the box would be closed by the time he got there. Why didn't the fat man ever leave his seat? Chase undid the belt and jumped up, but the fat man kept on sleeping. Chase stood watching him, wondering if he should just squeeze past, but his knees were rammed up against the seat. So that left waking him up. Luckily Andes was too preoccupied with whatever was in that box to notice him. Chase leaned forward. "Hey," he whispered. The man didn't move. "Hey," he said a little louder. The man grunted in his sleep, turned his head.

Chase tapped him on the shoulder. If it weren't for his massive chest heaving up and down, Chase would have wondered if their seatmate had kicked the bucket. For a moment Chase imagined this guy in the tiny bathroom, wedged on the toilet. What if he died in there? Sometimes Chase didn't like the thoughts in his head, and he'd be ashamed if anyone knew what he was thinking half the time, but he couldn't really help it. Something about this man dying on the toilet and the door having to be removed in order to get him out was fascinating to him. No wonder the man never got up to use the bathroom. If Chase were that fat, he'd never go to a public bathroom, and in private he'd do his best to make it quick. There would be nothing more humiliating for a fat man than to die on a toilet.

Chase was pretty sure it had happened on planes before. They called it the Mile High Club or something. He didn't know exactly why they called it that, because they should really call it something like the Six Feet Under While High Above Club. That would make more sense. Chase gave up on waking the man and went for option three, crawling over him. Unfortunately, this was the option that woke him up. "Sorry," Chase muttered, trying not to look at him.

"Huh?" the man yelled, opening his huge eyes and jerking his head back. Drool pooled on his chin. Chase scrambled off the man's knees and barely landed with his two feet in the aisle.

"Where are your manners? Where are your manners?" the man said.

Chase shrugged. Obviously it was a rhetorical question. "Sorry," he mumbled again. Didn't the fat dweeb realize he had tried not to wake him up? He was still looking back at the man, and trying to hurry away, when he plowed into Andes. The next thing he knew it was raining matchbooks. The little packets pelted Chase's face, neck, and head before hitting the ground. As he bent to pick one up, a piercing scream nearly ruptured his eardrum. Chase smacked one hand against his ear, and with the other continued reaching for the matchbook. But before he could touch it, a hand clasped his wrist like the Jaws of Life and yanked him up.

"Don't touch them," Andes said. "Don't touch them." Her face was flushed and feverish, and she looked poised to scream again. It was the same look she wore during the fire at the warehouse, when she was searching for him in the crowd, coming at him with that same desperate expression.

"Okay, okay," Chase said. "I won't touch them." She dropped his hand but held his gaze, as if she were silently begging him for help. She was still gripping the wooden box against her body. It was slightly tilted, but the remaining matchbooks were no longer raining down. Chase could see she was petrified of letting go of the box, yet was going to freak out if anyone else tried to pick up the ones that had already fallen. He glanced at the ground and started counting. There were at least twenty matchbooks scattered all over the aisle and a few poking out from underneath seats. Andes followed his gaze helplessly as the passengers around them started bending down to retrieve the matchbooks.

"No!" Andes screamed. "Nobody touch them. Nobody touch them." Her voice was ragged and high pitched, and laced with enough panic to freeze everyone in space. The stewardess who had been so kind to Chase earlier hurried up the aisle—she wasn't running, which was against regulations, but she was speed-walking, as if this were the more appropriate way to approach a passenger throwing a grand mal fit.

"Here," Chase said, reaching into his pockets. He pulled out a plastic Baggie.

"Do we have a problem here?" the stewardess asked, using her speed-walking voice as well. Chase noticed the other flight attendants were gathering in from each direction. Passengers were starting to whisper to each other.

"Matchbooks."

"Screaming."

"Look at her."

"She has a lighter?"

"No matches?"

"She's lighting matches?" The gossip gained momentum and soon the curious passengers morphed into bundles of para-noia. It wasn't long before the woman in 6F, a forty-year-old telecommunications analyst, screamed, "She's trying to blow up the plane!" In the meantime Chase stuck his hand in the empty plastic bag, the one in which Andes had put his only snack, Cheetos, which he inhaled before the plane even took off. Andes was still holding the box with one arm and trying to maintain her balance with the other, as the flight attendants began approaching from all directions, slowly but surely cor-nering her. Chase showed her his encased hand and waited for her approval, which came in the form of a slight, sickening nod. He immediately set to scooping up the matchbooks with his plastic-covered hand.

"Don't touch them," he instructed the other passengers as he picked them up. "Don't move your foot," he said to one man, "I've got it," to another. On hands and knees he began picking up the matchbooks and dropping them back into the little door on the box, as Andes tried to breathe and tried not to cry. The murmurs continued, and the flight attendants stayed uncomfortably in her personal space, but nobody made a move to stop Chase, whatever he was doing. At least the girl had stopped screaming. Finally, Chase dropped the last of the escaped matchbooks into the wooden box and held up his empty hands.

"They're back," he said in a reassuring voice. "They're all back." Andes nodded, and with trembling hands she secured the latch on the little door and snapped the gold lock back in place.

"Miss," the flight attendant said, reaching for the box, "You'll have to give that to me."

"It's okay now, it's over," Chase said. But it was too late. The attendant snatched the box away from Andes.

"Take your seats," she barked at them. "We're about to land. And when we do, the two of you are to stay in your seats. You will not deplane. Do you understand?" The box was now being marched to the front of the plane. A male attendant arrived to physically escort them back to their seats. The fat man got up to let them in, shaking his head in disapproval and showering them with spittle. The entire plane broke into applause when the naughty passengers were back in their seats. Andes sat next to the window, staring at the outside world as flames of humiliation crawled up her face. Chase reached over and buckled her seat belt before buckling his own. As tears dripped silently down Andes's face, Chase slipped his hand into hers and held it.

Moments later the stewardess was back, along with a male colleague. She thrust a sheet of paper at Andes and hovered over her while she read it.

IN-FLIGHT DISTURBANCE REPORT
Note: Your behavior may be in violation of federal
law. You should immediately cease if you wish to
avoid prosecution and your removal from this
aircraft at the next point of arrival—

"You have stopped the behavior," Chase said, reading over her shoulder. "She has stopped the behavior," he repeated to the attendants.

This is a formal warning that federal law prohibits—

Andes stopped reading and fought the urge to crumple it up.

"Are we going to have any more problems?" the male attendant asked.

"No," Andes whispered.

"Good." They started to walk away.

"What about my box?" Andes said. "You'll give it back, right?"

"You've deeply disturbed the other passengers," the stewardess said. "And you're only allowed four matchbooks on a flight."

"Makes perfect sense," Chase muttered. "Couldn't start a fire with just four, now could you?"

"Chase," Andes warned. "Don't."

"Little boy," the stewardess said. "Are you saying she was planning on starting a fire?" She turned to her male colleague. "Did you hear that?" she asked.

"He was being facetious," Andes said.

"Treating serious issues with deliberately inappropriate humor," Chase explained.

"It's just a collection," Andes continued, silencing Chase with a look. "They've never been lit. Not one of them—ever."

"I repeat, you're only allowed four on a plane."

"I didn't know that."

"Our rules are posted online."

"I'll know next time."

"How did you get them through security?"

"I just got through. They didn't say anything." The flight attendant finally walked away. Chase looked at the Passenger Disturbance Report and raised his eyebrows. Then he leaned over Andes as far as he could with the seat belt crushing into his stomach and took in the conglomeration of skyscrapers visible out the window as the plane headed in for a landing.

"For a world traveler," he said, sounding somewhat impressed, "you sure know how to cause a stir."

Chapter 16

As promised, the authorities boarded the plane. Andes and Chase were the only two passengers still aboard. The plane was stranded a half mile away from the terminal where planes carrying possible terrorists were required to park. Shuttle vans had already taken away the terrified law-abiding passengers. Andes was spinning through a wheel of emotions, but having already tumbled through embarrassment, she was now wading chest-deep in anger. This was ridiculous. She dropped her matchbook collection. Only four allowed to a plane, but she didn't know that and security didn't stop her. And yes, she might have screamed a little when strange, sweaty hands grabbed for her matchbooks, but it wasn't as if she had screamed anything threatening. And although she hadn't apologized to the kid, she was utterly humiliated he had been the one to act like the adult, trying to smooth everything over. They should've put a suit on him and hauled him over to the UN. Now she was weary and just wanted to get her box back, get to Sunnyside, and check into La Quinta motel on Queens Blvd.

Four men boarded the plane, swaggering toward them with

deliberate, yet clearly feigned ease, smiling as if they were approaching a pair of wild alligators loose on a children's playground. Two were dressed in regular business suits, one was wearing all black, and the fourth donned some kind of airport uniform. The man in black was visibly armed, and Andes suspected the suits were packing too. Chase jumped onto his seat.

"Cool," he shouted. "Can I see your guns?" That stopped the men in their tracks. Andes tugged on Chase's shirt and forced him back into his seat.

"Emily Cunningham?" Andes cringed at the sound of her name. She had changed it from Emily Tomlin to *Emily Cunningham* (her mother's maiden name) soon after leaving Starling. Then, a month after that, she unofficially changed it to Andes. Had she not bothered to change her last name, George Turner would have found her by now. Would that have been better or worse for her parents? It wasn't that she didn't like the name she'd been born with, but that was another girl, from another town, from another life. That girl had a simple wooden cross in her backyard with the dates of her birth and death on it.

"Who?" Chase asked.

"That's me," Andes said quietly.

"It is?" Chase asked. Great. If Andes was a betting woman, she'd put money on Chase not letting this drop anytime soon.

"Shh," she said.

"We need to see your identification." Andes handed them her passport, and Chase thrust out his Seattle Public Library card, which was handed back without an ounce of humor.

"Can I see your passport too?" Chase asked Andes. "I want to count how many countries you've been to." The man in the airport uniform holding the passport raised an eyebrow at Chase.

"She's a world traveler," Chase said. The man, eyebrow still raised, turned to Andes. She didn't waver from his gaze.

"Are you going to strip-search us?" Chase asked. Andes gave the kid another look. Who was the pervert now? She didn't say this either. "My dad is a fireman," Chase said.

"Your 'maybe dad,' " Andes corrected.

"You're only allowed four matchbooks on the plane," one of the men said as he handed Andes her passport back.

"I'm so sorry. I really didn't know."

"Security just let you through?"

"Yes."

"That's true," Chase said as if he had to think about it first. "That's true."

"We're going to hang on to your carry-on for a few days," one of the suits started to say. Andes didn't let him finish.

"You can't do that," she shouted. "You can't."

"We'll give you a case number and a phone number you can call to get an estimate on when and if we plan on returning your item."

"I have to have it now!"

"Homeland Security has the right to confiscate—"

"It's just a bunch of matchbooks! It's my collection!" Andes flew out of her seat. The men moved in with synchronized steps. She was going to lose it again, maybe even more than the first time. She couldn't go through this ordeal without her matchbooks, she just couldn't. The thought of not having the box by her bed at night, not being able to open the lid and smell the faint scent of sawdust, denied the right to run her hands through them, telling herself stories, touching the places where she'd been in her mind a million times, where she was living her best life, was unfathomable. She couldn't go to Queens without her collection. She wouldn't be able to handle it. Her mind was spinning to come up with something, anything to say to convince these men to let her matchbooks go, but her tongue wasn't co-operating, it was swelling in her mouth, crippling her speech. Luckily, the kid's tongue was working just fine.

"I have cancer," she heard him say. "Those matches are for a contest."

Stunned, Andes turned to Chase. He was speaking so softly and sincerely her first thought was: *He has cancer?* The men took a step back in unison as if Chase were contagious. "We've been planning this trip for a year," Chase continued softly, his big blue eyes staring straight ahead. "Matchbooks were sent to me from well-wishers all over the world." A single tear ran down his cheek. A part of Andes was yelling at her to put a stop to this, but the part that recognized the drama was working wouldn't let her. The suits were conferring in low tones, no doubt considering what bad publicity it would be to confiscate well-wishes from a little boy dealing with such big issues. After a few seconds, the largest of the four stepped forward.

"We're terribly sorry," he said. "We'll just take a few quick pictures of the item and fill out a little bit more paperwork before we return it to you. How about while we do that you can grab a bite in any of our airport restaurants, eh? It's on us."

Andes was grateful the posse of stern-turned-sympathetic Men in Black weren't around to see the "Cancer Kid" inhale two greasy cheeseburgers and a mound of spicy curly fries. As for Andes, she had lost her appetite wondering what they were doing to her matchbooks. Photographing them? Laughing at them? Touching them?

"So," Chase said between massive bites. "Why did you lie about your name?"

"It wasn't a lie. I made a life change."

Chase broke into her thoughts with a preemptory smile. "Somebody forgot to tell your passport about your life change, Emily Cunningham," he said. For a moment Andes couldn't breathe. Had he looked at her passport? No, that wasn't possible, she'd only handed it to the men, and it was still tucked in the little zipper pouch inside her purse.

"Still, it's not lying," Andes said. "Lying is telling someone, oh, I don't know, that you have *cancer*, Hector, when you don't."

"So it's not whether or not you lie, it's what you lie about?"

"My parents named me Emily. But when I left home I changed it to Andes."

"Why?"

"I was reading about the Andes mountains—"

"No. I meant why did you leave home?" Andes waited, illogically, to see if she would be saved by a bell. But nothing rushed in to ring, or tinkle, or even clank. It was just her, the kid, and the calories. Andes glanced at the curly fries. They smelled good. If only they'd had the technology, the Spanish Inquisition could have been spared a lot of bloodshed if they could have just bargained with curly fries. Andes stole a fry and sighed. They were going to have to find a place to live. She was going to have to regularly feed this kid. What in the world had she been thinking? What were they going to do if his father remained in jail?

For the first time since the fiasco began, she found herself thinking how much easier her life would be if Dave Jensen were his biological father. It would solve everything. She'd reunite the kid with his dad—*fireman, meet your prodigal pyro-son*—and she'd be on her way. It would be like the Hallmark movie of the week, except they'd have to get somebody really cute and a lot less cunning to play the kid. And if Dave Jensen wasn't his father? What then? *You're my responsibility,* she thought as she looked at him. For the first time, it really sank in.

"What are you looking at, Emily?"

"You have eyelashes a girl would kill for," Andes answered honestly.

"Ew." Chase threw a french fry at her. It wouldn't have bothered her so much had it not been smeared in catsup. She was wearing a brand-new white sweater set too. Perfect for the air-conditioned plane.

"Damn't," she yelled. She looked around for water, but they only had soft drinks in front of them. Chase didn't offer an apology and Andes was about to demand one when she noticed his posture. He was pulled back, shoulders hunched in; pre-flinch position. *No matter what, Emily,* she told herself, *never forget this kid is damaged.* She lifted her shirt to her mouth and sucked up the catsup.

"Ew," Chase said. "Pervert." But the words didn't matter; he was sitting normally again and laughing at her.

"Miss Cunningham?" The suits were back. They were carrying her snake box. "You're free to go," they said, handing it to her. They turned to Chase and flashed him enthusiastic smiles and mental pats on the back.

"We're truly sorry for what you're going through," they said.

"Thank you," Chase answered with a cough.

Chapter 17

Now what if my child was to git my gun and shoot it off? Am I to blame? Maybe. If I was to leave it out in plain sight all loaded and the like. Or if I was to hand that gun to my child and say, now here, shoot this. Then it's like I'm shootin' that gun myself, that's what I think. But what if I done kept that gun under lock and key? What if they done broke the glass and done took it without me seeing? What if they fetched the bullets from a box underneath my bed and loaded them bullets in themselves? What if it ain't even my gun? What if it were my neighbor's gun? You see? Everybody around here, they just assuming the parents are to blame. Now, I'm a God-fearin' man. And I raised my family to fear him too.

Now, I'm a Signs Follower. I believe God calls upon his children to handle serpents. He tells us in Mark 16. We've all witnessed the miracles of the Lord moving on his children. Now when I say children I'm talking about God's children, grown brothers and sisters, I ain't talking' about anyone under the age of sixteen. That's another thing you all got wrong, all you newspapers and the like. We don't let our children play with snakes. They ain't pets. We don't take 'em to church and put snakes on 'em. We keep the children in the back, not up front near the snake boxes. So whenever you hear that, it just ain't true.

I've seen men drink strychnine and dance with deadly rattlers wrapped around their necks. This ain't no foolishness on men's parts we're talkin' 'bout here, this is God-fearin' men in church when the spirit moves on them. This is God's children so moved by his faith, and guided by that faith, and swept up in that faith that they are called upon to prove God's love and power—we call that anointed by the Lord. You can't handle until you been anointed. That's the power of the Lord comin' over you, wrapping you in safety so you can handle deadly serpents and drink the devil's poison and live through it. And by God I've seen miracles you wouldn't believe. You just wouldn't believe the power in that room when the Lord moves on you. I've come close myself, and there will come a day when the Lord will move on me and I'll handle a snake, or drink poison, or handle fire, whatever the Lord moves on me to do—but make no mistake about it, this is only possible through the Lord, in church, when he moves on you. This ain't no game.

This ain't no joke. This is the power and the beauty the Lord is showing to his children who are willing to put themselves between him and death because that's how much they believe in the Lord, that's the power and beauty when he moves on you. You outsiders don't know us, but that don't stop you from writing lies. I don't keep snakes in my home. There ain't even a garden snake to be found in my shed. But all it takes is one kid sneaking out in the middle of the night without anyone knowin' or lookin'. And now I'm to blame? That ain't the Lord moving on that child, that's the Devil. And that ain't no joke. How come I ain't seen none of you papers write about that?

And as fer yer question, what do I think of what my daughter did? There's only one thing I can say. It ain't easy for a father to speak the truth about a situation like that, but I ain't gonna lie. I don't believe the Lord moved on my daughter to handle. She wasn't filled with the spirit of the Lord. She weren't anointed. I wish it weren't the truth, but I seen it with my own eyes. It weren't right. It weren't the Lord who told her to dance with that snake almost like she were in love with it. It was somethin' evil. A love for *a serpent! The creature the Devil sent to lure out our sins and cast us into eternal hellfire. Cast out of heaven into hell. Sure as I was standing there, I saw it with my own two eyes. What about what I done? The folks here have casted me out, but if it were their daughter and they had seen that look in her eyes as she danced with the snake, they woulda done the same thing. They think I'm crazy now. I ain't crazy. What do I think of my daughter? I don't have a daughter. The Devil done take her. My daughter is dead.*

Interview with Zachariah Tomlin
"Snake Girl's Father Speaks" by George Turner

Chapter 18

After the airport fiasco, it was a relief to arrive in Sunnyside, Queens. The cab rolled down Queens Blvd., treating the jet-lagged pair to 99-cent stores, small mom-and-pop pharmacies across from chain-store pharmacies, Irish pubs, discount furniture stores, a White Castle, Wendy's, a million local diners, and of course a Starbucks. Only the subway tracks running above their heads, splitting Queens Blvd. North and South, gave away the fact that they were in New York City. To their left a giant, rusted metal archway spelling out SUNNYSIDE sprouted in the air. Throngs of people milled up and down the street. Colorful fruits and vegetables from neighboring delis spilled out onto the sidewalk. People with baskets and babies maneuvered around each other with surprising ease, crisscrossing hands and hips to squeeze produce, like an understood game of Twister.

A food van, parked near the curb across from an ice cream truck, was selling gyros, Italian sausages, hot dogs, falafel, and tacos. Birds twittered and cheeped from cages hanging outside a tiny pet shop squeezed in between a 99-cent store (Everything 99 Cents or MORE), and a Peruvian chicken restaurant where

a dozen fat rotisserie chickens rotated in the window. Two bea-
gle puppies in the pet shop window were furiously digging into
the paper confetti lining the display case and completely ignoring the dark-skinned boy pressing his nose up against the glass
with longing. Farther down the street a man in a white flowing
robe was selling children's Bibles and plastic sunglasses from a
fold-out table.

"Look," Andes yelled as the number 7 train rumbled on the
tracks above them. The gleaming silver cars snaked along a
curve before squealing to a stop. "That's the subway into Manhattan," Andes informed him. And then just as she said it, she
looked up and saw the skyline spread before them. "There she
is," she said. "There's Manhattan." Chase didn't answer her or
even look up. He was furious with her for telling the cab driver
they were going directly to the motel instead of the firehouse.
She was still shaking from his tantrum; he'd screamed so loud
the cab driver pulled over, screeching to a halt on Queens Blvd.
As cars and buses and motorcycles whizzed past them blowing
their horns, the driver slapped his hands over the ears and
chanted, *Little boy scream he make me deaf, he make me deaf, he make
me deaf.*

Finally, Andes had to give him an additional twenty dollars to
keep going, and even then the driver only kept one hand on
the wheel; the other he kept plastered over his ear just in case
Chase started up again. Chase was quiet, but he had another
reason to pout now. Andes saw his face when she gave the driver
the additional twenty dollars. Money was another point of con-
tention between them. Before they left Seattle, Chase rummaged
through the sailboat, plucking stacks of cash out of every nook
and cranny. Apparently Jay was paid in cash, and as his drinking
progressed, he cared less and less about depositing it in a bank
and started stashing it in the boat instead. But his memory for
where he'd hidden all his money started to become a little
murky. Chase knew where every last dime was hidden, and by the
time he scavenged it all, they had a little over twelve thousand
dollars.

At first Chase absolutely refused to let Andes handle the

money. But she'd had her fill of Chase being in charge, and she was down to four hundred dollars of her own money. If the kid wanted to go to Queens, he was going to have to let her be in charge of the money, or he wasn't going. She promised him they'd keep a chart of their expenses so he would know where every penny went, and that seemed to placate him. She hadn't yet broken it to him that his father had promised her a salary as well. She figured she'd deal with that when the time came. She also had the feeling the kid was expecting her to eventually forget where the money was just like his father, and he was biding his time until he could sweep in and launch a silent coup.

As they moved along the boulevard, the driver frowning and continuously glancing in the rearview mirror, Andes scanned the surroundings for their motel. She hoped they were close. The driver looked feverish and unstable, one signature away from turning Sunnyside Queens into Sunnyside Farms. Just then, Andes spotted their motel up ahead. "We'll have a good night's sleep, and go to breakfast in the morning," Andes told Chase. "And then we'll make a plan."

"We don't need a plan. We just need to go to the firehouse."

"We'll talk about it in the morning." Chase folded his arms against his chest and clamped his mouth shut, exaggerating every movement before slumping against the backseat and letting his head fall against the window with a bang. The driver shook his finger and glared at Chase in his rearview mirror, but if Chase saw the scolding he didn't acknowledge it. Andes weighed her options. The kid was crying out for attention, and to make matters worse, he couldn't even come up with his own tantrums. First he'd mimicked her screaming fit, and now he was following it up with the Guillotine of Silence. He expected her to beg him to speak. Well, she'd had enough. Who cared if the kid didn't talk? Wasn't silence supposed to be golden anyway? And what about Jay's warning not to find Dave Jensen? With any luck he wouldn't even be around. Because she might be able to stall it until tomorrow, but there was no way she was keeping that kid away from the nearest firehouse for longer than one night.

The motel room was like a hand-me-down shirt that was start-ing to fray at the edges despite its just-cleaned smell attempting to mask its been-around-the-block smell, but not thrown away just yet because it still kind of fit. Chase didn't seem to mind the less than stellar accommodations. He was bouncing on the bed and flipping through the television. No wonder he was so happy; the motel room was twice the size of his sailboat. She wondered if he missed Seattle, or his father, but was too afraid to ask. She stretched out on her bed and stared at the ceiling. She should do some yoga poses. It had been a while. Maybe they would calm her down. Her snake box was tucked near the wall next to the bed. She was dying to open it again, but she didn't want to draw Chase's attention to it. She could see by the way he was eyeing it that he was already contemplating a break-in. She had other things she was dying to do too, away from prying eyes. It had been a while since she'd written a letter.

Andes grabbed a pillow from the bed, threw it up against the wall, and eased into a headstand. The back of her legs and the soles of her feet caressed the wall as she imagined every single drop of blood in her body rushing to her head. There, that was much better. The world had always made a lot more sense to Andes upside down. This was exactly what she needed. Now she could think about her mother and the letters.

This was definitely the longest she'd ever gone without writ-ing a letter. Would her mother notice? Even though they had all been returned to her, just the fact that it was her mother's own hands writing out *Return to Sender* left Andes clinging to a scrap of hope. Maybe this was her mother's way of communi-cating with her, telling her she still loved her. Otherwise why not just throw the letters out? Burn them? Andes would never even know if they'd reached her. Did her mother look forward to seeing Andes's letters in the mailbox? In her wildest fan-tasies, Andes imagined her mother carefully steaming open each letter and secretly reading them in her rocking chair by the fireplace before slipping them back in the envelopes and sealing them up. It was her father, Zachariah, who was prevent-ing her from reaching out to Andes.

Whenever she got the letters back, Andes would scrutinize the envelopes, praying to see signs of them being steamed and resealed. But the truth was, Andes was never sure about signs— and even though she didn't want to admit it, she was often incapable of seeing them. And now that she was once again news in Starling, she didn't know what on earth to say in a letter. *Dear Mom, Sorry I'm causing you trouble again, but why haven't you told them what's really in my grave?*

And did she really dare go and see George Turner? The last thing she wanted was to make a bad situation worse. If George Turner couldn't get the authorities to exhume her grave, then why should she step in? He would eventually leave them alone, wouldn't he? There was another part of her that was dying to confront him, punish him for the mess he'd made of her life. Andes suddenly became aware of how quiet it was in the room. Chase had turned off the television and was sitting in his bed, facing her. Even upside down, Andes could see the kid was upset.

"What are you doing?" he asked.

"What does it look like I'm doing?"

"Aren't you too old for that?"

"Why don't you try it?"

"You look stupid."

"So do you." Andes was ready to come out of the headstand, but stayed in position a few minutes longer just to prove her point. Then she came down with deliberate slowness and got into a calming lotus position. She had a feeling she was going to need it.

"What's wrong?" Andes asked, although she was afraid of the answer. Chase looked as if he were about to cry.

"What if my dad was killed in 9/11?" he asked.

"What?"

"He's a fireman. Lots of firemen were killed in 9/11."

"Oh, honey."

"You know I'm right. You know it's true."

"Chase, you are getting way ahead of yourself here."

"You said it yourself. He might not even be here!" Chase

jumped off the bed and started stomping around the space, half pacing, half speed-walking. Andes flashed back to her childhood, where she had acres and acres to run, trees to climb, vines to swing on, and creeks to wade or drown in.

"Come on," she said, uncurling her legs and standing up. "Let's take a walk."

"What?" This momentarily stopped Chase in his tracks.

"Let's walk it out," she said. "Come on."

"Walk what out?" Chase grumbled.

"Your fears," Andes said simply. "You've had a long day, a long plane ride, and a lot of new, scary things come up lately—"

"New, scary things?"

"And everybody knows that worries grow in the night."

"They do?"

"Yup."

"Why?"

"Because we're tired. Because they settle in and get all blown out of proportion. So let's take a walk, then pick up a little dinner, then take a bath, and then go to bed. Things will seem better in the morning."

"It's only six o'clock." Andes looked at the clock radio beside the bed. He was right. She'd forgotten all about the three-hour time difference.

"Then it's the perfect time for a walk and dinner, don't you think?"

"Why can't we just go to the fire station and make sure he wasn't killed in 9/11?"

"Chase."

"If we don't I won't be able to sleep. I'll be up all night."

"Walk. Dinner. Firehouse."

"You mean it?"

"Unfortunately," Andes said, "I do."

Chapter 19

"Here," Steve Newman said, heaving another heavy cardboard box on Dave Jensen. "Awaiting your sexy scrawl."

Dave groaned and immediately scoured the room for a place to dump the box. He eventually shoved it under the communal dining table near his usual spot. He tried to pretend he didn't hear his fellow firefighters chuckling. What in the world had he been thinking? He should have listened to his instincts. He didn't want to do that shoot in the first place. That was the trouble with women, they always talked you into things you were going to regret. When was this nonsense going to stop?

And no surprise, the ribbing he got from his siblings and friends was nothing compared to the barrage from his comrades at Engine 325. And the worst part was, he couldn't even blame them. If the shoe had been on the other boot, he would've been acting the exact same way. Worse, probably. Just imagining Steve or Johnny, or Mike—imagine little Mike—shirt off, hose in hand—

He told them he wasn't going to pose holding a hose like that, but then they got to him again. *It's for charity. It's for charity.* What charity was it? He couldn't even remember. Poor firefighters who didn't have anyone else to mercilessly throw shit on? He'd gone from being one of the most experienced and respected firefighters on the team to being a laughingstock. Jesus. BLAZING. That was the caption that ran above his photo— BLAZING DAVE.

The day after the calendar went on sale, he'd come into the firehouse and was treated to his image, blown up to billboard size and plastered to the side of one of the engines. Things went downhill from there. They made placemats, coasters, napkins, even shower curtains. Everywhere he turned in the station, there he was. He couldn't open his locker without facing his mistake. Six months later and they were still going strong. And so were the women. They were showing up at the firehouse at all hours, camera, calendars, and pens in hand. At first the guys loved it, until they realized the women were just there for Dave. Then they quickly turned it into more ridicule, and last but not least came the out-and-out resentment. One day he came in to find the four heaviest firefighters standing in front of the firehouse, stripped down to their underwear and boots, holding hoses just like his calendar pose—with six-pack stomachs drawn on their flabby, aging bodies with magic marker. Dave wished for a five-alarm just so the idiots would be in real trouble. Unfortunately that day not even a cat stuck in a tree.

He sat at the table and kicked the box. Six months. Six months and he was still signing these damn things. There was nothing to do but keep his head down and pray for the year to be over. And then there was Jenny. She was furious with all the female attention he was getting, like it was his fault. She was the one who forced him to do the charity shoot in the first place. The whole thing had been her idea, and now look where they were. And how she'd gone from this raving jealousy—bunny boiling, drooling, raving, jealous—to "let's get married and have babies," he'd never know. Couldn't figure out that transition in a million years. But there it was.

Dave kicked the box again. He'd like to take them out and burn them one by one, now wouldn't that be ironic? The only good thing about that damn calendar was that it had turned his shy, awkward little sister Pammy into the star of her junior high. Dave sighed as his fellow firefighters brought heaping plates of lasagna to the table.

"Not eating, Dave?" Steve asked.

"He's gotta maintain that six-pack," Johnny yelled from the other end of the table. The other men laughed with him; after all, it was his wife who baked the lasagna.

"My shift ends at seven, boys," Dave said. "Taking the little woman out to dinner." And that did the trick. The men nodded their understanding, and conversation soon moved on. Ever since Dave had started mimicking their speech, phrases like "well, me and the little woman," he'd gained a little more respect. Even though technically Dave thought "little woman" should be reserved for a wife. And Jenny was not his wife. Which was the whole purpose of tonight's dinner. He was taking her somewhere fancy. Somewhere public. Somewhere where he could look her in the eye and pick up on the conversation she'd started about their future and having babies. He had to make sure she understood exactly how he felt. Because it wasn't going to happen. Now now. Not ever. He liked Jenny. He cared about Jenny. He was physically attracted to Jenny. He just wasn't in love with her. Not enough anyway, not enough to marry her. She deserved better. Now if he could just find an easy way of letting her down.

Andes was simply enjoying the walk, taking in the sights. Chase, on the other hand, was studying the people of Sunnyside like an alien whose plan of attack was to assimilate before annihilating. He'd never seen such variety. Dominicans, Asians, Mexicans, Irish. And the food! In one block there was Japanese, Indian, Dominican, Korean, Chinese, and Irish breakfast, whatever that was. Was it a plate full of shamrocks? Because that would actually be kinda cool. He'd eat that. Then he'd go outside and throw up four-leaf clovers. Barfing good luck to us all! *Kiss me, I've puked Irish!*

He liked how the train ran over their heads too. That was kinda cool. But he wasn't quite sure why Andes kept harping on the Manhattan skyline. Seattle had a skyline too and the Space

Needle. So far he hadn't seen anything like the Space Needle, although he guessed the Empire State Building looked kinda cool. It would be even more cool if King Kong were to pick it up and squish it.

"Where do you want to eat?" Andes asked.

"Korean barbecue," Chase said, expecting her to make a face or scold him. Instead, her face lit up and she clapped him on the back.

"You read my mind, you good man," she said.

Great. He should have picked the shamrocks.

Sunnyside's fire station was only a few blocks away from where Andes and Chase ate dak galbi and samgyeopsal, which sounded way cooler than barbecued chicken and nonsalted bacon. It was located south of the main drag (Queens Blvd.), on Forty-third and Skillman near the historic Sunnyside Gardens. Andes read that writers and artists first flocked to the area as an alternative to overpriced Manhattan in the 1920s. Sunnyside Gardens was registered as a national landmark in the eighties and was a much sought after place to reside. It was strange to Andes that the natural beauty she grew up with and took for granted was in big cities a rare commodity to be fought over and paid dearly for.

"This is it," Andes said as they approached the fire station. She stopped. "I still think we need to take our time about this, kid. Ease into it." Chase kicked at a crack in the sidewalk while contemplating her comment.

"Let's just ask if he works here," he said. "Then we'll go back to the motel and make a plan." Andes smiled and touched him on the shoulder. He jerked away and ran full speed to the firehouse. *I could just run the other way*, Andes thought as she followed him. *The firemen will take care of him.* It was like she had adopted a notoriously mean dog from the pound just because it looked at her with big pleading eyes and wagged its tail at her, only to start snarling and snapping the minute she got it back home. Except Chase never did wag his tail at her; he snarled from the beginning, so she really had no one to blame but herself.

By the time Andes caught up with Chase, a man in his late sixties wearing jeans and a black jacket was coming out to meet them. It was no wonder either, since Chase was jumping up and down trying to see through the garage windows.

"Can I help you?" His tone was gruff, not mean necessarily, just slightly impatient and definitely to the point. Andes almost laughed; the tough-talking New Yorkers were just the kind of people fit to handle the kid. Chase stopped jumping and looked at Andes to take the lead.

"We just wanted to know if Dave Jensen still works here," Andes said, trying to formulate a reason why as she spoke. Was he an old friend? Distant cousin? Friend of a friend?

"Jesus," the man practically yelled. "When is this going to stop?" Andes frowned at the fireman, who had crossed his arms against his chest and stood legs spread out, as if barring the entrance to the fire station. He had furry gray eyebrows and a matching mustache, all thick and hairy, as if three aging caterpillars were using his face as their personal retirement community.

"Huh?" was all Andes could think to say.

"Does he work here?" Chase asked. He was jiggling in place, incapable of keeping his body still. The man eyed Chase while raising one bushy caterpillar inquisitively.

"Got you doin' her dirty work, huh?"

"What?" Andes said. She was totally lost. This guy was acting like they were playing some kind of practical joke—

Oh God. *Had* something happened to Dave Jensen? Did he die in some kind of tragic, local fire? If that were the case, she didn't want the man blurting the bad news out in front of the kid. She wasn't sure how Chase would handle it. Maybe she should pull the fireman aside and—

"He just finished his shift for a couple of days," the fireman said, interrupting Andes's thoughts. "And we're no longer allowing him to sign calendars outside the firehouse. You can get already signed copies at the coffee shop around the corner." *Calendars?* Andes was about to say when the man stopped her in an actual talk-to-the-hand manner. "And just so you don't go

getting your pretty head too far up in the clouds," he continued, "the answer is no. He's not single. He has a very nice girlfriend. But if you want to get your kicks like some kind of
teenager and tape him up on your wall, be my guest. Go to the
coffeehouse. But don't come back here. Understand?" Andes
nodded and grabbed Chase's hand before he could retort. She
could feel the tension in his grip, but she didn't loosen up until
they were far enough from the fire station that they couldn't be
overheard.

"I want to go back," Chase whined, looking over his shoulder.

"Listen to me," Andes pleaded. "You got your answer. Dave
Jensen is alive and now we know where he works. We also know
he's in some kind of calendar at the coffee shop, right?"

"I guess."

"So we get a cup of joe and see what he looks like. Then we
go back to the motel and make a plan. Remember our deal?"
Looking as if it pained him to do so, Chase nodded his consent.

"Do you think he looks like me?" he asked, looking in the direction of the fire station again. Andes sat on a nearby apartment stoop and pulled Chase down with her.

"We don't know if he's your father, Chase. And to be honest,
you and Jay have the exact same eyes." *Beautiful, blue,* she added
silently. Chase stared straight ahead, his jaw set in a line angry
beyond his years. He looked even more like Jay with that surly
expression, but Andes kept that to herself as well. "We should
call him," Andes continued. "Let him know we're okay."

"You call him," Chase said. "I'm not talking to him until I
know who my real father is." In a way Andes couldn't blame
Chase for being upset. Why hadn't Jay just taken a paternity
test? Was it because he didn't want to find out he wasn't the biological father? And what about his warning not to find Dave
Jensen? Maybe it was better the kid didn't want to talk to him;
imagine if Jay knew they'd been in Queens less than four hours
and they'd already tracked down his maybe-dad.

"Come on," Andes said. "Let's load me up with caffeine and
you with sugar." Chase treated her to a genuine smile.

"Yes!" He jumped off the stoop, clearing three steps and seemingly skipping the landing, his feet off and running before even touching the ground.

The Buzz was a quaint little coffeehouse on Skillman Avenue just a few blocks from the firehouse. It had a homey feel with brick walls displaying local artwork, clusters of leather chairs, and numerous nooks and crannies where one could lose themselves with a laptop and a giant latte. It was the anti-Starbucks, and it ex-emplified what Sunnyside, Queens was all about: the locals.

Chase immediately threw himself into an empty leather chair and barked, "Hot chocolate with whipped cream." Andes stood still and stared at him. When that failed to elicit an apol-ogy, she put her hands on her hips and glared. It wasn't a nat-ural pose for her, but she felt it was required for the task at hand. She wanted to see if she could work it with just a look, but Chase just stared back and before she knew it, Andes fell victim to a staring contest. The coffeehouse wasn't completely empty, but those that were scattered about weren't paying any attention to them. It would soon be one of the things they would appreciate about New York and New Yorkers, the free-dom to be a little insane in public without any scrutiny or judg-ment. A woman whisked behind them carrying a tray of desserts.

"*Por favor, mijo,*" she sang to Chase as she sailed by. "It means—"

"Puh-lease," Chase said. "I know." She shrugged and winked at Andes. She was a beautiful Latina woman Andes pegged to be in her late twenties. She exuded a positive and nurturing en-ergy. Andes liked her immediately. The woman whisked the tray behind the counter and was soon engaged in a conversa-tion with another beautiful woman at the register. Andes couldn't help but stare at the woman with a twinge of jealousy. She was hoping the rumor that New York was home to some of the most beautiful women in the world was a load of bull. But so far, no such luck. The customer was tall and buxom with straight jet-black hair, high cheekbones, and bright blue eyes. She looked like a model.

"Please," Chase said finally with disgust. "And a calendar." Andes grudgingly started for the counter.

"Oh no, no, no," the Latino woman said, leaning all the way over the counter and jumping into their conversation. "He may have used the word 'please,' but his tone was 'f-you mama.' You can't let him get away with that." She leaned over farther, spilling long dark curls over the edge, and directed her next statement to Chase. "We only serve hot chocolate to good little boys." Uh-oh, Andes thought, seeing the headline: SEATTLE BOY BURNS DOWN LOCAL QUEENS COFFEE SHOP. But Chase surprised her once again.

"Please," he said softly. Almost as if he meant it.

"Much better." The woman smiled and winked at Andes again.

"I'm Hilda," she said.

"Andes. And this is Chase." Chase treated her to a psychotic grin and Hilda wagged her finger at him until he giggled.

"Wow," Andes whispered. "You're good."

"I have a boy about his age," she said pointing to one of the adjacent rooms. "Alejandro." Andes followed her gaze to a where the boy sat eating a cupcake. It was almost as big as his head and piled high with pink frosting and rainbow sprinkles. Andes prayed Chase wouldn't ask her for one; she couldn't imagine what that much sugar would do to his cheery disposition. Sensing he was being talked about, Alejandro looked up and flashed Andes a genuine smile. She smiled back and gave a little wave, which he promptly returned. Andes wanted to ask Hilda if they could trade, but even though it was just a joke, she didn't want to take the chance of Chase overhearing it. She wondered if she should introduce the boys, but Chase, probably sensing this was her next move, had already buried himself in a newspaper.

"You have a reader," Hilda exclaimed.

"He loves books too," Andes said.

"Ah. As we say in Puerto Rico, *comiendo libros*. Eating books." Andes laughed.

"That's him," she agreed.

"Maybe he can rub off on mine." Andes turned to Chase in time to catch him mouth, "pervert." Andes shook her head and turned away again. No wonder parents were always saying "pick your battles." Chase would have exhausted anyone. He'd turn the Super Nanny into a crack whore. Andes giggled to herself until she remembered Chase's real mother was a crack whore, and then she felt guilty. Maybe she *would* get him a cupcake. Or was that being a bad parent? Plying him with sugar just to relieve her guilt over a mean thought? But she wasn't really his parent, she was just a professional escort. That wasn't the right phrase. Thank God he didn't hear that thought. He'd be mouthing "pervert" for the rest of his life.

Andes placed the order and tried to see if there was anything resembling a calendar lying around. The woman with the jet-black hair was still at the counter. And to Andes's discomfort, she was looking her up and down. Andes was wearing leggings, a tank top, and a simple cloth skirt. Even though she hadn't been to a yoga class for a while, she always dressed like this, telling herself it was so that she could go to a class at a moment's notice. The "model" was in high heels, a miniskirt, and a tight sequined shirt. If she wasn't a model, then she was a professional cheerleader. Or prostitute. Or a FBI agent posing as a professional model/cheerleader/prostitute. Or brilliant physicist who wasn't afraid to be herself. The brains (or boobs) behind Hooters. Andes forced herself to look away.

"Hilda? Do you have any calendars for sale?" Andes asked. The model turned her bright blue eyes on Andes and kept them there.

"Calendars?" Hilda asked over the sound of the espresso machine.

"Um, the firehouse said—"

"Oh. That calendar," Hilda cut in with a glance at the model.

"See," the model said. "I told you." Hilda rolled her eyes.

"It's for the kid," Andes said, glancing back at Chase, who was pretending he wasn't glued to every word.

"Yeah, right," Hilda said.

"No. It is."

"You don't have to say that on my account," the model said.

"Just give me a sec," Hilda said, placing Andes's latte on the counter and turning to make the hot chocolate. "I've got them back here."

"They're supposed to be right here," the woman complained, slapping the top of the counter. Hilda rolled her eyes again.

"I've got my hands full," she said. "You can come around and get one *for the kid.*"

"It is for the kid," Andes insisted.

"Should I give it to you?" Ms. Perfect said, emerging from the counter with an arm full of calendars and shifting them to one hip so her other hand was free to draw air quotes, "or are you still going with—'it's for the kid'?"

"Chase," Andes said. "Why don't you tell them—"

"I have cancer?" Chase muttered.

"Never mind," Andes said holding out her hand. "Can I just have the calendar?" Andes turned to take the calendar from the leggy beauty, but she was staring at Chase, mouth and eyes open like a cartoon character entering a surprise party. Chase was glaring at Andes, warning her. He didn't want her telling anyone he was searching for his father, and Andes would keep his secret—they were a team.

"He's joking," Andes said. "It was a very bad joke," she added for his benefit, "one you're never going to tell again, but a joke nonetheless. You're right. The calendar is for me." Since the woman wasn't moving, Andes reached out and pulled a calendar from the pile in her hand. To her surprise, the woman snatched it back and made a beeline for Chase.

"Hi, sweetie," she said, handing him the calendar. "I'm Jenny."

"Hi," Chase mumbled.

"Do you like firemen?" Chase glanced at Andes, then back at the woman.

"Yes," he said.

"How would you like to ride on one of the fire trucks and meet a real live fireman?" Andes expected Chase to say something sarcastic like *better than a dead fireman,* but he didn't. He'd quickly assessed this was a woman he could mold like putty.

"Golly," he said. "Could I really?" Jenny lunged at him, wrapping him into a hug.

"Yes, you can!" she said. "Yes, you can." She pulled back, opened the calendar, and held a page up to Chase.

"This who you were looking for?" she asked with a big smile. Andes took a step forward, taking in Chase's face as he took in the picture of his maybe-dad. This time the kid didn't say golly, or anything else. His face was serious and slightly pale. After a few minutes of staring at the picture, he nodded. "That's him," he said.

"Well then," Jenny exclaimed. "This is your lucky day."

Chapter 20

Little fires were boring. Little fires were child's play. It was time to move on to something bigger. There were plenty of abandoned buildings just waiting to burn, and this time people were welcome to slow down and watch. In fact, this next fire would be set from farther away by running a fuse to the scene, so it would be perfectly safe to have an audience. It would be fun to slip into the crowds and watch the flames shoot into the sky with everybody else. It was like a work of art. Then came the thrill of the fire trucks screaming down the street. And the firemen's powerful hoses blasting away at the flames were much more gratifying than a garden hose. Even so, something was going wrong. Each time was a little less satisfying. The next one would have to be bigger—better. Because every day that a fire wasn't set, life just wasn't the same. Almost not worth living. Too anxious, too restless, too dead inside. Still, it seemed like nothing could ever compare to the rush of that first little accidental fire. That was the feeling that must be ignited again! Patience. The feeling would come back. It must. And it would be simple. As simple as the flick of the wrist.

Chapter 21

Dave realized too late he shouldn't have picked a restaurant they both enjoyed to break the bad news to Jenny. But at the time he was simply thinking he wanted some of Amole's carne asada and he liked that the little Mexican restaurant was BYOB. That actually worked in Jenny's favor because it reminded him that one of the things he liked about her was that she liked to drink beer and go to Rangers and Yankees games with him. Of course, she was always dressed like they were going from the game to a fashion runway, but he didn't care; in fact, he was always happy to be seen with her. Although lately, he'd been the one getting the attention when they were out, which is why she was going to have to come to her senses and stop peddling those damn calendars. Problem was, how did you say, *No, I'm not going to marry you and have children with you,* and then expect someone to do a favor for you? Somehow, Jenny did it with him all the time. But she was sly about it, that was the key. Dave didn't know much about being sly, so he was on to plan B. Get her slightly drunk.

"Two six-packs?" she said as he picked up Corona for him

and Corona Light for her. "I'm only going to drink one beer," she said. "What about you?" This is what marriage would be like, Dave reminded himself. Constant scrutiny.

"I'll take the rest home," Dave said. Jenny practically lived with him even though she had her own apartment one block away. She refused to completely move in until they had a wedding date set, and Dave still called it "his" place. This had caused quiet a few arguments lately too. Dave set the beer on the counter and went for a bottle of tequila.

"What are you doing?" Jenny said.

"Look. I have the next forty-eight hours off. You're not working this weekend, are you?" Jenny's job was another source of arguments between them. When he met her he found her wild and exotic, probably a little bit dangerous, but when they became boyfriend and girlfriend he assumed she'd find another line of work. When she didn't, it started to bother him. He wasn't trying to be a prude or deny her her freedom, but he couldn't get the image of all those men staring at her out of his mind.

"Not this weekend, Dave," she said.

"So—let's have a little fun." Jenny made a face but no further comments. She was thinking with him drunk, it would be easier to ask him for her next favor. Not that there was any way he could turn it down, but alcohol wouldn't hurt. Jenny slipped her hand in his as they walked the few blocks to the restaurant. They were shown their usual table and soon they settled into a comfortable silence. *Maybe I can do this*, Dave thought. *Maybe I just have cold feet.*

"I met someone today," Jenny said mysteriously. He was a couple of beers and one shot into the meal, she was one beer and a tiny dredge of a shot behind. Jenny hadn't brought up marriage, or children, or the calendar. Dave was starting to feel as if he really loved her. Sometimes he was prone to overanalyzing, which was a funny trait for a fireman. Lucky for him, he was only like this in his personal life. On the job he was all action. But with his siblings, his mother, and his girlfriend, he couldn't help but obsess. Was she or was she not the right girl for him?

She was gorgeous and upbeat, but predictable. Dave liked the surprises in life, the what's-the-prize-in-the-cereal-box feel. Jenny liked everything mapped out, and she probably wouldn't buy the cereal until she knew exactly which prize she was getting. Whenever he tried to explain this to his guy friends, they gave him shit.

I wish my girlfriend looked half as good. As long as you can predict waking up next to her, what's the problem? And so on. But sometimes when Jenny talked, Dave found himself drifting off, thinking of other things. He didn't mean it, it just happened. She liked to go into excruciating detail when she told a story, such mundane detail he couldn't possibly stay interested. On their first date a year ago, he thought she was just nervous, and he found her need to fill him in on everything from what time it was when the story occurred, to what she was wearing, to what she ate for breakfast, absolutely adorable. That wore off after a couple of weeks. Since then he'd been trying, and failing, to subtly move her stories along.

"I don't *need* to know whether it was Tina or Kim," he'd say gently if she couldn't remember which one had told her the interesting tidbit she was about to relate. Or, "I don't know what used to be in the building where the coffee shop is now, but go on with the story." That's all he did, or tried to do, gently persuade her to move things along. But that wasn't possible for Jenny. It seemed the way she was hardwired, she couldn't tell the story without talking it out loud, and she had absolutely no filters whatsoever to weed out the minutiae that lulled the listener into a gentle but surefire coma.

"Was it Wednesday? I think so, but it could have been Thursday because it was right after my appointment with Dr. Hess and that was on Wednesday, but for some reason I keep thinking about my Jazzercise class, which is on Thursdays—oh, I know, I went around all day Wednesday thinking it was Thursday because I brought my Jazzercise clothes to work by accident—you know how I keep them in that purple bag right by the bed?"

And so on and so forth until he wanted to kill himself. Trying to interrupt her was like trying to stop a train hurtling down the tracks. Only difference was, the train, if you did manage to stop it, didn't get pissed off. Lately he'd taken to fantasizing about turning a fire hose on her while she talked, just to see if she could keep going through the blast of water. Dave Jensen wasn't a mean guy, although all of these thoughts he'd been having made him feel like he was, but he just didn't know what to do about it. And it wasn't until he fully realized that she couldn't change, would never change, that he'd really started obsessing over it. Due to whatever biological kink in her evolutionary chain, Jenny would never be able to tell a story any other way. And who was he to go around changing anybody? He knew there were things about him she wished she could change. He didn't cook, he wore socks way past their expiration date, and if allowed, he could spend an entire weekend watching *Ice Road Truckers*. Nobody was perfect. But lately, she'd really picked up on the fact that half the time they were together, he was daydreaming without even being aware of it.

"Did you hear what I just said?" Jenny demanded.

"Yup. Who'd ya meet?" Dave shoved his empty plate away from him and threw his napkin down. The portions were huge; he always ate too much.

"I was at the coffee shop, I stopped in there to check on the calendars, so it must have been about six-thirty because we were meeting at seven—"

Dave looked at the empty bowl of guacamole and wondered if they made it fresh or if it was store bought, and then he thought about the bet he had on whether or not Mikey was going to score with that chick from Jersey on their third date, and then he ran through the details for his mother's birthday party, and finally thought about his stack of unpaid bills.

"—and there was this little boy—oh, you should have seen him, Dave, he was skinny, but other than that you never would have known he had cancer—"

"Cancer?"

"You weren't listening to me again, were you?"

"I was, I was. I just missed that part."

"How could you have missed that part? The cancer part was the crux of the story, Dave."

Dave poured her another shot and inched it forward with an apologetic smile. "Sorry, honey. You know I just finished a long shift. I'm tired."

Jenny released the angry furrow in her brow and slid her hand across the table.

"I was going into too much detail again, wasn't I?" He squeezed her hand and they smiled at each other. She'd never be able to change how she told a story, and he'd never be able to listen to every single word. It wasn't ideal, but once in a while they were able to acknowledge and accept it between them.

"Coffee shop. Your calendar. Little boy in love with firemen. He has cancer. How's that?"

"That's great, honey," Dave said, kissing her hand. Then he dropped it. "Oh," he said, replaying it in his head. "That's terrible. I mean it—that's really terrible."

"I know. But you should have seen his little face light up when I gave him your calendar, honey." Dave felt a slight pressure building inside his head. They were suddenly talking about his calendar and kids in the same sentence. He really was tired; he hoped she wasn't building up to another ultimatum. And she wasn't touching the shot. This wasn't going the way he'd hoped.

"How old is he?" Dave asked, searching his mind for a way out of the evening.

"I think he's probably ten. I don't know for sure, but he looks Andrew's age—remember, Kathy's youngest"—Jenny stopped and slapped her hand over her mouth. It was so genuine and cute, Dave had to laugh. "He's about ten," Jenny said decisively.

"Well, that was very, very nice of you, honey," Dave said, looking around for the waiter. With a little luck they could pay the check and hit the sack.

"I'm not finished. I promise I'll make this quick." Dave stopped looking for the waiter, and the pressure in his head increased. She was using the same tone of voice she used to persuade him to do the calendar. Come to think of it, he'd been drinking Patrón that night too. All this time he thought he was the one hoping the sauce would relax her a bit—but what if she'd been playing him?

"Jenny," he said. "What did you do?"

"Nothing," Jenny answered quickly. "Just promised the boy you'd show him around the firehouse, that's all. Oh—and sign his calendar, of course."

"Jenny. Jenny, Jenny, Jenny."

"He has cancer, Dave."

"And I feel bad for him. But I can't have a kid hanging around the firehouse. Larry would flip."

"I'll talk to Larry." Dave closed his eyes and pinched the bridge of his nose. Larry loved Jenny. She'd have him eating out of her hands. One word from her and kids would be sliding up and down the pole all day. Then Larry would turn around and give Dave shit for it just to keep up his macho image. Oh no, she wasn't talking Larry into anything. If he wasn't careful, he was going to walk into the firehouse one day and find a surprise wedding on the agenda—his.

"No. I'll talk to Larry. I meet the kid outside the station—I'll tell you when—I sign his calendar, but that's it, Jenny."

"But—"

"I mean it. I work there. Don't you get it? That's my work. And I'm sorry I ever posed for that calendar."

"It was for charity."

"Well, I hope it was worth it, because it's certainly made my life hell."

"Which part, Dave? The money? The recognition? Gorgeous girls drooling all over you?" She was mad again, the furrow in her brow back. Great. Somehow her ideas always ended up being his fault. Why were relationships so hard?

"I'm tired, Jenny."

"I imagine chemotherapy and radiation would make a person tired too."

"Jenny."

"Just imagine it, Dave. Imagine being ten years old and facing

your own mortality. And all you want in the world is for someone you admire—someone you think is a hero—to show you
around his workplace. Maybe let you ride along on a call."

"Ride along on a call?"

"Maybe the last ride he'll ever take, Dave! Because his ten-
year-old body is turning against him. But don't do it on my account. You posed naked for a camera, maybe you're right.
Maybe that's all you can do. Don't worry about it. I'll tell the
kid you're too busy for him. You're too busy for a kid with cancer."

"No," Dave said. "Don't do that." Good God, she'd done it
again. "I'll check with Larry on my next shift, okay?" Dave said.
"I'm sure the guys would love to have him." Jenny slipped her
hand in his again and the check finally came. It would be a long
time before Dave would be able to let go of the image of the kid
sitting in a chair getting chemotherapy. The kid? He couldn't
even remember his name—had Jenny ever said his name?
What kind of father would he ever be? The kid, how imper-
sonal. Well, hell. Take the kid for a ride on one of the rigs, let
him slide down the pole. What harm was there in that? Dave
paid the check and tried not to worry. What was there to worry
about? But whether it was Jenny, the sick kid, or the Patrón,
something told Dave the answer was—plenty.

Chapter 22

"She fell in love with Millie the minute she laid eyes on her. She was the biggest, blackest snake in all of West Virginia."

"Why would anyone name a snake Millie?"

Andes flung herself back into a prone position on her bed and watched shadows from passing cars brush along the ceiling.

"Chase. It's not supposed to take me months to tell a story. You can't question every little detail." What she really wanted to say was, "What the fuck is wrong with the name Millie?" Andes was quickly learning that having children was a process of slowly covering up who you really were and what you really thought, because nothing, as it turned out, was appropriate for a kid's ears. He was growing bored of her travel stories, and she thought if there was anything a ten-year-old boy would love, it was snakes. But so far he'd been anything but impressed with her snake tales. What she wouldn't give to have a nice thick rattler here now, and give the kid a show. Although technically, you were only supposed to handle when you were anointed, besides which, she hadn't picked up a snake in a long, long time—but it was probably like riding a bicycle, and she knew she could summon God if only to see one other expression on the kid's face other than pious disdain.

Why did she name the beautiful diamondback Mildred? Not that Chase knew the story was true. If she couldn't please him with a deadly viper, then what could she please him with? Personally, she loved everything about snakes—which in the end had been her downfall. Long before she was allowed to handle snakes, she had been fascinated with worms. She'd forgotten that. She used to sit in the dirt for hours digging them up. She would pick them up, dangle them, hold a pile of them in her palms, set them back down and watch their rubbery bodies swirl and squiggle. She used to kiss them too, that was the dirty secret lingering in the back of her mind as she lay in the low-budget motel room in Queens with a ten-year-old blossoming Stalin. She used to hold piles of dirty worms in her palms, bring them up to her lips, and kiss them.

Why was she telling this story anyway? What she really wanted to do was read the newspaper article again and then Google the shit out of George Turner now that she was in his home turf, but she couldn't do it in front of the kid. Was he ever going to go to sleep?

"Millie," he muttered, rolling his eyes.

"Oh, forget it," Andes said.

"Well, it was better than the one about spilling maple syrup in an IHOP in Canada."

"It wasn't an IHOP. It was a Denny's. And there would have been a whale and streaking Mounties in that one if you hadn't interrupted me."

"Whatever."

"Whatever. Why don't you tell me a story, then?" Chase got out of his bed and padded over to hers. He stood in the space between the bed and the wall and stared at the far end where Andes's snake box was tucked away in the corner. He was pointing at it, she was sure of it; despite the cover of darkness, she could feel him pointing as sure as if it were her own hand outstretched in the dark. She knew the feeling well, longing for something you couldn't touch. She was so tired, yet excited. She loved being in a new place, she couldn't wait to go into Manhattan. She should be out tonight—painting the town red!

She should be flirting, and dancing, and drinking. Turning down offers to snort lines of little white powder, not stuck in 3A with this kid blatantly pointing at her personal things.

"Go to bed," she said. "Story time is over."

"I want to know what is in that box," Chase said.

"You saw what was in it. In the airplane, remember? Matchbooks." Matches. Maybe instead of the Millie story she should have told him about the time her father lit a blowtorch and eighty-nine-year-old Margaret Jessen from three doors down stuck her hand in it and held it there for five whole minutes? She didn't have a mark on her when she finally pulled it out, not a mark.

She knew why she didn't tell him—he was already too obsessed with fire, and because of this she should be sleeping with one eye open.

"Why do you collect matches?" Chase hammered.

Andes sat up. They weren't going to bed anytime soon.

"I just do," she said. "They're from all the places I've been. It's like taking a little piece of the country I've just visited. It's like writing on the wall—*I was here.*"

"But you're not leaving it, you're taking it with you," Chase pointed out.

"They're little packets of potential," Andes said quietly.

"Well, what else is in the box?"

"What do you mean?"

"Come on, I'm not stupid."

"I know you're not. You're smarter than me."

Chase shrugged, although he certainly didn't disagree.

"Why do you keep looking at the phone?" he asked.

"We have to call your dad."

"That's not the reason."

"Oh yeah, smarty pants? What's the reason?"

"I think you want to call someone but you're waiting until I fall asleep or take a really long shower."

Andes shrugged, although she certainly didn't disagree.

"Is it a boyfriend?"

"No."

"But it is someone." Chase sat at the end of her bed and the two sat in silence for a few minutes. Chase hadn't shown any interest in the television, which bordered on mental illness in Andes's opinion, but she also didn't want to be one of those parents who encourage children to ingest electronic garbage, so she hadn't brought it up either. Although, personally, she was dying to watch television, lose herself in an overblown drama. They were going to have to get an apartment with separate bedrooms and she was going to have a television in hers. She'd send him to bed with Shakespeare and she'd turn on *CSI.* Why didn't she just show him what was in the box? It wouldn't mean anything to him, most likely he'd just make fun of her. But she wasn't letting him open that box, not now, not ever. It was her past, the only link she had, and she was the only one who had a right to it.

"Come on," she said, edging toward the phone near the bed. "Your dad should be settled in Portland by now—"

"We should just call him Jay." Andes, who had already picked up the phone, set it down. She looked at Chase. This was going to be difficult. How could she tell the kid not to mention Dave Jensen to his father? That was like asking him to lie, right? But what if Jay was serious—what if he was going to make Andes "pay" for introducing them? He was in jail. What was he going to do, put a hit out on her?

"I won't tell him about my maybe-dad," Chase assured her as he acquiesced and reached for the phone.

"How did you know—"

"Because he'd kill you," Chase said softly.

True to his word, Chase didn't say anything to Jay about Dave Jensen. They didn't talk long, and Jay didn't even ask to speak with Andes. Chase hung up and seconds later started regaling Andes with facts such as how Manhattan used to be called New Amsterdam, and Andes was truly interested, but she didn't learn much, for the next minute he was asleep, and seconds after that a soft but steady snore filled the room. It was a comforting sound that soon lulled Andes into a deep sleep of her own. Unfortunately, her dreams would not be as comforting.

She dreamt she was in her grandmother's living room. Andrea Cunningham, Emily's maternal grandmother, was convinced God was a form of abuse in Emily's home, and she did everything in her power to take Emily away. One day, on one of Emily's weekly visits to her grandmother's, there was a stranger standing in the living room. He was tall, about her father's age, but thinner, and smiling. He was wearing khaki pants and a black T-shirt; he was handsome and smiling. Something about the way he looked Emily right in the eye and smiled at her made her shiver. She was thirteen, and even though she'd manufactured a few crushes on schoolboys and neighbor boys, Emily took one look at this smiling, handsome man, and fell instantly in love. She was suddenly ashamed of her braids and her long skirt and blouse. She kept her other clothes at her grandmother's, little treasures she looked forward to visiting: jeans, and sweaters, and hair clips. She would hurry and change as soon as she arrived. Why didn't her grandmother warn her they had company? Why didn't she let her change first?

"Emily, this is Dr. Warren," her grandmother said. Emily frowned. Dr. Warren? Was her grandmother sick?

"Call me Tom," Dr. Warren said, smiling and holding his hand out to Emily. Emily stared at the beautiful clean hand stretched before her, and put hers behind her back. They were dirty. She usually took long showers here too. Her grandmother didn't have a woods behind her house and a creek to play in, so Emily always came dirty and left clean. Now Dr. Warren was going to think she was a little girl with no manners, but that was slightly better than a dirty girl, so she couldn't let him see her hands.

"Are you sick?" Emily asked her grandmother.

"No, no," her grandmother said. "He's not that kind of doctor. He's a psychiatrist, dear. He specializes in . . ." She stopped talking and started wringing her hands, as if trying to squeeze out her next thought. "Cults," she said at last. Emily didn't catch the word "cult," or if she did, she didn't understand it.

"Your grandmother thought it might be helpful if you and I have a little talk," the handsome not-that-kind-of-doctor said. Emily didn't reply; in her mind she was imagining herself in her white jeans with her pink blouse and sparkly faux diamond barrette. Her fingernails were clean and painted.

"Grandma," she said. "I'd like to go upstairs and change."

"You have to wear those clothes every day, don't you, Emily?" Not-that-kind-of-doctor said. "Even to school?" Emily's cheeks burned as she thought of the routine of getting on that school bus in her long skirt, black shoes, and long-sleeved white blouse. Every single day. Her father had offered her the choice. She could stop going to school and be homeschooled, or she could go to public school but follow his dress code, the Lord's dress code, not anyone else's. It was only at her grandmother's house that she dared break the rule; her father knew the teachers at school, had even spoken with them, there were too many eyes, too many spies, there she would never be able to get away with it. Why was the doctor bringing this up? Grandma knew she couldn't do anything about this.

"Your grandmother's been telling me there are a lot of rules in your community," the doctor was saying. Somehow they were all sitting down now. Emily couldn't remember when they'd moved to the couch, but they were sitting down. There was even a plate of sugar cookies in front of Emily, her favorite, and she couldn't remember where they had come from either.

"Especially in church," the doctor was saying now. "Aren't there a lot of rules in your church?"

"The meetings?" Emily said, surprised. "No, not really."

"Emily, tell him about the—"

"Andrea," Tom said sharply. "May I speak to you for a moment?" The doctor and her grandmother disappeared into the other room. Emily quickly tried to work on her nails, using the nail on her right index finger to dig the dirt out of the nails on her left hand. She had only succeeded in taking care of her little pinky on her left hand when the doctor returned. This time, he was alone.

"Your grandmother and I thought it best if we talk alone," he said. They talked of many things. But Emily didn't remember everything. The last question he asked her was the one he had been building up to, and it would drive the rest of their conversation out of her head forever. "Now, Emily," he said, leaning as far forward on the couch as he could get and holding her gaze with all-knowing eyes. "Tell me the truth. They don't handle snakes in those meetings, do they?"

Chapter 23

"So have you tracked down the goods on that snake girl yet?" George Turner stayed glued to his computer so Jason Ebert couldn't see the look on his face. He'd asked him numerous times to stop calling her that snake girl, but that was never going to change, so all he could do was change his reaction, right? He'd read that somewhere but couldn't cite the source. All these years of researching stories and they were starting to blur into one soupy mess of faceless facts swimming about his brain—or treading water was more like it. Oprah or Deepak Chopra, who knew anymore? Some self-help shit that sold books but never really changed lives, because Greg was coming around to the reality that people didn't change, they just got older, heavier, more wrinkled, and started forgetting shit.

But George Turner remembered Emily Tomlin with a clarity that bordered on reverence. It had been almost a decade now. Who would've believed he'd still be working here, or Jason for that matter? Two fat, chain-smoking, knit-cap-wearing, dangerously-close-to-middle-age gossip-rag reporters. Still, it was a far better fate than the one Emily seemed to have succumbed to. George would never get over the guilt that he might have had something to do with it.

"The judge denied my request to exhume the body," George said, finally turning to Jason, who was moving papers around the desk so he could perch his fat ass on the edge. George wanted to yell at him, but it wasn't worth the effort. He just hoped he'd remember to Windex it later. Besides, he needed someone to talk to. "But get this, bro. The boy who died. Those snake freaks are actually contesting snakebite as the cause of death. Guess the kid had a heart condition as well," George said.

Jason snorted. "Yeah, well, if I had a fucking deadly cottonmouth wrapped around my neck I'd have a heart condition too. Not to mention a bladder-dick-just-out-of-the-swimming-pool condition as well. Jesus cult freaks. Damn. You get all the good stories."

George saw the picture of Emily in his mind's eye. Fifteen, barefoot, dancing with a snake. It was the baddest motherfucker he had ever seen, and she was actually cradling it in her arms. Her snake baby. The Blue Ridge Mountains framed her in the background, topped off by an achingly beautiful sunset. How could he *not* have taken her picture? It would have been a crime to miss that shot, a fucking crime! Although in doing so, he might have unwittingly precipitated another crime. It's not like he could have predicted it. He was just doing his job. George couldn't believe he hadn't won any awards for that piece—the picture alone was like a religious experience. For him anyway. The look of pure rapture on that girl's face, complete innocence and joy, and sensuality. The most amazing part was that the snake had curved its head toward Emily's cheek, and it was sticking its tongue out, as if getting ready to lick—actually *lick* the young girl's face. Nobody could've resisted taking that shot. George pushed it out of his mind. He didn't want to think about it now in front of Jason. He'd think about it later with a bottle of scotch.

"So what are you working on now?" George asked before Jason could grill him any further.

"I'll tell you what I'm not working on." Jason pouted. "The Upper East Side moms." George laughed and shook his head. A book club of young moms on the Upper East Side was recently busted for being a heroin ring. The story was taking front page in every newspaper and it had been given to one of the youngest reporters on their team, a young mom herself. The icing on the irony-cake was the book they were pretending to read was James Frey's *A Million Little Pieces*. Jason, not being the literary type despite claiming to be a writer, didn't grasp the irony. Apparently, he only remembered the stories he was covering.

"They've got me covering the new exhibit at the fucking Central Park Zoo instead," Jason complained. "All I can hope is that someone gets mauled by a billy goat or a penguin." George laughed despite himself, and then remembered something. He dug around his desk until he found the scrap of paper he was looking for.

"Then you can help me out," he said, handing Jason the piece of paper. Jason looked it over, none too pleased.

"Blazing Dave?" he said. "Nope. Not doing it."

"Come on," George said. "I'll owe you one."

"Why can't you do it?"

"I'm going out of town."

"Out of town? Where? Jersey?" George looked away.

"No."

"Back to snake country? Didn't Joe tell you to kill that story?" Joe was their boss, a twentysomething who further bonded Jason and George in friendship by their abject hatred of him.

"The boy's funeral is next week," George said. "I'm going to cover it."

"But what's the story? Especially if they're sticking with heart condition. And even that nobody cares about anymore. Besides, we're cutting out national stories, remember? We've got enough crazy locals to fill a paper. And Upper East Side moms dealing heroin is not only local, it's much hipper, bro." Jason lit a cigarette even though they weren't supposed to smoke in the office. George snatched it out of his hand and took a puff.

"Dude," Jason said. "What is it with you and that snake girl?"

Just for that, George didn't give the cigarette back. He shouldn't have said anything. "I mean, you wanted to bone her, okay—"

"It wasn't like that."

"No, dude, I get it. She was cute. And playing with that snake. That's fuckin' hot. That's deadly, man."

"Jason—"

"But she's dead, dude. She's been dead, what? Like ten years."

"According to the cross, nine years."

"Dude."

"But how did she die? Why won't anybody tell me how she died?"

"Because they don't want you to write about it, moron."

"I can't tell you what it was like. Seeing that grave. Just a simple wooden cross. With Emily's name."

"Dude. Nine years."

"I think Emily may have been murdered," George blurted out. "And it could be all my fault."

"Murdered. You got all this from a wooden cross in the backyard?"

"Remember her father? Mean son of a bitch. And even I couldn't have predicted the publicity that was going to follow. It was relentless. Let's face it. My article destroyed their lives. What if he went off the deep end and—"

"Murdered his own daughter? Dude." George crushed the cigarette out on the desk, which made him feel uncouth and disgusting, which in turn made him feel like a rebel, which made him feel slightly good. "You're really torturing yourself, aren't you?" Jason asked.

"Wouldn't you?"

"You were just doing your job. You were just telling the story."

"And it may have gotten her killed," George said.

"Dude. She played in the sandbox with snakes. That's what got her killed."

"I don't think so. Call it a hunch, call it whatever you want. I know there's a story there. I can feel it, Jason."

"Dude, we're second-rate reporters. We don't get hunches. And if we do, we drink them away."

"Not this time," George said.

"So what are you going to do?"

"I'm going to do my job. Find out who, what, where, when, and why."

"Dude. That's a lot of W's," Jason said, shaking his head. George shoved his things in his backpack and started for the door.

"And Joe's approved this?" Jason called after him.

"Fuck Joe."

"This could cost you your job."

"Fuck the job."

"All this for that snake girl. I just don't get it."

George bit back his anger. There was no use getting pissed. Of course Jason didn't get it. George barely understood it himself. He closed his eyes as his favorite memory of Emily assaulted him. Bright eyes, sensual mouth, flaming red hair. Arms stretched high above her head holding a deadly viper in her snow-white hands. Bare feet planted in the dirt, the snake's head curled around, his tongue stretched out and almost licking her cheek. It rooted him to the spot. It cemented his fucking feet to the ground. What did she call that snake? Mildred. George had never believed in God until that moment. Looking through that lens, taking that picture, was the most alive he'd ever felt. No. Beyond alive. As if there was something else out there. Beyond himself and the petty, daily things he wrote about; beyond the crushing, invisible weight constantly sitting on his chest. Bigger than anything he could have ever imagined. He felt it all right. Immortality. In those few seconds, looking at Emily's world through his lens, George Turner's mind opened up and for a few blissful seconds he believed. And he'd never felt it since. Not even close.

"Please," George said, going over to the trash and retrieving the crumpled piece of paper Jason had tossed in there. "Just do me this one little favor. I'll only be gone a few days, I swear." Jason reluctantly took the balled-up paper. He smoothed it out and read it over.

"Oh, fuck no, dude. Not the pretty-boy fireman."

"Please." Jason took the assignment and pretended to wipe it on his ass, which is how George knew he'd won. George tilted his head in thanks and walked out the door.

Andes woke to the smell of something burning and the piercing beep of the fire alarm. She bolted out of bed. "Chase!" she yelled. His bed was empty, the covers twisted and mangled. Panic gripped her until she saw him standing on a chair underneath the fire alarm.

"What are you doing?" she demanded. Now that her fear was relieved, she was furious.

"Trying to shut it off," Chase yelled over the unrelenting beeps. Chase couldn't reach the alarm, even from the chair, but it didn't stop him from trying. He was on his tippytoes, hand outstretched into a fist.

"What set it off?" Andes yelled, pulling a chair up beside him.

"I don't know." Andes traded places with Chase. It took several tries, but she finally managed to knock the cover off and rip out the battery. Chase scrambled back to bed. Then he flipped the television on, blasting the volume.

"Turn that down."

"We're going to have to buy new batteries," Chase said.

"I think that's the responsibility of the motel," Andes answered. She was still standing there, examining the fire alarm. She had smelled something burning. What was it? It was faint now, but still lingering in the air. It wasn't until she placed the cover back on the fire alarm that she found the culprit. A portion of the plastic was melted and charred black. Andes reached out. It was warm to the touch. "Chase," she said. "Turn off the television and come here." It took several seconds, which felt like hours, until she heard the television click off and he padded over to her.

"What?"

"Did you hold some kind of flame up to the alarm?" she asked.

"What?"

"Chase, the cover is melted. Did you do this or not?" Chase

maintained eye contact and Andes could see him wrestling with the answer.

"Don't get mad," he said.

"What did you do?"

"I didn't mean to burn the cover. I was just testing the fire alarm."

"With what? Matches?"

"Don't worry—not your matches. I took a book from the coffee shop. You want the rest for your collection?"

"No. But I want the rest, period. You are not to play with matches or lighters or anything else that makes fire."

"I was doing you a favor."

"By setting fire to the place while I sleep?"

"I told you I was testing the alarm. I wanted to make sure the batteries worked!" Andes came off the chair with her hand outstretched. Chase reached into the pocket of his shorts and handed her a book of matches. Sure enough, they were from The Buzz.

"Chase. Were you trying to—I don't know—maybe get the fire department to come to our hotel?"

"No. I was testing the batteries. You should be thanking me." *The boy's an aspiring pyro.*

"Well, now that we know the batteries work, can you make me a promise?"

"What."

"Don't do anything like that again, okay?"

"Fine."

"I mean it, Chase. If you have a concern like that again, you can bring it my attention first."

"I said okay."

Andes let it go for now. She was starting to get used to the slight shifts in Chase's tone, and, like a pianist dissecting a classical piece, she deduced he was teetering on the edge. The fact that he was trying to hold his cool touched her. She turned away before he could see she was on the verge of tears. Maybe she'd talk to someone at the firehouse about Chase's behavior. From now on, though, she was going to have to keep a closer eye on him, that was for sure. She hadn't even noticed him taking the matches from the coffee shop. Maybe she should set the kid up with a counselor too. Still, she wasn't going to jump to conclusions. What if people believed everything anyone had ever said about her? About her family? The humiliation of the world's judgment after the photo of her with Millie came out washed over her. The look in her father's eyes when he saw her next. Her grandmother's ultimatum. Her father picking up the axe and taking her to the shed—

"Are you crying?"

"Go to sleep."

"I won't do it again. I promise."

"Thank you." Andes closed her eyes. A few minutes later she heard his soft snores once again, but this time it was a long time before she feel back asleep.

Chase wasn't pushing to explore Manhattan, but Andes was determined to expose both of them to culture. She picked the Museum of Natural History as their first stop because what boy wouldn't want to look at dinosaur bones? But when she learned about their H_2O exhibit, she thought maybe fate was drawing them to the museum.

It was another contradiction Andes was well aware of, not believing in God but still looking for signs. But just because she didn't believe in God didn't mean she didn't believe in some kind of life force or inspiration that could be tapped into to provide guidance. And the next morning when she saw a man passing their motel window wearing a T-shirt from the Museum of Natural History advertising the water exhibit, she knew it was a sign. Water! What more proof did she need? It was exactly what the kid needed to get over his little fire obsession, a good dousing.

Even if it was only subliminal. Maybe the more Andes introduced water into his life, the less the budding pryo would play with matches. After the morning's fire alarm incident it certainly couldn't hurt. And then after the museum they could cross the street to Central Park, somewhere Andes had always wanted to go. No one in her family had ever been to New York City. Accordingly, no one else in her family would ever want to go to

New York City. The ironic thing was, New York City was such a conglomeration of oddballs that it was probably one of the few places where her family wouldn't have been ostracized. They probably could have marched up and down the subway cars handling snakes with barely a second glance from the seen-it-all-ites.

Hilda from the coffee shop told Andes she was on the subway one day and noticed no one under thirty was wearing any pants. She didn't know what the occasion was, National Show Your Boxers and Panties Day, perhaps, but New Yorkers barely looked up. Chase asked Hilda if she was wearing her pants and she cooed, "Oh, honey, I could eat you up," and proceeded to try. Hilda didn't look over thirty. Andes would have to find out her secret.

Of course, it wasn't until they'd taken two trains to the Upper West Side of Manhattan, and stood in line for tickets, and then stood in line for the bathroom and were finally entering the water dioramas that Andes realized the fatal flaw in her plan to extinguish the love of fire out of the kid. Chase grew up on a lake, on a sailboat. It was truly a "duh" moment, made even more humiliating by the extent to which she'd fantasized its brilliance, and she was just grateful no one else was privy to it. So while they might have soaked up an appreciation and awe for the planet's most precious resource, by the time they were done with water and wandering around the dinosaur exhibit, little else had changed. Andes was feeling small and helpless against the problems of the world, which in a strange way cheered her up. It was as if Tyrannosaurus Rex himself had leaned down and said, "Take it from me, kid, nothing lasts forever. Enjoy it while you can."

"Don't they make you feel small?" Andes asked Chase as they stood, necks tilted back, staring up the skeletal remains of the dinosaur. Chase didn't answer, which was how she knew he agreed with her. Then they were off to the gift shop where Chase bought a fossil, and Andes a packet of glow-in-the-dark stars, and then they were off to the bathrooms again before hitting Central Park.

But by now the museum crowd had swelled to twice its original size, and Andes was nervous about Chase going to the bathroom alone. She didn't know how they did it, single moms. She only had one ten-year-old kid to look out for and it was making her a nervous wreck. But they both made it out of the bathrooms alive, and headed down Central Park West to Seventy-second Street. As they reached the corner, Andes pointed out the Dakota, where John Lennon was shot.

"This is where he lived?" Chase asked.

"Yes."

"This is where Mark David Chapman shot him?"

Andes was surprised it continued to surprise her that Chase was a walking encyclopedia.

"Yes."

"Then the Strawberry Fields Memorial is nearby?"

"Let's find out." They crossed the street to the park, and within minutes were standing by the Strawberry Fields memorial, where roses adorned the IMAGINE inscription in the circular stone pattern on the ground. Tourists hovered around taking photos, making out, and playing guitars. Andes loved that there were people who had such a profound effect on others, they could make time stand still. It could have been the sixties or seventies.

The rest of Central Park didn't disappoint either. After buying hot dogs and sodas and chips, they promptly found a patch of grass in Sheep Meadow, where Chase informed her sheep really used to graze, and they sprawled on the ground without the slightest hesitation. Across the expanse of field, covered with bodies as if they were lying on the beach, Manhattan curled around them like a watchful parent. Andes didn't even mind that she hadn't thought to bring a blanket. The grass was soft and clean, and the July sun was warm and forgiving.

Andes wondered what Chase was thinking about as she watched him watch the people around them. She wondered if he had ever had his IQ tested; she wouldn't be surprised if it was off the charts. Chase caught her looking at him, and for a moment she feared he was going to say something to ruin her good mood. Instead he gave her a little smile and said, "I like it here."

"Me too," Andes said. *I like you too,* she thought, but this definitely would have ruined the mood, so instead she took another bite of her hot dog.

Chapter 24

The problem with living inside a small town outside of a big city was accidentally running into the very people you were trying to avoid. Andes wanted to control Chase's visits with his maybe-dad and secretly hoped after a while Chase would forget about him entirely. But when Andes and Chase were coming down the steps from their Fortieth Street subway stop in Sunnyside, they bumped into Jenny and Dave, who were coming up. Later Andes would wonder why she behaved so oddly, but she knew the answer lay in a thousand inconsequential but irritating little crumbs building up on her bedsheets. And one of the irritating little crumbs was how good-looking Dave Jensen was. Physically, Andes thought he was almost perfect, and she'd never been comfortable with in-your-face beauty. And although he was fully dressed today and in full living color, she couldn't help but to flash to the image of calendar-Dave, shirtless, black-and-white, Blazing Dave, holding a hose against his six-pack abs, water droplets drawing the eye to every muscle on his arms, stomach, and chest. He had a killer smile too, along with a full head of naturally curly hair and big, dark eyes. In person he was even more arresting.

Jenny was cooing something at Chase, but Dave was looking straight at Andes with such an open and friendly gaze that she had to look away. She was also irritated by the phony persona Chase was assuming. It was as if Jenny were Mary Poppins and Chase a chipper little English boy with a pocket full of smiles. Andes felt mean inside, because just a few seconds in their presence and all her good feelings about her afternoon with Chase was washed away in one giant gulp of jealousy. They were standing in an awful spot for a chat as well—people were trying to shove past them in both directions as they either ran for or away from the train. She had an urge to leave Chase with the two ambassadors of happiness and catch a train herself.

Suddenly Dave was reaching out for her and Andes was forced to look at him as they shook hands. It was an extremely awkward moment, considering handshaking was usually done when you first met and they'd been standing here for several minutes already.

"Dave," Jenny said as Dave shook Andes's hand, "this is Chase." Jenny then frowned slightly at Andes, whose hand was still entwined with Dave's. She yanked it back a little too hard and then felt like an idiot. "I forget your name," Jenny said to Andes, her smile fading slightly.

"Emily," Andes said. Then, like a bad cartoon, Andes slapped her hand over her mouth. Chase jumped up and down, pointing his index finger at her accusingly. "But I usually go by Andes," she said, quickly hoping the subject would just drop. She hadn't introduced herself as Emily in years. It must be the whole business with the passport and all the stress from traveling and George Turner—

"Well, they're both beautiful names," Dave said. Andes thought Jenny should have been more subtle with the dirty look she shot him, but she was no expert, so she kept her mouth shut. It was then Andes noticed Chase scooting up the stairs, positioning himself directly behind Dave. His legs were skinny and quick. His hand was sneaking into the pocket of his shorts. Jenny was talking at her, which was definitely the way to describe it rather than talking to her; Andes had the distinct feeling she had no more

input to the conversation than a lamppost. Even if Chase's movements weren't distracting her, Jenny's constant chatter was hard
to follow. Dave, on the other hand, looked almost pained, and
Andes knew in that instant he was no fan of Jenny's chatter
either. She was thinking this made him slightly more palatable
when she caught the glint of a blade out of the corner of her
eye.

Chase was wielding a pocketknife dangerously close to Dave's
curly hair. From the concentration etched in his lips and the
look in his eye, Andes knew Chase was seconds away from attempting a swipe. "Chase!" she screamed. Jenny kept talking but
Dave whipped around. Chase jerked his hand back behind his
head, his arm bent at his elbow, and he quickly feigned a yawn.

"Sorry," Andes said. "He's so tired. I thought he was going to
pass out for a second there." Andes moved behind Chase and
snatched the knife out of his hands while nudging him forward.
"I'd better get him home," she said, purposefully talking to him
like he was a child. "He needs a nap."

"Of course he does," Jenny said. "The treatments must be so
hard." Andes, who had started moving, didn't stop, but did slow
down as she tried to make sense of the words coming out of
Jenny's mouth. "At least he still has all his hair," Jenny added
cheerleader-style, forcing a smile and tilting her head. Con-
fused, Andes glanced at Dave's hair and then back at Jenny. Was
it remotely possible she'd known what Chase had been up to?

"Don't worry, little buddy," Dave said. "If you do lose your
hair, you'll still look great."

"Of course," Jenny said, crestfallen. "Of course you will." Having put enough pieces of the puzzle together, Andes was about
to set the record straight when Chase jumped in.

"I don't have cancer," he proclaimed. Dave and Jenny continued to stare at him, their expressions of pity intact. "And my
dad calls me little buddy," he told Dave.

"You have the right attitude," Jenny said, leaning down to
Chase. "Just imagine a healing white light wrapping around
you like a blanket." Chase didn't move his head, but his eyes
did slide over to Andes.

"Jenny, we should let them go," Dave said, putting his hand on her back and directing her up the stairs. She allowed herself to be escorted away, but a few seconds later dropped a business card down to Andes. It fluttered in the air and Andes would have caught it, if not for Chase snatching it seconds before it reached her hand.

"Call Dave for a tour of the firehouse," she yelled. "Even though you're perfectly, perfectly healthy," she added, bringing the pompoms back out. Dave looked down the stairwell at Andes and the two exchanged a look prisoners on adjacent cellblocks might throw each other when the warden came for lockdown. He raised his hand as if it were heavy, and smiled weakly.

"Yes, give me a call," he said. Then Dave and Jenny slipped out of sight, although they could still hear the ping of Jenny's voice echoing from above. Andes and Chase headed back to the motel in silence.

"What were you thinking?" Andes asked him when they were flopped back in their respective beds, staring at the ceiling. Andes was holding the pocketknife. She liked rolling the smooth pearl case through her slim fingers.

"It was the perfect plan," Chase shouted. "And you ruined it."

Andes held up the knife.

"These aren't scissors. I think had your perfect little plan succeeded you would have caused your 'maybe-dad' considerable pain and suffering." She knew as she did it that she shouldn't have called him maybe-dad, let alone put the words in air quotes, yet her already small dose of parenting patience had long run dry.

"You're right," Chase said after a long silence. "Scissors would be better. Or nail clippers."

"How about we let the man keep his hair and nails intact," Andes suggested. She was suddenly tired, as if she'd had no sleep since the Fourth of July. All the chaotic events since meeting the kid felt like one long miniseries without a commercial.

"What are we doing tomorrow?" Chase asked as if he expected her to have an agenda.

"We're going to find a place to live," Andes said, surprising even herself with the answer. From outside cars passed by noisily, and from the next room came the drone of the television. Andes wanted the boy to have, if not the American dream, then the American norm: his own room, a kitchen where he could stand in front of an open refrigerator complaining, and a living room where he could watch too much television.

"What's wrong with right here?" Chase asked.

"Wouldn't you like to have your own room?"

"I don't care."

It came back so easily, her annoyance, but she swallowed it. He had to care, he just didn't want to show it. He'd see. Once he had his own room, he'd see. Someday he'd thank her for everything she was doing for him. She might be dead by the time he did, but still, he would thank her. Besides, she wanted *her* own room, and she wanted to stand in front of a refrigerator agonizing over choices, and she wanted to flop on a real couch and watch television. They had enough money to find a rental for at least six months. Hopefully by then, Jay would be out of jail (maybe he'd even stay sober), and Chase could go back to Seattle. It was herself she should be worried about. What would she do?

She could travel. As long as she didn't think about flying over the ocean—long stretches of black depths waiting to swallow her whole—she could do it. But she wasn't going to think about it any more tonight. The knife became slippery in her palms.

"It's time," Andes said, sitting up and picking up the phone.

"I don't want to talk to him."

"You don't have to talk long."

"I don't want you listening."

"I'll dial the number and take a bath."

Even from the bathtub, Andes could hear from the clipped tones of Chase's half of the conversation that it wasn't going well. Then the television blared, and Andes disappeared under the water, wondering if there was any way she could pull off an accidental drowning. No one would blame her for leaving then. And the boy would be fine, wouldn't he? It's not like he needed her, per se, just someone. In some countries boys his age were already hunting and gathering.

She was startled when there was a knock on the door. Chase broke the news to her through the bathroom door that Jay was going into the hospital. She ascertained from the flu-like symptoms Chase was describing that Jay was experiencing alcohol withdrawal. She wondered if Chase did too.

"We'll send him a get-well card," Andes yelled through the door. "Don't worry, he's going to be fine."

"He doesn't sound fine," Chase said. Andes sighed. How was she supposed to have this conversation through a bathroom door with her hair full of generic shampoo?

"Sometimes people have to get really sick to get better," she yelled. Should she hurry out there? Would he be playing with matches? "Want to order a pizza?" she yelled. "Eat it in our pajamas?" There was silence. Andes waited nervously. She was tired, she didn't want a full night of arguing.

"Pepperoni," Chase said finally.

"Pepperoni," Andes said.

"But don't let them cut it," Chase said.

"What?"

"We can cut it ourselves," he yelled. "In circles." Andes slipped back under the water. In circles. Why not. Andes felt like she'd been turning in circles her entire life, so it certainly fit. They spent a rather pleasant evening eating pizza cut in choppy circles and watching television. They even fell asleep at a decent hour, but around three a.m. something made Andes sit straight up in bed. The kid was standing right next to her bed, in the dark. Her brain quickly processed it was him, but she screamed nonetheless.

"Chase?" she said immediately when he didn't move. "Chase?"

"I think I left the burner on."

"What?"

"At home. In the sailboat. I made hot chocolate before we left. Remember?" Andes tried to shake the grogginess from her brain, and her heart was still pounding from the scare.

"No, sweetie," she said, the endearment slipping easily off

her lips despite the fact she'd never used one with him before. "I don't remember that."

"What if the boat caught fire?" Chase said. His voice was nearing hysteria. "I think it did. I think it set the whole dock on fire." Andes flashed back to the warehouse fire. She could still feel the heat licking up the building, could smell the char of things burning.

"Chase. Gerry and Richard are looking after the boat, remember?"

"Do you think they put the fire out?" *I think if your boat had caught fire, they would have sent the Seattle police out here after you.*

"I don't think there was a fire, honey. But if there was, I'm sure they put it out right away." Andes felt for the kid, and she could relate. She used to wake up in the middle of the night worried that the snake boxes weren't locked, sure at that moment they were slithering out the tops of the boxes and steadily making their way through the grass to her front door, slipping under her sheets. People forget how much kids worry. And not over little things either, like what sugar cereal to eat for breakfast. Snakes and fire. Kids worried about the big things.

"Dad would be really mad." Chase sounded dangerously close to crying now, and Andes reached her hand toward him, yet stopped short of touching him when she saw him flinch.

"We'll call Gerry in the morning, okay?" she said as gently as she could. She was pretty sure she had Gerry's number around here somewhere.

"Can we call him now?"

"No. It's three a.m." Although there were still cars going by, and the occasional beep of a horn or the sound of a car door slamming, it was surprisingly quiet in their little motel. So quiet she could hear Chase breathing. For some reason this made her think of his health. Should she take the kid to a doctor for a physical? What if he got really sick in her care?

"Not in Seattle. It's only midnight there."

"That's still too late to call."

"If the boat's on fire it's not too late."

"Chase, if the boat was on fire, they wouldn't stop to answer the phone. Gerry would call the fire department and then he would call us, okay?"

"You don't even have a cell phone!" Chase yelled. "What kind of a freak doesn't have a cell phone?"

Andes swelled with anger. Not only because of the freak comment, but namely the reason she didn't have a cell phone was because she didn't have anybody to call. When she addressed him again, it wasn't lovingly.

"Chase, you need to go back to sleep."

"Even old ladies have cell phones." She had nothing to say to that, nothing at all. She wondered, briefly, if her grandmother had a cell phone. She hadn't spoken to her in years, not since running away to the Florida Keys.

"Go to bed."

"If my boat is on fire it will be all your fault!"

"Okay, I can deal with that. Because it's not on fire. Now go to bed!"

"I hate you." She realized as he stared down at her that he hadn't moved his body at all during any of his ramblings. Was he talking in his sleep? Would he remember any of this in the morning? She reached out to touch his shoulder. He didn't respond to her hand on him; rather, he turned away from her touch and headed back toward his bed. But instead of getting back in, he pounded it with his fist.

"Chase."

"I hate you, I hate you, I hate you."

"Chase, calm down."

He started pacing, muttering. "I left it on, I left it on, I left it on."

Andes quickly got out of bed.

"You'll feel better after a good night's sleep."

"No, I won't. I won't feel better until I know my boat's okay."

Andes sighed, picked up the phone.

"What's Gerry's number?"

"I don't know. I thought you had it."

Andes turned on the light. So much for sleeping. She went through her purse until she found a scrap piece of paper with

Gerry's number. "Do you want to call?" Chase shook his head, still pacing. In the dim light of the motel room she could see his hair was sticking straight up and sweat was beaded on his forehead. Andes gripped the phone, holding her breath until she heard it ring. "Answering machine," she called to Chase as she waited for the beep. Chase ran over and hung up the phone. "I was going to leave a message," Andes said.

"We have to do something," Chase said. "We have to do something." He was back to pacing, and this time his mutterings were louder as his feet padded back and forth across the faded carpet.

"Chase," Andes said. "You're tired. You need some sleep."

"I can't sleep if my boat's on fire!"

"What do you want me to do, Chase? Call the Seattle police or fire department?"

"No," Chase yelled as Andes moved top pick up the phone. "I'll get in trouble."

"Why? Why would *you* get in trouble?" Was this it? Was this the moment the kid was going to tell her he had been setting the fires all along? Andes's heart squeezed and she prayed he wasn't going to tell her any such thing. What would she do then?

"Because nobody will believe me that I just know my boat is on fire! They'll think I'm playing a prank."

"Then what? What can I do to help?"

"I don't know," Chase wailed as he started to pace faster.

"Listen," Andes said, talking almost as fast as he was pacing. "If there was a fire it would have been in the news, right?" Chase didn't entirely stop pacing but he did slow a bit and nod. "Okay, we'll find a computer and Google the news." Now Chase did stop and look at her with such hope in his eyes, Andes almost burst into tears.

"Now?" he whispered. "Now?" Regretting it even as she acquiesced, Andes nodded.

"Now." She let Chase put his jacket on over his pajamas and she quickly changed into sweats and slipped a lightweight jacket on herself and put on her flip-flops. Then she went to her snake box, unlocked it, and took out cash.

"It doesn't cost that much at an Internet café," Chase lectured.

"Well, there aren't going to be any open in Sunnyside," Andes said. "We're taking a cab back and forth from Manhattan."

"But—"

"It's three o'clock in the morning. We're not taking the subway." God, he was like a mini IRS agent. "We can always go in the morning," she said. Chase sighed and ran to his accounting notebook he kept in the nightstand drawer underneath the Gideon Bible.

"Fine," he said. "But we're getting receipts."

Chapter 25

"I thought we were going to find a place to live."

Andes didn't look back at Chase. Instead she addressed the whine facing straight ahead.

"We are."

"We're going to live in the post office?"

Seriously hitting a child would be wrong, but what about little slaps? Surely, little slaps should be allowed.

"We're going to set up a P.O. box so you can write your father." Andes touched the letter in her purse, mentally going through how she'd slip it in the mail without the kid noticing. It would come back, of course, they all came back, but writing to her mother made her feel grounded, connected to something. And there was always hope that one day she would write back, if only to tell her to stop writing.

"I'm hungry."

Andes closed her eyes. She had asked him just five minutes ago if he wanted to eat before going to the post office. She took his shrug to mean he didn't care. They were both tired. It was after five a.m. when they got back from the Kinko's in Manhattan. Of course they didn't find any news stories about a sailboat catching on fire; in fact, it was the opposite, there was an article on how the marina fires had ceased as of late. Still, Chase's obsession hadn't ended there. He wanted to print out every single article he found related to fires—awful headlines—but Andes wouldn't let him. Instead she let him pick three and print just those out, and that was only because she had to get back to bed. He picked: LIFE SAVINGS GOES UP IN FLAMES WHEN LOCAL RESTAURANT BURNS, SIX CHILDREN AND MOTHER DIE IN KITCHEN FIRE, and APARTMENT BLAZE IN THE BRONX KILLS 13 ILLEGAL IMMIGRANTS FROM HAITI. But that wasn't enough to make him happy. There were at least six more that he insisted he needed. Andes stood her ground. Chase didn't give up. He screamed at her in the Kinko's, continued screaming at her on the street waiting for a cab back to Queens, and even though he was silent in the cab, she could still *feel* him screaming at her. But he'd fallen asleep the minute they got back to the hotel, which was why they were both cranky and tired now, even though it was almost noon.

"We're going to the coffeehouse after this," Andes said. "You can eat there."

"The one with the fat kid?" Andes turned to Chase and gave him *the look*. She was getting quite good at it. She hadn't had much of a glimpse of Alejandro herself, just a quick glance at him, and he was an adorable boy, with a full face, cheeks you wanted to pinch—and yes, it was obvious he didn't lack for any good home cooking. Andes always felt a tug of love for chubby kids. She could only imagine the teasing they faced. How did anyone ever survive childhood, she wondered. She'd always been a skinny kid; her open wounds had more to do with the fat snakes she carried about her neck, but once her classmates found out about them, they were relentlessly cruel. The day the kids at school saw her picture in the paper . . .

All because of George Turner. And he was digging into her past again. The last time he'd caused her family this kind of pain, she'd been too young and too stupid to do anything about it. This time would be different. This time—

"Miss." The voice was loud and reprimanding, and Andes felt

the kid's sharp finger poking her in the back, urging her forward in line. She gave Chase another look and he gestured to the open window, where an impatient postal worker glowered at her. Little slaps. Yes, they should definitely be allowed, and there would be plenty to go around.

"Good morning," Hilda sang as they entered The Buzz. "*Buenos días.*"

"Good morning," Andes called back. Chase took a running jump and threw himself into one of the leather chairs.

"I'm hungry," he yelled. Andes ordered a breakfast burrito and an orange juice for Chase and a latte for herself.

"You need food too," Hilda said. "I'll make that two breakfast burritos." Andes smiled and didn't argue, she'd let the kid eat two. Just the thought of George Turner had turned her stomach; it would be hours before she'd be calm enough to eat. "Alejandro's in the little room," Hilda sang to Chase. "Go play. I'll bring your burrito." Andes waited for Chase to argue with her, but instead he ambled into the little room. Andes could only pray he would be nice to Alejandro. She liked the little boy, and she liked Hilda. They couldn't afford to alienate their only friends in Sunnyside. Or anywhere, for that matter. Andes picked up a couple of the local newspapers while Hilda busied herself behind the counter. The coffee shop was busy and there were at least two other girls helping Hilda out. Andes thought about how she'd spent her life bouncing from job to job. Waitressing, retail, telemarketing. Selling jewelry too, the only job she liked. But she hadn't made anything in a long time. There were probably marvelous bead and gem stores in Manhattan. She should get back to it. She took the newspapers over to a small table, resisting the urge to check on Chase and Alejandro.

After Andes had spent a few minutes scanning the rentals, Hilda came over with a latte and a burrito. Then she sailed off to the other room to serve Chase. When she returned, Andes resisted the urge to ask if he was okay. Hilda glanced at her pile of newspapers. "We're looking for a place to live," Andes explained. "We can't stay in a motel forever."

"This is a nice neighborhood," Hilda said. "Schools aren't bad either." Andes started to say they wouldn't be here by the time school started, but in the end decided not to. The less people knew about the two of them, the better. Andes didn't look up when she heard the bell on the front door jingle, but she saw Hilda roll her eyes. When she looked up, Jenny was flying her way.

"It's you," she proclaimed. "Hello."

"Good morning," Andes said politely.

"How's Chase?"

Andes glanced toward the little room where she could see nothing but two sets of boys' feet, swinging from the chairs.

"Nobody's screamed bloody murder yet," Andes said. Hilda threw her head back and laughed, Jenny looked slightly pained. She pulled up a stool and sat close to Andes.

"I wanted to ask you," she said lowering her voice to barely a whisper. "What hospital are you going to?"

"Hospital?" Hilda said loudly.

"I'll have a nonfat cap," Jenny ordered Hilda dismissively. Hilda walked away but not without a backward glance at Andes, who tried to throw her an "I'll tell you later" look. Andes turned to Jenny, pushing the Apartment for Rent ads aside.

"Listen to me. You overheard something you completely misunderstood. Chase is not sick. He does not have cancer. I won't even say it was a joke, because that would be a terrible joke. It's a long story. Suffice it to say—look at me—Chase does not have cancer. Okay? Do you get that?" *But he might be a pyromaniac* popped into Andes's head. Jenny sat unmoving, silently processing the information. Andes turned back to her latte and the want ads.

"Oh," Jenny said finally.

"But he still has his heart set on seeing the firehouse," Andes said. "So I hope that's not off the table." Hilda returned and set Jenny's cappuccino on the table. Some sloshed over the edge onto Jenny's pristine hands. She jerked them back as if she'd been scalded.

"Now what's this about a hospital?" Hilda barked in a voice you couldn't ignore.

"Total misunderstanding," Andes said. "No one needs a hospital." *Except maybe a mental hospital.* She had to stop thinking things like that. Yet she had to tell someone about Chase's behavior last night, didn't she? She'd have to talk to Hilda alone later; she certainly wasn't going to include Jenny in any of this.

"What are you doing?" Jenny asked, finally turning her attention to the newspaper.

"Chase and I are looking for a place to live," Andes explained. "Looks like we're going to be here a few months."

"That's fabulous," Jenny said with so much enthusiasm her drink sloshed again. Then she pulled the paper out from underneath Andes and hugged it excitedly to her chest. Andes looked at Hilda, who rolled her eyes again and walked away. "Dave's father owns a building right around the corner," she said. Andes said something like, really?, and Jenny spent the next ten minutes describing the apartment building, Dave's father, and Dave. "I'm calling Dave right now," Jenny said, taking a cell phone out of her purse. Andes had to admit, it would be a relief to get a place through someone she knew. Even though she had the money to pay for several months, she wasn't exactly the greatest applicant for an apartment. The only problem was, now she was going to have to make a bigger effort to disguise her annoyance at Jenny.

"Dave actually answered his phone, his cell phone I mean, because he has a work phone too for emergencies, and most of the time he'll answer that one, but not if he's out on a call because, duh, you can't really talk on the phone when there's a fire. Which there's not 'cause otherwise he wouldn't a' answered. Which means this was meant to be and he thinks his father does have a few units open, and of course he'd rent to you so he just gave me his dad's number, his name is Vernon, I'm just going to call him and see if he can't meet us—what time is it now? It's Saturday, right? I'm getting all the days mixed up—"

Andes put on her listening face and ate her burrito, slightly impressed that anyone could talk that fast and loose without crashing into something. Luckily, Jenny didn't seem to require much from the listener; an occasional head nod did the trick.

Soon she was on the phone again, although Andes couldn't quite follow where her conversation with her ended and with Vernon began. That would be Chase's grandfather, Andes couldn't help but think. If Dave was his father.

"It's all set," Jenny said, clicking off her phone. "Vern was showing an apartment today anyway. We're meeting him over there at two. Is that okay?" It took Andes a couple of seconds to realize Jenny was actually waiting for her answer.

"That's great," she said. "I really appreciate it."

"No problem. I don't work until seven anyway."

"Oh? What do you do?" Andes asked politely.

"I'm an exotic dancer." Andes almost fell off the stool. Not that Jenny didn't look like a stripper, for she certainly had the looks, but still, there was an innocent quality about her that she just couldn't match up. "But when it comes to kids," Jenny continued, "we just say 'dancer.' "

"Of course. Wow. So. How do you like that line of work?" What she really wanted to ask was how Dave liked it. Somehow he didn't seem like the type who wanted his girlfriend taking her clothes off for other men.

"It's a ton of money," Jenny said. "And it's a respectable place. I'm only topless, if you're wondering." Then Jenny was looking Andes over in a way that made her feel self-conscious. "I could get you a job there if you'd like," she said, matter-of-fact. Andes choked on her latte.

"Me?"

"Sure. Red hair is hot. And you're young. Plus you've got that cute tomboy look." Postcard to Mom: *Ghost Daughter makes good as a stripper in Queens.*

"Thanks, but, uh, I make jewelry." Jenny kept looking Andes over anyway. Then she reached for her neck. Andes wanted to pull away, but by that time Jenny was already fingering her necklace. It was black onyx with two bright blue topaz shining like eyes near the middle of the necklace.

"It's gorgeous," Jenny said. "I'll bet the girls at work would love it." *Yes*, Andes thought. *I could corner the market designing the perfect jewelry for strippers.* Actually, it wasn't a bad idea. She could have one of those candle-type parties but with jewelry and strippers instead of candles and housewives. Just her and a room full of exotic dancers. That wouldn't be intimidating at all.

"What does Dave think of your job?" Andes finally asked. Jenny fell into silence for once.

"At first I think it's what attracted him to me. We didn't meet at the club—Dave actually doesn't go to strip clubs, which is one thing I love about him, if you can believe it. But he didn't judge me either, you know. And I'm telling you, it's very modest. We are dancers. You should come sometime, you'll see what I mean. But lately he's started in on me about it. You know. Trying to get me to think about another career. I mean, I probably only have another couple of years before I'm too old anyway. Believe me, nobody wants to be an aging exotic dancer. I might go into nursing. One of my routines is in a nursing uniform. It's a hit. But I don't like how men start out liking things about you and then suddenly they're like, okay, now change, you know? I would never tell him to stop being a fireman even though it's really, really dangerous. I mean, he could die, you know? Every time I hear the sirens go by, I think, that might be the last time I ever see him. But you don't hear me telling him to become something else, because it's what he does. It's what he loves. And he could totally be a model. Well, you saw the calendar. He's hot. Oh. How long have you been standing there?"

Andes followed Jenny's question over to Chase, who was standing beside them with a look of consternation on his young face.

"Do you really think he could die?" he asked. Jenny looked appropriately mortified.

"Of course not," she said. "He's going to live a long, long time. But that's so sweet of you to worry for me."

"Dave's father is going to show us an apartment later," Andes said, cutting off any further conversation. "How does that sound?"

"Sounds like you're changing the subject and patronizing me all at once," Chase answered. Then he looked straight at Jenny. "And if I may ask," he said. "What's so exotic about a nurse's uniform?"

On their way back to the motel, Andes stopped at a Sprint

store on Queens Blvd. and bought two cell phones. She paid for a limited calling plan. "Why two phones?" Chase said on the way out. "Is one for me?"

"Who else would I call?" Andes said, handing him the phone. They walked the rest of the way in silence.

Chapter 26

This is how funerals should be, George Turner thought. *Simple.* The casket was made of pine, the church a one-room deal adorned with nothing but the midmorning sun casting a ray of light through recently cleaned windows, making the polished wood floor shine with God's blessing. Pots of flowers surrounded the casket, recycled tin cans filled with daisies, Indian paintbrush, and Queen Anne's lace, plucked from the fields behind the church. Someone was playing the guitar and clarinet outside, filling the space with a peaceful mourning sound. He could smell coffee brewing too, although he couldn't place the source. He'd love a cup, but going around asking for it would draw attention to his presence, which was the last thing he wanted. He'd have to tell someone he'd like coffee brewing at his funeral too. Coffee and Pilsner Urquell. And maybe a touch of ganja. He couldn't help looking around for Emily, on the off chance she didn't really die all those years ago, that they just wanted him to think she had. Of course, he couldn't be sure what she'd look like now, but so far no one had even come close to resembling the young girl whose photograph he housed in the pocket of his jacket, close to his heart. He'd expected other reporters or news coverage, but unless they were sneaking around like he was, the local news must have had something more important to cover than a nineteen-year-old man dying from a snakebite. He hadn't passed a single news van on his way out. He hadn't even been sent to officially cover the story. Was it a sign of progress that Americans were losing interest in the cultish religious practices of others, or was it the beginning of the end when the release of the latest PlayStation garnered more attention than a tragic, preventable death?

And that's just how George thought of it. Religious freedom or no, the death was preventable. Man should not handle deadly creatures in the name of God, or anything else. There had to be other ways to show your faith. Pray. Don't do drugs. Thou shalt not kill. Hell, give up sex. But rile up deadly snakes until they sink their fangs into your flesh? Come on. Didn't their fellow human beings owe it to them to put a stop to it?

Even if they didn't let the children handle the snakes as they proclaimed, the children under the influence of this religion were going to grow up thinking it was normal. He couldn't get Emily's face out of his mind. The expression on her face. Pure rapture. Dancing with a deadly reptile. It was Nike-shoe-wearing, Kool-Aid-drinking stuff, and she had been raised that way. He'd have to remember to drop the grudges he'd held against his parents—at least they'd given him the basics. Don't play with fire, don't do drugs, don't drive drunk, oh and in case the fancy ever strikes you, don't pick up a venomous snake and hold it up to your face in the name of God. He was getting worked up now, and the funeral was starting. People were crammed in on all sides of him now, just when he was starting to sweat. He tried to pick up pieces of conversation around him, but there were so many voices in the room, some of them singing, some of them praying, others seemed to be chatting about the weather or this or that, he just couldn't get a grasp on anything but the fact that his clothes were really tight, and he was sweating, and all he really wanted to do was get the hell out of there. Nobody else was wearing a necktie, so why the hell was he?

"Brother?" A round-faced man next to him passed him a basket filled with coins and crumpled dollar bills. George held the basket with one hand and reached into his pocket with the other. He didn't have anything but a couple of pennies and a cheese cracker. He palmed the pennies and dropped them in the basket with his fist close to the bottom, hoping no one would notice his meager offerings. Then he passed the basket to the woman next to him and snuck the cheese cracker in his mouth. God, he was hungry. He wondered if they were all meeting at somebody's house after the service and if they would have food. Not that he was trying to get something for nothing, but a good reporter had to infiltrate such things. They wouldn't serve snake, would they?

A prayer was starting. The man standing near the casket didn't look like an official preacher, at least he wasn't dressed any different than the rest of them. He was reciting from the Bible. George wasn't a believer. He'd never understood how the masses just accepted the Bible, or the Koran, or Dead Sea Scrolls, or Area 51 as the Word of God. Obviously they weren't reporters, or they would require a little hard evidence to support their facts. All the crazy things man did in the name of God. Didn't that raise their eyebrows? How many wars had been fought in the name of God? If there was a God, George was pretty sure none of them had ever heard from him. Hell, even the politicians played the God card to get votes. In a way, he didn't blame people. He even sympathized with their need to believe in something, anything. You certainly couldn't count on mankind or nature or even luck to get you through most days. He touched the picture of Emily through his jacket. Such ecstasy on her face, a bliss he had never known.

The preaching was over now and the musicians from outside the church were moving in, filling the little room with the sounds of a guitar, clarinet, cymbals, and a couple of violins. As they walked up the aisle, their pace stayed steady, but the music grew more upbeat. The preacher waited for the music to play out before raising his voice in thanks and praise.

Then the people around him started to join in, clapping their hands, stomping their feet, answering the prayers with shouts and Amens, and Yes, Brother. George wished to God one of his buddies were here to share this. It had the energy of an African American church, but with nothing but dough-white faces. A woman ran to the coffin and threw herself on the ground in front of it. She was writhing and speaking rapidly, but none of the words made any sense. *Speaking in tongues,* he thought. *Holy shit, she's speaking in tongues.* This was good stuff, yet he hadn't even brought his camera. He was worried it would be a dead give-away, and of course, he was right. But still, to get a shot of this!

Two men walked up the aisle carrying two large wooden crates, navigating around people dancing and stomping. They literally had to step over the woman writhing on the ground spouting incomprehensible gibberish. They nodded to the preacher as they lifted the crates onto the stage and set them next to the coffin. George's body knew what they were seconds before his brain had time to digest it. His stomach clenched and his heart jump-started. No way, no way, no fucking way. Part of him wanted to run, part of him wanted to kill himself for not getting a cell phone with a camera, part of him wanted to call somebody to listen to this, just to listen to it. The boxes were set down against the back wall. George couldn't take his eyes off the crates. *Snakes on a Plane,* he thought. *Snakes on a fucking fundamentalist plane!* Doubt any of these folks had ever seen the movie. This was wild. The news fucks in this town were crazy. This was the shit! They were actually going to handle snakes at a funeral where the kid died from a snakebite. This was the shit!

Suddenly George's stomach did more than clench, it started to downright flare. God damn it. He wasn't going to miss this. He wasn't going to miss this! He grabbed the bench in front of him and bowed his head. He was grateful that the out-of-control crowd allowed him to audibly moan without drawing any stares. Must have been that greasy diner, that cunt-licking, greasy diner. What had he even ordered? Well, he'd just sit here and shit his pants if that's what it took. He wasn't going to miss this for the world. "Help me, God," he said. "Help me, help me, help me." Whether it was the clenching, or the praying, or pure will, he felt his stomach ease up a bit. He lifted his head just as the preacher neared one of the wooden crates, and lifted the lid to a chorus of Hallelujah. Then in one fluid motion, the preacher bent over, reached into the box, and produced a thick, leopard-like snake. He dangled it like a rope between his hands, turned around, and held it out as if offering it to the congregation. The snake lifted its head and shook its tail. George thought he was going to pass out.

The preacher raised the snake into the air and took a few steps forward. George was so fixated, it took him a minute to notice others had joined in, and now there were at least five or six snakes held in various hands, squirming their way toward the casket. George could feel the sweat pouring out of his armpits. He had never hated himself more than he hated himself in this moment for not having his camera. And then, as snakes were draped one by one on top of the coffin, George looked at one, just as it swiveled its shiny head around and stared him directly in the eye. *I know who you are!* it hissed. Then it opened its massive jaw, probed the air with its tongue, and shook its tail like a musician's rattle. Unable to look away from his beady black eyes, the snake spoke again. *Die, sinner!* That was when all conscious thought left George's body. He slammed into a brick wall of blackness, silently slid off the pew, and slumped to the floor.

"What are we doing here?" Chase asked as they entered the Calvary Cemetery in Woodside. Woodside was just north of Sunnyside, gaining its nickname, "Suicide's Paradise," from the two large cemeteries that bordered it like immortal bookends. When Andes shared that little tidbit with Chase, he rolled his eyes and said, "Figures."

"We're just taking a walk," Andes said when Chase whined again.

"It's a cemetery," Chase yelled. "It's gross."

Andes kept walking.

"Some of these graves date back to the 1700s," she said over her shoulder.

"So? Gross and old."

"You think the statues are gross?" Andes said, pointing to an angel with her hands clasped and her head dropped shyly to the side. Chase responded with a loud sigh.

"I love cemeteries," Andes said. "It puts everything into perspective."

"What? That we're going to die?" Chase sneered.

Andes stopped, turned, and caught Chase before he slammed into her.

"No," she said. "That we're still alive."

"Some of us knew that coming in," Chase said, looking over her shoulder instead of in her eyes.

"Let's pick someone's grave and visit them," Andes said, venturing onto the lawn and peering at the headstones. Chase stayed at the outer edge of the lawn, kicking the curb with his shoe.

"You want to visit skeletons?" he yelled.

Andes didn't answer right away. She was kneeling before a headstone, trying to make out the names and dates.

"No," she explained lifting her head and looking at Chase. "I want to visit the memory of a person."

"A person you never met."

"That's right."

"A person who can't hear you."

Andes shrugged and moved to the next grave.

"You don't know that."

"Do you see dead people too?" Chase mocked.

"Nope," Andes answered. "Just cranky living ones."

"This is why you don't have anyone to call on your stupid cell phone," Chase pointed out.

"The faster you stop whining, the sooner we'll leave," Andes said.

"Seriously?"

"Yes. We just have to find one grave, pay a little visit, and we'll be gone."

"Then pick one."

"I still hear attitude in your voice." They rounded a bend

where mausoleums stood like miniature temples from an ancient empire. Several had gorgeous stained-glass windows inside. Even Chase was looking them over with interest.

"Why are so many of them from Ireland?" he asked.

"Sunnyside was—and is—home to a lot of Irish immigrants."

"Have you ever been to Ireland?"

Andes opened her mouth to tell him a tale of the rolling hills of Donegal, but stopped.

"Not yet," she said.

"How about this one?" Chase was circling a large Celtic cross. Andes joined him and they read the fading headstone. Michael Murphy. From County Cork. Born in 1813, died in 1903. "Wow," Chase said, doing the math in his head. "He lived to be ninety years old."

"Perfect," Andes said, sitting down next to the grave. Chase remained standing. Andes ran her hand along the headstone, enjoying the roughness and the warmth beneath her fingertips. Then she closed her eyes and centered herself with deep breaths.

"Now what are you doing?" Chase complained.

"Saying hello," Andes answered. "You try it."

"That's stupid."

"Hello, Michael," Andes said. "Top of the morning to you."

"That's really, really stupid," Chase said.

"I'll bet you were a family man," Andes continued. "Hardworking. Smart. Liked to read. Liked to tell jokes. Liked to go to the pub now and then." She whispered the last part, although she knew Chase could still hear her. "I wonder what you would think of the world now," she continued. "I'd say it's changed a bit since you left us."

"Left *us*?" Chase said. "*We* didn't know him."

"You're living on prime real estate now," Andes continued, unfazed. "It's a beautiful cemetery."

"But all your neighbors are *dead*," Chase added loudly. Andes fixed Chase with a look before turning back to Michael Murphy.

"I wonder how you died."

"Who cares how he died?"

"I hope you had a full and happy life."

"Are you crying?"

"I wonder if you would have rather died in Ireland."

"What kind of question is that?"

"Ireland was his home, Chase. See? Born in County Cork, Ireland." Andes pointed out the line on the headstone.

"So?"

"So just because people moved here and made great sacrifices to have a better life for their kids, doesn't mean they didn't miss home. Doesn't mean they wanted to die in Woodside, Queens. Maybe he wanted to die in County Cork where he was born, okay?"

"You're yelling at me."

"I'm sorry." Chase didn't answer, but after a moment he too sat down and stared at the headstone.

"If he wanted to go back home to die," Chase asked, "why didn't he go back home?"

Andes looked up at the Manhattan skyline hovering in the distance like giant headstones and then let her eyes fall back over the rows and rows of headstones in front of her, seemingly stretching into eternity. She found it both immensely comforting and inherently sad.

"Sometimes when you leave a place you call home, you can never go back," Andes whispered. "And you know. You know in your heart of hearts you can't go back. Even if you try, it's too late. They wouldn't even take you back. Imagine! You don't even want to be there, but you still know if you did—even if you did—they wouldn't want you back. They wouldn't take you back."

"Oh," Chase said. "I thought it was because they didn't have air travel back then and taking a boat back and forth to Ireland wouldn't have been financially or physically possible, especially if Mr. Murphy here was an old man at the time."

"Yeah," Andes said, biting back the tears that threatened to fall. "That too." Chase was still staring at the headstone. "You say something," Andes encouraged.

"Sorry you're dead," Chase said after a moment. It may not

have been the toast of the year, but his voice was quiet and sincere. "Can we go now?" he asked. Andes held up her index finger. She knelt by Michael Murphy's grave and bowed her head. When she was finished with her silent prayer, she leaned in and softly kissed the headstone. Chase teetered on the edge of derision, but at the last moment kept his mouth shut. He even waved at Michael Murphy's grave as they walked away.

"Have you ever been to a funeral?" he asked her as they were walking out.

"Yes," Andes said. "I've been to a lot of funerals."

"A lot? How many?"

"Oh, at least a dozen."

"You know a dozen people who died?"

"Yes. They weren't all family or friends, though. You see, I lived in a small town where everyone knew each other. It was very family oriented. So when anyone in the community died, we all went to the funeral to show our respect."

"Do you ever go back to visit?"

"No."

"Why not?"

"That's a complicated question."

"I can handle a complicated answer."

"I know. But I don't think I'm ready to give it." Chase shrugged, but she could tell he was hurt.

"My parents were very religious," she said. "And they weren't very accepting of anyone who wasn't. The truth is, I'm not welcome there anymore."

"Because you don't believe in God?"

"Because I don't believe in *their* God." They walked out of the cemetery and back onto Queens Blvd., where city life sprouted around the cemetery like weeds through a sidewalk. Cars whizzed by them, and even though they were safely on the sidewalk, Andes moved so she was closest to the street.

"That wasn't so complicated," Chase said.

"Good."

"I'm hungry."

"Again? We just had tacos."

Chase shrugged. "What can I say," he said. "Death makes me famished."

Andes looked at her watch. They had a few hours to kill before they were to see the apartment anyway.

"So what you want to eat?" she asked.

"How about cheeseburger empañadas?" Chase asked.

"*Sí, señor,*" Andes said. Chase rolled his eyes, but his giggle betrayed him. He ran ahead at full speed. If Andes had looked away, she might have missed the object fall out of his pocket. Instead of calling out to Chase, she reached the spot where the object had fallen out and picked it up. It was a black lighter with a Playboy Bunny. *Have you seen my lighter, Chase?* She heard Gerry's voice in her head as clear as day. *I always put it in the same place, and yesterday after you left, it was gone.* Andes curled the lighter in her palm and squeezed until it hurt. Her appetite, along with her good mood, had been utterly extinguished.

Chapter 27

He'll have to tell me, Andes thought as she watched the kid inhale his cheeseburger empañadas. *Of course, by the time he realizes the lighter is gone, he'll probably just think that he lost it. So no reason to confess after all.*

"How come you're not eating?"

"I lost my appetite."

"I told you the cemetery was stupid." *Did you start the fire at the warehouse, Chase? Should I be sleeping with a fire extinguisher?* She had made up her mind that when they visited the firehouse, she would talk to Dave. Maybe he could help her shed some light on this. Of course, she had to bring it up without out-and-out accusing the kid of anything. On the other hand, she couldn't just sit by and wait for an explosion. She could tell Dave partial truths—Chase was overly fascinated with fire, did he have any suggestions on how she could handle it? Maybe a little tough love, a little fire safety class à la Smokey the Bear. Too bad there was such a thing as child labor laws—otherwise she'd sign him up to be a fireman. Let him work it out of his system. See how much fun it was to watch someone's entire life go up in flames.

God, that was awful of her, she was just tired and angry at Chase for having Gerry's lighter. She didn't want to face facts. She wanted there to be some other excuse—some innocent reason for why Chase was Mr. Heat Miser. Was she going to have to pat him down day and night, make sure he wasn't packing heat?

"Seriously, what's wrong with you?" Andes's internal meanderings were interrupted by the harsh tone in which Chase delivered the question. It was a spur-of-the-moment reaction, taking the lighter out of her pocket and putting it on the table.

"This fell out of your pocket," she said. Chase grabbed it before Andes could stop him. He shoved it back into his pocket.

"Thanks," he said.

"Back up to the loading dock, buddy," Andes said holding out her hand. "Give me the lighter." Chase picked up his last empañada and shoved the entire thing in his mouth. "Chase. Now." He chewed with his mouth open. The kid was a genius at gross-out warfare. "You're ten years old, Chase. You don't need a lighter."

"You're twenty-five," Chase answered, his mouth still full. "You don't need a cemetery."

"Give me the lighter."

"You have a whole crate full of matches. You don't need my lighter."

"Your lighter? Don't you mean Gerry's lighter?"

Chase closed his mouth, looked away, and swallowed.

"Chase, your behavior is starting to concern me."

"How come you wouldn't let me see your passport?"

"What?"

"At the airport. You wouldn't let me see your passport. How come?"

"We aren't talking about that right now. Give me the lighter."

"No."

"Chase, you are not going to keep that lighter."

"Says you."

"Yes, says me. Now give it here." Andes couldn't believe how angry she felt. Before she met this kid, she liked to think of herself as Zen. Of course, she hadn't done yoga in a million years; that was something she was definitely going to change once they had a place to live. But right now, even breathing deep didn't do anything but make the blood coursing through her veins pump faster. What was she going to do if the kid didn't give her the lighter? Manhandle him? Throw a fit? Call the police? Say, *Wait until one of your fathers gets here?*

Maybe she should've let him cut off a lock of Dave's hair. If he was the boy's father, all she had to do was hand the kid over and she'd be out of here. Then she realized she did have a little bit of leverage.

"You know the apartment we're looking at today?" Chase didn't answer, but he did narrow his eyes. "I was going to let you have the bedroom and I was going to sleep in the living room. But if you don't give me that lighter, we're going to have to share a room so I can keep an eye on you." She held her breath while he contemplated it. Finally he dug into his pocket and threw the lighter across the room. Andes gave him a warning look, but without further comment calmly walked across the room and picked up the lighter. And she also decided to ignore what surely sounded like "bitch" as she did so. But this time, instead of being angry, it only made her incredibly, incredibly sad, and for the first time since she'd started getting to know him, she wondered if she should be just a little bit afraid.

Andes was pleasantly surprised to see Hilda and Alejandro waiting in front of the apartment building when they arrived fifteen minutes early for their appointment. "I thought you might like some reinforcements," Hilda said with a bright smile. Andes had gone over their budget. They had ten thousand dollars. She knew NYC rents were high; the place they were looking at was a steal for $1,200. Still, their money was only going to stretch so far. Andes was going to have to get a job, and she had no idea what to do with the kid while she was working. For a moment she envied Hilda, who seemed to take Alejandro with her everywhere she went; on the other hand, the poor kid was probably bored to death. Chase was actively ignoring Alejandro, turning his attention instead to a group of teenage boys walking by with a basketball.

"Alejandro," Hilda said. "Show Chase your new game." Alejandro smiled and pulled a Game Boy out of his pocket. Chase exchanged a look with Andes and she silently commanded him to play nice. As the boys huddled over the game, Hilda took Andes's arm and whispered in her ear. "You're getting better at this," she said. "You've got the look down."

Andes laughed, grateful for an ally.

"So is Dave's father showing us the apartment?" Andes asked.

"No," Hilda said. "I think it's the super. And it's really Dave's stepfather—not that that matters."

"Oh?"

"Dave's real father passed away a long time ago." Hilda opened the door to the lobby. Andes loved the older brick building, it was prewar, with curved arches and a certain *je ne sais quoi* you just couldn't find in its modern counterparts.

"This is a nice building," Hilda said, checking out the decorative fireplace and glittering chandelier in the entrance. "Nicer than my building."

"Why don't you trade us if you like it better?" Andes said. "We just need a temporary place to crash." Even as Andes made the offered, she prayed Hilda would turn it down. The truth was Andes didn't want a temporary place to crash, she wanted a home. And just because the kid was here temporarily didn't mean she had to be, right? She was starting to like New York. And Hilda seemed like someone who could become a true friend.

"Ah, *mija*," Hilda exclaimed. "We have so much junk I'd never survive a move. Besides, it's not too bad, and even one street over can mess up where the kids go to school. You should check if Chase gets to go to Sunnyside Elementary with Alejandro or Woodside."

The super was coming toward them. He was a tall, thin man with a goatee and glasses. At first she thought he was older, in his forties or fifties, but as he drew closer she realized he was more her age.

"You're here to see 4B?" he asked without so much as extending a hand.

"That's right," Hilda said, striking a hand-on-hip pose. *Attitude*, Andes thought, *I need to work on my New York attitude.*

"Follow me," the super said, shoving both hands in his pockets and shuffling toward the elevator. *If we take the apartment, Chase and I will take the steps every day,* Andes promised herself. It had been so long since she'd done any kind of regular workout.

"This is nice," Hilda said over and over as they walked through the apartment. Andes was pleasantly surprised. The apartment had a dining foyer, a large kitchen, a large living room, and an equally huge bedroom. You could have almost split the bedroom in two, but Andes wanted real distance from the kid, so she was already thinking she'd either take the dining foyer as her bedroom or they'd split the living room. The kitchen was big enough for a little eat-in table, so she was leaning toward using the dining foyer as her bedroom. Like in the lobby, the entrances were curved arches. Even the little built-in bookcase in the dining foyer was shaped like a rainbow. There were plenty of windows, but they faced an alleyway between sides of the apartment building, so their view was pretty much a brick wall. It didn't matter; it was nicer than anything Andes had ever lived in. And it could be hers. Well, theirs—but then when the kid moved out, the whole place could be hers.

"How much?" Hilda said with a tone of slight disgust.

"Fourteen hundred," the super said.

"We were told eleven hundred," Hilda lied. "She's a friend of Dave's father." The super shrugged.

"Then it's eleven. I was just told to show it to you."

"No harm, Papi," Hilda sang, hitting the super on the shoulder so hard even Andes winced. "Tell Mr. Jensen she'll take it, but we'll have a list of things to clean up first." Andes watched in amazement as Hilda pulled a notebook out of her purse and started scribbling things down as she went through the apartment again, this time like a blind woman, touching and tasting and turning everything on. Chase and Alejandro were still immersed in the game, and Andes noticed with dismay it was Chase who was commandeering the toy while poor Alejandro looked on with a big, innocent grin.

"Chase," Andes said a little harsher than she'd intended, "why don't you let Alejandro play and tell me what you think of our new home?"

"Home?" Chase said, jerking his head up and shoving the game into Alejandro's waiting hands. He didn't move from his spot or even look around. "The motel is next to McDonald's," he said.

"Why don't you go into the bedroom," Andes said. "It's humongous. And it would be all yours."

"Humongous," Chase imitated.

"You should take the bedroom," Hilda told Andes. "You let the boy sleep in this little cubby," Hilda said, twirling around the dining foyer. "It has a nice bookshelf too for toys." Andes smiled at her.

"No," she said. "He gets the bedroom."

"Whatever," Chase said. He turned to the super, who had opened the window in the kitchen and was smoking a cigarette. "You shouldn't smoke in our house," Chase yelled. The super shrugged, took another drag on the cigarette, and threw it out the window. Chase folded his arms across his chest and glared at the guy. "So," he said in a voice older than his years, "where are the fire exits in this joint?"

The fire engines were just returning to the station when Chase and Andes arrived. The firehouse doors were thrown wide open and a truck was waiting to back in, while a hose from another was being unraveled and reset. Chase and Andes stood and watched the men efficiently working in tandem, like Olympic swimmers rehearsing for a synchronized event. Even Andes had to admit she understood the excitement, and Jay was probably right, what ten-year-old boy wouldn't be fascinated by fire? The thought of Jay reminded her of his warning, and here they were again, stalking the kid's maybe-dad. But she was the one in charge now, she was the one taking care of the kid, the one who had just found them a place to live. And if the kid was playing with fire, who better to get acquainted with than the ones who made a living putting them out?

When there was a lull in the activity, Andes grabbed Chase's hand and they ducked behind the truck to where most of the firefighters were standing, hoping she'd spot Dave. Chase, meanwhile, was eyeballing the inside of the fire station like a kid peeking in on a woman undressing, eagerly soaking up every inch while battling the deathly fear she'd pull the curtain closed at any second. Andes was otherwise occupied. She had never been around so many good-looking men at the same time. She had a sudden, guilty urge for sex. She wanted to be thrown against a fire truck or even slammed to the ground. When was the last time she was even kissed? And then she remembered, it was Jay, inside a burning building. The oddity of it all made her laugh. Chase threw her a look of disapproval, and she might have used that moment to pick a fight with the kid had it not been for Dave spotting them. He was taking off his helmet and gloves. He was sweaty, but not covered in soot.

"Hi," he said, approaching the two of them. "Would you believe ten fire trucks just raced to save a suicidal dog?" Andes laughed a little too loud even though she had no idea what he was talking about. Chase threw her another look, and this time added a reproachful shake of his head. Andes wanted to cry, and scream, and she wanted to beat the shit out of the kid. It wasn't her fault that being around strangers made her nervous. In fact, she wouldn't be here if it weren't for Chase, so couldn't he just once show a little gratitude? Did Dave say something about a dog committing suicide?

"So there's this dog," Dave said when Andes and Chase continued to stare at him expectantly. "Owners left their window open and apparently the neighbors spotted the pooch teetering on the edge of the window. Six stories, so it wouldn't have been a pretty fall. But by the time we got there, pooch was curled up on the fire escape. Personally I think he could've gotten back in, but hey—it's the taxpayers' money, right?" Andes laughed again.

"What kind of dog was it?" she asked.

"A depressed one," Chase said. Dave laughed and patted Chase on the back.

"A mutt," Dave said. "About yea big." Dave held out his hands a little less than shoulder width apart.

"So the canine wasn't even on fire?" Chase asked.

"Nope, just needed a paw up," Dave said, laughing at his own joke. "So, Chase, just let me change out of these clothes and I'll show you around a little, okay?" Chase nodded and went back to ogling the engine that was finally backing into the station. Andes felt a hand on her arm. She looked up to find Dave smiling at her. "You too," he said. Andes felt her face flush, something she really hated about herself, and realized she had no idea what he was talking about. Her too, what? "You get the tour too," Dave clarified when she didn't speak.

"Great," Andes said. Her voice came out with a little squeak. She cleared her throat. "Great," she said in what she hoped was a more normal approximation of the word.

True to his promise, Dave literally only took a few seconds to change. He must have been wearing jeans and a T-shirt already underneath his bunker gear, as Andes and Chase soon learned it was called. He walked them around the fire engines, showed Chase the pole but apologized he couldn't let him slide down it, showed them the sharpening devices for their halligans—the sharp sticklike tool used to break into houses. He showed them the oxygen tanks, the gear, and he opened the door to one of the engines so Chase could look inside the cab. He explained the different jobs firemen were assigned to—there was the captain, the chauffeur, the door control position, the nozzle position, the backup. Chase was listening intently, but Andes didn't hear anything past "nozzle." Unfortunately it made her think of that calendar pose Dave did all over again, and after that she lost complete control of her thoughts.

She had to remind herself of three very important things. One, Dave had a girlfriend, Jenny. Jenny was the one who helped them get the apartment. Two, Dave might just be Chase's father, and she'd already almost slept with his other father. The kid would probably need serious therapy if she were to get involved with this one as well. Of course, the kid didn't really know anything about her and his other father—unless of course he was in the warehouse that night. And if that were the case, she had bigger things to worry about then him seeing her smooch his dad.

But third, she was way, way, way out of her league. She was, whether she liked anyone to call her it or not, a freak. And even if he didn't have a girlfriend and even if he wasn't Chase's maybe-dad, there was still the undeniable fact that he was a nice, normal, incredibly hot guy, and she was just a girl who used to dance with rattlesnakes.

"We call those guys probie—basically means rookie—but we're all a team. We all have to keep the bay clean, and do our jobs. Even if we're just sitting around playing cards, we're always on the ready." They had done a little circle around the fire station and were now coming back out to the entrance. It took Andes a minute to realize Dave was showing them out.

"Thanks for the tour," she said, sticking out her hand. "Oh, and the apartment. We love it." She nudged Chase to thank him.

"The apartment?" Dave said.

"Oh. Yes—your father's building? I thought—"

"Which building?"

"Forty-eighth Avenue and—"

"That's my building."

"Oh. Well, we're on the fourth floor."

"I'm on the fourth floor." Andes stopped talking. It was obvious he was processing way smaller bits of information than she was trying to reel off. "Four B?" he asked. Andes nodded. "I'm across the hall." As soon as she said it, Andes felt something hard stepping on her little toe. She yelped and jerked her foot back, then glared at Chase, who was subtly trying to hide the foot that had just crushed hers.

"I'm right across the hall from you," Dave exclaimed, oblivious to the attempted mauling.

"I didn't realize," Andes said, turning back to Dave. "Jenny heard we needed a place to live—"

"Jenny? Right. I should really pay more attention when she talks." Dave erupted in nervous laughter.

"If it's not okay—" Andes glanced at Chase's feet as she said this.

"No, no. I just forgot. That's all. That's great. So. Welcome. Neighbors."

"Thanks for the tour."

"Anytime." Dave's smile and eyes stayed on Andes until she looked away. Neighbors, Andes thought as she and Chase walked to The Buzz. They were meeting Hilda, who wanted to celebrate their new home by having them to her place for dinner. She also had some things she said they could take for their apartment if they wanted them. *Neighbors*, Andes thought. *Thou shall not covet thy neighbor*. Well, one thing was for sure, Jenny certainly wasn't threatened by Andes if she was moving her in across from her boyfriend. Which meant she probably spent a great deal of time there as well. Which meant nonstop chatter. Then there was Jay. What would he think if he knew not only had Chase met his maybe-dad but would now be living across from him?

This wasn't good. Andes knew it, yet she felt there was little she could do to stop it. At some points in life, you just had to concede; most of the time, life just wasn't under your control. As they walked along, the pain in Andes's toe flared anew.

"Why did you stomp on my foot?" she demanded suddenly.

"I dunno," Chase said. "I thought maybe you shouldn't be telling him where we lived."

"You didn't think he was going to figure it out when he kept running into us from across the hall?" Andes asked. Chase opened his arms in exasperation.

"That's why I stopped," he said. Thank God she had Hilda. She needed Hilda and an entire bottle of wine. The boys could entertain themselves, watch mindless television, swing from the fire escape, she really didn't care. It was a good thing she wasn't a real mother. She just didn't have it in her to constantly care.

Chapter 28

The minute Hilda opened the door to her apartment, Andes knew they were entering a real home. Warm colors lathered the walls in a perfect blend of paint, family photos, and folk art, the smell of home cooking wafted from the kitchen, and a lingering feel of laughter filled the air. It was the exact feeling Andes yearned to capture for herself: a place she created, a home where she belonged.

"You're coming in," Hilda said, taking Andes by the arm and pulling her inside. Andes handed Hilda a bottle of wine, a red from Chile the man at the liquor store had recommended. It was such a trivial thing, bringing a bottle of wine to a dinner party, but it made Andes feel grown-up. Chase had already disappeared inside. Andes could hear Alejandro's excited voice gushing from the other room.

"Do you mind if I save this?" Hilda asked, holding up the bottle of wine. "I thought we'd start with margaritas." The apartment wasn't huge, but the bedrooms were at the end of a hall leading away from the front door, and the living room and kitchen were down a second hall off the right of the front door, so the ultimate feeling was one of space. Like the apartment Andes had just taken, there were natural curved arches leading into each new space, tall ceilings, and wood floors. Hilda had numerous colors splashed about; throw rugs, plants, and family photos lining the hallway. Unlike Andes's family photos, there were no snakes in any of them.

Hilda took Andes past the living room, where the boys were sitting on the floor hunched around Alejandro's new electronic game. Hilda smiled and wagged her fingers at them even though they weren't looking. Then she led Andes through a beaded curtain, stopping to do a little mamba step as she passed through it and into a nice-sized kitchen, where a pitcher of margaritas stood prominently on the kitchen counter next to a stovetop full of sizzling pans.

"Oh my God," Andes said. "It smells so good in here."

"Enchiladas, rice and beans, and just enough steak to make us feel like the King of Queens," Hilda said with a laugh. She tucked the wine away on the counter and pulled two margarita glasses out of her cupboard.

"Cheers," she said, clinking the empty glasses peremptorily against each other.

"So what's it like living in the same building as Blazing Dave?" Hilda asked with an exaggerated naughty look.

"Across the hall, no less," Andes said with a laugh.

"Oh my God," Hilda said. "I changed my mind. I do want to trade." Now that Hilda had opened the door to the conversation, Andes wanted to ask a million questions about Dave, but she didn't want to admit to anyone that she was thinking about him in any kind of romantic or sexual way. He was someone else's girlfriend, he was Chase's maybe-dad.

"When are you moving in? Do you need a truck? Wait—do you have furniture?" The questions were so rapid-fire and fluid, it was almost as if Hilda was singing a song. Andes laughed and gladly took a sip of her overflowing margarita. "I'm a mom," Hilda explained. "Sometimes I only have three minutes to grill Alejandro about his day. Forgive me." She poured chips and salsa into bowls and disappeared through the beaded curtain and into the living room. She certainly was a mom, Andes thought. Multitasking. She was going to have to get used to it. Maybe. Either that or speed up her pace finding out if Dave was Chase's real father.

"You want chips?" Hilda said, returning. "Dinner is at least an hour away. I like the enchiladas nice and crispy around the edges."

"I'm fine with this," Andes said, holding up her margarita.

"Me too," Hilda said, gesturing to the dining table.

"Is there anything I can do to help?" Andes asked politely, even though it was obvious the bulk of the work had already been done.

"Just sit and give me some gossip," Hilda said. They sat at the wooden dining table drinking their margaritas and momentarily falling into a shy slice of silence, women on the verge of becoming friends, searching for something impressive to say.

"Gossip," Andes repeated, as if there weren't a trace of it in her life. For a split second she was overcome by the urge to tell Hilda absolutely everything, even though she was barely two sips into her margarita. She'd never had a real girlfriend, not really. For a brief time in high school there was a girl, Amanda. She was from a family much like her grandmother: wealthy, cultured, well-read. She lived a few houses down from her grandmother and had no idea about Andes's secret life. So for one whole year Andes had a good girlfriend—that is, until Amanda wanted to know why they only talked on the phone one weekend a month, why she only visited Andes at her grandmother's, why she'd never been invited to Andes's real home. Amanda severed the friendship the day the newspaper article hit the stands, and Andes had never found the same kind of female companionship since.

But that was all so long ago, another lifetime, and Hilda was a grown, vivacious, multitasking woman. Surely, Andes could tell her almost anything.

"Can I ask you a personal question?" Andes asked. Hilda spread open her arms, slightly sloshing margarita onto the tiled floor.

"I'm an open book, missy," Hilda sang with a wink.

My chapters are on lockdown in the Vatican Library, Andes thought.

"Is Alejandro's father in the picture?"

"Oh yes." Hilda pointed out the tiny kitchen window behind them. It overlooked several apartment buildings, a series of brick walls and black rooftops, interspersed with a smattering of city-planted trees. "He lives three blocks that way," she said. "With his wife and kids."

"What?"

"Might as well tell you now so you can decide if you want to be friends with the town whore."

"Hilda."

"Ramon and I, that's Alejandro's dad, Ramon Miguel Antonio Martinez. Isn't that a beautiful name? Ramon and I were a torrid affair." Hilda leaned forward and lowered her normally boisterous voice. "I got drunk on my twenty-first birthday and Ramon and I fucked in a bar bathroom fifteen minutes after he walked in and bought me a shot of Jagermeister."

"You're kidding." Hilda shook her head and then nodded toward the living room.

"I almost named him Jag," she said. Andes laughed, but not too loudly, hoping Hilda would continue her sordid tale.

"Of course, I didn't know he was married at first," Hilda said. "And Ramon was ten years older than me, and such a charmer. By the time I found out—six months later—I didn't care. Well, I did. But I couldn't stop. I was his mistress for three years. Three years. And probably still would be, if Alejandro hadn't happened."

"He broke up with you when you got pregnant?"

"No, Ande," Hilda said pronouncing her name without the *S*, "I broke up with him." She smiled then, a tear almost forming in her eye, but she kept it out by what seemed to Andes as pure strength of will.

"I didn't want Alejandro to grow up a secret. Ramon did. He already had three kids with his wife, who I suspect knew about me but didn't make a fuss as long as no one else knew. But it's funny, the minute I felt him growing inside me, I knew I had to do better for him than I was doing for myself. I knew I had to come clean about the affair, and Ramon had to choose. But I would not bring my boy up in shame, or secrecy, or lies. You see? Motherhood made me a better woman. And that's what I tell myself on those rare nights when I let myself feel sorry for me, pity party *por uno*—because there are nights when I miss Ramon so bad I want to crawl over to his place, crawl, on the ground, on my hands and knees like a mangy dog, and beg him to come back." She took another pause, a breath, a drink.

"How did his wife react?" Andes asked.

"She flipped, of course. Pretended she knew nothing of the affair. I'd just started the coffee shop. For the first six months I had very few customers. She made sure of that. She screamed the child wasn't his, couldn't be his—even though I'd never slept with another man. Anyway, it's a long time ago. Long enough."

"What's she like with you now?"

"Still nasty, but it's quieter. She's nice to Alejandro. At first she tried to get him to stay with them. But not because she wanted him, she just wanted to hurt me. Ramon, the only good thing I can say about him, Ramon talked her out of it. He's not as handsome anymore either. Big belly. Disappearing hair. That helps too." She laughed again, and so did Andes.

"So there's never been anyone else?"

"I'm a mom, now," Hilda said. "With a full-time business. I'm not saying Ramon is still the only man I've ever slept with. There are always men. But there's never been that fire, that passion." By the end of Hilda's tale, Andes had drained her drink and Hilda was pouring her another. Chase and Alejandro crashed through the beaded curtain, Alejandro carrying the empty chip bowl, holding it up like the Holy Grail.

"We're still hungry," he announced. Hilda rolled her eyes and mouthed, "boys." Andes looked at the chubby boy and couldn't help feel sorry for him, even though she wouldn't want her new friend to know it. Hilda had made the best of a bad situation. How could Alejandro not feel a little strange knowing his father had a wife and kids, a family he wasn't really a part of? She knew just how he felt, and she had a sudden urge to hug the boy. Chase was staring at her. She glanced at him and was instantly "outed" by the smirk on his face. He had perfected this look, something hovering between anger and sarcasm, something meant to shame. He glanced purposefully at the empty margarita glass in her hand and then at the half-full pitcher on the counter.

"Dinner will be in a half an hour, *mijo*," Hilda said.

"But we're bored," Alejandro said.

"Why don't you play your guitar?" Hilda asked. Alejandro turned instantly red and stole a glance at Chase.

"You play guitar?" Andes said. "That's wonderful. I'd like to hear it." Alejandro's face remained the bright shade of red and Andes immediately regretted saying it.

"Chase went to the firehouse," Alejandro whined. "He rode on a fire truck. At like a hundred and twenty miles an hour." When Hilda and Andes remained mute, Alejandro threw open his arms. "Like two hundred miles an hour!" he shouted. Andes looked at Chase, who was staring straight back at her. "More!" Alejandro finally said out of exasperation and a total lack of understanding of how many miles per hour it would take to impress these two women. Andes opened her mouth to inform him that Chase had not ridden on a fire truck, but then closed it again. What was it they said? Boys will be boys.

"Very nice," Hilda said to Chase. "Lucky boy."

"I want to ride on the fire truck," Alejandro whined.

"I'm sure you do," Hilda said. "Put it on your list." Alejandro nodded; the answer seemed to satisfy him. He turned to Chase. "Want to go to my room?" Chase shrugged, kicked at the rug beneath his feet, and then glared at Andes again.

"I'm sure he'd love that," Andes said. "A half an hour goes by so quickly."

"Why don't we have drinks?" Chase asked.

"I have Jarritos!" Alejandro yelled running to the refrigerator. "Do you like Jarritos?"

"I don't know," Chase said. Alejandro pulled two lime green soda bottles out of the fridge and held them up like a boy on his first hunt, proudly displaying a dead deer. Chase shrugged like he didn't care but promptly held out his hand for the soda.

"Can we, Mom?" Alejandro asked before handing it over. Andes noted that Chase didn't ask her if it was all right.

"Why not," Hilda said. "Tonight is special. We welcome new friends!"

"Okay with me," Andes added, although Chase had already twisted open the bottle and taken a swig. As the boys raced out of the room, Andes could only hope Hilda hadn't heard Chase's derisive grunt.

"What's his list?" Andes asked when the boys were out of sight.

"His list of things he wants to do. I think it's over twenty pages now. It's a good technique. You can steal it if you'd like." Andes nodded politely, but the thought of what Chase's list might look like terrified her. Her own list wasn't any better. Even if it started out innocent, it would turn into a list of revenge. Starting with George Turner. He should be back in town soon. She was going to have a face-to-face. Whether they wrote it down or not, everyone had a list. And confronting George Turner had been burning on hers for years. This was the year she was going to do it. Hilda would be proud of her.

"So," Hilda said. "Now you know my dirtiest secret. Your turn," she said. Andes laughed and pretended to think.

"Well," she said. "I don't normally talk about this. But once when I was in Rome . . ."

George Turner opened his eyes and saw heaven. The sky was vast and blue, the mountains gray and immovable. His head was swimming back into focus, the faces peering down at him were scrunched into one strange-ass hybrid of tiny noses and eyes and a mirrored mouth. After a few seconds he realized he was looking at the faces of children, four of them to be exact, whose heads were hovering about him in a semicircle. The last thing he remembered was passing out in church, but now he was lying in a field. He wanted to yell at the children to back away, but his throat was dry, and so instead he closed his eyes and hoped they would just go away. They did not.

"Give him some air," a harsh female voice commanded. Soon

thereafter, Greg felt the children's shadows pass over him. In their absence, bright sunlight assaulted his face. He rolled his head to the side and opened his eyes a smidge. The woman who scolded the children was standing a few feet away holding a shotgun. She was at least six feet tall, and dressed in a long black skirt with a white blouse that buttoned all the way up her neck. Her long gray hair fell to her waist. George couldn't think of a single thing to say. *Is that a shotgun against your thigh or are you just happy to see me?* Luckily, the woman spoke first.

"What's your name?" She ran it all together and it sounded foreign to his ears, as if she were playing at an accent: *Wutsyername?* It was a distinct dialect of these parts he remembered well. Some people made fun of it, but George had always found it endearing, musical even.

"George," he managed to say. "Name's George."

"What are you doin' in these parts?" George lifted his head up a half an inch and looked at the outside of the one-room church. Inside, the funeral was still going on. The children who had recently fled from him were sitting on the steps to the church, two perched on the top, two on the bottom.

"I came to pay my respects," George said.

"You a reporter?"

"Can I have a glass of water?" He let his hands drop to his chest, suddenly overcome with weariness. Music and voices drifted out from the church, laughter erupted from the boys on the steps. Everything came back to him. "Snakes," he said. The woman shifted the shotgun, lifting it to her shoulder, and pointed the barrel straight at him.

"Git," she said, moving the shotgun in the what George assumed was the general "git" direction. *I would "git,"* George thought, *if I could just sit up. Can't git if I can't git up.*

"Emily," George said out loud even though he didn't mean to.

"What?" The woman moved another step, the gun moved with her.

"I once met a girl from around here named Emily. She was the youngest serpent handler ever."

"Zachariah's girl?" the woman asked. George lifted his head again and pretended to think.

"Tall? Big man?" George asked. The woman seemed to hesitate, as if it were a trick question.

"He used to hold meetings," George explained wondering whether or not he should say "meetin's."

"That's Zachariah. He don't preach no more. He don't even attend meetins.' "

"Does he still live around here?" George dared to ask. "I'd like to pay him a visit."

"He ain't had a visitor in a long time."

"Guess he's due for one."

"Nobody hardly talks to that man anymore," the woman said in a whisper. "Poor girl. That man done went crazy all them years ago. Just pure crazy."

"I can do crazy," George said. "I'm from Queens."

Chapter 29

Outsiders call it snake handling, whereas we call it serpent han-
dling. Our churches are plain, but our faith has more embellish-
ments than any stained-glass winder or gilded statue of Jesus.
Fire, and prayer, and hands clapping, and them guitars and
flutes, and whatnot a goin', and voices raised in rapture. Them's
the beauty of our temples, and holiness weren't never meant to be
whispered, rather the Lord wants us to shout it out and praise
him at the top of our voices. Sometimes we hold our meetin's at
night under the stars near the fire. How can you get any closer to
God than that? Especially when the moon is fat and glowing from
the inside, and the air's got a tangy taste that stays on your
tongue, butted up against the mountains. Severe and everlasting,
them mountains. Black as a sinner's heart at night and gold as
an angel in the mornin'. An' the cricks gurgling to wash away
our sins. It is a religion of people, passing on heart to heart,
mouth to mouth, hand to hand givin' to the Lord and offering up
his will when he moves on us to do so. When he anoints us to do
so. It ain't us handling them serpents, it's the Lord handling them
through us, showin' us the way with his glory everlasting. This is

what you want to call crazy? Then you's callin' the Lord crazy, and I ain't got enough of an army to defend that accusin'. No matter how big you build your houses, or how many TVs you worship, the Appalachian Mountains will outlast you all, and God will see to the sinners.

Zachariah Tomlin—from the files of George Turner

Between their suitcases and Andes's snake box, it didn't take long for the two to pack up their belongings at the La Quinta Motel. Then they headed over to McDonald's for a greasy good-bye. Chase eyed the box the entire time, once in a while daring to touch it with his foot. They were meeting the super at the apartment at nine. It was only eight a.m. Andes was excited about their new place, but suddenly feeling very foolish that they would have nothing to sit on or sleep on for a while. They were going to have to buy air mattresses and maybe some dishes. And groceries!

Andes almost wanted to cry at the thought of having her own kitchen and doing something other people did every day—buying groceries. Chase had spoken to Jay on the phone last night and he was out of the hospital and back in custody in Oregon. Chase told him about the apartment and Jay seemed pleased. Andes spoke to him briefly as well. Jay was polite and hopeful about an attorney Richard and Gerry of all people had hired to help him out. He didn't ask anything about Chase's maybe-dad, and she didn't volunteer anything. He mentioned that Vicky would be furious he'd missed the last payment and ordered Andes to send it. She pretended to write down Vicky's address. Maybe jail time was going to be good for Jay all the way around. He was sober, had been for a while, and he was finally going to stand up to Vicky, even if he didn't know it. They needed all the money they had for themselves—did Jay think it was going to last them forever? Andes needed to get a job. Maybe she would start making jewelry again and have a little stripper-jewelry party.

"When are we going to find out if Blazing Dave's my dad?"

Chase asked her. Andes didn't know what to tell him. They really didn't have much of a plan. And there was no way paternity could be proven without a test.

"When we get to know him better, we could start by asking him about Vicky," Andes suggested, making it up as she went along. "No offense, but we don't even know if your mom really dated him."

"It was when she was younger," Chase said. "She was pretty and nice back then." Andes wanted to ask him how he knew that, but she didn't want to upset him.

"You don't talk to your mom or dad at all?" Chase asked suddenly. "Because you don't believe in God?"

"It's not that simple," Andes said.

"Why don't you just pretend to believe?"

Andes put down the rest of her McMuffin. It was heavy and hard in her stomach. They shouldn't be eating this crap. She was doing a terrible job taking care of the kid. She suddenly wanted to cry.

"I did pretend," Andes answered as she folded up the remainder of her sandwich. "I just didn't convince anyone." It was a lie, but how could she explain that the exact opposite was what ruined her family? How could she explain that she believed so much she dared to be better than her father? That somewhere along the line, impressing him had come to mean surpassing him? Had she even been aware of it herself? All she'd known, really known for sure, was that her father—the most devout man she'd ever met—was terrified of snakes. And no matter how gifted a preacher he was, and oh, how he was, he never made a move to reach for the snake boxes lining the back wall of the meetings. Instead, he watched as his brothers and sisters in the Lord became so moved, so anointed, that they would prove their faith by handling the snakes, drinking poison, holding hot coals. But Brother Tomlin did not. And the only one who knew why was Emily.

She alone saw the way her father's throat would tighten at the sight of the reptiles, how he would never look directly at them (as if they were the sun), how he could barely breathe until they were put away. Where the sight of them made her tin-gle, they made him cringe. Where she wanted to reach out and touch their sleek skin, he wanted to recoil. The man who was never proud of her. The man who over the years would put her down the well over and over again, who would rage that her red hair was from the devil, who made her mother cower, who made her mother weak. The all-powerful Zachariah Tomlin had a weakness. It was as deadly a poison as humans could ever possess—knowledge of another's deepest weakness. And once Emily possessed it, she couldn't let it go.

"Had enough to eat?" Andes said, dragging herself out of the past. Chase burped out his yes. Andes didn't scold him; instead, she laughed. This was move-in day. He'd have to do a lot more than that to get her goat. He could burp the Gettysburg Address for all she cared.

"Looks like we're not the only ones," Andes said as they rounded the bend in front of their new apartment building. Parked in front of the building was an enormous moving truck. Two men were finagling a bulky mustard-colored sofa down the ramp. "You distract them, I'll steal us a couple of beds," Andes joked. Chase rolled his eyes and squelched his laughter. Andes pinched him.

"Pervert," she yelled before Chase could get it out of his mouth first. This time he did laugh, even though he rolled his eyes again. She wanted to hug him, but that was probably asking too much. One little hug could ruin their rapport for the whole day. She'd only gotten away with it twice, and both times were right before bed when he was so tired he couldn't say anything sarcastic. She'd kissed him on the cheek once too, but he'd been fast asleep then. Since the movers were using the side entrance, Andes and Chase entered through the main doors. Chase had already impressed on her that they needed to practice going down the fire escape. She had almost forgotten about her decision to talk to someone at the fire station about his behavior until he brought up his plan to run practice fire drills in their home. A fire extinguisher was going to have to be on the list too—maybe she should strap it directly to Chase's back.

"Looks like we're going to have to take the stairs, kid," Andes said when the movers beat them to the elevator. She didn't complain when Chase dropped his suitcase and ran for it. She simply picked it up and added it to her own load. It was slow going with two suitcases and a snake box. She could hear Chase's feet echoing above her as he ran. After she'd trudged up two sets of stairs, she could hear a male voice bantering back and forth with him. Then she heard footsteps running toward her, and looking as if he'd just rolled out of bed in gray sweats and a black T-shirt was Dave Jensen. Looking at him gave Andes the feeling of swimming underwater for a long, long time, then coming up to take her first breath. Looking at Dave was like taking that first breath. She didn't know why that was, but it wasn't exactly a feeling that instilled confidence in her.

"Hey, neighbor," he said with a big smile. "Let me help you with that." Andes kept a strong grip on her black duffel bag carrying the snake box, but she reluctantly let him take the other two suitcases.

"Thank you," she said. "You don't have to do that." Dave made a sound like it was nothing.

"I could carry you too," he threatened. As they neared the fourth floor Andes heard the movers carrying on. She had an absurd jolt of jealousy, as if it should be their moving day and no one else's. Just before they reached her floor, she heard a familiar voice ordering the movers around.

"*Mijo*, don't get in their way," she said. "I am not telling you again, go play down the hall. *Vámonos, vámonos*, both of you."

"Hilda?" Dave smiled at Andes as she took in the sight before her. The movers were taking the furniture into her apartment.

"Surprise!" Hilda said. "Don't be mad. You're not mad, are you? You said you had nothing and let me tell you, *mija*, my friends were like 'I have a couch' and 'I have a bed' and 'I have a lazy, good-for-nothing husband.' We didn't take that one— but everything else we took off their hands. It's like *Extreme Makeover Puerto Rican Thrift Store Edition*. You mad? Whatever you don't want, Dave will throw it out for you," she added with a punch to Dave's arm. Andes didn't say anything, she couldn't speak. She threw herself into Hilda's arms, hoping she wasn't going to cry. Nobody had ever done anything like this for her before. She was going to have furniture! But she was also going to start bawling in front of Dave, and she didn't like the thought of that either.

"I don't know how to—"

"It's nothing. You might hate it."

"Thank you." Andes wiped her eyes and turned to Dave to thank him for taking her suitcases. Their eyes locked and continued to hold even as they moved out of the way for the movers, who were bringing in a bed. Andes looked away first.

"Beds too?" Andes said.

"Wait until they're done. I was hoping to have it all done by the time you got here, but somebody was late," she shouted in through the open door.

"Traffic on the BQE," one of the movers shouted right back. Hilda rolled her eyes and then leaned in to Andes and whispered, "Did you see that one? He's kind of cute." Andes smiled back and pretended not to notice Hilda glancing at Dave and then slightly raising an eyebrow at Andes.

When the movers were gone, Hilda, Alejandro, and Dave left Andes and Chase alone as well, but not until promising they'd come back soon for dinner. Andes walked around her new furnished home like someone in a beautiful dream, praying silently, as Chase padded behind her, that he wouldn't do or say anything to turn it into a nightmare. As Hilda pointed out, the furniture wasn't brand new, but it was clean and nice and completely functional. Up close she could see the mustard sofa was sprinkled with little white flowers, something straight out of the seventies, but it was large and soft, and smelled nice. Someone had obviously cleaned it. The wood pedestal dining table looked like the wood in the kid's sailboat, although Andes kept this to herself, in case he was homesick.

There was a leather blue La-Z-Boy in the living room, which Chase had already claimed. It was perfectly fine with Andes— she was going to lounge on the couch with a romance novel. And even though Hilda was appalled Andes was giving Chase the bedroom, she respected her wishes. Chase's room had a bed and a dresser, as well as a boxful of games and books.

Andes was relieved Chase was exploring the other rooms. She didn't want him to see her eyes filling with tears. Of course, the books were way too young for Chase, but the thought touched Andes nonetheless, and *she* could always read them. There was a bed for her too, which as she asked, they put in the dining foyer, and the dining table went into the eat-in kitchen. Maybe she'd make a nice curtain all the way around her bed so that you wouldn't see her bed from the living room. In addition to the furniture, there were boxes of dishes, and two throw rugs.

Hilda had also brought doughnuts, and Chase was happily devouring his third. Andes set up the coffeepot, which again thanks to Hilda came with everything necessary to make it. She plugged a clock radio into the kitchen outlet and started the coffee. It had been an exciting morning, the start of something new, with the help of new friends, actual friends. Andes was feeling overly emotional; she felt like the luckiest woman in the world today, yet she wanted to cry. And despite a myriad of distractions, she couldn't keep from running every encounter she'd ever had with Dave Jensen over and over again in her mind. It was nothing, she tried to convince herself, just a simple crush.

She had just taken her first sip of coffee when her cell phone rang. Her first thought was that it was Chase calling her from the bedroom to thank her profusely for all the sacrifices she'd made for him. "Thank God we've finally reached you." It was Gerry; Andes would have recognized his booming voice anywhere. "We've got a problem," he said. A little voice whispered in Andes's ear to hang up. So what if they had a problem? Why should their problem be her problem?

"I can't really talk now."

"The Seattle Fire Department is building a case against Jay for the warehouse fire," Gerry said. Andes felt guilty that with that one sentence, she felt lighter, freer. *I'll have to enroll the kid in school,* she thought. *PTA meetings, school pictures, model rockets on the fridge.* They weren't at all unpleasant thoughts.

"Wow," Andes said. "Thanks for letting me know. Chase can stay here as long as it takes—"

"Andes," Gerry said. "We both know Jay isn't the one setting the fires." As Andes digested this, another voice came on the line.

"Hi, Andes, it's Richard."

"We're on speaker," Gerry said. Andes went to the cupboard, opened it, and stared at the bottle of tequila Hilda had stashed there as Richard and Gerry gushed out the gory details in perfect stereo. The fire department was building a case against Jay, and Jay wasn't defending himself against the accusations, which could only mean one thing—they had been right all along, Chase was the one who had been starting the fires. Gerry and Richard had hired a lawyer to help Jay—it was the least they could do, for the kid—and now that Jay wasn't fighting back, there was only one other option. Chase needed to turn himself in.

"Excuse me," Andes said, breaking back into the conversation.

"We can help you with the plane tickets," Richard said.

"No," Andes said. "No."

"Andes," Gerry said. "The kid needs to face this. He needs help."

"Where's the proof?" Andes demanded. "You don't know if Chase had anything to do with those fires." *Thank God he doesn't know about his lighter*, Andes thought. "And if he did," Andes heard herself add, "he's fine now."

"What do you mean he's fine?" Richard asked. Andes could tell by the tone of his voice that he was clearly alarmed. In fact, they both sounded like two old worry warts. Busybodies. *He's laughing now, did you know that?* Andes wanted to tell them. *He has his own room. We have a fridge. And I've hugged him twice.*

"It's not like getting over a cold, Andes. Playing with fire—"

"Pyromania," Richard interrupted.

"Pyromania," Gerry continued, "is a very serious affliction."

Affliction, affliction, affliction, Andes repeated in her head.

"Jay," Richard cut in again. "She has to call Jay."

Get a lock of Dave Jensen's hair. Get the paternity test. Maybe Jay isn't even his father. If Dave was his dad, he could fight for the kid.

"Andes, you have to come back to Seattle immediately. We'll

pay for the tickets. And we know an excellent child psychiatrist—"

Andes didn't even realize she hung up the phone until she
heard it snap and saw it flattened in her hand. She was still
standing in her kitchen staring off into space when it rang
again. This time she set it in a nice pot of African violets on the
windowsill and ran into Chase's bedroom. He was on the floor
going through his box of games. *He's mine*, she thought. *He's
mine and he's not going anywhere.* She would talk to Jay. If he was
already defending the kid, he was damn well going to continue
to do it. If Chase was starting fires, it was Jay's fault and he knew
it. Chase wasn't going to pay for his parents' mistakes anymore.
Not when he had his own room and books, and toys, and friends.
And a goddamn refrigerator.

"Chase," she said. "Where's your cell phone?"

"Why?"

"The store called. If we trade them in now, they'll give us better ones."

"I'm fine with mine."

"With more games. And colors to choose from." Chase
shrugged, still engrossed in his box.

"Where is it?"

"I don't know," Chase said. "Check my backpack." Andes started
for the backpack, but Chase, suddenly interested, beat her to it.
He held the phone in front of him as it started to ring. Andes
snatched it out of his hand before he could answer.

"It's a prank call," she said as Chase watched her with suspi-
cion.

"How do you know?"

"Because I just got one myself."

Chase held out his hand.

"I'll deal with it," he said. But Andes was already heading out
of the room and into the kitchen. She swiped her phone from
the plant and before she could talk herself into a more reasonable course of action, she was already standing over an open
toilet and dropping the phones into them. Chase watched from
the doorway as his phone continued to buzz in the bowl, a sax-

ophone blowing out a sad and distorted tune. Chase joined Andes at the toilet and the two stood staring into the abyss. "Two steps forward and one giant, disgusting step back," Chase said.

"Now what?" Gerry asked when they gave up on getting a hold of them again.

"We have no choice," Richard said, picking up the phone. "We report a kidnapping."

Chapter 30

The first night in their new place was alive with sound. Chase's excited ears tuned in to every car horn, creak, and hiss. An hour after attempting to sleep, he began appearing at the foot of Andes's bed saying, "What's that?" after every new noise, as if Andes was conducting the orchestra of sound. There was no fear in his voice, only an analytical interest, that of a scientist cataloging the results of his experiment.

Andes, on the other hand, had something other than noise on her mind. Earlier, on their way home from canvassing the 99-cent stores, she had seen Jenny running out of the building in full-blown tears. She didn't even stop when she saw Andes and Chase, struggling under the weight of their black plastic bags filled to the brim with just-starting-out crap. Andes couldn't help but wonder if Jenny had a fight with Dave, and she couldn't deny feeling a crumb of hope that the two had broken up.

After all, it would mean they wouldn't have to run into Jenny as much, get assaulted with conversation at every turn. At least, that's how Andes explained her desire to break them up. But deep down she knew it was a lie. She knew the truth was in the glances she and Dave shared that day; one of them had lasted seven whole seconds, neither of them looking away until they heard footsteps behind them. And he lived just across the hall. Even now, as she tried to deal with Chase, she was thinking of Dave. Was he home now? Just on the other side of that wall? Or was he at work? She knew anytime she or Chase heard fire engines racing down the street, they would immediately think of Dave.

"Earth to Emily," Chase said. In the dark, the boy was slightly easier to deal with, having only to hear his disgust conveyed through the tone of his voice, the omission of the matching facial expressions a pleasant reprieve.

"What is it, Hector?" Andes replied.

Chase threw himself on the end of her bed.

"I can hear something like water leaking," he said, his voice deep and thoughtful.

"It's an old building."

"Yeah, but remember how at the museum they said millions of gallons of water a year were lost to common household leaks?"

"I don't remember that," Andes admitted. At least he wasn't on about fires. She was learning to be grateful for the small things.

"Well, they said it. We need to find the leak."

"In the morning. Right now you need to go to sleep." Andes had decided after their last midnight raid to Kinko's that she would never again indulge one of these nightly excursions, even if it meant letting the kid have a full-blown fit.

"Why was Jenny crying?" he asked suddenly. Since he didn't mention it at the time, Andes had assumed he'd either not seen her or not recognized her.

"I don't know. Go to sleep."

"Do you think my maybe-dad hit her?" Andes sat up and tugged the chain on her bedside lamp. The low-wattage bulb caked the room in a mustard yellow haze. Chase's shadow loomed large on the wall behind them.

"Why would you say a thing like that?" Andes watched his shadow move with the shrug of his bony shoulder. Personally, if anyone in that relationship were to get violent, Andes was sure it would be Jenny. Dave had an overwhelming nice-guy air, despite his model good looks. Maybe it was his profession, but whenever Andes thought about him, she felt safe, as if she were wrapped in an invisible cloak of protection. It wasn't an entirely welcome feeling; she hadn't realized how unsafe she'd felt until she met Dave.

"Maybe he just yelled at her," Chase said.

"People can have disagreements without hitting or yelling, Chase," Andes said, hoping her voice sounded comforting and reassuring. "And people cry for lots of reasons." Chase perched at the edge of her quilt and managed a nod. He began to pick at the stitching with his dirty fingernails. They were too long too. He needed a trim. Was she supposed to tell him to trim them? If he refused, was she supposed to insist? She would leave the nail clippers on the bathroom sink tomorrow, see if that did the trick. "Hilda left us a box of books," she said when it became apparent Chase wasn't going back to his own bed without a nudge. She gestured to the Harry Potter book peeking out from underneath her pillow. "If you can't sleep, you can read."

"I know," Chase said. "I've already started *The Amityville Horror.*"

"Probably not the best thing for bedtime, kiddo."

"Can I sleep here?"

"No. You have your own bed, your own room. I didn't plant myself in the dining room just so you could sleep in here."

"Fine," Chase said, sliding off the bed. "But if something unseen squeezes you in the middle of the night, all the water in the apartment turns black, and suddenly you're covered in flies, don't come crying to me."

"I'll keep that in mind." Andes snapped off the light and listened to Chase stomp back to his room. She fell asleep with random, unpleasant thoughts floating about her head, like pieces of debris bobbing along in a stream. It must have been the kid's comments about black water and flies that led to Andes's nightmare. Her father's larger-than-life shadow loomed on the wall in front of her. He looked exactly as he did on that last day, raising an axe high above his head, the recently sharpened blade twinkling from a spot of sun shining in through the shed's one tiny window. But it wasn't the axe that rooted Emily to the spot, it was the expression etched into her father's face. A fury she'd never seen before, the last stop before madness. His eyes bored into hers as he brought the axe crashing down.

She woke to the sound of a piercing scream and sat straight up in bed. Chase, despite his threat that she was on her own if calamity befell, ran out of his room and to her side. Andes scrambled out of bed. The noise seemed to be coming from the hall. The two inched toward the front door. Had they moved into a dangerous building? Was someone trying to break in? Gerry and Richard would use this against her. They would be armed with their child psychiatrist, and Chase would be forced to admit that his first night in his new home, he was allowed to read a horror novel and was awoken by burglars, but he couldn't call 911 because his cell phone had been tossed in the toilet. It was at this critical moment that Andes realized she did not have the makings of a good mother. As they crept to the door, Andes held her arm out to keep Chase at bay. Her heart was pounding and her hands were trembling as she lifted the latch to the peephole. She saw Jenny standing at Dave's door, pounding on it with both fists, and screaming in a drunken rage. "Open the door, you bastard," was the only bit clear enough for Andes to make out.

"It's Jenny," Andes whispered when Chase tugged on her nightshirt. Dave was either the soundest sleeper in the world, or he was at work. "Go back to bed," Andes said. "I'm going to bring her in."

"Here?" Chase asked alarmed. "You're bringing her here?" Jenny fell into a heap by Dave's door, but her wailing continued. It was either bring her in or let one of the neighbors call the police. Surely, irritated fingers were already dialing 911. Then again, it was New York, the city where everything seemed to go as long as you didn't get in anyone else's way. Well, Andes wasn't a New Yorker, and the woman was totally losing it. She gently pushed Chase back and opened the door a crack.

"Jenny?" The heap ceased her wailing and peered up at the interruption.

"Andes," Jenny cried. "You live here now." The wailing started anew. For a moment Andes tried to reconcile Jenny's comments, which was challenging given the racket. *You live here now.* Is that why Jenny was crying? Wasn't she the one who orchestrated the move to begin with? Andes padded over to Jenny, put her hands on her shoulders, and tried to nudge her to stand up.

"Come inside," she said.

"He dumped me," Jenny wailed. She raised her head a tad and screamed at the door. "He fucking dumped me."

"Shh," Andes said. "I have a kid." The minute she said it, she prayed Chase wasn't listening through the door, which was exactly what he was doing. The way she said it sounded proprietary, *I have a kid*, as if she had given birth to him herself.

"Sorry," Jenny said, clutching onto Andes and trying unsuccessfully to bring her wail down to a whisper.

"Come on, get off the floor." Jenny allowed herself to be hauled up and partially dragged as she stumbled along in grief-stricken compliance. Although he was sitting on his bed and hiding behind *The Amityville Horror*, Andes knew Chase was glued to every word gushing out of Jenny's mouth, and she tried in vain to redirect it.

"That total bastard," Jenny yelled. "I loved him. I wanted to marry him. I wanted to have his babies. I know that's what this is all about. He's terrified of being a father. He doesn't want kids—"

"Shhh."

"He's adamantly refusing to combine his gorgeous DNA with this," Jenny said sweeping her hands over her body in a need-I-say-more fashion. Andes couldn't help but imagine Jenny doing her stripping routine. And although Andes would never be the type who would dance naked in front of salivating men aiming clammy dollar bills at her G-string, she did wonder, briefly, if men would be more riveted by Andes's imperfect little body dancing naked with a six-foot cobra slung between her breasts, or perfect-bodied Jenny dancing sans snake. It was just one of those passing thoughts that she would never have answered in her lifetime. Jenny was still talking.

"Imagine what our children would look like. I mean really—seriously, are you imagining right now? We're talking cataclysmic beauty." In the dark, in the other room, Chase had partially shut his bedroom door and was peering into the full-length mirror hanging on the back of his door. He wasn't sure what cataclysmic beauty looked like, but he was pretty sure he didn't have it.

"I'm sure he's not terrified of having kids," Andes said loudly. Why did adults always forget that children's radars were constantly scanning? "In fact, I think he'd be a great father," she yelled even louder.

"Andy," Jenny said.

"Andes," Andes interrupted.

"Believe me," Jenny continued, "if he doesn't want to have children with *me*, he doesn't want them period."

"A lot of people don't want children," Andes said, moving to get Jenny some water and aspirin. "But the moment they have them, they can't imagine what their lives would be like without them." Jenny followed Andes into the kitchen and plopped down at the table while Andes prepared the water and aspirin.

"Are you saying what I think you're saying?" Jenny asked. With the water running, Andes didn't exactly hear what Jenny said, and it was getting to the point in the evening where she didn't care.

"Are you?" Jenny asked. "Is that what you're saying? Because if you are, I like it—no, I love it! I was thinking it myself but then I thought it might be kind of sneaky, you know—but it's not. It's not at all. It's just helping someone who is terrified get over their fears."

"Uh-huh," Andes said setting the water and aspirin in front of her. In her mind she was gathering up the extra sheets and blankets for the sofa; obviously Jenny wasn't in any condition to be going anywhere. She wondered if she should put a bucket beside the sofa just in case. She'd give the chatty stripper a place to sleep, but she drew the line at cleaning up vomit.

"I'm going to do it," Jenny squealed. "That is, if I can get him to do it at least one more time. Sometimes it doesn't take, though, the first time."

"Drink this, I'm going to get the sofa ready," Andes said. Chase was standing at the doorway with his book when Andes went past to get the sheets.

"Go to bed," she said.

"You said I could read," Chase replied.

"You're not really reading," Andes said.

"How do you know?" Chase demanded.

"Well for one thing, boy genius, you're holding the book upside down." Chase glanced at the book, threw it down, and stomped back to his bed.

Back in the kitchen Jenny watched microscopic particles swirl around her water. She dipped her finger in, imagining the dust particles were eggs and sperm, and her finger Dave's beautiful penis. Get pregnant. She'd had the plan all along, but until tonight everyone she'd told had been absolutely horrified. But not this Andy girl. Andy had pointed out what Jenny knew all along.

Of course Dave wanted her babies. Of course he'd be a wonderful father. He was just terrified. He was terrified because his father died in a fire leaving eight children behind. Dave, being the oldest, had to step in, be like a father. He was just afraid—but he was born to do it. Jenny wouldn't be doing anything underhanded. She wouldn't be trapping him. She would be freeing him. Freeing him from his own fears. She would be giving him a family, for God's sake. For the first time all day she finally felt some relief. She was going to get Dave back the old-fashioned way. She had the oven. Now all she needed was the Jensen-seed bun.

Chapter 31

Alejandro cupped his hand around the surprise in his pocket as Chase talked, biding his time, waiting his turn. What a new and delicious feeling. He didn't have the words to put to it yet—if he did, he would have said: *unbridled anticipation.* All he knew was that he was very, very, happy—giddy with excitement. The only problem was it was making it that much harder to understand what Chase was talking about. Still, he made sure to smile and nod his head a lot, even more than usual, just to make up for the fact that he wasn't really listening. He'd seen his mom do this with almost everyone who came into the coffee shop, and it really worked because most of the time, they came back. Chase didn't speak any Spanish, but other than that, he seemed to know a whole lot more about the world than Alejandro. Today, he was talking about snakes and drinking poison, something Alejandro knew absolutely nothing about. If this had been a normal day, Alejandro would have been listening really hard, and then he would have tried and failed to say something just as cool about whatever Chase was talking about. Then Chase would have given him that look, the one that always made Alejandro feel shame. But that wasn't going to happen today. Because today he finally had something cool to tell Chase—something that might even make them friends. Alejandro found it when he was walking home from swimming.

His mother didn't know this, but he hated swimming. He didn't like how his stomach hung out over his trunks. He didn't like how everyone tried to swim far away when he got ready to jump in the pool. He knew people were laughing at him, and most of the time he just pretended he was laughing too. But he was not. Not ever really laughing. Because you didn't have to be as smart as Chase to know the difference between kids laughing with you and laughing at you. The kids at the pool were laughing at Alejandro. And they had good reason to laugh too; this is what made Alejandro really burn.

Sometimes he got water up his nose. Sometimes he accidentally kicked girls swimming behind him. Sometimes his shorts got stuck so far up his butt he had to pick them out. Sometimes he smacked his belly so hard on the water it stung for days. But today he was happy he went. He was happy because on his way home, he spotted a really cool lighter just lying in the middle of the sidewalk. He picked it up, expecting it to be a dud, but to his astonishment, when he flicked it—poof—a little flame shot out.

He'd wanted nothing more than to flick, flick, flick, all the way home, flick, flick, flick, away all the kids at the pool, but he'd waited. He didn't want it to run out. He shined it up with a shirt from the back of his closet. It was black with cool red and orange flames shooting up the side. When you flicked it a little red light beamed through the flames. He'd been waiting all week to show it to Chase. He knew some kids at school last year who had knives. He'd watched them one day draw the blade across their stomachs, wincing but not moving until a thin trail of blood trickled from their cuts. They weren't faking either, Alejandro saw the pain in their eyes. Then, still bleeding, they pressed their cuts together. Blood brothers.

Even if they had asked, even if the boys had invited Alejandro into their circle—which they certainly did not—he always knew he would have been too afraid of the pain to pull the blade across his belly. He didn't like knives and he didn't like blood. But walking home that day, holding the lighter that went poof, he started thinking. Fire didn't bother him too much. He was thick-skinned. A few times he'd touched the burner at home and barely felt it. Fire, he could probably do. He and Chase. Burn brothers. It might not exactly be the same as blood, but it might be the closest he'd ever come to having a real friend. A friend. *Mi amigo.* It was the only thing Alejandro had never put on his list; the one thing he wanted more than anything else in the world.

Before long Chase and Andes settled into their little nook in Sunnyside as if they had lived there all their lives. They knew most of their neighbors, at least to say hello, they were known by name at the bakery across the street and the Thai restaurant around the corner, and they knew the names of at least four neighborhood dogs. Additionally, they knew the idiosyncrasies of every single 99-cent store in the area, and there were a dozen if not more. Some carried better frozen Popsicles, others even had frozen food that wasn't too bad—Andes liked the lemon fish, Chase liked the chicken tenders. The one around the corner was best for stocking up on cleaning supplies, and the one on the north side of Queens Blvd. near Ariyoshi Sushi was good for greeting cards and knickknacks. Besides shopping and eating, they went for walks, spending as much time outdoors as they could. And to Andes's relief, Chase seemed to actually be warming up to Alejandro.

There was a little park around the corner from them, and although Chase was too old for the swings, Andes bought him a basketball and a couple of times a week the two of them would go to the park, Andes with a romance book, Chase with his basketball. They'd invited Alejandro several times, but he always got bored with the basketball and would join Andes on the bench, where he'd try and touch a pigeon with a long stick. On the days Hilda joined them, Andes wouldn't bring her book. Instead, the two of them would chatter and gossip. It was on one of these bench visits that Hilda asked Andes if she would like to work a few days a week at The Buzz.

"Are you serious?"

"Of course," Hilda sang, examining her fingernails. Today they were longer than Andes had ever seen them and painted a deep purple. "I need the help and you need some experience on your résumé. Not to mention a little cash coming in, right, *mami*?"

"You got me there."

"And I'm finally getting a new baker's oven this summer," Hilda said, clapping her hands together. "You should see this thing. It's a sleek Jaguar, *mami*. I'm so in love with this oven, they can toss me in and bury me in it when I die."

"I was excited for you a moment ago," Andes said. "But you've gone over the edge." Hilda threw her head back and laughed. Then she stomped her feet and shook her head and laughed some more. Andes glanced at Alejandro, who was smiling at his mother, but when he caught Andes looking at him, he rolled his eyes.

"And there's food left every night to take home and I won't take no for an answer," Hilda said, coming out of her laughing fit and jumping right back into the conversation.

"I'll take it."

"That's it? You don't even know how much I pay."

"Gotta be better than zero."

"I like you. No worries. I pay fair. And Chase can hang out with Alejandro. You want to start tomorrow?" Alejandro, who'd been silently trying to prod pigeons, suddenly shifted on the bench with a loud cry. "What's wrong, baby?" Hilda cooed.

"I don't want him there," Alejandro said, flipping the stick back toward Chase, who was battering the basketball into the cement with ruthless energy.

"Alejandro!" Hilda said. "I thought you'd love a boy your own age to play with."

"He's loco," Alejandro said, shaking his head and drawing the word out in a loud whisper. Hilda snatched the stick out of Alejandro's hands, snapped it in two, and winged it perfectly into the nearest garbage can.

"Sit up," she ordered and he did. Then she spoke to him in rapid-fire Spanish, complete with hands shooting up in the air now and again for emphasis. When she was done, Alejandro looked at Andes.

"I'm sorry," he said. "*Lo siento.*"

"It's okay," Andes said with a forced smile. What she really wanted to know was what exactly Chase had done to make Alejandro call him loco. She was dying to ask, felt it was perhaps even her duty to ask, but Hilda wasn't asking—and she knew her son better than anyone. Maybe Alejandro went around calling everyone loco.

"Can I go get a Popsicle?" Alejandro asked, pointing his stick in the direction of the 99-cent store.

"In a minute. I've been on my feet all day," Hilda said.

"I'll take him," Andes volunteered. "If you don't mind keeping an eye on Chase."

"Just don't let him talk you into anything else," Hilda said, waving them on.

Andes tried to chat with Alejandro on the way but he was unusually quiet. Once inside the store he went directly to the freezer, pulled out a Popsicle, and turned away from her. Andes took out Popsicles for the rest of them and started for the register. Alejandro was standing behind a rack of T-shirts. His head was bent down. Andes drew closer. Alejandro had his shirt lifted up and was holding the Popsicle against his belly.

"Alejandro?" Startled, he lifted his head, but he didn't move the Popsicle. "What are you doing, sweetie?"

"Nothing," he said. His lips started to tremble and his eyes and nose started running simultaneously.

"Let me see," Andes said. She took the Popsicle away. Alejandro cried louder, but he didn't stop her from examining him. A patch of Alejandro's stomach was covered in a burn blister the size of a fifty-cent piece. Andes gasped and immediately put the Popsicle back on the wound. *He's loco.* Oh no. No, no, no. "What happened?" she asked. "How did you get that burn?"

"At the pool," Alejandro said a little too quickly.

"You did not," Andes said. "Did Chase have anything to do with this?" Alejandro looked away. "You have to tell me," she said.

"He was supposed to do it with me," Alejandro cried. "But he wouldn't."

"Do what with you?"

"I used a lighter. We were supposed to be burn brothers." Andes couldn't believe what she was hearing. Chase had deliberately cajoled Alejandro into burning himself? She paid for the Popsicles and put her arm around Alejandro.

"Let's go," she said.

"Wait." Alejandro stopped in the middle of the sidewalk. "You're not going to tell my mom, are you? Please don't tell my mom." Andes wrapped Alejandro in a little hug.

"You didn't do anything wrong, sweetie," she said. "And you need to see a doctor. And Chase is not going to get away with this. He has to be punished."

"Punished because he wouldn't burn himself too?"

"Punished because he tricked you into burning yourself."

"How did he do that?"

"Honey. All this business about burn brothers or whatever, he just made up to get you to do that to yourself." Alejandro dropped his head. Andes gently guided him forward. "It's not your fault," she said.

"Mom won't let him near me again if you tell her," Alejandro said, his tears starting all over again. "Can't you punish him in private?"

"She needs to see that burn, Alejandro. You need to go to a doctor."

"I'll tell her I did it all by myself. I'll tell her I found a lighter and I wanted to see if it worked, and I was flicking it and I accidentally burned my stomach."

"I can't let you do that."

"Please. Please. I don't have any friends." Alejandro stopped walking and threw his Popsicle to the ground. "Don't tell her. He'll hate me. He'll hate me." Alejandro dropped to the sidewalk and sobbed. Andes knelt down next to him.

"Honey. Anyone who would do this to you isn't a real friend anyway," she said. "And I'm so sorry he did this to you."

"Then don't tell my mom. Please. Just punish him in private, okay? And tell him I'm not mad. Tell him I still want to be friends."

"Let's just get you to your mom so you can take care of that burn," Andes said.

Andes stood a few feet away from Chase, staring at him until he looked up. "What?"

"Put the ball down. We're leaving," Andes said. Chase glanced over at the benches.

"Where'd they go?"

"Hilda took Alejandro to the doctor," Andes said. Chase threw the ball and started walking ahead of Andes. "Don't you want to know *why* she's taking him to the doctor?"

"No."

"Hold it right there." Chase stopped walking but he didn't face Andes. She walked around until she was in front of him.

"Listen to me very carefully," she said. "I've been trying. I've really been trying to give you the benefit of the doubt. But what you did to Alejandro—"

"What I did?"

"Chase, I saw the burn on his stomach. He didn't want to, but he told me what happened."

"What did he say?"

"I want to hear it from you." Chase's hands curled into fists at his side. His face was red. Andes knew he was gearing up for another fit, but she wasn't going to back away this time.

"I didn't do anything," Chase said. "He found a lighter. He wanted us to be burn brothers. I told him he was an idiot. He put the lighter on his fat stomach and held it there for like forever. Then he expected me to do the same thing. I said no freaking way. He's a fat freak."

"Stop it. Stop calling him that, and stop lying!"

"I'm the liar? I'm the liar? I hate you."

"What about the fires at the marina, Chase? What about Gerry's lighter? What about the articles you print out on fires? What about putting up a lighter to the fire alarm in the motel?" Andes hadn't meant to confront it like this, in a giant wave, but it was too late to take it back.

"You think I set those fires, don't you? You're just like the rest of them."

"Then explain it to me."

"I'm just trying to stop them. Okay? I'm trying to stop the fires."

"How did the fires start, Chase? Who set them?"

"I'm not telling you. You don't tell me your secrets, I'm not telling you mine."

"Those aren't secrets, Chase. Those are serious crimes. If you know who's doing it and you're not telling—"

"I hate you—"

"I heard you the first twelve times. You hate me. Okay, I get it. Now tell me who started those fires. Is it your father, Chase? Is that why you don't want to tell me?"

"You're just like the rest of them," he said again. And then before Andes could react, Chase took off. He was a fast kid even when he wasn't trying, but with adrenaline pumping through him, he was unstoppable. It took Andes a few seconds to react. At first she assumed he'd stop somewhere ahead, wait for her with his usual silent treatment. Or she thought he'd come racing back to her, yell at her, pound on her with his fists. But instead, he kept running. A huge wave of panic swept over Andes the moment she could no longer see him. She broke into a run, knowing as she headed in the same direction that if he didn't want her to, she would never catch him.

Chapter 32

Andes ran up Greenpoint Avenue in a blind panic. A few times she stopped to ask if anyone had seen a boy go running by, but all she got were shakes of the head or strange looks. Every possibility ran through her mind at once. *Did he go back to the apartment? Did he go to the fire station? Did he slip into one of the numerous stores lining the avenue?* She was in full-blown tears, and truly terrified. Anything could happen to him. She was responsible. She'd been a fool to ever accept this kind of burden. She couldn't imagine never seeing him again. She couldn't imagine calling Jay and telling him his son was missing. She couldn't imagine facing Dave and telling him he might have had a son all this time and she never said a word. She stopped running and started yelling his name. She was going to have to call the police. She could call Dave instead, but was that just an excuse to see him? It wasn't until she got to Queens Blvd. that she realized where Chase might have gone. She took a right and started running again.

The feeling of relief that flooded over her when she saw him sitting in the cemetery was overwhelming. She stumbled up to him and collapsed by his side. "You scared me to death," she said, her tears starting again.

"Then I guess you're in the right place," Chase said.

"Don't ever do that again."

"I didn't tell Alejandro to burn himself."

"Look at me, Chase." It took some effort, but he finally met her eyes.

"I believe you," Andes said.

"All right, then," Chase said, getting up. "Let's go home." Andes realized as they started walking out of the cemetery, it was the first time he had ever called their apartment *home*.

Jason Ebert threw his last cigarette to the ground and crushed it out before reaching the firehouse. The afternoon sun was slowly releasing its squeeze, and the blue sky was glazing down a shade. Jason couldn't wait until this interview was over so he could walk over to Astoria, famous for Greek food, and grab him some gyros. Staying in Sunnyside and knocking back a pint of Guinness wouldn't be bad on a summer's evening either, but he had to be at the Central Park Zoo at the crack of dawn for the penguin feeding.

Blazing Dave hadn't returned any of his calls. There wasn't even a story there, just an editor at their loser paper who thought running a picture of the guy without his shirt would garner more female readers. As if the paper was ever going to be more than a two-bit gossip rag. Not that he was complaining. He'd long ago given up on wanting to work for the *Times*; he'd heard too many stories of reporters having to cover complete shit just to pay their dues. And although one could argue it was all shit he was covering too, at least it was local shit—nobody was sending him to Albany to cover reforms in education. But on this day it wasn't just his lousy job or even Blazing Dave eating at him, it was this snake business with George. Why wasn't he returning his calls? Was he still there? What had those freaks done to him?

Jason didn't want to get in his car and drive out there—he hated going anywhere, actually—but short of calling the West Virginia police, he didn't know what to do. Although given his last conversation with George, he didn't think foul play was involved as much as brainwashing. George sounded almost . . . religious. At first Jason was convinced George had been putting him on when he said, "The Lord is showing me the way, Jason. The signs are lit and glowing." Jason thought he heard music in the background.

"Is that a fucking banjo?"

"Jason, I don't swear anymore, so please don't use that foul language with me." Jason laughed, still waiting for George to 'fess up to the joke.

"What, you get bit by a snake, asshole?" Jason asked. "Are you wearing Nikes and drinking fucking Kool-Aid, dude?" George hung up. That was the last he'd heard from him. Brainwashed by a fucking snake cult. Jesus. It wasn't fair. Why did he always have to be the one dealing with this shit? Just then he saw Blazing Dave, walking with a group of firemen out of the station and down the street. Jason followed. When they reached the corner, Dave went into a coffee shop on the corner and the rest kept going. Jason waited a few minutes and then slipped into the coffeehouse after him.

Andes had been waiting for this moment. She knew Dave was bound to come into the coffeehouse eventually, and truth be told it, had been with that thought in mind that she got ready every day. And not just in case he came to the firehouse—she lived across the hall, one never knew when they would get a glimpse of each other. Chase hadn't commented on her lip gloss and still modest but slightly lower cut blouses, and how it was taking her double the time to fix her hair. But he had taken to squinting and smirking at her, which was definitely worse. Still, she wasn't going to let a ten-year-old ruin her crush. She was already prepared to defend herself; if Chase asked what she was doing she would say she was doing it for him, making an effort to get to know his maybe-dad.

Yet despite all the preparation, she was still caught off guard when Dave walked in. She would forever remember how the jingle of the door on that warm summer evening filled her with inexplicable joy before she even turned to see him. It was as if they'd both been waiting for the moment, which of course they had, and in their endorphin-flooded brains, two weeks since Dave's breakup with Jenny was long enough to wait. Chase was in the other room with Alejandro, and Hilda was in the storeroom, and the patrons couldn't have cared less, but had anyone been watching, they would have known as Dave drew near the counter that the two had already fallen one step in love, and there would be no easy way to back out of it now. Any reservations Andes had about getting involved with Dave dissolved with the ring of a bell, and as for him, he had to be with this unique and wonderful girl—it was as simple and complicated as that.

They exchanged shy hellos and Dave ordered a coffee and a scone, but all the important bits were said through their eyes, and through the purposefully accidental touching of their hands when Andes handed Dave his change. And although she would try to capture every minute detail in bed later that night, the gist of it was that after a few moments of pleasant stalling, Dave asked Andes on a date for the following Friday evening and Andes accepted without hesitation or the social norm of playing hard to get. A few minutes later the bell jangled again, and Dave was gone. Andes hummed to herself as she cleaned. Nothing could bother her tonight, not even the overweight man in the blue baseball cap who was watching her every move.

Chapter 33

No matter what was to follow, they had that night. And in the end, can one ever expect any more than that? So beautiful and filled with new love, a night where the rest of the world disappeared. They were so in tune with each other, infatuation invaded their bloodstreams like a drug. A night, a person, a place. A night where Andes let go of her worries: the stench of New York in August, sidewalks littered with cigarette butts, a dirty drunk man passed out on the sidewalk, snakes shedding skins in her dreams. Tonight she was carefree and life was thrumming through her full force. New love, like freshly fallen snow, is fleeting, but no one can deny its breathtaking beauty, its ability to inspire belief in magic, and no one, were they lucky enough to have it come their way, would ever give it up. Even knowing the pristine ground would soon be marred with the footsteps of life didn't deter Andes; it simply made every second of their glorious date precious.

She given up her own life ever since meeting the kid on the dock. She came to Queens because she thought she was doing right by him, and now she was on a date with the man the kid was seeking out, and it was the most selfish thing she had ever done, but she couldn't help it. To say Chase had not taken the news that she was going on a date with his maybe-dad well was akin to saying the Atlantic Ocean was a little bit wet. By the time she'd left Chase with Hilda and Alejandro, he had already taken a vow of silence. Hilda had gently urged her on, of course not knowing the real reason Chase was so livid, the crazy web she and the kid were spinning. And Andes didn't tell her; instead she escaped into the night through the small opening her life had offered her, hoping she would be able to smooth everything out with the kid in the morning. And so she and Dave went to Chinatown and walked hand in hand through narrow streets strung with lights, and restaurants teeming with people, deaf to all noise except the sound of their own stories and laughter.

Before going to the real restaurant, they ducked into a tiny café where Dave swore they made the best dumplings in the city. They ordered just a taste, and he wiped soy sauce off her when it dribbled down her neck and threatened to stain her new blouse, the one she had bought just for him. They laughed out loud at everything the other said, they listened to each other's stories as if they were their own. As they chatted and walked the streets, an unusual slice of pink cut through the slowly darkening sky, slicing through the middle like a creek dragging a girl's hair ribbon into its depths. They stopped to listen to live jazz drifting out of a lounge, and before they reached the restaurant, Dave pulled her into a hidden alcove by a faded brick apartment building and kissed her. The bricks rough and warm against her back as he leaned into her, their mouths tentative and sweet, slowly growing stronger as the kiss increased. It was nothing like the awkward fumbling she'd shared with Jay, or the stolen moments with Keith, or any of her other brief, unfulfilling love affairs. Dave pulled back, looked into her eyes, and smiled.

"I'm sorry," he said. "I had to do that. I never would have made it through dinner." And again they were hand in hand as he led her to the restaurant. The outside was nondescript; a squat brick building with darkly stained windows. But inside it was a Chinese palace, with winding staircases, plush red carpet, glittering chandeliers and statues of gold. A large pond with exotic fish lined the center, ending in a waterfall. Andes drew a breath and Dave laughed and drew her in at the waist. "I thought you'd like it," he said. "It's one of my best kept secrets."

"How could you keep this place to yourself?" Andes asked as a hostess dressed in a red silk gown led them to a corner table for two. An intrusive thought eked into Andes's mind; she wondered how many times he had come here with Jenny. And although she certainly wasn't a friend of the girl, she couldn't help but feel bad that she was falling in love with a man who had only so recently broken someone else's heart. But when they sat down and looked into each other's eyes across the candlelit table, Andes let her worries melt away. She was going to start enjoying the here and now, starting here and now.

"You look deep in thought," Dave said.

"Actually very shallow," Andes said. "And I intend to wade myself out." Dave laughed and didn't ask her to reveal any more than that. After admitting there really wasn't anything she didn't like to eat, she accepted Dave's offer to order for them, down to the bottle of wine. He was as nervous as she was, and it was the perfect touch to a completely enchanting evening. *It's okay*, she said to herself as the evening started to pass all too quickly, *I'm having a wonderful time. I deserve to have a wonderful time.*

The drinks flowed and so did their tongues. Their chests resonated with so much laughter that as the night grew, nearby patrons took to giving them looks, some because they felt the pair's laughter was interfering with their evenings, others because they wanted to savor a few vicarious drops from the two so obviously in love. But as Dave took the top off a pot of steamed dumplings (Dave wanted her to compare them to the first place they'd tried them), Andes froze as she watched the steam rise to the ceiling and disappear. "Reach in," Dave said. "They won't bite." The heat tickled her underneath the arm, yet she couldn't move; it was as if she were cemented in place. There was something in the slithering motion of the steam that triggered her. It was such a silly, simple thing, yet it happened so fast, she didn't have time to think, she simply reacted.

She'd managed to push this memory away for nine years. She'd been so diligent, her mind had constructed little walls, then layered them with brick, and with each passing year it grew higher and higher until she barely thought of it at all. Of course it wasn't perfect, there were days she could feel the wall giving, a little chip here, a crack there, but it never completely crumbled.

But tonight, she had let down her guard, and a tiny fracture had sliced into the wall. It was just a sliver of space, but that's all it took. His words were the key that sprung the rusted lock of her memories, and the wall came crumbling down on her and the restaurant disappeared. She was no longer in her new blouse sitting across from a beautiful fireman in New York City. She was barefoot and fifteen in West Virginia. The meeting room was packed. George Turner sat in the back row with a camera hidden underneath his baggy corduroy jacket. It was a night of gentle heat and pulsing music, an achingly beautiful summer night. Brother Wayne was in a good mood and his voice was booming. People were jammed in tight. The spirit was moving in early, several women were speaking in tongues, and the musical instruments were being played in an improvisational fashion, and building to a crescendo, teetering on the edge of *something*. And nobody felt it any stronger than Emily Tomlin.

"It's going to bite somebody today for sure," Thomas Hunley said, leaning over and whispering directly in her ear. Emily tried to scoot over—his breath smelled like Swiss cheese and baloney, and beads of sweat were rolling down his pale, fat cheeks. He was pointing to the lone snake box sitting slightly askew against the back wall. Emily rolled her eyes. The boys were always going on about snakebites, mostly to rile the girls. "It is," he insisted. "We've been poking it with a stick all day. It's spitting mad." Alarmed, Emily searched Thomas's face to see if he was telling the truth. Whenever Thomas lied, his nostrils flared and his cheeks burned bright red. But his face was still and pale, his nostrils relaxed. Emily looked back at the snake box and tried to imagine what was going on inside. Snakes that were hissing mad would be coiled and alert, and they would waste no time striking. Emily stared at the snake box as if everyone's life depended on her. Death was in that box, coiled and hissing, sitting slightly askew against the back wall, waiting to strike. And she alone had the power to stop it. It was a sign. Some people missed them because they weren't chosen, or their minds were closed to the Lord's mysterious ways. But Emily's mind was open, and the Lord had been trying to talk to her for some time now. Sometimes the signs were drifting in dreams, or clouds, or riding the high notes of a flute. But sometimes, they were a little more subtle, and much less poetic. For sometimes, God spoke through chubby cheeks and breath that reeked of processed meat. And tonight, he had spoken to her. Death was in that box. And nobody knew it but her.

Dave was good in a crisis, there was no arguing with that. That didn't mean he was any more equipped to deal with a screaming woman than the regular Joe. His first thought was that the steam was somehow burning her arm, and all but her vocal cords were paralyzed by unbearable pain. Yet as he ran his hand over the pot to take hers, he barely felt the steam, just a little lick of wet, a caressing kiss of dew. "Andes," he said as gently as he could as she continued to scream. Everyone was looking, but that didn't bother him, so much as the helpless feeling engulfing him. It was as if she were stuck in some kind of epileptic fit, except she was convulsing vocally instead of physically. He was ashamed at his next fleeting thought, that a physical fit would have been less embarrassing.

Waiters were running over, but Andes didn't seem to notice. Finally, Dave picked up his water glass and threw it in her face. He wasn't trying to be mean. He was a fireman—dousing the problem came naturally. And it seemed to do the trick. Although Andes's mouth remained open, the sound suddenly ceased and a collective relief hovered over those who had been holding their ears. Dave sat holding her hand, watching her. He felt lost once again. The only other time he'd thrown water on anyone, they'd been on fire, and quite grateful for his actions.

"Whatever it is," Dave said, sliding a napkin over to her, "it's okay." A hint of a smile played across Andes's face, but Dave knew it was a sad smile, an embarrassed smile. His confidence returned and he suddenly felt warm and protective of her. He leaned across the table so only she could hear his whisper. "When I was ten," he said. "I was in love with this girl named Heather. She was the prettiest girl in class. It was fall and I'd been dreaming about her all summer. I never knew your heart could really do that—just start beating like mad just from looking at a girl. But Heather did that to me. I thought others could hear it, see it even just jumping out of my chest when Heather would enter the room." Dave stopped to smile at Andes and tap his hand over his heart in a rhythmic demonstration. "And this day, I was called to walk up to the board and write a math problem. It was number thirteen too. Unlucky thirteen.

"So I'm up there at the board, writing away, almost done with the equation, when I hear the teacher call on Heather to put number fourteen on the board. And the only spot available on the good old chalkboard was the one right next to me. And I'm almost done. But just hearing her name and realizing any second she was going to be standing right next to me literally paralyzed me. I kept telling myself, erase it, erase the problem and start over, but I couldn't even move. And she wasn't even standing next to me yet, so it was just the thought that any minute she would be standing next to me that did it. It was the end of August. The hottest time of the year in New York. So for that first week—and only that first week back to school—we were allowed to wear shorts.

"And I'd drank a huge thing of orange juice that morning because my mom had just bought it and I was mad at her for something so I stood right in front of the fridge and just started chugging it when she was out of the room. Then next thing I know, there's Heather right beside me. Long brown hair down her back, arm stretching up to write number fourteen in chalk. And just like that my heart started beating. Thump, thump, thump." Dave stopped talking and sat back, but his smile rambled on.

"And?" Andes asked when he didn't continue.

"And what?"

"What happened?"

"That was it. Oh—I got the problem right too."

Andes couldn't believe that was the end of the story.

"I thought you were gearing up to tell me something really embarrassing—like you peed your pants or something—so that I would be less embarrassed," she said, slightly disappointed.

"Peed my pants? At thirteen?"

"You said you drank a lot of orange juice."

Dave smiled again and leaned forward.

"No," he said softly. "I told you that story because I've spent the rest of my life waiting for another girl who could make my heart beat just by looking at her. And I had just about given up. Thought it only happened to teenagers with out-of-control hormones. Thought I'd have to grow up and settle for someone who didn't trip my cardiac trigger. And then I met you," he said.

Dave picked up a napkin and started dabbing water from Andes's face.

Chapter 34

By the time Andes remembered she'd forgotten to ask Dave's advice on Chase's obsession with all things fire, it was too late; it was hours past their date. Chase didn't utter a word on the way home, and even Hilda looked appropriately rattled. Apparently, despite her best efforts, Chase hadn't budged from the corner of her apartment all evening. He wouldn't speak, eat, or play. Hilda refused to take money for "watching a statue," and she didn't waste any time showing them to the door. "What's going on?" she managed to whisper right before showing them out. "What's wrong with him?"

"There's nothing wrong with him," Andes said, surprised how defensive the question made her feel. She knew Hilda meant well. Yet a stubborn rock in Andes's throat prevented her from opening up and spilling all her fears about Chase.

"He needs to see somebody," Hilda said. "To help with his head." Shame quickly covered by anger welled up in Andes, but she held it at bay.

"He's homesick," Andes said as she glanced at Chase, who was standing in front of the elevator, giving no signs of listening. "Thank you for watching him."

"A houseplant would have been harder to watch," Hilda said with a shake of her head. There was sadness in her voice when she bid them good night. Chase and Andes rode the elevator down in silence, and heaviness sat over them like a dense fog. Was it less than an hour ago Andes was deliriously happy?

She knew exactly what would make Chase snap out of his pity-party. It was sitting right in her purse, yet she didn't produce it right away. The truth was his silence was a welcome reprieve. Once he did start talking he was going to grill her about her evening with Dave, and she wasn't quite ready to share. Except for her breakdown at the end, it had been a wonderful evening. And how nice he had been about her freaking out, how unbelievably sweet. And the best part was, he didn't run away from her. Of course she was deeply ashamed at her outburst, but she could have no more controlled or predicted that than she could have stopped a summer storm from rolling in and overtaking a sunny day. But just like the storm, it was over, and the best thing to do was put it out of her mind. So in her reruns of the evening, she would conveniently slice out the bad bits as if she were editing a film. On their short walk home, she replayed the evening over and over again in her mind while Chase still didn't say a word. The minute they entered the apartment Chase went to the corner of their dining room and stood facing the wall.

"I don't really live here," he said. "So I'm just going to stand here."

Andes changed out of her clothes and into her pajamas. She washed her face and brushed her teeth. She turned down Chase's bed and then her own. Then she went to her purse and using a cloth napkin removed the cup she had taken from the table at the Chinese restaurant. She stood in the corner next to Chase holding the cup. "I'm not thirsty," he said when a few minutes of silence had passed.

"It's not for you," Andes said. "Not to drink out of, anyway." Chase turned away. "It's evidence," Andes said. "Your maybe-dad drank out of it." Chase turned back.

"DNA?" he whispered.

"DNA," Andes confirmed.

"Now what?"

"I found a lab online. Now we send it to them along with your DNA and we wait."

"How long?"

"Seven to ten days."

"Does it really work?"

"They say it does."

"Does he know?"

"Of course not."

"You did this for me? That's why you went out with him?"

"It's one of the reasons. Now get to bed."

"Seven to ten days." Chase smiled at her and started toward his room. But instead of feeling happy, Andes was weighed down by a sudden dread and nagging feeling of guilt. Dave had been so nice to her, and she swiped his cup off the table like a common thief. What would he think of her if he knew she was keeping this secret from him? *Chase thinks he might be your son. That's why we're in Queens.* That's what she should have said first. *Your son may also be a pyromaniac.* That's what she should have said next.

"Chase." The kid stopped but waited with his back to her. "I think you should call Jay."

"He hasn't called me."

"Well. What about writing him a letter?"

"He hasn't written *me* a letter. And we even have a post office box." Andes couldn't argue with that, she knew the feeling all too well. Instead she drew close to Chase but stopped short of touching him.

"We'll figure this out in the morning," she said.

"No," Chase replied. "We'll figure this out in seven to ten days." He gave her another little smile and then touched her on the arm with the tip of his index finger. "Good work," he said. "I'm proud of you."

That makes one of us, Andes thought as she watched him disappear.

Four of them were missing. She was sure of it. Argentina. France. Russia. Germany. Gone. Red. Green. Blue. Faded yellow.

Dancer. Le Roue. Danka. A cap pulled low. She went through the box twice. Somehow, Chase had managed to pick the lock and put it back on. She waited until he was in the bath to sneak into his room, and began to pick through his things. Dirty clothes, Game Boy, books, an endless number of T-shirts and shorts and underwear. He didn't like to wear socks, so there weren't many of them. Where were her matchbooks? She tried not to panic when diving her hands into his little pockets yielded nothing but gum, lint, and a few stray rocks. Had he thrown them away? Or did he have a hiding place? Was he squirreling away fire-starting paraphernalia, waiting to use them? Hilda was right, the kid needed to talk to someone. Hell, *she* needed to talk to someone. The two of them were going out with Dave this evening. She would find a way to confide in him. He would be able to help Chase. The kid was just stressed, that was all. They hadn't heard from Jay in over a week. The last time she'd tried to call the prison she was on hold for a long time and then disconnected. After that the phone had been busy. Andes went back to her snake box and looked at the lock. It wasn't damaged in the least. It couldn't have been easy to pick. She'd better get to the bottom of it before he drained her collection match by match. If he'd taken four matchbooks, how was she to know he hadn't violated the others? Ripped out individual matches? She was going to have to check them one by one.

The water in the bathroom shut off. Soon he'd be coming out, towel wrapped around him, dripping water all the way back to his room. She always dried off the floor after him, and he never seemed to notice. Pick your battles. The water she would swallow, but she wouldn't eat fire. Tonight, Dave was going to hear all about Chase's little problem. And finally, she wouldn't be so alone.

For a kid supposedly crazy to find out whether Dave was his real father, Chase was doing a remarkable job of appearing to be the kid who couldn't care less. They had been at the movies for twenty minutes and he'd only grunted at all of Dave's efforts to get to know him. Andes wished she hadn't showed him the cup or mailed it off to the lab the next day. Chase would have been talkative if he was still trying to ascertain Dave's relation to him. Or maybe Chase was uncomfortable by the way Dave was looking at her, or maybe he'd noticed Dave's repeated attempts to hold her hand. It was awkward, Andes realized. After all, Chase had first known Jenny to be Dave's girlfriend, and despite her nonstop chatter, Jenny had always gone out of her way to be nice to the kid. Andes hoped Chase would be enthralled with *The Black Stallion*; she was thrilled when she found a theater was playing the old classic. She loved the first scene on the ship, the tiny horse won in the poker game, the silhouette of the real majestic black stallion standing on the ship with the ocean roaring in the background, the threat of the upcoming storm.

Yet during her favorite bits Chase wasn't even watching; he was playing a game on his watch. She felt angry and ashamed. Even after she covered his watch with her hand, he simply yanked his wrist away, twisted his body so that it was hanging over the seat, and continued to play. Well, screw him. If he was going to be himself, she was going to be herself. She leaned nearer to Dave and slipped her hand in his. In the dark, he brought her hand up to his lips and kissed it. Andes didn't have to turn toward him to know that Chase was watching.

After the movie they decided to go for pizza. It was a nice night, and they took their time walking. Dave asked Chase what he thought of the movie and Chase launched into a detailed explanation of how the book was much better. Dave didn't say much after that. On their way to the pizza place, they passed the local park where Andes read her romance books and Chase played basketball. A stray ball sat at the base of a tree. Dave picked it up and tossed it to Chase. He dropped it. "Want to play a quick game?" he asked. Chase said yes, the first sign of eagerness he'd shown all evening. And so even though Andes would've liked to play too, she pretended she would rather just sit and watch so the kid could have some alone time with his maybe-dad. She took a seat on a bench as the two played. A few minutes later a man sat at the other end of the bench. She didn't look directly at him, but out of her peripheral vision, she could see he was wearing a knit cap, which was a very odd accoutrement for such a warm summer evening. The smell of stale cigarette smoke clung to him, and had she not already been on the edge of the bench she would have scooted farther down. She was contemplating moving to another bench when he spoke.

"Nice night," he said. Andes glanced at him. He was overweight, looked to be in his thirties. He didn't seem drunk, but perhaps he was the type who could hide it well.

"It is," she said.

"You from around here?"

"I am now."

"Ah," he said. "A transplant."

"Something like that."

"I'm born and bred." *Just ignore him*, Andes thought. She buried herself in her purse and pulled out her new phone. It reminded her how stupid she'd been, throwing their old cell phones into the toilet. When checking her phone and silently berating herself failed to divert the stare of the stranger, she dug a quarter out of the bottom of her purse. What was she going to do with it, she wondered. The phone had been a better distraction. *Stay away from me, you psycho—I have twenty-five cents and I'm not afraid to use it!* A blowtorch, a mason jar of battery acid, and a copperhead would've served the purpose, but you work with what you have. She took the phone out again, but this time it, along with the quarter, fell from her hand. She heard the phone skate along the ground. That was all she needed, to break this one. She couldn't afford a third one. She bent to retrieve the phone and the quarter, but she couldn't see it. She pawed along the ground for a few minutes, feeling like an idiot. Finally, the stranger got off the bench, walked a step, and bent down. When he returned, he pretended to pull the quarter out of her ear. Far from being amused, Andes was starting to get creeped out. Where was her phone? As soon as she found it, she was definitely getting away from him.

"It's right here," the stranger said, holding her cell phone out like an offering. "If it was a snake it would have bit ya." Startled, Andes looked up. He met her gaze and held it. It could have been a coincidence, but Andes didn't believe in coincidences. He was speaking softly, almost whispering, but to Andes he was screaming. His eyes were the nicest thing about him, sparkly and blue. Stripy bits of blond hair stuck out of his cap. He needed a shave and there were dark circles under his eyes, but they were kind eyes nonetheless. They kept her from running away. He was looking at her as if he cared, as if he was concerned.

"Buddy of mine I work with," the man said. "He's been on this gig for a long time. No one's even heard from him in over a week." Andes wanted to run but remained rooted to the spot. Dave had noticed the man by now, she could tell by the frequency with which he was glancing over.

"Last I heard," the man continued, "my buddy was in West Virginia. Starling, West Virginia." Andes held her breath and lost herself in the sensation of her heart pounding out of her chest. She could no longer hear the dribble of the basketball or the thunk as it hit the backboard. Sure enough, when she looked up, Dave and Chase were making their way over. The man reached into his pocket, took out a business card, and handed it to Andes.

"Unless you want everyone else hearing your business, you're going to want to call me," he said. "You're going to help me find George." Something clicked in Andes's mind. The sun, the snake, the snapshot.

"George?" she said. "George Turner?"

The man let out a low whistle.

"Hot damn," he said. "It is you." The man leaned toward Andes until they were face-to-face. "He thinks you're dead, you know. He thinks your father murdered you. He's there right now asking all sorts of questions and not returning any of my goddamn phone calls."

"No," Andes said. "No."

"You have to take me there. We have to tell him you're alive and get him out of there."

"Never," Andes said. "I'm never going back."

"Well then," the man said. "I guess everyone's going to find out snake girl's alive. Been faking her own death all this time.

Allowing the outside world to think her own father's a murderer. You know a boy was just bit and died, don't you?" Andes didn't answer, or move, or blink. "Look, it's not like I don't pity you. I would have run away from those crazy fuckers too. But whatever voodoo they got goin' on down there, they're using it on my friend. That is, if he's still alive."

"Stop it. It's not like that," Andes said. "It was never like that." Dave and Chase were only a few feet away.

"Well, I don't know what it's like. But I need George back. And you're going to help."

"Andes?" Dave called. "You all right?"

"So either you're coming with me or I'm going to start digging. Everyone has secrets, darling. And I'm going to dig yours up one by one and shine a great big light on them."

You have kind eyes, Andes wanted to say. *They fooled me.*

"Hey," Dave said, wedging himself in between Andes and the man. "Who are you?"

Jason Ebert backed up, still talking as he did so.

"I'm going to write everything there is to write about you," he said, pointing at Andes. "When I'm finished you'll be famous again. Snake girl rises from the dead." He yelled the last part, raising his hands high above his head. Then he thrust his business card at Andes again. Silently, she took it. As she left she swore she heard him hissing under his breath. Chase must have heard it too.

"Snake girl?" Chase asked as Jason ambled away. "Why did he call you that?"

"I'm not sure what he called me," Andes said.

"He called you snake girl."

"He probably wasn't in his right mind, Chase," Dave said. "Sad fact about a city park. You get a lot of freaks. You all right?" he asked putting his arm around Andes.

"Whoa, whoa, whoa," Chase said, yelling and pointing at Andes. "She doesn't *tolerate* the word 'freak.' "

"Oh," Dave said. "I just meant—"

"It's all right," Andes said. Chase glared at her. "How was the game, boys?" she said with forced enthusiasm.

"I suck," Chase said.

"You just need practice," Dave said. "We could play once a week if you'd like." Chase shrugged, but Andes knew from the tiny smile on his face he was pleased. "You hungry?" Dave asked, catching Andes around the waist.

"Starving," she lied. She tried to clear her mind as they walked to the pizza shop. The air was gentle and only slightly clinging. The sounds of people out on a summer evening gurgled like music along Greenpoint Avenue. The smell of pizza dough drifted lazily about. Chase was actually skipping ahead and humming. The most beautiful man she'd ever met put his hand in hers. And Andes had never felt so sick and frightened in all her life. It just couldn't get any worse. Up ahead, she heard Chase yell.

"Jenny," he shouted down the street. "Jenny. Over here."

And with that, Dave abruptly dropped her hand.

Chapter 35

It surprised Andes, the fear pouring off her fireman friend. Apparently, he was brave when encountering the scorched, but not the scorned. She wasn't sure if he had purposefully dropped her hand or if it simply slipped off because of the sweat pooling in his palms. Andes had to admit, she wasn't feeling exactly innocent and secure either. Dave started walking slightly ahead of Andes, as if they weren't together. Chase nabbed Jenny at the corner right in front of the pizza shop. From the looks of it, Jenny had been heading around the corner. Had Chase not screamed out her name, she simply would have disappeared down the street, and the three of them would have slipped unseen into Marabella's Pizza. It didn't matter what she had given up for the kid, or how much she had done for him, apparently it wasn't enough, it was never going to be enough. He was never going to be thankful, or grateful, and he was certainly never going to give her a break. He must have known exactly what trouble he was stirring up when he yelled Jenny's name down the street. How could he do this to her? It felt like a slap in the face.

Although Jenny was bent down, smiling at Chase, one shot of her blue eyes was all it took to see the jealous rage boiling underneath. Despite the eccentricities of the mountain people who raised her, Andes had no experience with violence. She curled her fist at her side, warming it up, just in case she was going to have to throw a punch. From the way Dave was reacting, he wasn't going to be coming to her rescue. Andes was much smaller than Jenny, so if Jenny came at her, she planned on ducking and ramming her head into Jenny's solar plexus. You never knew what life was going to throw at you. A minute ago all, Andes wanted was a slice of pepperoni pizza.

"Hey," Dave said as they approached. "We were just coming in for pizza after shooting some hoops. Right, buddy?" Dave rustled Chase's hair.

"That's great," Jenny said with false enthusiasm. She turned to Andes. "And you're tagging along?"

"They're on a date," Chase said, smoothing his hair back into place. Jenny stood tall and folded her arms across her chest. She stared directly at Dave.

"This is why you broke up with me? Because you wanted to date? Or because you wanted her?" Andes moved over to Chase, put her hand on his back, and pushed him in the direction of the pizza shop.

"I'd better get him fed," she said. She turned to Dave, hoping he would tell her he'd meet her inside.

"Good game, buddy," Dave said. "We had fun. But just for future reference, that wasn't really a date. A date usually involves just two."

"Like when you two went out Friday night," Chase snapped back. Andes pushed Chase again.

"Go," she said. "Get a table." She turned to Jenny.

"I needed a break from the kid. Hilda agreed to watch him and Dave knew of a good Chinese restaurant. He's making it sound like something it's not." She hated herself as the words were coming out of her mouth. What a coward she was. Why didn't she just say what she felt? She had the time of her life with Dave. She might be falling a little bit in love with him.

They laughed, and talked, and kissed, and the world disappeared. She made his heart beat just by looking at him. Right? Isn't that what he said? But he wasn't saying it here and now. And she wasn't going to stand there and let Dave be the only one to reduce what was going on between them to nothing but neighborly gestures.

Andes turned back to go into the shop when she heard Dave say, "The kid needs a man around, that's all." She turned back around.

"He has a father," she said. "He's been around the kid his entire life. That is, until a few months ago. He's not a charity case."

"Andes, I didn't mean that—"

"He just meant he's not dating you," Jenny said. This had gone too far. Andes looked at Dave, waiting for him to say something. His jaw was set and he was looking away from her, away from both of them.

"I'm sorry," Dave said at last. "But I need to talk to Jenny in private." Andes nodded and slipped into the pizzeria. On rubber legs, she wobbled over to the booth where Chase sat.

"Let's get the works," he said.

"Okay."

"Don't let them cut it."

"I know."

"Get a glass and we'll—"

"I said I know." Cut it in circles. *Funny*, Andes thought as she made her way up to the counter. *My entire life is turning in circles. I'm spinning and not making any headway. I keep returning to the same place with different people. Unattainable men, unavailable kids, friendships that dissolve. I'm a snake eating its tail.*

The only good thing about Jenny ruining her date was it temporarily knocked her meeting with the reporter right out of her head. It wasn't until she dug into her pocket to pay for the pizza that the business card fell out. She bent down, picked it up, and in a flash it was back. George Turner was in Starling, and according to Jason Ebert, he hadn't come back, wasn't returning phone calls. It was rare, but it did happen sometimes that outsiders wandered in and found some comfort in the mountains, the magic, and yes, in the meetings. But Turner wasn't there seeking God. He was seeking her. He might even be spending time with the parents she hadn't seen in seven years. The mother who sent all her letters back. The father who took an axe and—

Andes felt a tug on her shorts. Chase was standing by her side looking at her.

"Are you mad at me?" he asked.

"Why do you ask?"

"Because you're not moving." He was right. She was holding a tray of pizza in her hands and standing in the middle of the restaurant like a statue. "We don't have to cut it this time," he added reluctantly. The tears came unexpectedly. Andes dropped her head and sobbed as Chase took the tray out of her hands and guided her back to the table. She felt the weight of the world settle in her chest. She forgot Jason's business card was in her hands until she felt Chase edging it out from underneath her fingers. For the next few minutes she knew nothing but her own tears and the relief that came from shedding them. When one of the pizza guys made their way over to see if she was okay, Chase waved him away. "Low blood sugar, buddy," he said. "She'll be better soon." The pizza guy started off. "And," Chase shouted after him, "she wanted these cut in *circles*."

That night Chase brought Andes her doll, Rose. "Your wooden box was open," he lied. "I thought you might want her."

"I'm too old to sleep with a doll," Andes said, taking Rose in her hands anyway. Chase shrugged.

"I won't tell," he said, crawling into her bed. She wanted to ask how he really got into the box, and she wanted to grill him about the matchbooks, but she was so tired. Too tired to be angry with him, too tired for another fight. And he was trying to comfort her. She wasn't going to punish him when he was being kind. Chase picked up her Harry Potter book, opened to where she had it bookmarked, and began to read out loud.

Andes's first thought, when she threw open the door the next morning, was that they were going to a funeral. Alejandro was wearing a somber suit, and Hilda was dressed head to toe in a tight black dress with impressive cleavage.

"Nice hat," Andes croaked, pointing at the wide brim circling Hilda's head like a UFO. Hilda stepped in, Alejandro trailed behind.

"Get dressed, amiga, we're taking you to church."

"I'm not going," Chase yelled from the bedroom. Hilda threw her arms up and squealed.

"He speaks, he speaks!" she yelled. "See. Just the thought of church is healing you, little one. Now get dressed, because we are going to church and then we're going for tacos and you two are coming with us." Andes looked at Alejandro, who simply stared back until Andes made a silly face and then his chubby little face broke into laughter. Impulsively she reached down and gave him a hug.

"*Vámonos!*" Hilda cried. "God and tacos are waiting!"

We need some dress-up clothes, Andes thought, grateful they were sitting toward the back of the church. All Chase had to wear was dark blue jeans and a plain green T-shirt, and Andes had a skirt that would be perfect for the taco guys, but probably a little too short for the Lord's liking. Next to Hilda and Alejandro they looked like beggars plucked off the street. It was mostly a Latino crowd, and Andes was happy to note despite the somber outfits, they were a lively crowd and the service was filled with song. No one even seemed to notice Chase slumped down in his seat, kicking the pew in front of him. No one, that is, except Andes. Lately, everything the kid did was magnified, and she couldn't help but feel his every action was a bad mark on her. Which is why she found herself leaning over and whispering threats in Chase's ear.

"Sit up straight and stop kicking the seat or no tacos." The statement was probably reasonable, but her anger made her feel as mean as if she had threatened him with a lot worse than taco deprivation.

"We don't even speak Spanish," Chase whined. "We have no idea what they're saying. And why are they so freaking happy? It's annoying."

"They're giving thanks to God, okay? And God makes some people happy. It's the same in every language. Seriously, stop kicking that bench."

"I'd rather go to the cemetery, wouldn't you?"

"We're here to support Hilda and Alejandro."

"You think they'd at least be wearing sombreros," Chase said, looking about. Andes rolled her eyes and suppressed a giggle. Alejandro was sitting up straight and singing. Hilda had her eyes closed, but she too was belting out the song. Andes never realized what a beautiful voice she had. The song ended and the crowd was immediately silent. Heads bowed. A prayer started in Spanish. The words were unfamiliar, but the cadence was the same. Andes felt her lips moving as prayers from her past slipped through. She closed her eyes. After a moment she felt Chase kick her. Suddenly she realized her arms were elevated. She opened her eyes. She was holding her hands high above her head, and spread out, as if she were handling. The prayer stopped. All heads turned to her. She had been speaking in tongues, lifting an invisible snake. Hilda's eyes were open wide, her mouth dropped open. Some of the people didn't look so happy anymore. In fact, a few looked downright angry. They thought she was making fun of them.

"Snake girl," Chase whispered to himself as he touched the business card he'd tucked into the pocket of his shirt that morning.

"What are you doing, *mami?*" Hilda whisper-yelled. Andes could see by the expression on her face that she was mortified.

"She's been taking Spanish," Chase yelled. "But she's not very good." Chase elbowed her. Andes dropped her hands.

"*Sí, sí,*" she stammered.

"*Lo siento,*" Chase yelled into the crowd. "Sorry, amigos." The kid might have stopped there, but everyone was still staring at them like an accident they couldn't turn away from. Chase raised his hands and his voice, like a host of a party encouraging his guests to go home. "Go with God," he said. Everyone continued to stare. Chase raised his hands and voice even more. "He grants you serenity. Loves all his little children. God is good!

Good is God. God grant me the serenity! His are the footprints in the sand when you thought there was only one 'cuz you were on his back or something! May the wind be at your back and not coming out your—"

Andes slapped her hand over Chase's mouth, although from the looks they were getting no one really understood the kid anyway. Chase licked her hand. Andes yelped and jerked her hand away. Hilda threw them a look of pure horror.

"Just go," Hilda said. "*Vete.*"

"You heard the lady," Chase shouted. They hurried to their feet and started down the aisle to the exit.

"I'd better get a freakin' taco," he said as they hit the door. "I think I've earned it."

They lay in the Calvary Cemetery next to James and Mary Cunningham from County Cork, Ireland, eating their tacos and looking up at the sky. "I just thought of the perfect sermon," Chase said. Andes waited patiently. "What does an agnostic insomniac with dyslexia do?" Chase asked eagerly.

"I don't know."

"Lies awake at night wondering if there really is a Dog." After a moment, Andes giggled.

"Yes," she said. "That would've gone over well." Chase snorted.

"Hey," he said. "What were you doing back there?" Andes wished he hadn't asked her that with her mouth full. She tried to swallow, but the bite was stuck in her throat.

"I used to go to church," she said. Chase sat up as if sensing a confession was forthcoming. "Our church was very different from others, Chase."

"Bet they didn't sing in Spanish," he muttered.

"No," Andes said. "But we spoke in tongues."

"Ew," Chase said. "Like cow tongues?"

"I didn't say we ate tongue," Andes said. "We spoke in tongues. It means sometimes when the Lord moved on us—"

"Moved on you?"

"Yes. It means the spirit enters you and lifts you and you feel like a balloon floating through the sky. And all you want to do is give thanks. And sometimes when you're caught up in this feeling you might start speaking in a language nobody has ever heard of. It's called speaking in tongues."

"That is so weird. You're making this up, right?" Andes was going to ease into the bit about handling fire, drinking poison, and handling serpents. Yet it wasn't going to happen now.

"Yeah," Andes said, lying back down. "I can see how others would think that." She felt a shadow pass between her and the sun. Chase's face was directly over hers.

"Well, you must think that too," he said. "Because you don't go to church anymore." Andes opened one eye. She didn't like looking up the kid's nostrils so she shut it again.

"Sometimes," Andes said. "I don't know what to think. Sometimes I just try and make my mind a blank."

"Ah," Chase said, finally moving away and allowing the sun to pour over her face once again. "That explains a lot."

Chapter 36

By the time George Turner snapped her picture, when she was fifteen, Emily Tomlin had actually been handling serpents for five years. She was the youngest handler Starling had ever known, but that would never make the history books. Instead, as her prowess grew, her legend would be passed mouth to mouth, in excited jabbers, hushed whispers, and downright awe. As word spread, so did attendance at the meetings. Everybody wanted to see the young redhead turn venomous reptiles into docile garden snakes. The snake whisperer.

It all started that one night, that one meeting when Thomas Hunley leaned over and whispered in Emily's ear. He'd poked and prodded the snake into a fit, he told her. Whoever touched it next would surely be bit, probably even die. Then Emily watched her father step toward the snake crate with the expression of a man determined to face his fears once and for all. Emily didn't have time to think this time. Death was in that box. The Lord moved on her to save her father. The snake wouldn't hurt her, she knew it in her bones. But it would surely sink its fangs into her father. The Lord was moving on her, and this time she wasn't going to hesitate. His hands were reaching for the lid when Emily slipped in behind him. Before he could react, her small body was hovered over the box, and she was the one prying open the lid and going for the snake.

Back in the pew, Thomas Hunley's mouth was hanging open as he watched the young girl lift the sleek, black reptile out of the crate. The sight of it, open-jawed and thrashing, paralyzed her father. The normally gregarious congregation was struck mute as they watched Emily move with the snake. Her father thought she was trying to humiliate him; she understood that now. But back then she was only trying to save his life.

As she moved with the serpent, she felt voices and hands from far away reaching out to stop her. But the voice of the Lord was louder. She felt a slight swell in her belly and groin, and sweat caked the edges of her forehead, but a great song pounded in her chest. She had no fear of the snake. She placed one hand close to its head, and the other she held just beneath the heft of its body close to the tail. Its head whipped around as she lifted it, its tail gave a violent, upward flick. Her father stumbled back, his hand covered his eyes, his body turned away. He was going to be sick. Emily met the eyes of the snake.

It's all right, she told it. *You're all right.* The jaw still opened, the tongue still flicked, but in the next blink of its eye she saw that the snake understood her. She lifted her hands higher as voices around her began to chant and the music swelled underneath her. Tears ran down her cheeks as she felt the snake relax in her grip. Its tail wrapped around her hand, and a collective gasp rose from the pews, but Emily did not panic, nor did the snake squeeze. Instead, its head came to rest on her palm, and it closed its eyes. In the time it took for the young girl to glide across the stage, the snake had fallen asleep.

When the Lord moved on her again, she walked it back to the snake box and gently laid it inside. It had only been thirty seconds, but to those watching it had been a lifetime of suspense. And only when the lid was securely back in place did anyone dare to breathe. And then came praises and clapping and screams. From everyone, that is, except the man collapsed against the back wall. Emily stared at the stranger whose blood ran cold through hers. He was still clutching his head, but he managed to lift his eyes and catch her gaze. A cold, sick fear spread through her. It was painfully clear. The Heavenly Father may have loved her, but the earthly one was filled with nothing but hate.

To look at Zachariah Tomlin, one would assume nothing scared him, and certainly couldn't imagine anything keeping him awake at night. He was bitterly disappointed the Lord only saw fit to give him one child, and a redheaded daughter at that. But he made sure his wife and child were obedient, and his household was always orderly. Emily was about ten years old when she started to change. Zachariah saw her insolence grow with each passing day, and yet the more discipline he imposed, the more she rebelled. Whenever he spoke to his wife about their growing problem, she insisted the answer lay in more meetings. But there was something else Zachariah noticed about Emily—she was fascinated by serpents. And this was the something that kept him awake at night. Somehow, his daughter knew. She knew the six-foot-four, two-hundred-twenty-pound, God-fearing, coal-mining man was terrified of snakes. And his four-foot, seventy-pound, redheaded daughter was not. He had seen her lingering near the crates at the wee hours of the morning, when she thought no one was around. He'd heard her whispering to them, reaching in to stroke them, as if they were pets. Her flaming red hair had struck fear in his heart. It was the color of fire, it was the shade of the deepest depths of hell.

His wife had placated him, assuring him she was from God. But now he knew better. As hard as he tried to deny it, he was convinced the devil was working through his daughter. He remembered one morning, coming around the corner of the shed, and suddenly there she was in front of him. Barefoot, standing in his way, the sun lighting the strands of hair on fire. She was holding a four-foot rattler. She held the snake out to him, as if this was the very moment she had been waiting for.

"Would you like to hold him, Daddy?" He'd never struck his daughter in his life. Had she not been holding the snake between them that day, he knew, by God he knew he wouldn't have been able to stop his hand from making contact with her face. Eye to eye he saw firsthand the evil in his only child. God was testing his faith through his own flesh and blood. He knew then she needed to be cast out, or she would destroy him.

"You are committing a sin, Emily," he told her as calmly as he could.

"The Lord moved on me to handle," Emily said. "He told me to pick him up. See?" She jostled the snake; it moved lazily in her hands.

"Put it back. Then come right back here."

"I can teach you. I can teach you so that you're not afraid." There. She'd gone and done it. Spoken aloud what was between him and the Lord. From that second on, Zachariah began planning how and when he would cast her out.

"Put it back," he ordered. "Then come here. Every second you waste is going to cost you."

It would be the first of many "overnights" in the well.

George Turner was startled by the change in Zachariah Tomlin. The man was nothing like the strapping figure he'd met seven years earlier. He looked as if he'd aged twenty years. He'd lost weight; he walked stooped over with a cane. His hair, once thick and black, had gone completely white. He lived alone in a disheveled house that used to be tidy and filled with the scent of cooking. He always carried a shotgun and a bottle of whiskey. He hadn't been to meetings in over five years; he was an outsider in an outsiders' community. But he was starting to talk to George about Emily. In fact, he spoke about her as if she were still alive. He was gearing up for a confession, George was sure of it. He could feel it coming. He knew now, with absolute certainty, that Zachariah Tomlin had indeed murdered his own daughter. And he, George Turner, small-time potatoes, was about to hit pay dirt. He knew it. He knew there was a reason he'd stayed obsessed with the redhead all these years; she was his ticket to fame. That was something he shared with Zachariah, their obsession, albeit for different reasons, with Emily.

He knew Jason was worried about him, thought he'd succumbed to the snake lovers. The thought made him chuckle.
Oh boy, the laugh they would have over that when the story
broke. He needed these people to think he was one of them, he
needed to break this from the inside out. Although he *was* kind
of getting to like the meetings. He was even getting used to the
snakes, and so far no one had been bit. And with the amount of
handling they were doing, even George had to admit that was
sort of a miracle. Of course he was a bit weirded out when
Brother Lyle drank that nasty stuff out of a jar, said it was battery acid. But come on, it must have been something else. The
man drank it down and kept on dancing. George thought
about slipping the glass into his pocket to have it tested, but
what did it matter. They could have their little fantasy world.
He just wanted Emily's story. He wanted the truth.

Yet so far, every time he asked Zachariah how his daughter
died, the man would launch into another story of the evils of
his daughter. But there was hope. The stories were progressing,
he wasn't just telling the same one over and over again. There
was definite forward movement. And George, little by little,
shot of whiskey by shot of whiskey, was leading Zachariah Tomlin right to Emily's grave. But he'd better do it soon. The old
man was really losing his mind. Just the other day he grabbed
George by the arm and stared into his eyes like a madman.
"Emily," he said. "You can help. You can bring her back to me."

"That's not in my power to do," George said earnestly.

"She has to come back," Zachariah insisted. "I have to finish
it. I have to finish it." And then the old man went out to the
grave and just stood there staring at it. It was nightfall before he
came back in.

"Next week we'll be a little crowded in The Buzz," Hilda said.
"The kitchen area will be closed off, so we'll all have to squeeze
in behind the counter. Pretty much coffee drinks only, but I
might bake a plate of cookies at home to sell." Hilda was having
a new baker's oven put in at The Buzz. She and Andes were sitting in Andes's kitchen while the boys played in Alejandro's

room. It was the first alone time they'd spent since the burn brothers incident, and Andes was fighting the urge to hover over them.

"I can bake here too," Andes heard herself say, although she'd never baked anything in her life. Her mother, instead of teaching her to cook, always sent her out of the kitchen, preferring her to do it herself. Or maybe part of her wanted a different life for Emily, didn't want to prepare her to be a wife slaving away in the kitchen. Emily liked to think that was the real reason.

"Ooh," Hilda sang. "Learning to bake cooookies for your new man?" Andes laughed out loud. "*Mami*, look at your face. You are like a red kite. Blushing, blushing, blushing. Going to float up to the ceiling at any minute. Oh my God. You are in love."

"No," Andes said quickly. "Don't put it like that." The look of horror on Andes's face was so genuine, the two women broke into laughter again.

"They're fine, *mami*," Hilda said when Andes looked toward Alejandro's bedroom again. "Look at you. You're even more overprotective than me." Andes's laugh was nervous this time. She couldn't imagine what Hilda would do if she knew Andes was keeping a secret about her son.

Chase's good mood disappeared after their guest left and for the second week in a row there was no phone call from his father. Andes finally agreed to call the jail herself. After being transferred umpteen times, she was finally given to Officer Landau.

"Are you related to Mr. Freeman?" the officer asked her.

"No, but I'm taking care of his son." She heard papers rustling in the background and a gruff "hold on."

"You're not the boy's biological mother—Vicky?"

"God no," Andes said. "Why? What has she done now?"

"Do you know a Gerry Ward?"

"No."

"Or a Richard Barnes?"

"Oh, Gerry and Richard. From the marina. Yes, I know them. Why?"

"What is your name?" Andes hung up. Even after she did it, she couldn't believe she'd done it. Why did she just do that? It was something about the way the officer was only asking questions and not answering them. Still, she hadn't really planned on hanging up, her hand just took on a life of its own and snapped shut the phone. What had she just done?

"Where's my dad?" Chase demanded.

"I don't know," Andes said. "We got disconnected."

"No, you didn't. You hung up."

"It was a figure of speech."

"Was that a cop?" Chase asked. "Did you just hang up on a cop?" Andes turned away from Chase.

"I need Gerry's number," she said. Chase muttered to himself as he went to look for it. He came back with his address book opened to the G's. Andes's hand shook as she dialed the number. She would just say they had been truly disconnected. There was no way he could prove they weren't disconnected, could they? She reached Gerry's answering machine.

"We're on vaycay!" she heard Richard and Gerry yell together. She was waiting through the message, ready to leave one herself when the two started belting a familiar song. "Start spreading the news. We're leaving today—"

Andes hung up. Chase snapped the address book shut and shook his head again. "You're starting to develop a habit," he said and stomped out of the room. Where was Jay? Why was the police officer treating her like a criminal? This must have something to do with Gerry and Richard. Why were they coming to New York? Or was Vicky causing trouble because she hadn't received her last payment? Jay told her to continue to pay her even while they were in Queens, but Andes didn't do it. Even Chase didn't know she'd missed the payment. She hadn't entirely meant to—of course, the woman didn't deserve it and it made her furious she was getting away with it—but still, Andes had simply forgotten all about it. Chase reminded her the night before, of course, but there was always so much going on—

Should she call the police back? And say what? They still hadn't told her where Jay was and why he was no longer contacting them. She opened the drawer next to the phone and pulled out Jason Ebert's business card. There was this matter hanging over her head too. Snake girl's alive and well in Sunnyside, Queens. Well, alive at least. And if that reporter was getting cozy with her family, then she had to go and put a stop to it. All her years away had been leading her back to this, leading her back home. She put the card in the drawer and shut it. But not tonight. Tonight she was going to tell Chase about her Kenyan safari, read a chapter from Harry Potter, and go to bed. But after a few minutes of reading the same sentence over and over, Andes put the book away and picked up her cell phone. She hadn't done anything wrong and the Seattle police had to tell her what was going on.

Chase sat in the dark trying to hear the thoughts and breath of his father three thousand miles away. He was surprised by the things he missed. The ragged catch of his dad's breathing, the cadence of his cough, the timbre of his voice at night, after work, after too many beers. He even missed the smell of beer, because that reminded him of his dad. He might drink too much, but Chase knew he didn't have it bad. His dad always worked hard, always came home. Functioning alcoholic. Maybe not everyone was meant to self-actualize. It was a nice thought, but the flaw in the plan revolved around the mundane humanness of us all. At first it was his father's trouble with the law that had worried Chase the most. How was his dad going to get along in prison? Especially in the mornings. His dad was really grumpy in the mornings. Now the exact opposite was bothering him, and that didn't make any sense given that he missed his dad and all. But it was too soon. It shouldn't be happening this soon.

Earlier, Chase had heard Andes on the phone when she thought he was sleeping. From her end of the conversation, Chase pieced together that his father was out of jail. The lawyer Gerry hired had "pulled something." A rabbit out of a hat,

Andes said. Or was it "out of thin air." Chase couldn't remember. The point was, his father was out of jail. And yet they hadn't heard from him. Chase heard worry in Andes's voice. Why hadn't Jay called to let them know he was out of jail? Was she afraid she was going to be stuck with him forever? Did she want him gone?

Chase reached under his pillow with both hands, scooped his palms around the little pile underneath, and pulled it toward him as if his hands were a plow, tilling the field. He had six of them now, and so far she hadn't noticed. It had been a little risky, handing her the doll. But she'd taken it without a word, without a reprimand. She was keeping secrets too. He wanted to know them all. He wanted to know if she loved him. He wanted to know if he was going to live with her. It had been looking like it. For a while it had been looking like it. He could have grown used to her, he knew this. But not now. His dad was out.

Chase took the Dublin House and flicked it open. He wanted to light one in bed. He wanted the scratch, the whoosh, the smell. Fire at his fingertips. *Abracadabra. Look what you started.* Look what you started. Maybe it was in his blood. Maybe he had the DNA of a firefighter, he had fire inside him. He liked the jolt of fear the hot flame delivered to his body. How his thoughts would race and he would chase after them. His father, Jay, was thinking of him this very second, he knew it. He could feel it. The two of them had always been connected in this way. Chase couldn't explain it, they just always had this way about them. His father wasn't in Oregon or Seattle. He was closer. Much closer. Chase knew Andes was worried Jay was abandoning him.

Yesterday he'd heard Andes talking about schools for the fall. As if they were going to be together. As if she would be walking him to school or seeing him off to the school bus. As if their bare refrigerator would soon be covered with pictures and drawings, and homework, and report cards. As if their social calendars would fill with birthday parties, and swimming lessons, and basketball games. Just one. Maybe he could light just one. As if they were a family. His dad would never fit in now. She was in love with the other one. Blazing Dave. Chase leaned over the bed and flicked. Scratch. Whoosh. He held the tiny flame under his chin. He could feel the heat licking his skin. The smoke curled up past his mouth, his nose. His engorged shadow-head fell across the floor like a giant beach ball floating on the ocean. Chase knew there could only be one reason they hadn't heard from Jay. He was coming. Now Chase just had to figure out what, if anything, he was going to do about it.

Jay sat in bed talking to Chase. He had too much to say, and so little time. He'd done it, he'd partially slipped out of his sentence thanks to Gerry and his lawyer. Someone else's money. Gerry had an ultimatum, of course, one Jay had no intention of following. But he was out and now he could make moves. Make shapes, his mother used to say. Get up. Get moving. Make shapes. *Your son needs help*, Gerry had said. *I know what he's done. You'd better get there before he sets anything else on fire. She's protecting him.*

She's protecting him. That wasn't exactly true, now, was it? Vicky was out of rehab, and hell hath no fury like those recently reformed taking stock of their lives. Reclaiming, regretting, raging to make up for everything right now. Even now he heard her voice echoing in his head. *I want my son back*, she'd said. *I want my son back.* Her son? Where was she when Chase was two years old? Three? Four? Five? Six? Seven? Eight? Nine? Ten? *Ready or not, here I come.* Jay wanted to down a six-pack. But he'd been sober for forty-five days now, which might be the only thing he had going for him if this was heading for a custody fight.

He thought of his wretched past with Vicki. She'd run her mouth off about the fireman. When she'd first started bragging about him, it was just to make him jealous. And it worked. Back then, it worked. But back then she was pretty and had a figure and a working brain. Before she melted, rotted, disappeared. It didn't matter. It had always been a threat hanging above his head. That someday she'd get clean, waltz in, and take over like he hadn't been the sole parent for an entire decade. And between a definite bias in the courts for the mothers and his dodgy past coming back to haunt him, what chance would he

have if she really did want to take Chase? If only the girl had
sent the check like he insisted. Yet he couldn't entirely blame
her. This is where the whole thing was headed, had always been
headed. It was time to confront it.

He might be at the wheel, but he had never really been driving.
It was time. Jay wondered if Chase knew he was coming. They'd
always had that kind of connection between them. And what
about Gerry and Richard? He told them not to go, but they'd
gone anyway. Their yacht was all closed up. He thought about
what they'd shown him. The articles they'd printed out after
Andes left. Snake cults and matches from eBay. It wouldn't be
long now. Chase was his son. And he was coming for him. He
just had to get there before the others.

Chapter 37

"I'm so sorry about the other day." He said it casually, quietly, as they weaved in and out of the tourists swarming Times Square. Andes had been waiting for over an hour for the subject to be brought up. But now that it had, she didn't want to talk about it. She wanted to lose herself in the flashing neon lights and tall buildings. She wanted to make a game out of scrambling out the way of the careening, beeping, swearing, taxicabs. Her eyes couldn't stop wandering. There was so much to look at, so much to take in, she was drowning in stimulis. One of the buildings had a globe perched on top, the other a glowing clock. Electronic billboards blared and flashed, and a million little lights reflected every color of the rainbow into the windows of passing cars. She could feel the energy of the city. It was as if it were alive and breathing, pulsing around her, pulling her along.

Chase was running up ahead of them, which had terrified Andes until Dave put his hand on her back ever so lightly and said, "I'm keeping my eye on him. I've got it." He was protecting her with this statement. *He could be yours,* she should have said. *He could be your flesh and blood. Would you be so calm then, watching his head disappear into the crowd?* What would he do if she just let it slip? He was apologizing to her, but she was the one holding a life-changing secret from him. Yet the test results would be in their P.O. box in a few days. Wasn't it better to wait until they were sure?

Dave stopped suddenly and pulled her toward him. Over the blare of a horn and the shriek of young girls he said, "It's over with Jenny. You need to know that. I ended it." Andes nodded, not trusting her voice to speak. "It's just—she's in so much pain—"

"I know," Andes said. "It's okay." And maybe it was, and maybe it wasn't, but really, what else could she say? She looked away from Dave in time to see Chase running back to them, his long bangs flapping like a the wings of a bird. She should have them cut. His face was flushed, his lips were moving.

"Andes," Chase said, grabbing her hand. "You have to see this." He was remarkably strong, pulling her through the crowd. She barely had time to eke out apologies to the shoulders, and handbags, and torsos she was bumping into as he pulled her farther down the street. She saw what was coming in clipped frames, like photos in an old slideshow bouncing double images on the screen before settling into focus. Ray's Pizza, lovers kissing, a woman with tight purple stretch pants showing too much cellulite, a muscled man, a tiger tattoo. And then she saw the man, boy really, standing in front of Dunkin' Donuts. A thick, slick, glittery body was draped around his neck, the head and tail trailing down his chest. A pale yellow stripe ran through the middle of its mosaic-like skin. People were gathered around snapping pictures with BlackBerrys and Sidekicks, and iPhones. Chase was still holding Andes's hand; together their palms were slick with sweat. The man-boy with the python had a deep tan and green beer-bottle eyes. He smiled at Chase. Chase looked at Andes with such expectation it almost broke her heart, despite that his interest was purely selfish, he was testing her, he was goading her, he was trying to "out" her.

"Whoa," Dave said, coming up behind them. "Look at that."

Andes hated herself in that moment for hating Dave. She hated
that he was so casual, she hated that he was so clueless, she
hated that he knew nothing about her. But the kid did. Why
else bring her here? If it was the snake Chase was interested in,
why were his anxious eyes fastened on her? De-milked, she
wanted to say. This one isn't filled with poison. This one's bite
isn't deadly. You could dance with this one until dawn and it
wouldn't prove your faith in God. Chase had pieces of the puzzle but not a picture. He was trying to form it now with gestures
and show-and-tell and unasked questions. "I'm not too fond of
snakes," Dave said, still lingering behind them.

"She is," Chase whispered. "She's snake girl."

"What?" Dave asked. "Snake girl?"

Andes didn't answer Dave. She was searching out Chase's
face, studying him as if seeing him for the first time. The article, Andes thought. She'd been keeping it in the snake box. Of
course, he'd been stealing matchbooks, rifling around in there.
He'd taken out Rose. And he'd read the article. So he knew.
What did it matter anyway? But it did. She'd worked so hard at
keeping her past at bay, under lock and key. It was the only way
to cope with it. Visiting it once in a while, circling around it, but
never landing, holding out hope without confronting it, writing letters her mother never opened, collecting matchbooks to
places she'd never been, this was her life. Now George Turner
had infiltrated her home, and his friend was threatening her if
she didn't help him get George out of the clutches of "that
snake cult," and the boy she thought she loved was holding a
mirror up to her unearthed past.

*They've brainwashed him. That snake cult. I'm going to get him
and you're coming with me. Or the whole world will know. Why do they
think you're dead? Why is there a headstone in your backyard with your
name on it?*

They don't handle snakes in those meetings, do they?

Snake girl.

Ripped open, exposed. Love someone and they'll find that
spot. The spot that hurts, the spot you spend a lifetime protecting, the spot that when open may prove that you're not really

who you think you are, who you want to be, who you should have been.

Snake girl, that's who she really was. Emily. A life she thought she'd buried. Piece by bloody piece. She couldn't hold it back anymore, she couldn't stop the memories from crashing in. Her father. The axe. Held high above his head, the blade glimmering in the sun. *It was so beautiful*, she hated herself for thinking. Just before it came down, the tip of that axe was beautiful in the West Virginia sun. And even worse than that was the beauty of the blood that soon covered it, soaked it, drowned it.

"Daddy!" She'd screamed it. Over and over she'd screamed.

"Andes?" Was she screaming again? Now? Like she had in the plane? Like she had in the Chinese restaurant where she and Dave were in love, if only for one night? Like she screamed in her dreams? She didn't think so. She didn't think she was screaming now. Dave's hand was on her shoulder.

"You don't like snakes either, huh?" he said. And then she knew. He should go back to Jenny. She would have told him this if she could move her lips, will her vocal cords to form words.

"Aren't you going to do something with it?" Chase demanded.

I still love you, she wanted to tell the kid. *It's not going to feel like it for the next few days, but I still love you.*

"What exactly did you have in mind?" she asked the kid, feigning ignorance. But something else in her moved her toward the snake. She wanted to touch it. It had been a long time since she felt a soft sandbag around her neck. But it's not deadly, she's not in church, she isn't that girl anymore.

"He's leaving," Chase said as the man with bottle-green eyes walked away with the snake. "I want to see you touch it."

"Pervert," Andes said, nursing a glowing ember of satisfaction after seizing upon the opportune moment to throw that one back in his face. It wasn't very adult, but nothing that felt that good ever was.

"What's going on here?" Dave asked.

"Freak," Chase said.

Andes turned to Dave.

"He's all yours," she said. Then she picked a direction and started walking. She could hear Dave calling after her, but she didn't stop. She would go home—no, back to the apartment, it wasn't home, it never would be home. She would pack her things, she would leave a note. *To Whom It May Concern. Dave. Hilda. Jay. He's all yours.* She heard him running behind her, but how this was possible in the din of Times Square, she didn't know or care. He was running, perhaps calling out her name, but she still didn't stop. Perhaps she wasn't hearing him so much as feeling him. Anger and desperation walked with her, cloaking her in their need, so even as she turned around and squatted to catch him, her chest was receiving his blows. She heard him clearly now. He was yelling it over and over again as he hit her. *I hate you. I hate you. I hate you.* Which is how she knew he loved her.

Dave rushed in from behind, a blur in the background. She held out her hand to stop him. It was five minutes or an hour, but eventually Chase was still. She could feel his heart beating against her breast. She cried into his hair. It smelled like discount shampoo. They sank to the sidewalk, still holding each other. She didn't care about the people struggling to make their way around them. Chase laid his head on her shoulder. Dave stayed at a distance. Leaning against a wall. Watching them.

"Don't leave me," Chase says. "Don't ever leave me."

"I don't know how that's going to be possible," Andes said. "I have to go home."

"Then I'm coming with you," Chase said. Dave walked toward them and knelt down.

"Where are we going?" he asked.

"West Virginia," they answered in unison. Dave nodded.

"Then let's go pack," he said.

Andes called Jason and they agreed to set off for West Virginia the next morning. He would drive. Andes was grateful Dave was coming with them. She didn't know how she was going to survive the car ride there, the anticipation, the second thoughts. Dave would be a welcome distraction. The three headed home from Times Square in silence. The cab ride over the Queensboro Bridge was filled with the Manhattan skyline and their separate thoughts. Andes was thinking they should go back to their place and order in. Thai food, or pizza, or Argentinean steak, or Puerto Rican spit-roasted chicken, or Mexican. Whatever the boys wanted. They would have a fun, relaxing evening, they wouldn't think about tomorrow. But life had other plans.

Jenny, Hilda, and Alejandro were by their apartment door, huddled in wait. Alejandro was crying, but Hilda and Jenny looked furious. Gripped in Hilda's right hand was a black garbage bag. Jenny was holding a manila envelope. Andes had the feeling she should be dreading the contents of each equally, and wasn't sure where to look first. But Alejandro's tears disturbed her the most. So did the look on Chase's face. He definitely recognized the garbage bag. Andes felt a prickly dread creep up her spine.

"What's wrong?" Andes asked as she braved the next few steps to her front door.

"We're not coming in," Hilda said. She pulled Andes's welcome mat toward her with her sandaled foot. Her toenails were painted a sparkly purple and Andes wanted to tell her she liked them. She wanted to tell her she was glad they were friends. She wanted to sit down with Hilda with another pitcher of margaritas, or maybe mojitos, and tell her a little bit about herself, about Emily. If not for the fact that it was likely to be the reunion from hell, she would have invited them to West Virginia. There were places for boys to run, she wanted to say. There were vines that swung out onto the river. There were rocks you could swim out to, pull yourself up on, and lie with your belly flat against the warm stone. Baking in the sun listening to the river gurgle. Woods to run through. Mountains framing the sky. Campfires—

One by one Hilda began removing items from the garbage bag. It was hard to recognize most of them; they were all covered in black soot and char. A tennis shoe, a spatula, what appeared to be a Mickey Mouse alarm clock. Mickey's ear was completely melted and dripping down the side of his face as if the mouse needed a shave.

"That's enough," Andes said, but Hilda continued raining items out of the bag, obscuring the word "Welcome" on the mat.

"You were in a fire?" Dave asked, going into professional mode.

"Oh my God," Jenny said.

"I thought they were playing handball in the courtyard," Hilda said. "They told me they were playing handball." Alejandro was looking at the ground. Tears rolled down his chubby cheeks and he was gasping for breath. Andes leaned toward him.

"Leave him," Hilda said. Next she pulled out a clear plastic bag and held it up. Inside were Andes's missing matchbooks. Hilda dropped them to the ground. It took every ounce of self-restraint Andes had not to drop to the ground after them. The last item Hilda pulled out was a wad of newspaper articles.

"He's a reader, all right," Hilda said, glaring at Chase. She thrust the newspaper cut-outs at Andes.

THREE DIE IN KITCHEN FIRE

BRONX APARTMENT BUILDING ABLAZE

FLAMES CONSUME LOCAL FLORIST

"I agree this needs to be looked into—" Andes began. Hilda was holding up her hand.

"You knew," she said. "You knew he was troubled." Hilda yanked up Alejandro's shirt and lifted a section of his stomach. Andes felt for him, how humiliated he must feel. But Hilda was on a warpath. She pointed to his burn. It had faded slightly, but it was still visible. "Burn brothers," she said. "How dare you."

"Chase didn't do that," Andes said.

"Stop it," Hilda yelled. "You don't know anything. You don't have a right to say anything. You're not a mother. How could I have forgotten? You are not a mother."

"Now wait just a minute," Dave tried to interrupt.

"He's a pyromaniac," Hilda said, talking to Dave but pointing at Chase. "He set fires in Seattle."

"You don't know that," Andes said.

"Well, they do." Hilda pointed to the recess of the hallway, where Gerry and Richard stood waiting.

Chapter 38

Hilda left, dragging Alejandro still crying behind her. Andes tried to talk to her, tried to explain, tried to tell her she didn't know the whole story. But Hilda was gone. Andes sent Chase inside, refusing to their surprise to let Richard and Gerry inside. Dave, however, refused to leave. So did Jenny. She was still clutching her envelope, waiting her turn. They sat in Andes's living room while she stood outside the door with Richard and Gerry.

"We're just trying to help," Richard pleaded. "The boy needs help."

"You have no proof," Andes said. "And I think Jay's been setting the fires. Not Chase."

Richard and Gerry exchanged a look.

"That's why Chase is so obsessed with them," she went on to explain. "Wouldn't you be if you knew your father was a danger to himself and others?"

"Did you ask him? Did Chase tell you it was his father?" Gerry asked.

"No. But it makes sense. Come on. What ten-year-old boy could pull this off?"

Richard picked up the melted Mickey Mouse clock.

"A very smart ten-year-old boy," Richard answered.

"Chase said Alejandro's the one who's been playing with the lighter. Burning the toys."

"My God," Gerry said. "You are completely snowed over, aren't you?"

"What if I'm right? What if it is Jay?"

"Let the boy talk to a psychiatrist," Richard said. "They'll figure out what to do from there."

"Before he really hurts someone," Richard said.

"We're doing you a huge favor," Gerry added. "Jay is on his way here. He was only a day behind us. Vicky too."

"Vicky?" Andes said, ready to explode. "His crackhead mother?"

"She's been clean for the past forty-five days," Richard said. "You wouldn't even recognize her."

"She's really coming along. She wants to see her son," Gerry added.

"I'll bet," Andes said. "She just wants the money. I haven't been sending the checks."

"This isn't your problem anymore," Richard said. "Let his parents handle it."

"Chase isn't a problem," Andes said. "He's a boy."

"He's not your son. Don't you get that?"

"How did Jay get out of jail?" Andes demanded.

"He's out on bail. The charges aren't serious though—"

"Arson?"

"They didn't charge him with arson. He admitted Chase has been setting the fires."

"No. It's not true. He's just saying that—"

"They'll be here tomorrow. That's all we came to say. The boy needs help. I guess you really need to be a parent to understand that." Andes shut herself in her apartment without so much as a good-bye. She could still see Richard and Gerry standing there, in stereo, emoting expressions of pity. She rushed past Dave and Jenny, who were perched on her couch, and ran into the bedroom. Chase was packing a bag.

"He's coming, isn't he?" he asked without looking up.

"Yes," Andes said. "Chase." He stopped, T-shirt in hand, and waited. "If you tell me it's you, I won't be mad. I'll be with you every step of the way and make sure you get help." She sat on the bed, took the T-shirt out of his hand, and pulled him to her.

"Do you know why that man called me snake girl?"

"Because there was a picture of you in the newspaper holding a snake?" *The picture you found in my locked box along with my matchbooks.*

"It was a religious practice. They call us serpent handlers. We handled them in meetings, when we felt we were filled with the spirit of the Lord. The snakes were venomous. One bite could kill you. But where I'm from, they believe you'll be all right as long as the Lord has moved on you. Some people called us freaks. They thought we were ignorant. Evil, even. I was one of the youngest handlers. I had a way with the snakes. But my father didn't. My father, a preacher, was terrified of them." Chase began to pack again. His movements were quick and furious.

"People do bad things when they're frightened, Chase. People do things that could hurt others. But you know what's the worst part? The worst part is making someone else keep that secret. Because it infects you. It eats you up."

"What happened?" Chase asked. "What happened between you and your father?"

"Andes?" Dave was standing in the doorway with Jenny. The manila envelope was in his hand. "What the hell is this?" he asked, thrusting it at her. Andes took the envelope and opened it. Inside were the DNA test results. Chase and Dave were not a match. Silently, she handed it to the kid.

"It's a federal offense to open someone else's mail," she said to Jenny.

"Chase gave me the key to your P.O. box," Jenny said. "He wanted me to open it." Andes looked at Chase.

"You're not supposed to be with him," he said, pointing at Dave.

"I don't understand," Dave said. "You thought Chase was my son? And what? Where did you get my DNA?"

"The restaurant," Andes said. "I took your cup."

"Jesus." He ran his hand through his hair, turned away. "It was all an act."

"No," Andes said. "That was the best date of my life."

"Why do you think he's my son?"

"Do you remember a woman named Vicky?" Andes didn't know her last name. She turned to Chase. He shrugged. "Blond hair. Lives in Seattle now. Got into drugs."

"None of that rings a bell."

"She said she slept with you ten years ago."

"And that's why you came out here? To find me? This whole time?"

"Yes." Andes turned to Chase, and gently took the report out of his hands. "Are you okay?" she asked.

Chase nodded, tears in his eyes.

"He's my dad," Chase whispered. "Jay is my dad."

"Yes. And he's on his way here," she added. Chase resumed putting clothes in his bag.

"Then we have to get out of here," he said.

"You can't come with me, Chase. Your father is coming for you. And your mother."

"I hate her."

"Richard and Gerry said she's getting better. She's been clean and sober for months now." Andes could barely force the words out of her mouth. She really wanted to take the kid and run.

"I'm going with you," he said. "You need me. You need me to face your father."

"Chase—"

"If you let me come, I'll tell them. I'll tell everybody the truth. I promise."

"Chase," Andes said. "You can't just make a promise and expect me to believe—"

"I swear on Michael Murphy's grave," Chase said. He held her gaze.

"Okay," Andes said. "You're coming."

"Do you have a picture of this Vicky?" Dave asked. But Andes didn't answer. She was already dialing a number on her cell phone. When Jason answered, she told him if they were going to do this, they had to leave now. He said he'd be there in twenty.

He spent two, maybe three days preparing. Zachariah might have been crazy, but he was methodical and focused. There were fifty of them in all, but Emily would never know this. By the time he was done, it was impossible to count. She remembers how they covered the floor of the shed. They were piled on top of each other, a heaving, slithering, hissing mass. Still, they did not frighten her. But the axe in her father's hand did. He rigged up a harness for her and hung her on the wall of the shed in between a shovel and a rake. It was too tight; the harness dug into her crotch and into her armpits. She knew better than to ask him to loosen it, she knew he would just make it tighter to spite her. It would have been pitch black had it not been for one diamond-shaped window at the very tip, near the roof. Through it the sun shone on the blade of the axe, spotlighting it like the star of the show.

George Turner was awake by four-thirty. There was something about the morning mountain air that spoke to him, called him from sleep, found him wide-awake before the sun could make its ascent. Back in New York he had loathed mornings, and back then (as he referred to his previous life in New York), morning meant any time before noon. He even developed a finger blister from repeatedly jabbing the snooze button. He couldn't really function until after noon—many pots of coffee later. The coffee here was just as strong, but he drank it out of a tin cup, no foam, no sugar, no milk, no shit. They had taken to calling him Brother Turner. He kind of liked that too. His own siblings didn't even call him brother. He was getting used to the meetings too. He'd seen snake handling half a dozen times or more now, and not once had any of them been bitten. He took long walks in the woods. The other day he stripped down and swam in the river. He'd lost ten pounds. His story was changing. These people were misunderstood. This was as good a life to live as any. The only person he was slightly worried about was Zachariah Tomlin. He thought he was getting close to a murder confession, but instead the man was increasingly crazy, speaking as if his daughter were still alive. And not only alive, but coming back.

He'd heard bits and pieces about the Tomlins from the others. How Elizabeth Tomlin had left with another man soon after Emily was gone. How Zachariah stopped going to meetings, started keeping to himself. How he could be seen standing outside in the middle of the night by her grave, holding various items: a baseball bat, a shotgun, a rusty axe. He didn't like to talk about snakes either, which is why George was convinced Emily had died of a snakebite. But it no longer seemed like a story, it was the past. She should be allowed to rest. Zachariah was already in a prison of his own making, already tortured by the past. And George couldn't imagine the authorities swarming in and around them, ruining the evening music, or the morning walks, or the swelling excitement George felt whenever they handled serpents. Of course, he still sat in the back by the door. Just in case. No. Whatever happened to Emily Tomlin was in the past. This was the present. And he was home.

Andes forgot that Chase hadn't traveled much in his young life, and was surprised to see how much the drive thrilled him, even though to her there was nothing exciting about I-95 or I-75. Chase, on the other hand, was waving at truckers, pointing out road signs or bumper stickers or anything else he deemed an oddity. Soon it would be dark, and Andes was hoping he'd sleep. Jason Ebert wasn't much of a conversationalist. He kept his eyes on the road and hadn't said much other than to give them a heads-up when they were passing a rest stop. Chase wanted to stop at every single one until Andes explained they were only going to stop if he actually had to go to the bathroom. At last he did fall asleep.

"So," Jason said as he turned the radio down. "If you're alive, why is there a grave in your backyard with your name on it?" Andes rested her head back and closed her eyes. She didn't have to answer his questions. Or she could make up something else. Emily was also her grandmother's name, something like that.

"My father's way of saying I was dead to him," Andes said instead.

"Wow," Jason said. "That's rough."

"Uh-huh."

"So it's just an empty grave?"

"I didn't say that." Jason swerved into the lane next to him. Andes yelled and gripped her door.

"Watch it."

"Sorry." Andes glanced in the backseat. Chase's eyes were firmly closed, which was how she knew he was awake.

"So who's in the grave?"

"Are you here to dig into my past or get your friend back?" Jason looked in the rearview mirror at the boy. Then over at Andes. George was right. She was beautiful. She was feisty too. He liked that in a woman. He tried to suck his stomach in, but it made it difficult to concentrate on driving.

"There's a rest stop coming up," he said.

Chapter 39

She didn't know that day was going to be the day. She didn't know there was going to be a reporter. From the lift of a snake, to the click of the shutter, to the newspaper tossed on her grandmother's front porch the next morning. They don't handle snakes in those meetings, do they?

Just hours into the next day, her grandmother's black Lincoln Town Car pulled into the Tomlins' yard. It was the first and last of such visits. She stayed in the car and spoke only with Zachariah through a partially opened window. Twenty minutes later the Lincoln Town Car pulled away, leaving a swirl of dust in its wake. Zachariah stood in the yard staring after it. Emily crouched by her window watching him. There had been others coming and going since the picture of Emily was printed in the paper. Authorities, reporters, protestors. But none of them scared Emily more than her grandmother. What did she say to him? Why was he just standing there, staring off into space?

When he did turn around, he looked right at her. Then he walked off the property and didn't return for three days. Emily's mother was frantic during those three days. Emily caught tearful pleading on the phone, and several conversations with the man in a suit that came to the door. An attorney hired by her grandmother. Emily knew this without asking. She'd been caught on camera, underage, handling a deadly viper. She'd brought great harm to her community. It didn't matter that God spoke to her, told her she would be safe. That he moved on her. To the outside world, they were freaks. And now, because of her, they had the ammunition they wanted—the freaks were endangering their children. Forcing them to handle poisonous snakes.

On the evening of the third day after her grandmother's visit, her mother came into her room and told her to pack her suitcase. She was not to live in their home anymore. Her grandmother had agreed not to press charges if Emily came to live with her. Her father wanted to see her before she left. He was in the shed.

When Emily went to the shed, her mother did not follow. She watched her daughter from the window. When Emily disappeared into the shed, she pulled the curtains closed and turned away.

"Are we there yet?"

Andes couldn't believe it. This was the part of the drive she loved the most. The narrow winding roads along the woods, the mountains drawing near, green fields stretching into the distance. But Chase was tired and cranky and not having any of it. The closer to home, the fewer cars for him to scope out and the farther away the rest stops.

"So how are we going to do this?" Jason asked. "How do we get him out of this cult?"

"They're not a cult," Andes said.

"You don't call drinking poison, handling fire, and wrestling deadly snakes cultlike behavior?"

"Poison?" Chase said sitting straight up. "Fire?" Andes shot Jason a dirty look. He shrugged an apology. "You drank poison? Handled fire?"

"No," Andes said. "I didn't."

"But you handled deadly snakes."

"Yes."

"Cool." Jason chuckled. Andes threw him another dirty look.

She wished Dave were here. When they left Jenny was still cling-ing to him, confident that now that he knew about Andes's be-trayal, he would go back to her. And maybe he would. After all, he wasn't there, was he? And could she blame him? Stealing his glass from the restaurant, keeping the real reason they'd come to Sunnyside from him. She wouldn't have forgiven herself ei-ther. Just like she'd never forgiven herself fifteen years ago. But maybe the old adage was right. Maybe there was a first time for everything.

They were so close now, passing familiar sights: the corner store, the apple orchard, the scenic overlook, the river. Andes's stomach was in her throat. Ambivalence clutched at her as hard as she was clutching the door handle. This was home. She also wanted to run. Chase took to watching her like a surgeon oper-ating on a live patient for the first time. Had George already spoken to her parents? Did they have any inkling she might be coming? Did they care? She wanted to scream at Jason to stop the car. But it kept on rolling. All these years and she was home. As she guided Jason's car up a partially hidden dirt road lead-ing to her house, Emily Tomlin did something she hadn't done in nine years. She prayed.

I'm going to move here, George Turner thought. He'd grown up a city boy, born in the Bronx—who knew he could fish? You could see the stars at night too, they were magical. This was what life was about. He hadn't had a drop to drink since he'd arrived either, and he didn't miss it. And in the meetings, there was this girl. Woman. She'd smiled shyly at him the other night. But just as George had been losing interest in Zachariah, local gossip was kicking it up again. He was hearing rumors about the boarded-up shed in the Tomlins' backyard. The snake inci-dent, everyone called it. The hushed voices, the looking away. George couldn't imagine what it was. None of the folks seemed at all put off by the serpent handling, so whatever this was with Zachariah must have been big. Was it something that hap-pened before or after Emily died?

He was standing near the well, pumping water and trying to

work up the nerve to check out the shed, when he heard a car pull into the drive. He knew the sound of that car, the rut of the muffler. It would be good to see Jason. He'd take him to a meeting, show him through the woods. He'd send a message back home with him. He could get Jason to ship some of his things. Because one thing was for sure. He wasn't going back.

Chase held her hand as the car pulled up the drive. Andes squeezed it back. "Just pull up over there," Andes said, pointing to a side yard next to a cabin.

"This was your house?" Chase asked.

"Yes," Andes said.

"Not much bigger than my sailboat." Jason shut off the engine. It was quiet, barely six a.m. There were no lights on in the house.

"Jason," Andes said. "Can you stay here for a minute?" Jason put his seat back and nodded.

"I need a little nap anyway," he said. Andes opened the car door and waited for Chase to follow her. She began to walk around the property and he followed. They passed a well. Andes stopped and stared down it for a moment. Then she turned to Chase.

"There were a lot of things about my childhood that weren't very pretty," she said. "Just like yours. But I'm here to face them. I'm here to face my father. And then we're going to go back to Sunnyside and you're going to face yours. Do you understand?" Chase looked down the well.

"I don't want to get anyone in trouble," he said.

"I know. And no matter what he's done, your father loves you. And he raised a really smart boy. And sometimes, no matter how hard it is, you have to do the right thing. He might not understand today, or even tomorrow—but someday I think he will. And you can start living your life without the burden of terrible secrets. You got that, kid?"

Chase nodded.

"Let's go visit a grave," she said, standing up and taking his hand again.

"Another one?"

"Just one more," she said as she started to walk.

"Whose is it?" Chase asked.

"Mine," she replied. "But this time, we're going to need a shovel."

She was slightly surprised to see the shed was still standing. In the light of day it looked harmless. Just an old shed, far removed from the one in her nightmares. Once painted green, the sides were faded and splintered, and had it not been boarded up all those years ago, the door would have been falling off its hinges. A musty, decaying smell hung in the air. It screamed neglect. If she had stayed, she would have personally burned it to the ground. Andes stared at the multiple two-by-fours nailed across it, contemplating how she would pry them off. She was in no hurry. She had to pry off the boards barring her memories first.

Some memories linger in the back of your mind, resurfacing when you're tired, or sad, or had too many glasses of wine at a party. Some are wedged like ice in the brain, always there but frozen in place, only to be thought of when chipped away at or temporarily thawed. Other memories, like what happened on that day in the shed, exist on all of those planes simultaneously, and change you to your core.

"Open it," Chase said. Andes closed her eyes briefly, then she tried the first board. It was weak with age, and creaked as it gave. Chase joined in, and together they ripped away the remaining three planks. She opened the door. The first thing she looked at was the wood floor. She didn't know why she expected to see anything other than splintered wood and tools. She could see the marks the axe had made in the floor. Her eyes roamed the walls looking for the hook where he'd hoisted her up, harnessed above the slithering floor where she could watch the axe fall on the heads, and bodies, and tails of the snakes, over and over and over again. She often wondered if she had been tall and big, too tall to hang, where would he have put her? Would he have forced her to watch at all? Was it simply because of her slight stature that she was subjected to the horror?

"There's a shovel," Chase said, taking a step toward it. Andes held out her hand to block his passage, but he simply went through. Andes cried out, a great wave of grief escaping her mouth. Chase faced her, holding the shovel. He was dying to know what it was all about, she could see it in his face, but front and center was the concern he felt for her. She couldn't tell a ten-year-old about what she'd seen. She couldn't tell him about the screeching, or the blood. She couldn't tell him about the smell, the vapors released from the decaying flesh, how their heads and tails continued to twitch long after they'd been severed. Her father covered in blood and guts and slimy bits of snakeskin, never letting up on bringing the axe up and then down and then up and then down. Sweat pouring off his body in the biggest display of madness she had ever seen.

She waited for him to die as well. She saw the venomous snakes bite at her father's legs, snapping and thrashing as they tried to escape their fate. Their fear and rage spewed out of their mouths in a cacophony of horrifying hisses. She would never forget those terrifying exhalations as long as she lived. They bit at everything they could. The walls, the axe, her father. She waited for him to fall into the pit of snakes and die. Blood splattered on her dress, her face. She didn't know why she didn't just close her eyes—she tried, of course, but the sound amplified without sight was much worse. She didn't know how long it took before every last one them was dead, because in her mind it was forever and a day. Her father wasn't aware of the time either, for he kept hacking at them long after each snake had died a million deaths and nothing remained but the odd twitch of furious nerve endings sputtering out the end of their life and refusing to let go like ghosts seeped in revenge, stuck between this world and the next. Later, she would learn her father had protected himself by wrapping his entire body in Ace bandages and several layers of clothing. When it was over he stood in the yard and unraveled the layers of protection one by one like shedding his own skin. Then, naked, he examined every inch of his body with a flashlight, just to make sure there were no puncture wounds. His daughter did not see any of this. She was still hanging in the shed. He left her dangling above the dead snakes all night. The next day he came to take her down. She had soiled herself, but he didn't let her go inside to bathe right away. Instead, he handed her a shovel. He told her to dig a grave in the backyard, her grave. It wasn't until he deemed the hole big enough that he told her it was for the snakes. He made her pick the dead snakes up off the floor of the shed piece by piece and drop them into the grave. Then she covered it with dirt. Her eyes were swollen with tears, but most of all she was exhausted. She did everything he told her, grateful he wasn't going to kill her. All she wanted was to take a bath and go to bed. For his final touch, he put up a cross. EMILY TOMLIN was carved across the horizontal plank along with the date of her "death."

"Pack your things," he said. "You're dead to us now."

He watched her from the window in the kitchen. She and a boy stood by the grave, furiously digging. The man who'd been visiting made as if to stop them. Zachariah held up his hand.

"Let them be," he said.

"Who is that?" George asked. "Why are they digging up Emily's grave?"

"That is Emily," Jason said, reaching for the nearest whiskey bottle. He'd been talking to George for fifteen minutes, trying to get him to come to his senses, and he'd been holding back, keeping Emily as the ace in his hand. The time had come to play it.

"What?"

"She's not dead, dude. I found her in Sunnyside, Queens."

"Then—who's buried there?" He turned to Zachariah, who was still staring out into the yard. "Who is she digging up?" he demanded.

"There won't be anything left of 'em," Zachariah said.

"Who? There won't be anything left of who?"

"The snakes," Zachariah said and went back to his chair. George started for the door. He couldn't believe she was alive. He had to see her up close. "Take one more step, boy," Zachariah said from his chair, "and I'll shoot you dead."

* * *

These are the things she would take with her. Running bare-foot through the woods, tearing down dirt hills, plunging into the deepest end of the river. Cool water enveloping her body. Pushing down into the river until the silt bottom caressed her toes like a million butterfly kisses. The Blue Ridge Mountains proud, and strong, and inky blue. The sun setting her hair on fire, inflaming her cheeks. The music of the mountains, and the rapture of the meetings. The feeling of belonging, of brother-hood. Pork chops and red gumdrops; the love, even if brief, from her mother. Tall green trees, and low, moaning valleys. Yes, and the snakes too. Their sleek soft skin, their seductive slither, and the doorway to the universe they threw open when she held them in her arms. These are the things she would remember. The rest she would leave behind.

"It's just a bunch of dirt," Chase said as he dug up another clump.

"That it is," Andes answered. They were covered in it and ex-hausted. Andes held the cross with her name on it across her chest as they lay beside the hole.

"What are you going to do with that?" he asked.

"I'm going to burn it," she said. "Want to help?"

"Aren't you afraid of me around fire?"

"No," she answered.

"You think I know, don't you. You think I know who set those fires."

"Yes."

"Are you going to make me tell?"

Andes rolled over until she was face-to-face with the kid.

"It's your secret, Chase. But know this. Secrets are prison. If you don't release them, you'll never be free."

Chase stared at the sky.

"It's nice out here," he said.

"Yes."

"Are you free now?" he asked, looking at the hole.

"It's a start."

"It's a pile of dirt."

"One man's pile of dirt is another man's start."

"You're still kind of weird."

"I know."

"Emily?"

"What?"

"I didn't mean that."

"It's okay."

"I like you."

Andes threw the cross down the hole and reached out for Chase's hand.

"Hector?"

"What?"

"I like you too."

"Pervert."

Andes started it with a giggle. Chase followed. The sun bathed their faces. Their stomachs rose and fell for quite some time. They laughed long and loud. *I'm laughing over my grave*, Andes thought. Nothing had ever felt so good.

When it was all done, Chase and Jason waited in the car. Zachariah stood on the front porch, gun in hand, staring at Emily. She stayed in the middle of the yard. It was hard to believe how frail he looked, how old. It was hard to remember how frightening he used to be.

"I heard Mom left," Emily said. Zachariah looked off into the distance. He put his gun on the rail of the porch. He fiddled with the tie on his robe.

"Yep," he said. "A ways back now. A ways back."

"My letters?" she asked. Zachariah looked her in the eye.

"She did what she was told," he said. "Up until she left." Emily nodded and turned away, not wanting him to see the tears in her eyes. Despite everything, she had hoped for some kind of miracle, some kind of reconciliation. She longed to see her mother again. She wanted to touch her, she wanted to look her in the eye, she wanted to whisper forgiveness, she wanted to give her another chance.

Emily started for the car.

"I've got an address," her father said. "If you want it." Emily stopped. Should she? Could she stand to write more letters, ones that might also be "Returned to Sender"? *Yes*, she thought, *I can.* It was her life. Her mother might reject her again, that was the plain truth. That was something she couldn't control, and she was strong enough to take it if it happened again. But was she strong enough to face herself if she didn't do what was in her heart to do? That was a different matter altogether, facing yourself. This was her life, she couldn't let fear make all her decisions. "I think she'd like to hear from you," her father said, clinching the deal. "She don't do what she's told no more." Hiding the faintest of smiles, Emily turned back to her father and followed him into the house.

Chapter 40

It was easy enough to get into the apartment. All one had to do was mention the pending kidnapping charges against Andes. The doll had to burn, that was clear. The woman named Hilda had not been very nice. When questioned, she said an awful lot of bad things about Chase. The woman owned a coffee shop around the corner from the fire station. It would be kind of exciting—lighting a fire right under the firemen's noses. And it had been way too long since they'd watched anything burn. One could already feel the flames, hear the crackle; adrenaline coursing, it was the biggest high ever. This time, this time it would feel as good as the first time. Maybe even better. Flick, whoosh, roar. This would be it, this would be the big one. First the doll. Then the coffee shop. And then they would stop. Someone had a kid to raise.

Chapter 41

Police precinct
Sunnyside, Queens
Present day

"**I** asked the kid who's been starting the fires. You want to know what he said?" Andes didn't produce an answer. She had a feeling one was forthcoming. "At first we were sure it was the kid," the officer continued. "But apparently you two were out of town when Hilda Morita's bakery caught on fire." Andes pretended this was the first she'd heard about the fire. The new kitchen Hilda put in The Buzz had gone up in flames just yesterday. Thank God everyone had escaped unharmed. But even though the fire trucks were just next door and were literally there within seconds, there was substantial structural damage. Hilda would have to wait for the insurance money to start over. Andes first learned about the fire from Hilda herself—she'd called her from her cell phone on her way back from West Virginia. Andes had offered to help, and to her enormous relief, Hilda agreed. What started out to be a quick apology phone call lasted hours as Andes opened up to Hilda about her family and her trip with Chase to dig up the grave; then it was her turn to hear about the bakery catching on fire, and Andes wasted no time coming up with ideas of how to help Hilda get back on her feet, starting with volunteering Blazing Dave to put on a bake sale. She called Dave immediately and he had agreed, although one of his stipulations was that he wanted to have a long talk with Andes when she got back, something she was extremely nervous about. She certainly hadn't expected Dave to show up at the police station. She'd begged him to leave, but as far as she knew he was still sitting out there, waiting for her. But right now, she had other things to deal with.

Jay and Vicky were sitting in an adjacent interrogation room. Vicky was trying to charge Andes with kidnapping and Jay was trying to talk her out of it. "The kid said to tell you he's not sure he's ready to set himself free," the officer said. "What does that mean?" Andes closed her eyes. There was a knock on the door. The officer yelled his consent and when Andes opened her eyes again, Dave was standing over her. She'd almost forgotten what a beautiful man he was. He was smiling at her now; she couldn't help but smile back.

"I remembered who she was," Dave said. "Vicky."

"You're speaking of the boy's mother?" the officer asked. Dave nodded.

"She was never my girlfriend," Dave said. "She was our number one suspect in a series of local fires." Andes, who had been drifting in a semi-dream state, snapped to attention.

"What?"

"She was always hanging around the fire station," Dave said. "Overly interested in what we do. Always showing up to fires we were putting out like a murderer visiting the scene of their crimes. But by the time we'd gathered enough evidence to try and charge her, she was gone."

"Oh my God," Andes said. The officer stood.

"Then there must be a file on her," he said.

"There is," Dave answered. "They're getting it now."

"Looks like it's going to be a long night."

"Is she free to go?" Dave asked.

"Almost. Once we talk to the boy's mother about these fires, I'm sure pressing kidnapping charges will be the last thing on her mind. But she's going to need to stay here a little longer," he said, gesturing at Andes.

"Then can you give us a second in here?" Dave asked. The officer thumped Dave on the back.

"Anything for Blazing Dave," he said.

"I'm sorry," they both said once they were alone.

"Please," Dave said. "Let me. Just in case your 'I'm sorry' was 'I'm sorry but I never want see you again.' " Andes waited. Dave took a seat across from her. "I'm usually not a corny person," he said. "I'm very practical, in fact. That night—our first date— that was the best night of my life. But even before that, I was drawn to you. To be honest, it kind of pissed me off. I didn't know if it was just pheromones or whatnot messing with my brain every time I looked at you. Thought of you. And I'm taking a huge risk here because maybe you don't feel the same way. But I've never once looked at someone else and seen my whole future laid out before me like I did with you. I'm showing what an idiot I am here, I realize this, but I looked across the table from you that night and I saw marriage, and children, and Christmases, and school plays, and quiet dinners at home. I saw grandchildren, and great grandchildren, and our two wrinkled hands holding each other until the day I die. I go first, by the way, in case you're wondering. And if you don't feel the same way, I'm prepared to walk out that door. Because now that I know the feeling is possible, I wouldn't want anything less for you. Or Jenny. Or anyone else. Because it's true. I never believed it was true. But when it's the one, you know. You just know."

Dave stared at Andes for a moment, swallowed, and then looked away. "Your turn," he said. Andes took his hand across the table.

"Let me introduce myself," she said quietly. "My name is Emily Tomlin, and my passport is blank."

"Then we're going to have to do something about that, Emily Tomlin," Dave said, smiling. Andes smiled back, but Dave could see it was a smaller smile, one bracing against disappointing him.

"No," Emily answered. "*I'm* going to have to do something about that." She reached across the table and took Dave's other hand. "I had the best night of my life that night too. It was magic. But it wasn't real life. I've been out of touch with the real me for so long, I'm afraid it's going to take quite some time to catch up." Dave squeezed her hands and then let go.

"How much time?" he asked, trying not to sound too needy.

"I don't know. First, I'm going to travel, and then—well, I just don't know. This might sound totally crazy, but for the first time in my life, I'm in love with the idea of not knowing where I'm going, not searching for anything in particular. Because this time, wherever I go, there I'll be. The real me. I'm sorry. Sounds corny, doesn't it? I can barely keep from cringing as the words come out of my mouth. But it's how I feel."

Dave laughed, although it didn't quite reach his eyes. "It did sound a little corny," he admitted. "But your face lit up while you were talking. That's all I needed to see. I'm happy for you. I really am."

"Me too," Andes said. Dave leaned across the table and kissed her.

"Send me a postcard," he said. And this time, Emily knew it was said by somebody who really cared.

"*This* is a temple?" Chase whined. They were standing on a patch of dirt in the city park across from their apartment. Andes had put down a few pieces of memorabilia. A picture of the two of them. A candle. Gerry's lighter. A stub from the Natural History Museum. A lock of Chase's hair. *The Amityville Horror.* Harry Potter. They stood staring at the objects for a moment.

"Now what?" Chase said.

"Now we light the candle." She handed Chase the lighter. He touched it to the little flame.

"Now what?" he asked again as the little candle glowed.

"Now we send our prayers—or wishes, if you'd rather call them that, to the Universe."

"You're weird."

"We've established that many, many times."

"What kind of wishes?"

"We wish your mom will get help."

"She's going to jail."

"I know. But she recovered from the drugs and maybe she can recover from her . . . proclivity to pyromania." Andes wished she could take the words back, for Chase burst into tears.

"All this time I thought it was my dad," he sobbed. "And my dad thought it was me."

"I know, honey. You were both protecting each other. You love each other a whole lot. But you're both going to be okay. And now he's sober and that's a very good thing."

"But I didn't free myself," Chase said. "I thought it was him and I didn't tell. My mom even burned your doll, and Hilda's kitchen, and I thought it was my dad—and I still didn't tell." Chase's face was flushed, the veins on his neck bulged, and the words poured out of him in a frenzy of grief. Andes wrapped her arms around him without hesitation, and this time he didn't pull away.

"It's not your fault," she said, pulling back and forcing him to look her in the eye. "We found out who it really was before you'd come to the decision to tell. That's all. Look how long it took me to tell my secrets. And maybe deep down, you knew it wasn't your dad. You believed in him. Just like I believed in you. You know what that's called, kid?" she asked softly. "That's called faith, Chase." She put her hand over his heart. "And that's something you never want to lose, kid. Never, ever, ever." Chase blinked and then nodded.

"I'm sorry about your doll," he said. " And Hilda's kitchen. And—"

"You're not responsible for your mom's actions, kid," Andes interrupted. "It's not your fault," she said again, for she knew it was something he was going to have to hear a lot before he started believing it. She'd have to remember to tell that to Jay.

"But what if it's in my blood? What if—" Andes gently placed her hand over Chase's mouth.

"My father did a lot of crazy things too, kid," she said. "And that's not in my blood. Not an ounce." Chase looked down at their temple. There was a slight breeze and it took the candle out.

"So what do we do now?" Chase asked, watching the faint line of smoke curl up from the candle and disappear.

"We get you home," Andes answered. The two brushed off their dirty knees but didn't make a move.

"What if I don't want to go home?" Chase asked after a minute. "What if I want to stay here with you?"

"Don't talk like that," Andes said, biting back the tears she'd tried to keep from falling. She didn't want him to see her cry. She didn't want him to know she'd had a whole life planned out with him. A vibrant life filled with school plays and field trips, and holidays. And now, just like the little candle, the flame on the life they had lived in her imagination had been snuffed out. And she had no idea how she was going to bear it. "I need you to help me face this. And I won't face this if you talk like that, okay, kid?" Andes was openly sobbing now.

"Okay," Chase choked out. "Will you visit?"

"And write, and call, and e-mail, and text, and fax," Andes said. "And send loads and loads of postcards." Chase gulped and tried to wipe away his tears with his dirty fingers. The sight of his pain was worse than anything Andes had ever felt. She considered grabbing him—running off with him—they could take a train to anywhere and start over.

"Your father loves you so much," she said. "You're his life."

"Come with us," Chase said. "You can live in the houseboat." For a moment, Chase's sadness disappeared and he grew excited. For a moment, Andes considered it.

"I have a passport to fill up, kid," she said. "But you and me? We'll always be connected. No matter how far apart." Andes pointed at Chase's heart and drew an invisible line between them.

"You're so totally weird," Chase reiterated. At least he had stopped crying. He looked down at their temple. "A homeless person is going to take these things," he said.

"Probably," Andes said as they started to walk away.

"Well, all I can say," Chase said when they got a few feet away, "is that he'd better not read *The Amityville Horror* before bed."

"Here's hoping," Andes agreed. Chase slipped his hand into

hers. As they crossed the street, neighborhood noises filled their ears. Cars passing, children laughing, the bell on the Thai restaurant dinging; it sounded a little bit like music. A little like the blues, only less sad, slightly more hopeful. And the last strain of the song was joined by the kid's voice, quiet but clear as day as they made their way across the street.

"I love you, Emily," he said.

"I love you too, Hector," she replied.

SUNNYSIDE BLUES

Mary Carter

ABOUT THIS GUIDE

The suggested questions are included to enhance
your group's reading of Mary Carter's
Sunnyside Blues

DISCUSSION QUESTIONS

1. Andes is not Emily Tomlin's birth name. Where did the name come from? Why did she choose this name and what does this say about her?

2. In the beginning, Andes's heart is set on renting the little houseboat. Shortly thereafter, she's fantasizing about living on a sailboat. What does this say about her? What is she really searching for?

3. What does "home" mean to Andes, and how is her search for it symbolized in the novel?

4. Chase and Andes do not get off to a good start in their relationship. Does this make Andes more or less willing to look after him? How does their relationship change as the novel progresses? How are they similar? How are they different?

5. Despite his homophobia, Andes is attracted to Jay. Why? What does she mean when she says she's "always belonged with the outsiders"?

6. How does Emily's past affect her present life? Is she religious? How does her attitude toward snakes differ from her father's?

7. What role does Emily's mother play in her childhood? Is she just as responsible for the abuse Emily endured? More? Less? Why? What influence did her grandmother have on her growing up? Did she make things easier for Emily or harder?

8. What purpose do the bedtime stories Emily tells Chase serve? Does he believe she's telling the truth or does he think they're just stories?

9. The plane ride from Seattle to Sunnyside is a first for Andes and for Chase. Who fares better? What role do

they take on during the ride and how do their roles shift mid-flight?

10. What does Andes's matchbook collection mean to her? What does Chase think of it? Why does Chase lie to the authorities about the matchbook collection? Does the lie change the nature of Andes's and Chase's relationship? If yes, how so? If no, why not?

11. Why does Emily visit the graveyard? How is Chase influenced by the visits?

12. What role do "secrets" play in the novel? Which characters are keeping the deepest secrets? How is it hurting them?

13. Is Andes in love with Dave? Would she be more or less in love with him if Chase weren't in the picture?

14. How does the neighborhood of Sunnyside, Queens, affect Andes and Chase? Do they fit in there? Why or why not?

15. Does Chase really want a new father? Is he happy with the outcome of the paternity test?

16. Has Andes's father changed by the end of the novel? If yes, what actions does he take that suggest this? If no, what actions does he not take that suggest this?

17. What is the significance of Emily's relationship with Hilda?

18. Will Chase and Andes keep in touch the rest of their lives? Will Andes return to Sunnyside, Queens, after she travels the world? Will Chase's father remain sober?

19. Are Chase and Andes better off for having met each other? Do they love each other? How do each of them change as a result of having met?

20. Does Andes think Chase has been setting the fires? If so, why doesn't she say anything? If not, who does she think is responsible?

21. Several characters in this novel are protecting secrets they think the others are keeping. Which characters are covering up for each other and why?

22. What is the significance of Andes digging up her own grave at the end? What does this do for her? How does this relate to Chase and the secrets he's been keeping?

23. What is the significance of the little temple Andes and Chase build at the end of the novel?